Praise for Mary Ann Marlowe's *Some Kind of Magic*

"Marlowe makes a name for herself in this hilarious and sexy debut. . . . It's filled with frisky sexy scenes set to the backdrop of rock music, and Marlowe makes the chemistry scientific and literal in this fun read."

—*Booklist* STARRED REVIEW

"Fun, flirty read about a magical romance . . . a lighthearted pick me up. Eden and Adam's chemistry was so electric—I rooted for them the whole way!"

—*FIRST for Women*

"This love potion romance, which pairs up the lead singer for a rock band with a biochemist who's also an amateur singer/songwriter, is light and fluffy."

—*Publishers Weekly*

"This fun, romantic and sexy novel explores the instant connection that manifests between two people and what happens next. The chemistry between Adam and Eden is instant and electric, and watching them bring out the best in each other gives the story warmth along with the heat. . . . This love story will make readers smile!"

—*RT Book Reviews*

"Frisky, Flirty Fun!"—Stephanie Evanovich, *New York Times* bestselling author of *The Total Package*

Please turn the page for more praise for *Some Kind of Magic*.

DATING

BY THE

BOOK

Books by Mary Ann Marlowe

Some Kind of Magic

A Crazy Kind of Love

Dating by the Book

Published by Kensington Publishing Corporation

DATING

BY THE

BOOK

MARY ANN MARLOWE

KENSINGTON BOOKS
www.kensingtonbooks.com

KENSINGTON BOOKS are published by

Kensington Publishing Corp.
119 West 40th Street
New York, NY 10018

All Kensington titles, imprints, and distributed lines are available at special quantity discounts for bulk purchases for sales promotion, premiums, fundraising, educational, or institutional use.

Special book excerpts or customized printings can also be created to fit specific needs. For details, write or phone the office of the Kensington Sales Manager: Kensington Publishing Corp., 119 West 40th Street, New York, NY 10018. Attn. Sales Department. Phone: 1-800-221-2647.

Kensington and the K logo Reg. U.S. Pat. & TM Off.

ISBN-13: 978-1-4967-1822-8 (ebook)
ISBN-10: 1-4967-1822-4 (ebook)
Kensington Electronic Edition: July 2019

ISBN-13: 978-1-4967-1821-1
ISBN-10: 1-4967-1821-6
First Kensington Trade Paperback Edition: July 2019

10 9 8 7 6 5 4 3 2 1

Printed in the United States of America

To editors: for shaping our words
To book bloggers: for sharing our works
To readers: for inhabiting our worlds

Chapter 1

The vandals had struck again. With a shaky *R* scrawled on the window pane, they'd redubbed my bookstore the Mossy Stoner. Hilarious.

This sort of thing never used to happen in the sprawling metropolis of Orion—"the small town with the big heart." But over the past few months, I'd scraped unwanted paint off the window three times. At least the latest effort was somewhat clever. Three weeks ago, they'd doodled a crude dick and balls under the *Y*. *Kids*.

I fetched my maxed-out Visa card and scratched at the graffiti, thankful they'd only defiled the glass. If they'd painted on the wood, I would've gone Javert on the miserable twerps.

Once I'd more or less rectified the problem, I fished out my keys, but the front door refused to open even when I bumped it with my shoulder. Great. Another problem to fix.

I gave one good hip slam, and I was inside. All at once, a sense of home settled over me. I breathed in the peace like a meditation.

Every morning, as I walked across the threshold into my sanctuary, I said two prayers. First, I'd offer up thanks to the gods for the bookstore that was (mostly) mine now. Second, I'd send out a plea to the universe to drive customers my way so I could keep it. I'd already sacrificed so much to fulfill my dream, failure would be beyond heartbreaking. It would crush my soul.

Six months ago, my fiancé had begged me to abandon my small-town business and follow him to his preferred life in the city. Stubborn as always, I chose to stay. Ever since our paths had forked, I inhabited a strange new dimension where one-half of my dreams could come true, but at the cost of the other, like an ironic twist out of an O'Henry short story. Yeah, I had my bookstore, but because of the same, I'd lost one husband. I wasn't even a widow; I was a never-married. I should have been Mrs. Peter Mercer. Instead, I was still Miss Madeleine Hanson.

I dragged a couple of tables outside with sales books, then grabbed my sidewalk sign and knelt down to chalk in the daily deal. TAKE AN EXTRA 15% OFF CLEARANCE BOOKS. As much as I hated practically giving books away, my shelves were bursting with unsold merchandise.

A gentle breeze stirred, and I closed my eyes to appreciate the dawning warmth of the morning sun, but then I caught the aroma of fresh-baked croissants from Gentry's French bistro, and my nose wrinkled. The no doubt delicious pastries smelled rancid to me, since they would lure all the morning traffic away from my pitiful café.

As if my thoughts had conjured it, a white panel van pulled up to the curb, and I shaded my eyes to watch Max Beckett jump out. He waved, then skipped around to the back, hollering, "Wanna give me a hand, here?"

I trudged over and let him stack a pair of boxes in my arms before he lifted three more. I nearly dropped them, thrusting the front door open. Max followed me to the counter where I inspected the contents. An assortment of muffins, croissants, and other pastries made up the bulk of the baked goods. The boxes I'd carried contained two whole cakes, marble pound and double chocolate.

"How much do I owe you?"

He produced an itemized receipt. As I scanned it, he leaned against the display fridge and said, "Have you considered my proposition?"

I raised my eyes and snorted. "Not so much."

He sucked on the inside of his cheek for a second. The light caught in his hair, revealing layers of browns and reds and auburns dancing together in a combination any colorist would envy, a combination I envied with my ordinary chestnut.

"It would be good for business, Maddie. *Both* our businesses."

His innocent act didn't fool me.

He claimed he wanted to expand his catering business, the one he ran with his mom, into my bookstore to get a foothold in town. He claimed it would help my bottom line, too. And maybe it would, but it drove me insane that he thought he had all the answers. Always giving me advice I didn't ask for. Like when he'd expressed his concerns about my impending wedding last year.

It only irritated me more when he turned out to be right. Sometimes—usually—I couldn't help suspect he had ulterior motives.

I just needed to figure out *why* he wanted to insinuate himself into my business. "How would it help me?"

"If we open a legit bakery here, you could draw in more customers."

"I already sell your baked goods. Try again."

He sighed. "Maddie, I've got a degree in marketing. Look at what I've done for my mom."

That was true. She'd focused on the occasional wedding cake until he stepped in with new ideas, and now they cranked out orders for local restaurants and special events.

"I don't see how that's relevant to my situation."

"I've got ideas. Ways to make better use of your space and grow your customer base."

Just like he'd done with his mom's business. I narrowed an eye at him. My stink eye. "You're trying to take over my bookstore, somehow. Is that it?"

He must have counted to ten before answering. "We wouldn't be taking it over. We'd be forming a partnership."

A partnership implied a relationship of equals, but ever since high school, Max had patronized me with unwanted advice when he wasn't straight up trying to best me. It wasn't like I hadn't also studied marketing, and I liked running my business my way.

"Our current arrangement works for me."

We had a solid routine. I placed daily orders, he and his mom baked in their kitchen, and Max delivered the food. I sold their baked goods at a markup. And I didn't have to give any control to Max.

"Come on. You have this amazing kitchen going to waste. Imagine if I could come in at night and bake? I could even open the store early and catch more early morning traffic."

God knew I needed to find some way to increase revenue, but what he was describing sounded a lot like ousting me. I didn't want to give Max a chance to pull a fast one on me. "I'm doing just fine, thanks."

Red spots dotted his cheeks, and I knew my resistance irritated him as much as his pushiness infuriated me. "It's almost like you've completely forgotten all the things you wanted." His tone softened. "Maddie, you lost a fiancé, but you haven't lost your bookshop. Not yet."

I tilted my head at that last dig. "You don't think I can do this?"

He bit his lip, and his chest rose and fell, like he was practicing some new age breathing technique. It pissed me off that he could keep his emotions in check better than me. Score one for Max.

Suddenly, his face lit up, and no trace of conflict remained. "Oh, Mom wanted me to give you this." He opened a pastry box and pulled out a small cupcake with off-white frosting and held it aloft, a wondrous talisman discovered in another realm. "Try this." He arched an eyebrow, in challenge or concession, I couldn't tell.

I glared at him and popped the entire cupcake in my mouth. As if I'd suddenly give in just because he—

"Oh, my God."

His green eyes shone like emeralds. "You like it?"

It was a burst of strawberries. It went down so easy. "What *is* that?"

"It's a mini strawberry shortcake cupcake. Mom's been experimenting." A smile curved the corner of his lip.

I shrugged. "It's okay."

"Uh-huh." His eyes crinkled. "I've seen you hanging around our back door like a stray dog begging for scraps whenever mom used to start gathering strawberries."

I never knew how he could make me drop my defenses and laugh, like when we were kids. He was right, though. I was a sucker for his mom's shortcakes.

He chuckled, knowing he'd won a tiny victory. I blew a raspberry.

"Mind if I bring some tonight to your book club? Push them on your captive audience. Advertising."

Always an angle. "Sure. Whatever."

When I walked him out, I propped open the door to let in some air and invite customers to venture in without having to battle the fortress of the sticky portcullis. Max turned and said, "Have you tried oiling the hinges?"

He acted like he was my dad. Or a more capable older brother even though we were roughly the same age.

I gritted my teeth and tried out his deep breathing technique. "Thanks. I'll give that a try later."

The weather was so nice, I couldn't stay disgruntled for long. Inside, I tuned Sirius radio to the Coffeehouse station and hummed along as I replenished the muffins from the batch Max had delivered. Then I sat back and waited for patrons to pour in.

The Mossy Stone had stood on this tree-lined street for thirty-seven years, since long before my parents had adopted me and brought me to Orion, population two thousand. I'd purchased books here in my youth, and I wanted to keep selling them as long as I could.

As such, the business student in me fretted over the immediate emptiness, but the book lover in me wanted it to stay quiet forever, so I could hide in the corner and read every book on the shelves like I had when I was a kid.

My initial love of reading was born sitting cross-legged on

the floor as Mrs. Moore, the original owner, licked her fingers and turned the page of *A Wrinkle in Time* or *The Indian in the Cupboard*.

My mom started taking me to our small library up the street when I was old enough to read on my own, but that was about as well stocked as a wet bar in a dry county, and I was a voracious reader. So Mom started letting me buy one book a week from the Mossy Stone. It wasn't until later that I understood the meaning behind the store's name. By then, I'd begun to grow moss myself from sitting immobile in the reading corner.

I savored the musty smell of the old space and the old books. I basked in the muted glow of sunlight that filtered through the antique windows, illuminating ghosts. Dust floated among the high rafters, and the wooden floorboards squeaked in the Mystery section, giving it a bit of spooky ambiance. There wasn't enough room to create a dedicated children's space since the coffee shop consumed a good third of the entire store—and accounted for two-thirds of my revenue—but the cozy corner with soft inviting chairs was a relic of my youth.

There was a space on the front wall, between the new arrivals, where I intended to shelve my own novel. Spending so much time among books had eventually worn off on me, and I'd tried a hand at writing myself, like so many others. Fortunately, I'd managed to land a book deal, but I hadn't made my author identity public yet. I'd decide whether to confess that once my novel was released in a matter of weeks. And then only if it met with a positive reception. That thought gave me a thrill of excited, nervous butterflies.

But that was in the future. For today, it was business as usual.

It wasn't long before one of my regular customers, Charlie Hamilton, strolled in and waved as he crossed over to his favorite table near the front window. He'd sit there grading or working on his laptop all morning, punctuated by long periods of time resting his chin in his hands and watching people pass on the sidewalk outside. *Ah, the life.*

I hollered over, "The usual?"

He looked up from plugging in his computer cord. "Thanks."
I kept one eye on Charlie while I pressed espresso into the filter.
As a quintessential college professor, Charlie had constantly
disheveled dirty-blond curls. He kept a close-trimmed beard and
wore black round glasses you'd feel compelled to call *spectacles*.
He reminded me a little bit of Indiana Jones at the beginning of
Raiders, cute in a super nerdy way. But I'd be shocked to discover he went on any adventures. Except in his own mind. Like
me, he kept one foot firmly rooted in the fictional worlds he'd
experienced. We both found life a little more tolerable by imagining we lived a fluid existence, part in and part out of reality.

If Charlie were a character in my fantasy novel, he'd either be
the scribe or the droll sidekick. I dubbed him: Charlie the
Chronicler.

When I set his latte between a legal pad and his cell phone, he
pushed a chair out with his foot. "I don't think the romance in
Pride and Prejudice would fly in the real world. At least not the
modern world."

That was typical Charlie. He didn't much go for small talk.
He started up mid-conversation. He wasn't from here, but since
he'd started working at DePauw, he'd made Orion his home. I'd
grown fond of him and looked forward to talking to him about
literature and his English classes.

"Why not?" I sat and rested my elbows on the table. This
could be a good topic for our book club tonight.

"It isn't exactly sparkling with chemistry."

I laughed. "You're joking. I find hate-to-love romance sparks
the most chemistry. You have to admit it's hot."

He rolled his eyes. "If you say so. I find it kind of lacking."

I was about to accuse him of being a robot when across the
room, my phone went off with the throwback ringtone associated with my author email account: *You've got mail!*

"Excuse me." I stood, and he returned his attention to his papers.

With trepidation, I ducked behind the cash register to check
my phone. Emails to my author account could bring great news,

like: "*Congratulations! We're going to make an audio book!*"
But they could also bring terrifying, challenging work. "*You
need to rewrite the last third of your novel.*"

This email turned out to be neither—just a disappointing
Google alert. Junk.

I'd set up a search on my pen name and the title of my as yet
unreleased novel to catch any mention on blogs, but this alert
came from some site spoofing a bootleg of my book. I forwarded it to my editor, disgusted at jerks who would try to scam
other people by using my creative output as the bait.

Then I saw another link below the first. I clicked it, unaware
that three innocuous words were about to flip my world upside
down.

Chapter 2

✶✶✶

Funny how so many life-altering moments are accompanied by three little words.

I love you.

Kiss the bride.

Hold my beer.

The three words of advice my editor imparted when she sent me my advance copies were: *Don't read reviews.* Nevertheless, I settled on the stool behind the cash register and scanned the blog post, blood pulsing in my fingertips, hoping to see the words *"Brilliant first novel"* and some ego-stroking praise. The few advance reviews I'd already read had been fairly glowing, so despite the prevailing wisdom, I'd started to look forward to the external validation.

The teaser in the email read: *"Review of Claire Kincaid's The Shadow's Apprentice,"* and led to a site called the *Book Brigade.* I'd never heard of it, but then again, I hadn't recognized the last few blogs I'd come across. Authoring was all new to me. I had so much to learn.

My high school English teacher liked to say the author is dead, and, in literature classes, that was usually literally true, so I never gave much thought to the fact that modern-day writers were living, breathing, in-the-flesh real people with feelings and possibly very strong opinions about wrong interpretations of their works. I figured JK Rowling had better things to do than peek her head into a lecture and listen to arguments about the overarching themes in *The Prisoner of Azkaban*.

That was before I crossed the Rubicon from reader to writer. Now reviews gave me a weird thrill. Knowing someone out there was reading my book, I couldn't resist spying on their reactions.

Today was my reckoning.

I scanned the review, and my heart stopped in my chest when I hit the final verdict: *Three solid stars*.

Objectively, I knew most people would consider three stars good enough, and I tried to tell myself it was one disheartening review, not a presage of doom. But I had lofty, and apparently unwarranted, aspirations of literary praise, awards, and interviews with Terry Gross on *Fresh Air*. My career was over, and it hadn't even started.

Rest in peace.

Like a straight A student receiving a C, I wanted to challenge the teacher.

My three word reaction: Not gonna read.

I barely registered when Charlie gathered his things and approached the counter to pay for his latte. I wiped my eyes and took a deep breath. I didn't have the luxury to wallow. I had a business to run.

He paused and cleared his throat. "Are you okay?"

I reached for the stubborn resilience of Anne Shirley and straightened my spine. "I'm fine," I lied.

He narrowed an eye, not convinced. "Gotta go teach, but I'll return before book club."

His shadow lingered in the archway of the door a beat after his body disappeared, but then it grew longer again. I half expected Charlie to emerge, searching for something forgotten, but instead Layla Beckett filled the doorway.

Thank God.

Layla, my best friend, roommate, and confidante, was the only person in town, other than my mom, who knew about my burgeoning side career as an author. I'd eventually confessed to her on pain of death to keep it a secret because I needed her mad skills to help set up my website and show me how to use Twitter to promote myself when the time came. At least I knew I could count on her to read my early drafts with gentle suggestions that wouldn't destroy my confidence, unlike some people around here. In high school, I once asked Max to read a funny short story I'd written. I just wanted to make him laugh, but he turned it into a teaching opportunity and offered me unsolicited advice on tightening the language. I vowed never to let him read anything I wrote ever again. Hence my need for Layla's utter discretion.

Layla spent the better part of her day staring at the computer screen, managing a band's unofficial fan forum, and writing blog posts. She understood the benefit of keeping a dual identity, though she kept her anonymity in reverse. She'd never hidden her passion for her pet band around town, but she fiercely protected her real-life identity from the strangers she met in her forum. She didn't think of them as strangers, but rather as portable friends. Nonetheless, she went by an alias and never shared identifying information. I couldn't understand how one could get to know anyone camouflaged behind a screen name.

"Can you do me a favor?" I pulled up the *Book Brigade* as she crossed the store to the register. "Some stranger hiding behind an alias left me a review. Would you read it and tell me what you think?"

I handed her my phone, and she squinted at the tiny print on the screen. "Who's Silver Fox? Guy or girl?"

"No idea."

"One sec." She clicked the username to the bio page and pronounced, "He." She clicked back to the review. "Should I read it aloud?"

I put my hands over my face and peeked between my fingers. "Sure."

"Here we go." She waggled her eyebrows as if she were talking about doing something fun and mischievous, like sneaking out late at night. I guess it's always more fun when it's someone else's execution. "'Review of Claire Kincaid's *The Shadow's Ap-*

prentice.' " Layla reached over and touched my wrist. "I still think it's awesome you took your birth mom's first name for your pseudonym."

She seemed less impressed that I'd used my adoptive mom's maiden name as well.

"You are killing me, Layla." I wasn't going to survive if she peppered every statement with commentary. "Can you just read straight through?"

She turned her attention back to the phone. " 'I received an advance copy of this book in exchange for an honest review.' " She lifted her eyes. "Who sent the free copy?"

I grumbled. "Not a clue. I'm guessing my publicist wanted to get the book out there ahead of the release."

"Okay. Let's see what this Fox character has to say." She cleared her throat. " '*The Shadow's Apprentice* is a quest fantasy with a side of romance. I went into this thinking it would be a Tolkien knockoff as the novel opens with a visit from a mysterious wizened old man seeking a willing assistant to journey with him across the land to defeat a distant foe. But the similarities with other quest novels often serve to upend expected tropes, which leads to some surprising and amusing twists. The apprentice chosen to follow the old man is a commoner, a woman named Lela, who has a well-timed sense of humor, and her confidence and power grow stronger over time.' "

She stopped again. "Lela? That's almost Layla."

"Yeah, he got their names wrong. Keep going."

" 'A love interest is introduced, but the attempt to shoehorn in a romantic arc proves a lackluster effort at best. The wooden rapport between Dane and Lela—' " she cackled " '—left me unsatisfied. I've felt more chemistry between my kitchen appliances. It's so stilted that I'm left suspecting the author hasn't had a single romantic experience.

" 'The world building—though filled with info dumps and heavy exposition—was the strongest aspect. For a debut novelist, Kincaid shows a deft hand at creating a real sense of depth in culture and geography. There were times it seemed like she'd read a real Wikipedia page about some custom and felt the need to show her research. That these were fabricated elements impressed me on an intellectual level, but these were also the places that took me out of the story and made me wish to know less about the *Creed* and more about what is driving Dane and Lela on their journey.

" 'Overall, a promising debut, though for me it fell flat. Three solid stars.' "

"Hmm." Layla tilted her head at me. "Not a terrible review at all."

I gripped a napkin and twisted it. "He hated it."

"I disagree. Did you hear all the praise in there? A promising debut, Maddie."

"It fell flat." By the end of the day, I'd probably be able to quote the entire review like it was *The Hitchhiker's Guide to the Galaxy*. If only it had been that funny.

"It's only one reviewer. And honestly, you're hearing only the critical bits. You know how subjective opinions can be."

"I do know that. But how can his critique be valid when he doesn't appear to have read the book? He didn't even get the character names right."

"Maybe fantasy isn't his thing."

"He took specific issue with the romance." I scrunched up my face to fight tears, swallowing the frog in my throat. "You read it. Did you find the romance believable? Am I such a failure at life, I can't even tell if my fictional romance rings true?"

"Let it go, Maddie. You're likely to encounter much more brutal reviews once it's released. If you're lucky enough to get readers."

Gut punch. "Ouch. Thanks for the vote of confidence."

"Just saying. Champagne problems. It's a part of the deal, Mads. You should see what people say on my fan forum about Adam's new music. And that's coming from his fans."

I loved that she took criticism of that band personally. "I'm just irritated."

"Remember. You signed up for this. You can't now complain that your diamond shoes are too tight." She handed me back my phone.

"Come to book club tonight?" I'd been asking her for ages, but Max had gotten all the Beckett bookworm genes.

She wrinkled her nose. "Nah. I only came over to get you to make me a latte. I just got up."

I didn't chastise her for sleeping all day. The girl was a recluse and a night owl who only occasionally risked full sunlight. I fixed her a to-go cup and slipped her one of the leftover apple crumb muffins.

Once Layla had left, darker thoughts rolled in like an army of orcs. Business was slower than I would have liked, but a few patrons came in, ordered coffee, and sat at tables talking or reading their devices, without buying books. The mail arrived, bringing an energy bill that had me wanting to crawl up to every customer on hands and knees and implore them to purchase the *Game of Thrones* box set.

And winter was coming. Eventually.

As the day went on, I returned to the review like a moth bashing against a fluorescent light. I'd let an anonymous reviewer get under my skin, and the words *wooden rapport* ping-ponged around my brain, but the jab that truly rattled me was: *It makes me suspect the author has had no romantic experience.*

Ha. *You know nothing, Silver Fox.*

Granted, my last great romantic experience had ended in crushing humiliation. But, my main characters, Rane and Lira, had a better love story than I'd ever personally known. As my own relationship collapsed, they'd become surrogates I poured all my frustration into.

I'd *felt* their attraction. Had I failed to convey it on the page?

I began to panic over the impending book club. How could I carry on a literary discussion of a classic while half my brain obsessed over my own literary incompetence?

By the time the sunlight grew burnt orange and faded, I was deep in a pity party. I slipped outside to drag my sales table back in and caught sight of the chalkboard sign that now read:

I LIKE BIG BOOKS AND I CANNOT LIE.

I chortled, wondering if it had been like that all day. At least I knew I could blame that bit of vandalism on Max.

The bell tinkled as Charlie burst through the front door like a battering ram. He rubbed his shoulder. "You should really fix that."

He laughed to diffuse the criticism, and I tried to shake off my despair. It was time to put on a good pretense for the bi-weekly Friday night book club.

With a fake but hospitable smile, I crossed the floor. "Ready to plunge into *Pride and Prejudice*?"

I was so pleased when Charlie started coming to the book club since the only other man who ever showed up was Max. But while Max used the gathering as a chance to advertise his wares, Charlie legitimately loved to argue about books. Plus he gave me an excuse to take a prolonged detour into the classics.

We moved closer to the circle of chairs where the rest of the group would soon gather.

Charlie took a seat, pushing his glasses into place. "I'm looking forward to comparing it to modern romance."

If Jane Austen were alive, would she care to hear Charlie's opinion? Would it hurt her fragile ego if he said her book was filled with too much exposition? Did real authors eventually develop a thick skin for criticism? Or did they just get better at *shoehorning* in the romance?

Charlie set the book on his lap and tapped his index finger on the binding. We weren't usually the only two at the book club, and I dreaded facing a one-on-one conversation with a legit English professor when I'd lost all confidence. I was a total fraud leading a discussion group on literature when I couldn't even get four stars from a third-rate blog.

I'd been tempted from time to time to confide in Charlie about my novel in the perhaps naïve belief that my skin was thick enough to withstand his literary criticism—or perhaps arrogantly confident there would be none. Now I imagined him taking a red pen to whole passages, saying, "*This romance doesn't ring true. Delete. Delete. Delete.*"

I doubted I'd ever want to share this secret with him or anyone else. I couldn't even handle judgment from a total stranger. At least I could take comfort in the fact that I was forging my own destiny, running a bookstore on my own. I didn't need some blogger to validate me or anyone else to help me succeed in my business. I would prove to all the doubters that my potential was limitless.

I was no damsel in distress in need of a hero to rescue me.

These were the words I told myself so I could fake it until I made it. Deep down, my faith balanced on the edge of a knife.

Thankfully, the bell jingled wildly again as Shawna Brooks, proprietor of a high-end boutique two doors down, thrust the door open, followed close behind by recently widowed Midge Long.

I counted heads. "Where's Letitia?" Our town karate-slash-dance instructor was usually punctual.

When the door opened again, I was disappointed it was just Max, come to use my book club for his own professional advancement. If I was being honest, I'd formed the club to breathe life into my own struggling business.

I started to raise my voice to start the group, but Max approached the mingling mass, offering a plate of his mini cupcakes.

Midge followed my gaze and cried out, "Oh, Max. Look at those beautiful works of art. Are those for us?"

Whatever order I might have imposed was lost in the excitement of a dozen extra-small cupcakes. I should have opened a daycare.

"Remember," said Max, "next week, we'll have strawberry shortcakes, so make sure to beg Maddie to order enough for everyone."

I knew what he was up to. He was planting the idea in their brains that my bookstore was a conduit straight into Max's kitchen.

He cut his eyes over with a mischievous grin, like he could

just pretend we'd forged a joint LLC and he was simply building brand loyalty. I couldn't begrudge him hustling to drum up business, when the truth was, by coaxing customers to come in, he was helping me, too. But it was just another gambit to gain access to my store and benefit his own growing business.

I shook my head and walked toward the chairs. Channeling the pride of Elizabeth Bennet and the self-determination of Jo March, I clapped my hands. "Can we go ahead and get started? We can mingle after the book club."

Our motley group convened in the circle of assorted chairs. While everyone scooted around, I took a seat between Midge and Shawna and began.

"You've all read *Pride and Prejudice* I hope." Nearly every head nodded. Midge grimaced, but I didn't call her out. I knew she mainly came for the company. There was a good chance she'd at least seen one of the movies. I continued. "I want to start by talking about the title if that's okay. What do pride and prejudice mean to you in this novel?"

Charlie, ever the professor, raised his hand and dove into a lengthy theory about individual desire versus societal pressure. Charlie relished the role of literary expert, so I let him ramble on for a few minutes. I was about to wrest the conversation back when Shawna interrupted. "Let's get to the good stuff. How hot is the chemistry between Lizzie and Darcy?"

She could have plunged a dagger in my heart, reminding me that Silver Fox had written: "*I've felt more chemistry between my kitchen appliances.*"

That nasty review got nastier in my imagination. It was like poking my tongue at a painful cold sore, and I was unable to stop myself from the torture.

I pulled my long braid forward and twirled it around my finger, anxious. Had I been as delusional as Professor Lockhart? *Was* I a hack?

There was a pretty even split between those of us who believed the longing and desire in Austen's romantic tension and those who found the romance two-dimensional and unconvincing. The fact that even Jane Austen could be torn apart by a difference in opinion improved my mood slightly. Maybe I'd get a better review by someone less obviously heartless.

Max got in the last word on the topic. "If she hadn't been so *proud,* he might have been able to help her out a lot sooner."

I suspected he'd only stayed to use the discussion to tell me how to live my life. He hadn't even answered the question.

Rather than humor him, I decided to move on. Right as I landed on the perfect topic, the door swung open, and all heads jerked toward the sound, eyes lit up, and Shawna actually stood. I turned around to see what all the fuss was about. Dylan Black, known to his childhood friends as Dylan Ramirez, stood in my bookstore looking directly at me with his piercing blue-gray eyes.

Chapter 3

Dylan was immediately surrounded by everyone, crowding him, demanding to know everything at once.

"When did you get in?"

"How long are you here for?"

"Are the rumors true?"

He answered or evaded questions with charm and a staged chuckle. "Tonight. A month. What rumors?" He kept glancing at me sidelong as he moved farther into the store, like a rock star surrounded by paparazzi. That was half right.

With his raven-black hair and long dark eyelashes framing those stormy eyes, it was no wonder the record studio had opted to package him like he'd recently walked away from a Latin boy band. Over the years, he'd grown even more attractive, and photographers knew how to work with him to take his image into the sphere of erotic fantasies.

Despite all the hoopla, he was just Dylan to me. Once upon a time, he'd been my boyfriend, but rivers of water had passed under burnt bridges since our last kiss years ago. Things had never been the same between us since he'd climbed on a Greyhound bound for New York City, guitar slung over his back like the quintessential musician leaving home, insisting he'd never return to the small world of Orion.

And yet, here he was, and not for the first time, though I hadn't seen him since Christmas.

He scratched his jaw and smiled. "Hey, Maddie." His voice sounded like sandpaper, like he was recovering from a debilitating illness. He dropped into a chair. "Sorry to break up your book club, but I knew I'd catch you all here."

"Not a problem. We were just discussing *Pride and Prejudice*. I think you might remember it?" We'd studied the book in AP World Literature. I didn't mean to sound like a chastising schoolmarm, but his sudden intrusion had me searching for the proper reaction. The last time he'd come home, I was about to be married, and he was preoccupied with his music, as always. Had he come here to see me or catch up with the rest of the gang?

Dylan said, "Please. I'd love to sit in. Don't stop on account of me."

As if a force field broke, the others slowly came back and took their places around the circle, and I picked up my notes with a shaky hand.

"We were just talking about the romantic tension between the leads." I gave them a chance to settle down, but the energy in the air had changed, charged. I read the question on my notes, feigning business as usual. "It's notable that Lizzie's love for Darcy grows despite a lack of direct contact through much of the book. Is this realistic? What is her love ultimately based on?"

Shawna blurted out, "His ten thousand pounds yearly," in the voice of the foolish mother from the movies, and everyone laughed.

"Funny," said Max, not laughing. "But I think it's because she was finally matched in intelligence and wit, and it drove her mad."

He was taunting me, recalling how we'd vied for the best GPA in high school, but also getting in a dig at Dylan, as if intelligence and wit had played no part in our attraction. That assumption was both rude and wrong. He'd never taken the time to get to know Dylan and mistook quiet for shallow, but I knew how deep those waters ran.

Charlie exhaled ponderously. "On a practical level, Darcy

ends up proving his own so-called love for her beyond a shadow of a doubt through his actions, by saving her family's honor."

I gave him the stink eye. "His *so-called* love?" Charlie didn't hold out hope for romance, but sometimes his cynicism pushed the bounds of plausibility.

Dylan cleared his throat. "She may not always be in contact with Darcy, but she knows him."

He rubbed the sexy day-old stubble on his chin. Had he learned that calculated move from copious photo shoots? As a writer and a connoisseur of scruff, I lamented the dearth of words to describe the beauty of a man's facial hair. It made my fingers itch with the desire to touch.

He found me gawking and flashed his professionally whitened smile at me, like a perfect toothpaste ad. "She has his letter after all. Reading his words, she recognizes a soul like her own."

He could have been describing us. We were a study in opposites, Dylan and me. In high school, he rode a motorbike and played guitar. I was a bookworm who lacked the courage to look at nonfiction boys. But I knew him by his words. When Dylan sang his lyrics to me, there'd been no hope for my virginity.

I caught Shawna watching me, watching Dylan. I knew it was only a matter of time before the town would start speculating on my own swooning heart. But I was made of tougher stuff than when I was seventeen, when my body had only recently developed enough to attract the male gaze and glorify in such attention.

Midge sighed. "That's absolutely beautiful, Dylan." I dragged my eyes back to my discussion guide, but Midge went off script. "It's so lovely to see you again. What's brought you home?"

Dylan had the grace to cast an apologetic wince toward me, but everything eventually revolved around Dylan. He was a gravitational force, and becoming an honest-to-God star had only fed the bonfires of his vanity. "Well, Ms. Long. I was ordered to take a break, get some fresh air and home cooking."

Before it could turn into the Dylan show, I asked, "You should come back to the book club in two weeks. We'll be reading *Jane Eyre*."

He pressed his lips together. "I will . . . If you promise to come out to see me perform at the Jukebox in a few weeks."

When did everything become self-promotion?

But he got the desired response, and Shawna and Midge started hounding him about his music. I stood, stretched, and walked to the register to give them all the hint that it was time to buy the next book and leave. My ploy worked, and everyone but Dylan lined up.

Dylan reached into his messenger bag and produced a flier for his upcoming show. "You mind hanging this somewhere?"

Was that why he'd stopped in?

I frowned as he turned toward the door. I thought he might hang around a bit and catch up, and it hurt that he was already taking off. Though what did we have to talk about anyway? The days we'd spent together were in the past. So were the nights.

He paused and said, "I'll stop by tomorrow."

As I rang Charlie up, Shawna gushed, "That boy could make me consider cheating on Rebecca." My eyes must have been saucers because she added, "Apologies, Maddie. But you did let him go."

Midge bought her copy, saying, "It's never too late." Then to my horror, she added, "If I were fifty years younger . . ."

After they bought their books and left, the noise in the store dropped back to near total silence.

I exhaled. That had been a crash course on why I'd never date a rock star.

But it did nothing for my private thoughts that echoed Shawna's. And I wouldn't even be cheating on Peter. So why wasn't I rushing after him?

I shook my head, recalling what that reviewer had said about my fictional romance. *"It's so stilted that I'm left suspecting the author hasn't had a single romantic experience."*

Boy, was he wrong. I'd had *two*. Did it count if both had ended in failure when I refused to give up my own dreams to follow theirs?

If that's what love was, Silver Fox could keep it.

* * *

With the store empty, I started to close out the cash register. I stacked the cash and packed it into the security deposit bag, rubbing my eyes and humming a Beatles song. I nearly jumped out of my skin when a voice harmonized with mine.

"Shit, Max. You scared me to death."

He'd taken up a spot on a rickety old stool that had been in the store since we were kids. He had a dog-eared copy of *Huckleberry Finn* on his knee, like he was killing time. He stretched and flipped the book facedown, still open, and I cringed for the dilapidated spine.

He sat only a couple of feet behind the register, and I caught the scent of cinnamon and brown sugar, as if his mahogany hair itself were a confection from his kitchen. Muffin-head Max.

"Crazy seeing Dylan tonight, huh?"

I closed the cash drawer and grabbed the security deposit bag and my purse. "Why are you still here?" He'd never spared a thought for Dylan.

"I thought you might want to go grab a slice of pizza."

"Not hungry," I lied.

After I flipped off the lights and moved to the front of the bookstore, I turned with my hands on my hips, waiting for him to take a hint and clear out. He slipped off the stool and crossed the room in three strides. Streetlight and shadows streaked his face. My gaze lingered on the slight scruff across his jaw, my biggest weakness when it came to objectifying men. If I hadn't known him since he'd worn diapers, I might have pictured him as the hero of some paperback romance as he closed the gap between us with hooded lids, obscuring his clear green eyes.

"Ah. You're mad about this morning." He exhaled ponderously. "I know I'm trying too hard. I'm really sorry. Okay?"

I wasn't mad. I was tired. Everything had been a competition with him since high school. Only one of us could be valedictorian after all. I didn't want my bookstore to become another prize in an unwinnable contest.

"I'm not mad, Max."

He snickered at the accidental movie title, but I rolled my eyes. It wasn't even close to the first time we'd heard that particular joke. Layla had even given us the hashtag #TeamMad-Max, shipping her twin brother and her best friend since we were kids, as if that was ever going to be a thing.

"If I promise to drop it tonight, will you come hang out with me?"

He couldn't fool me with his change in tactics. He thought he could wear me down, but I wasn't going to hand him the keys to my kingdom.

"Come on." I held the door open. "I just want to go home."

He went out into the night before me.

Three words I wouldn't be saying to Max Beckett anytime soon were: *Let's work together.*

He walked me home, though there was no need for the escort. Crime in Orion was limited to jaywalking or rolling a stop sign. Or lately graffiti. Anyway I lived right across the street from my bookshop, a block from his apartment. It wasn't my ideal living situation. I'd pictured myself with Peter in my dream house at this point. But since he'd left me with my unwanted freedom, I'd had to figure things out for myself.

Layla found herself with a similar need for cheap, independent housing. We'd roomed together in college, but while I headed to Indianapolis after graduation, she'd moved home, right back to her childhood bedroom. It was that or room with Max. When I found myself homeless, we'd agreed to move in together to split costs.

I would have preferred to find a way to live alone above my bookstore. I'd managed to make the upstairs space into a rugged office where I sometimes escaped to write, but without a shower, it wouldn't be an abode anytime soon.

At least my short walk to and from work forced me to get exercise out among other people.

Max talked about the bridal party his mom had made a cake for. "They're tying the knot by that old covered bridge out Route 36. You know the one?"

"Mm-hmm." Peter and I had driven over there on one of our

dates. The bridge didn't go anywhere, but it made a quaint land-mark, a romantic destination. We'd picnicked along the side of Big Walnut Creek.

I didn't want to talk about Peter. Not with Max. Not yet. Probably not ever.

As I opened the door leading up to my apartment, Max waited as if some lunatic was going to materialize out of thin air at the last second to assault me.

"Tell Layla to give me a call. See if she might want to go with me when I take the cake out on Sunday, okay?"

"Will do."

"Maybe you'd like to go, too?"

Thanks to a stupid town ordinance, the bookstore was closed on Sundays, so I'd be free to hang with Max and Layla like old times. The three of us had been inseparable once upon a time. But there was no way in hell I'd spend my day off captive to Max's enterprising suggestions. He'd probably bring a poster board, complete with pie charts and a laser pointer. Pass.

"Sorry, no. I'm gonna go hang out with my mom." That was likely true.

"See you tomorrow morning." He edged back.

I spared him one last glance before closing the door, and in that moment, I could see a dozen younger versions of him super-imposed one on top of the other, and nostalgia hit me so hard, it took my breath away. Why was life so complicated?

The light was on in Layla's bedroom, so I tapped on the door, and it creaked open. She sat in bed with her laptop propped on her knees, like always.

"Hey." She set her laptop aside and stretched.

I never would have predicted she'd become such a huge music nerd. We'd grown up watching her dad perform in dad bands, usually in her basement but sometimes at the pool clubhouse. It was equal parts mortifying and hilarious. He'd play Clapton of course. Layla hadn't come by her name by accident. He also played a ton of Beatles to please Mrs. Beckett. Now he came out to perform at my café sometimes. He was good. Not Dylan good, but I liked it when he played.

It wasn't until a new band ended up at the Jukebox one night that she truly caught the spirit of music fanaticism. Then she fell in whole hog.

After high school, she avoided a real job by writing freelance music articles and scrounging up ad revenue on the website she founded. She and I went off to college to study business on our parents' dime. Afterward, I immediately found an entry-level job in Indianapolis making use of my degree, but fortunately for her, the band she followed had had a meteoric rise in popularity over the past few years. Now, she doubled down on contributing articles and driving traffic to her site. She was fairly successful at it, but reality was knocking, and it was obvious to me that she couldn't sustain this lifestyle forever.

Not that I could talk. I'd walked away from my exciting career in product management to take a chance on a risky venture. At the time, I'd assumed I'd have financial security in the form of a supportive, employed husband. Stupid assumption.

Layla pulled her feet up to make room for me on her bed, her bent knees forming a tent under the sheet. "You here to vent about Peter?"

She'd listened patiently as I passed through the five stages of grief since Peter left, and although she'd never exactly taken sides against Peter, she continually half joked about her crazy notion that now that Peter was out of the picture, her dream of matchmaking me with her brother so we could become sisters would finally pay off.

For that reason, I didn't mention that Dylan was home.

I dropped into the space she'd cleared. "Oh. For once, it's not that."

She winced. "Sorry, honey. Have you heard anything from him?"

That was a kick to my slowly healing heart. Ever since my fiancé, my groom, my husband-to-be failed to show up to our wedding, leaving me humiliated at the altar, all we ever did was fight over the business we shared. He'd given me a simple choice: Sell the bookstore and leave Orion to join him in Indianapolis, or he'd walk away.

I'd called his bluff. He'd called off the marriage.

The funny thing about ultimatums is that they seem like a great bargaining tool until you're left living with the logical extreme of your negotiation tactic. In my case, I'd told Peter if he left me, he shouldn't bother coming back. He hadn't bothered to.

"Not since he sent me my last bank statement." I heard how pathetic that sounded, and my shoulders slumped. "I think he's waiting for me to fail." Waiting for this alternate universe to collapse under its own weight. He'd never believed I could keep the bookstore going another year, so I pictured him biding his time until I was forced to crawl back and concede. I thought if I could prove him wrong, he'd be the one crawling to me. We were both as stubborn as my sticky front door.

The end game that scared me most was that one day, when he was done waiting, tired of playing with my heart and my future, he'd call in his loan. At that point, I wouldn't be able to pay him back, and I'd lose it all—both the bookstore and Peter.

The clock was ticking.

But I wanted to show them all. I could do this on my own.

She nudged me. "Earth to Maddie. What did you need?"

I blinked and recalled what had carried me to her threshold. "It was about that reviewer."

"Silver Fox?" She snorted. "Who does he think he is? George Clooney?"

I smiled, but I was still too angry and upset to laugh about it yet. "I keep thinking about him getting my character names wrong."

"And?"

"And maybe I should write him and ask him if he even read the book."

Her eyes went wide. "No. Do not under any circumstances do that. Do not engage."

"I just want to know."

She kicked off her covers and rolled over to swing her legs onto the floor. It was a miracle of Grandpa Joe proportions whenever she got out of bed. I pictured her dancing around, singing "I've Got a Golden Ticket" in her nightgown. Her knees didn't so much as buckle as she headed to the kitchen. She stopped at the door.

"If you want to mess with him, do it the old-fashioned way. Create an army of sock puppets to hide behind and dispute him in the blog comments." She shuffled out the door. "You want half a frozen pizza?"

I got up to follow her, dreaming up some convoluted plot that would place me face-to-face with Silver Fox. He'd show up at a book signing and introduce himself. I'd play it cool at first, but when I signed his book, I'd write, "*Let me just shoehorn in this signature.*" He'd attempt to defend his review, but I'd point my finger in his face and—

"You coming, Maddie?"

Layla stuck her head around the door, and I shook myself into reality.

Once we'd eaten, I set a bottle of beer on my nightstand, climbed under the covers, and pulled up my bookstore blog to write a post about the book club's discussion of *Pride and Prejudice*.

I put on Dylan's album in the background, and for a solid half hour, allowed myself to scan the images of him that came up from a Google search, trying to find the boy I used to know in the slick photo spreads or the grungy concert shots. I paused when I found one showing him way back at the start of his career, fresh faced and innocent, still looking like the boy I'd once thought I loved.

Then they'd polished him into someone I barely recognized. At first he'd been miserable. He sent me the photos they'd shot for his album cover with an angst-ridden letter, followed by drunken phone calls. And then he slowly became that other person, the phone calls grew less frequent, and Dylan Ramirez ceased to exist.

Sighing, I closed out the browser and tried to get some random miscellany accomplished. I checked the schedule for the week since school was out and I wanted to advertise a teen summer reading group. I finished off my beer and went to grab another, yawning. It wasn't late, and I had a newsletter to lay out. Before I started that, I sent an email to an author about an upcoming signing event at the store.

It was close to midnight when I opened my last beer and my work-in-progress sequel. I wasn't dumb enough to write with a buzz on, but I giggled, leaving myself passive-aggressive comments to Silver Fox in the margins.

What does some sixty-year-old virgin know about romance?

These would either be hilarious or pathetic in the morning, but it felt good to take out my revenge with my mighty pen—like slaying a dragon. It was a relief to finally laugh about it.

Chapter 4

Morning light filtered in red through my closed lids, and I woke with a slow awareness that the chiming sounds were in fact my alarm and not an invasion of customers opening my shop door in a massive stream. My head throbbed like I'd been slamming back beers. Maybe I had been.

Calling in sick isn't an option for a sole proprietor, so I rolled out of bed, fighting an urge to barf. I half crawled to the kitchen and fell into a chair.

Layla appeared in the kitchen doorway. "Did you successfully drown your sorrows?"

"What are you doing up so early? Have you been up all night?"

"Crazy rumors are swirling. Had to make sure everyone on the forum was behaving."

She started grinding coffee, and the pounding in my head increased. I groaned.

She cast a concerned look my way. "How late did *you* stay up?"

"Uh." I cast my mind back to try to remember when exactly I'd finally put the computer away. "I had this dream that I got into a taxi and the driver was that reviewer. I gave him a piece of my mind. It was kind of cathartic." That's what I got for burning him in effigy before going to sleep.

She opened the fridge. "Can I fix you something to eat?"

"Nah. I'll grab a muffin and coffee at the shop."

I took my time showering away my hangover. On mornings like this, I was glad I was the shop's owner. Nobody could yell at me if I rolled in a little late. Not that I had many mornings like this. I hadn't gone on a bender since—well, since Peter ditched me with a church full of friends and an uneaten wedding cake. I ate the cake, then made use of the open bar in the reception hall. I figured the deposit was nonrefundable.

When I returned to my room, I found Layla digging through my closet. Not at all ashamed to have been caught, she said, "I need to borrow something professional." She sorted through my slacks and blouses like she was going through a sales rack. "Wow, Maddie. I didn't know you owned so many dresses."

I'd built an extensive career wardrobe, but the dresses were for after work. Peter would take me to cocktail parties with friends and corporate events with colleagues. We looked dashing together, though people would often assume he had fifteen years on me. The sprays of silver highlights in his hair lent him maturity and a weird advantage in his business. Women twice my age would flirt with him right in front of me, and men who didn't realize he was barely thirty would nod approvingly at me as evidence Peter had landed a hot young trophy wife.

Later that night, in the privacy of our apartment, those dresses would hit the floor, as we undressed each other, laughing at how stuffy those parties were, at how we'd never let ourselves get sucked into that world. We'd be in it, but not of it. That was the plan once upon a time.

Layla fanned out the red fabric of a slinky cocktail dress, probably imagining how it would look on her. Or me. I'd bought those dresses in another time. Another place. It wouldn't have surprised me if Layla reached behind my wardrobe and brushed the fir trees of last Christmas. If I walked through, could I step into my old life exactly the way I'd left it six months before?

When Layla unearthed a black polka-dotted A-line from the very edges of history, my heart squeezed. I'd worn that one year ago when I'd dragged Peter to our first and last bachata class. Halfway through the lesson, Letitia announced we'd be switching partners. Peter scanned the room, and his gaze came back to me. He pulled me close and whispered, "I came here to dance with you." Rather than make the best of an awkward situation, he walked out, leaving me in the impossible position of either finishing the class without a partner, or worse, quitting on Letitia as well. It was our first fight over Orion. He apologized later, and I forgave him, but we never went back for another lesson. Only in hindsight could I recognize it as foreshadowing our final break.

I should have donated all those clothes a long time ago. "Take what you want. I have to go."

Layla laid a hand on my wrist. "Everything okay?"

"Fine," I lied. "Stop in later, okay? Get out and prove to the world you're still alive."

When I descended the stairs and exited out my front door, I was met by Saturday morning in Orion. Out on the sidewalk, kids in white karate uniforms dragged huge duffel bags up the sidewalk in one direction while little girls in pink leotards headed in the other, toward Letitia's for dance lessons. I'd spent plenty of time myself in her studio, either learning rudimentary martial arts or ballet. Later, my mom pressured me into taking ballroom dance with other teens. Max and I giggled our way through the Foxtrot.

Letitia stood in the doorway of her studio chatting with parents. She waved, and I yelled, "Where were you last night?"

She called over, "I had a date!" and a chorus of young kids responded in a singsong *ooOOoo*.

"Anyone I know?"

"No! I met him online."

Ridiculous. I couldn't believe anyone could build a real relationship on the Internet. Between Layla and now Letitia, I knew it happened, but it would be so much harder to get to know someone that way.

Across the street, a few customers enjoyed the beautiful morning at small tables outside Gentry's. If I had opened on time, would they be sitting in my café instead?

I looked both ways before crossing Main Street toward my

own bookstore, waving at the parents herding their children toward their cars or to the library or elsewhere. Some of the younger kids would show up to my bookstore for story time later. Parents might then buy my coffee and pastries. Maybe even a book or two.

If I could inspire one of those kids to become a lifelong reader, I'd feel satisfied I'd done something good. My attempts at a teen reading group had so far fallen on deaf ears. Most of the older kids had jobs during the summer. When they weren't working or vandalizing my storefront, they'd either hang out at Anderson's eating pizza or run around outside unsupervised, much like Max, Layla, and I had done when we were younger.

Even with all our adventures, I'd always found the time to read. During the school year, I'd established a familiar habit of taking a detour to the bookstore before walking home. Mrs. Moore would show me the latest books to arrive or point me to an overlooked classic. We'd sometimes talk about the books we'd read—our own small book club.

My allowance was always earmarked for a new book, and as soon as I'd finish one, I'd donate it to the library so someone else might encounter the same worlds I'd walked through. Sometimes Max, my constant shadow back then, would turn around and pick up my castoffs and follow me to the Mossy Stone to sit on that rickety old stool and eavesdrop on my discussions with Mrs. Moore, always ready to contradict our interpretations.

When I'd visit from college, I could count on Mrs. Moore to recommend some mindless fun reading to pass the holidays. I assumed she'd always be there, and it never occurred to me that I'd one day replace her.

After Mrs. Moore died, I came home and walked into this bookstore, breathing it in, letting the peace settle over me, the sense of belonging, of being home. Remembering. And I swear the bookstore remembered me.

I dearly wanted to buy the shop, but Peter convinced me to focus on working my way up the corporate ladder rather than throw away borrowed money. Wes Moore, the eldest son, took over and tried to keep his mom's business afloat. Books were never his passion, and whenever I'd stop in, it was apparent he wasn't happy. As a result, the store he'd cleverly renamed Read Moore Books wasn't thriving.

One day, without consulting Peter, on pure gut instinct, I approached Wes with an offer. At first Peter rolled with my change in plans and even helped me get the financing to buy the store. His down payment and co-signature secured the mortgage, making him a silent partner. At least, he didn't interfere with how I ran the business. Not at first anyway.

Wes seemed relieved to be able to let the place go to someone who would love it.

And I did love it.

Every time I walked inside, the air of my youth enveloped me. I'd traveled to many distant lands while curled up in the corner nook. It was only fitting that the store itself could transport me in time.

I fetched my keys and fumbled for the right one. A couple of skateboarders came out of nowhere and nearly knocked me over. I glared after, resisting the urge to shake a fist.

After a good thrust, the door opened. I went to flip on the lights and a soft jazz station, then started a pot of coffee

My phone buzzed with a text from Max. *Stopped by, but the shop was closed. Everything okay?*

A sinking feeling of guilt hit me. I should have been here early enough to take care of business instead of pulling an all-night pity party over my writing, which let's face it was more a hobby than a career.

I shot off a reply. *Here now. So sorry. Could you stop by when you get a chance?*

In my kitchen, I had a surplus of double chocolate muffins nobody had bought the day before. They'd have to do until Max arrived. It was close to lunch anyway, and I had a small menu of sandwiches I could make. Most people just ordered coffee anyway.

As I restocked one corner of my display unit, my phone blurted *You've got mail!* and I wondered who was trying to reach me through my author account so early.

I played a game of anticipating whether the email would be something fun, like finding out my agent had sold movie rights, or mundane, like a newsletter from a writing organization. Since it was Saturday, I put my money on the latter.

After I fixed my own coffee and muffin, I grabbed a seat in the café to catch up on all my missed notifications.

The subject heading waiting for me made me nearly choke:

Subject: Re: Silver Fox review

I set the phone down, unsure if I wanted to read on. I thought my rant had all been a dream, just drunken fantasies playing out in my subconscious. Evidence would seem to prove otherwise. Apparently, I had emailed Mr. Silver Fox, and I had a nauseatingly good idea what I'd written. None of it good. Layla was going to give me hell.

The bell over the door jangled, sparing me from mustering the courage to find out how badly I'd fucked up. The arrival of a potential customer cheered me up until Gentry Lamar poked his gray-haired head in. "Madeleine?"

"Over here."

He strode in, all business. "Madeleine, are you aware that door is a fire hazard?"

Ever since Gentry had been elected president of the town council, he considered himself president of Orion. Nobody else wanted the position, so we were stuck with the dictator. Emphasis on dick. He was mostly harmless, though, and it was easier to let him handle organizing town events. We paid the price with his prissiness.

"What do you need, Gentry?"

He pursed his lips. "I thought we'd talked about leaving our 'Buy in Orion' flags up through Labor Day. I noticed *yours* is not hanging outside your door. Have you taken it down?"

Those stupid flags. "I may have taken it down."

"Your shop stands out as the only one not participating in the Chamber of Commerce's efforts to promote local business."

He had a way of both whining and commanding at the same time. The word I wanted was *needling*.

I hadn't even taken a sip of my coffee. "If I promise to put it up, will you stop berating me?"

He scowled. "I was not berating you. I'm simply pointing out a deficiency. I'll thank you for correcting the problem."

I waited, but he didn't leave. "Is there something else?"

"Yes. Could I get an assortment of muffins to go?"

My face must have looked cartoonishly shocked. "Gentry, you sell your own muffins."

He'd always had a better selection of muffins and croissants and scones than I did. Plus Max told me he'd hired a nightly pastry chef. He probably had all kinds of fancy breakfast pies and extravagant donuts.

He scanned my paltry leftovers. "Yes, but we've run out."

Was he serious? Or psyching me out? The only way Gentry could have run out of muffins would be if his business was booming. Maybe I ought to rethink Max's offer to set up shop in my kitchen.

If Gentry wanted to pay me full price for Max's stale muffins, I should have let him. After all his money was as good as anyone else's. But I couldn't very well run a coffee shop with nothing to feed people. "No, Gentry. Those are for my customers. You know that."

He looked around slowly. "What customers exactly?"

I bit back a blistering retort, vowing to take out my frustration later in writing. Everything was fuel for my fiction.

On his way out, Gentry paused. "I'm glad you've reconsidered the sign. And fix this door. I'd hate to have to report your shop as a death trap."

No, he wouldn't. He'd been nagging me about every aspect of my store since I'd moved in, from the peeling paint on the windowsills to the minuscule crack in the foundation where that damn dandelion kept creeping back. He'd made it no secret he would love to buy me out so he could demolish the bookstore and turn this space into a bed-and-breakfast to accompany his small restaurant. He'd need to drive me out, but there was little chance of that. Didn't stop him from measuring for curtains whenever he stopped in.

The minute Gentry left, I turned the deadbolt to keep the door from closing all the way, intending to investigate the atrocity in my inbox, but Max's van arrived. I started to tell him I probably only needed half as many muffins now, but I was interrupted by the arrival of little chatterbox Lucy Rhodes and her taciturn brother Dallas. The bell jingled again and again as parents steered their children in and crowded into the small corner cubby.

Sweet little cherubs sat on their knees with parents standing behind them, chatting with the other adults. I perched on a beanbag, eye level with the kids, and picked up the copy of *Stuart Little* we'd been reading aloud. I continued with great dramatic intonations until everyone was giggling and rocking with joy as Stuart was lowered into the drain, one of my favorite scenes. Hopefully, nobody could tell half my brain was occupied. What had I written to Silver Fox? Did I even want to know?

As I turned the page, I glanced at the parents. Some listened in, eyes gleaming, possibly hearing the story for the first time or remembering when they had. Some stared at their phones or whispered with another parent. Max had taken up residence on that stool and listened intently as if he had a vested interest in Stuart's adventures.

It reminded me of sitting with him on this very floor, listening to Mrs. Moore read to us. It reminded me of why I'd wanted to buy the bookstore in the first place. I wished I could push out my adult concerns and just read to the children, but as soon as the chapter ended, I switched on business mode, recommending titles the parents might like. At the end of the day, it was the kids who mattered, but the ultimate cynical goal of the Saturday reading was to get bodies in the door. Thankfully several parents bought a book or two, and the beaming faces of their children acted like a balm to my soul. I couldn't feel too bad for wanting to sell something that would make them happy. It didn't hurt that I was also addicted to the drug I was pushing.

Chapter 5

Soon after the kids and Max had left, Charlie entered, holding the door for Layla. Charlie went to his table in the corner, but Layla strode right up to the counter looking surprisingly bright and cheery for the late morning. Rather than the Brooks Brothers she'd been eying in my closet, she had on her yoga pants and a worn-in T-shirt. At least she'd left the apartment.

She gave the pastries in the display a once-over. "Could you make me a latte?"

While I ground the beans, she pointed at Dylan's flier. "Hey, Dylan's playing here?"

"Yeah. He's back in town."

"He's already here? Did something happen?"

I shrugged. It did seem weird he'd shown up suddenly, weeks before a planned performance. Nobody had mentioned any health issues with his parents, and he looked fine. Very fine. "No idea. You wanna go to the show with me?"

"Hell yeah. Maybe I'll shoot some video and upload it to my website." She meandered to a table without offering to pay. I didn't protest. She'd fed me often enough.

Once I'd poured the steamed milk over the espresso, I followed her and dropped into a chair across from her, watching Charlie work out of the corner of my eye. He sat, intently squinting at his laptop, writing, pausing, thinking, hitting backspace, writing again. Behind his computer, he'd stacked papers he'd probably started grading for whichever English course he was teaching. Neglected now, a few sheets had slipped off the top and inched across the surface of the table, toward freedom—and an undeserved zero for whichever student would swear he'd turned in his mysteriously missing work.

I turned to Layla and whispered, "So, I may have done something bad. Really bad."

"You drunk texted Peter again?" She sipped the coffee.

God, that would have been worse. I needed to remember that real life and book life had different levels of calamity. "Not in weeks. You're close."

She dropped her shoulders and gave me a dead serious look. "You emailed that reviewer."

"Bingo."

She closed her eyes and looked toward the heavens. "Why do I exist if I can't even help you thwart your inevitable fate?"

"I know. I thought I'd dreamed it, but he replied."

She sat up. "He did? What did he say?"

"No idea. I haven't had a free moment, and I'm too chicken-shit to read it."

"Dare I ask what you wrote?" She looked almost happy at this turn of events, like she did when reading Internet conflict between people she didn't even know.

"I think I insulted him."

She held out her hand. "Give it here."

I slid my phone over and immediately chewed on my thumbnail. Fortunately, some customers approached the counter, so I was saved the live play-by-play. I rang up the orders and chatted for a minute with each person, locals all.

When I returned to the table, Layla had set the phone down. I swallowed rising panic. "Well?"

"I think you should read it without me interpreting it for you." My stomach lurched. "That bad?"

She tilted her head side to side, red waves oscillating gently, as though weighing the proper response.

I scrunched my face up like I'd done when my mom would try to make me eat creamed chipped beef, aka "shit on a shingle."

But the deed was done. Ignoring it wouldn't make it go away.

Holding a lungful of breath, I clicked on the Sent folder first to assess the damage before I read the response. I psyched myself up by reminding myself they were only words. What was the worst thing that could happen? Layla would have told me if the guy had made any threats to reveal my email on his blog. Or worse—drop my rating to two stars.

I counted to three, then read my own poison pen missive.

Mr. Silver Fox,
I wanted to thank you for taking the time to read and review my novel, The Shadow's Apprentice.

Relief washed over me. I'd managed to be more professional than I'd feared. The email continued.

But let's be honest, you didn't read the entire book, right? You skimmed it, sure. You're probably one of those snobs who sneers at fantasy romance as if it's inferior, so you decided to make a personal attack on the author. However, you don't know the first thing about my experiences.

The blood drained from my face. It hadn't been a dream. If I'd written that . . . My hands went cold suspecting what was to come.

Who are you to disparage my romantic life? Going by your chosen screen name, I'd guess you're some sixty-year-old virgin whose romantic prospects are busy swiping left. For your information, I was involved in a long-term relationship throughout most of the writing of this novel. How does your vast expertise compare?

Ouch.

I glared at Layla. "Why did you let me read this disaster?"

She laughed and nudged the phone closer. Was she enjoying this? "You only pulled the Band-Aid halfway off. Read his response."

I pinched the bridge of my nose. "You're dead to me."

She rolled her eyes. "Hey, I didn't make that mess. You need to face the music. I promise it won't kill you. You should totally see the kinds of emails and comments I get all the time."

That didn't convince me at all. "Yeah, but that's different."

She shot me a look of wounded disbelief. "How?"

"They aren't attacking you personally."

"The hell they aren't. Just because they don't know who I am doesn't mean they aren't trying to hurt me. People are even more vicious when they think they're anonymous."

Like an ostrich sticking its head in the sand, I reasoned that if I didn't read Silver Fox's response, it would cease to exist. But when I returned to my inbox, it was still there. I could see the preview without opening the email:

Ms. Kincaid, How awesome to hear from an author. You're quite welcome for the review. Normally, my reviews don't elicit . . .

The sarcasm came through loud and clear. I pushed back my chair. "I can't do this now."

"Suit yourself." She swallowed the rest of her coffee. "Could I steal a bottle of water? I'm gonna ride my bike over to see my parents and help them install an entertainment unit."

The bell over the door rang, and Dylan walked in, looking more disheveled than he had the night before. His scruff gave him that same rakish look that had caught my attention when I was seventeen. The tattoo snaking up his forearm reminded me of his eighteenth birthday when he'd whispered promises of moonlit adventure in my ear. As he'd gotten older, he'd cultivated a sexiness that should have ensured him a much bigger career, lights and cameras. Though maybe that was just the marketing.

I gave him the hug he'd avoided last night. He always smelled musky with a hint of sandalwood, and breathing him in took me back in time to stolen evenings in his arms when sleeping was the last thing on our minds. I braced myself against the powerful invitation to disappear into his warmth.

Layla stood. "I'll be home later if you need moral support."

Dylan turned the chair around and straddled it. "Moral support for what? Resisting my legendary magnetism?"

I snorted. "Sure. Let's go with that."

Layla shouldered her backpack, then gave me a look I couldn't interpret. It looked like a warning, but she needn't worry. Dylan had outgrown whatever had passed between us. He could have any girl he wanted.

Then again, if anyone could seduce me without trying, it would be him.

When we were teens, Dylan staked a claim on me as if he'd picked a rose the moment it was in bloom. One day after a class on poetry from the Romantic period, he stopped by my desk and said, "If you really want to read romantic poetry, you should check out Pablo Neruda. Have you ever read him?"

I hadn't, so the next day, he copied a translation of the poem "I Do Not Love You" and slipped it into my hand. In hindsight, that Neruda poem summed up our entire relationship perfectly. In those days, we simply existed with no words or rationale to define us. We'd never had to name what we felt until the present slipped into the past and it was time to grow up and let each other go.

"How've you been, Maddie?"

How had I been? Alone. Barely getting by. "Good. You?"

"Not too shabby." His shirt rode up as he stretched and yawned. I forgot my manners and stared at his hip bone peeking out of his pants. I didn't need to rely on my imagination to envision what lay behind all that fabric.

"Why are you really here, Dylan?"

His cocky grin slipped. "The label is pressuring me to write another hit song. They told me to take a break and come back when I had something to show them."

"And Orion is the farthest place in the world from New York City?"

"Something like that." He propped his elbow on the table and crinkled his eyes like we were alone in his parents' shadow-dappled barn, not sitting in a sunlit café. "You should come over tonight. I could use some inspiration."

I knew Dylan meant "inspiration" as a euphemism.

He cocked an eyebrow. "Come on. It would be like old times." He licked his lips and skimmed his eyes along mine. My imagination ran wild, and Dylan was ripping open my bodice as I dragged my hands through his raven black hair. But I wasn't wearing a bodice, and there were a couple of teenagers peering through the front window.

I flushed. Was I really considering a one-night stand? I was pretty sure I needed more than a lay, and I doubted his interest in me extended beyond his bed, let alone Orion. It hadn't when we'd parted ways before.

And he'd leave me obsessing over a ghost.

I sighed, an author bereft of words to express a rejection I wasn't exactly sure about. "Dylan."

He remained an electrical arc away. Charisma was never Dylan's problem.

"Think about it." And as if the answer hadn't mattered anyway, he shrugged and stood to leave. "I've got to head out."

I watched him through the picture window as he mounted his motorcycle, and my thighs tingled with memory and longing for the bad boy. My dormant sexuality stirred and began to awaken.

When afternoon gave way to evening, Max and his dad sauntered in. Mr. Beckett liked to play his guitar to the small audience, and I loved it when he'd come in. Max carried the stool over to the café and helped set up. Their similarities were so stark, I could imagine what Max would look like in another twenty-five years with a dad bod, except while Mr. Beckett wore cargo shorts and a T-shirt emblazoned with I SHOT THE SHERIFF in Jamaican colors, Max dressed more conservatively in a nice pair of dark jeans and a short-sleeved gray-blue pinstriped button-up oxford with a white undershirt peeking below the collar. He'd always leaned more preppy than punk, more nice guy than bad boy.

Max caught me staring and twisted around like what held my attention might be behind him. Upon discovering nothing but an exposed brick wall, he spun back. But before he could read too much into my wandering gaze, I averted my eyes and walked away.

Mr. Beckett broke out his repertoire, starting with "Oh! Darling." People sat in the café—couples enjoying an evening together and paying the musician in the corner no mind. That could have been me with my husband, whispering endearments, flirting, and looking forward to sex. Right now, the lack of sex was the bigger tragedy.

When I went outside to roll shelves of discounted books in, I guffawed at what Max had chalked on the sidewalk sign.

Q: WHY ARE APOSTROPHES TERRIBLE TO DATE?

A: THEY'RE TOO POSSESSIVE!

We were approaching the summer solstice, so the evening light lingered. Voices carried from up the street near the Jukebox where most people would be heading to dance to a real band. I watched Mr. Beckett through the window. He seemed perfectly content with the situation.

Next door, couples enjoyed the cooler evening temperatures while dining al fresco on the sidewalk outside Gentry's. I suddenly recalled my promise to rehang the town's pitiful commerce sign. I went to the back room to find the step ladder, but Max intercepted me as I lumbered through the store with my hands full.

"Let me do that."

I accepted his offer and relinquished the ladder.

Once he'd hung the sign, he asked, "Why's the deadbolt turned on the door? It's gonna damage the frame."

Had he just noticed? "Because if I don't prop it open, I'm afraid I'll be stuck inside forever."

He grimaced. "You're gonna make it worse."

He disappeared into the storeroom, emerging a minute later

with a bright orange toolbox. He opened and closed the door once or twice, then he ran his hand along the edge. He was tall enough, he didn't even rise onto his tiptoes to skim the top. Had he always been so tall? I would have needed a stool to reach so high.

As if reading my mind, he climbed the step ladder to examine the top of the door. He scratched his neck. "That's weird."

He descended and produced a hammer and chisel from the toolbox before clambering back up.

I saw what he was about to do and yelled, "No, Max!"

He shot me one bossy glance and laid the chisel on the wood. Just one more thing he'd take care of without paying any mind to what I wanted, like he knew better. With a blow, he skimmed off a layer, splinters and paint flying in every direction. He stepped down and tested the door. It opened and closed without resistance.

He bent and picked up a broken shard. "Come here."

When I approached, he asked, "Has anyone messed with this door lately?"

"How would I know?" People came in and out all day, and I didn't always watch it. "I haven't."

He held out the wood. It was light brown, not at all the mossy green of the rest of the door. "Shims like this are used when a door is first hung."

"You think it's been there all this time?"

"Maybe." He frowned. "Usually those are placed in the door-frame, not on the door. This appeared to have been epoxied down."

"Maybe someone once tried to patch it?"

"Maybe." He shrugged and went to grab the broom to sweep up.

As we dumped the debris into the trash, Mr. Beckett finished performing and began packing. Max raised his eyebrows. "You up for a movie? Looks like they're playing *Zoolander 2* at the Bijou."

The Bijou was our local dollar movie theater, which doubled as a playhouse, a town hall, and the location of the high school band concerts, choral extravaganzas, and talent shows. Half the seats were broken, the screen was smaller than some TVs, and we had a single movie option, a bad one. It made for an excellent experience overall, especially since the opening reel dated from the 80s and featured burn holes, Arsenio Hall jackets, and not a single mention to silence our cell phones. Max and I would pretend we were film critics and snark all the way through, trying to outdo each other and laughing until I feared I might hyperventilate and pass out.

Normally, that would have been a hard yes. But I'd lost my appetite for mocking another person's creative output. Besides, the deadline for my second book loomed over me, and I'd grown morbidly curious to read Silver Fox's email.

I said good night to Max and Mr. Beckett, then closed out my cash register, dismayed as always at how little had come in for book purchases and how much for coffee and food sales. I was grateful for the income, but it only proved Gentry's point further. My bookstore might no longer be relevant. Gentry argued that we needed a bed-and-breakfast more.

It didn't help that the town council had decreed we close on Sundays. Our heaviest influx came on Saturdays. If I could open Sundays, the bookstore might flourish. Or at least not falter.

I walked over to Anderson's to order myself baked ziti to take out, hoping pasta would take the sting out of what I had to do. The little pizzeria had long been a place for teens to hang out, and tonight was no exception. I waved to Ross as I paid his wife Linda, making small talk about the heat and how business had been.

When I got home, I ate, changed into my pajamas, put the laptop on the table, and paced around it like it was a crime scene. Finally I gritted my teeth and opened the email I'd been dreading all day.

Ms. Kincaid,
How awesome to hear from an author. You're quite welcome for the review.
Normally, my reviews don't elicit such colorful responses. Or

really any response. Because in case you missed the memo, you sent a book out into the public, and now the public gets to have an opinion about your work. It's up to you if you want to follow it around explaining to people how they're reading it all wrong, but I wouldn't advise that. If you want to show that emotion to your reader, here's an idea: Put it in the book.

Yes, I did read your entire book. I wouldn't put my name on a review if I hadn't. That would be a disservice to our readers—my intended audience. And no, I'm neither sixty years old, nor a virgin, though I contend neither of those would disqualify me from knowing plausible romantic chemistry. I concede that it must be difficult to pull off a solid romance, but you chose to include one, and as such, as a reader, I want that element to work as well the rest of the book. Readers looking for a fantasy romance will want to know if this is the book for them.

If I disparaged your personal life, I do apologize. However, your word choice implies that your long-term relationship is possibly in the past. I'd guess it wasn't a love for the ages? No shame in that. Not every romantic relationship is something to write home about, or write a romance novel about. Maybe you should just stick to the fantasy aspect. You might be better suited to that.

And don't berate reviewers. Most of us aren't vicious. We're just honest with our own opinions. If you have trouble with that, perhaps you should find a way to avoid reading the comments? Or get out of publishing.

Cheers,
Silver Fox

My adrenaline was pumping, and I wanted to explode, scream, email, or even call Silver Fox and rail against his insulting tone. I got up and stomped around, muttering curse words and trying to keep my brain from forming a cohesive string of sentences I might write back. I wasn't sure I could refrain from responding. How dare he?

Rather than white knuckle my desire to type a furious reply, I grabbed my purse and ran outside. Nothing but the restaurants and bar remained open this late, but I needed to walk and clear my head.

I passed Shawna's Manic Pixie Seam Girls dress shop. Four mannequins graced the display window showing off a gorgeous wedding gown and a trio of stunning formal dresses. My gaze lingered wistfully on the wedding dress, remembering the day I'd let Shawna sort through an array of possible choices for my gown. She'd cried when I came for my final fitting. I thought at the time it had been for joy. Lately, I wasn't so sure.

The sounds of music and crowds met me as soon as I approached the corner. I passed the Jukebox with most of its flaws obscured by the night. The marquis needed a power cleaning, and the front vestibule had the faint smell of vomit. Still I felt nothing but love for the old place. Memories rushed at me like a shattered kaleidoscope. Dylan had started out playing that venue, high on possibilities.

I used to love the old church at the end of the block. It dated back to the founding of Orion and had a deep history from the many christenings, weddings, and funerals. I'd insisted on getting married there, and now my own history stained those walls.

I jogged down the little hill leading to the path by the stream. The gazebo was empty and dark. A perfect place to calm down and think.

As I watched the black water ripple in the moonlight, I took stock of all the things I knew to be real in my life—my friends, my mom, my shop—and a book review wasn't one of them. Silver Fox had no power over me here.

I resolved to do what I should have done in the first place: Forget about him and let it drift away, like the gurgling brook below.

One day at a time would become my mantra as I resisted the siren call of risking my career and reputation on another suicide note to my new arch nemesis. I would not respond to Silver Fox. I would not take his bait. He'd just have to wonder how his words had landed.

Chapter 6

✖✖✖

Sunday, after church services ended, Gentry required all the store owners in town to meet at his restaurant to plan the Fourth of July activities coming up in less than a month. He put me in charge of writing the newsletter. Yes—Orion had a newsletter.

When the meeting ended, I stretched and unlocked my phone to check notifications. The volume was down, and I'd missed a call from my mom, but I was heading over there anyway.

I had a few emails in my personal account, mostly garbage, but there was a new one from Peter with the subject, "*May Finances.*" I groaned. The last time I'd talked to him, a couple of weeks earlier, we'd been texting about the insurance policy of all the boring things, and he just stopped responding without so much as a "*talk to you later.*" So I'd made another four or five replies before realizing I was talking to myself. Typical. If only he'd correspond about more than the monthly financial analysis.

With dread, I opened his email and scanned it. He'd pasted in a small spreadsheet with a breakdown of last month's income versus expenses. The outflow was more than the inflow, again. I'd covered the last deficit with a transfer from my savings account. I had to make the mortgage payments—which included interest on Peter's down payment loan—and pay for electricity and WiFi. I had to buy coffee and milk and bread and, of course, books. I couldn't tighten the budget much more. I'd already scaled back on promotions, which went against everything I'd learned in business classes. It was hard to justify the outlay of cash when I couldn't see an immediate return.

He added:

Your credit is stretched, and I know you don't have a lot of cash on hand. If you can't increase revenue, you're going to need to cut expenses. Look at how much you're paying the Becketts for food you could easily make yourself. You need to sever ties with them and save the money.

Oh yeah. He would love for me to sever ties with Max. He'd never liked Max from the minute they'd met. I always figured it was because Max never liked Peter. But Peter was wrong. Sure, I could save money if I made two dozen blueberry muffins every morning. Ordering from the Becketts allowed me to offer a variety of different items. I'd be baking nonstop. And I couldn't simply stop selling food. Peter had to know that I earned more revenue on food than I spent. He had to know his advice would plunge me faster into ruin. That was probably his intent.

The end of Peter's email made me sit bolt upright.

I read your blog last weekend, and I have to say, your write-up on Pride and Prejudice *made me think about us. Anyway, I picked up a copy and reread it over the weekend.*

I scratched my head and tried to recall what I'd written. Other than him looking down on me and my small town, what comparisons could be drawn? Was he trying to say I was being stubborn and irrational? Did he believe his motivations were all noble and good if I'd just open my mind? Was he waiting for me to conclude I'd been wrong all along and admit defeat? To give everything up and integrate into his world?

He'd be waiting a while.

I wasn't even sure how to respond to his comment, and I definitely wanted to ignore his financial input, so I gathered my things and began the walk out to my mom's to help her in the garden and talk. It was almost two miles to the edge of the sub-division where Layla, Max, and I had grown up. It was another mile or so out to Dylan's parents' farm if I kept going.

As I walked along the thin country road past shoulder-high fields of corn, I had such a strong memory of my days riding my bike back and forth between my house and Dylan's. Or riding on the back of his motorbike.

The blue sky stretched on forever to the horizon, unbroken by a single cloud or chem trail. A slight breeze stirred the tops of the corn. The phrase "knee-high by the fourth of July" was a lie. The stalks would soon get so tall it would creep me out to walk alone beside them, lest a demonic child or dead baseball hero should emerge. Today, the tops of houses in the subdivision beyond peeked over the farthest edge of the field.

At the bend in the road, a crazy, twisty oak with a massive trunk stood like a landmark for locals to give directions by. "*Go yonder past the great oak . . .*" When I was little, I used to think this was the origin of the Berenstain Bears' *Spooky Old Tree*. I could still imagine dragging a ladder up to it and climbing in to find a great sleeping bear.

The occasional car passed, and I stepped into the ditch. The driver would wave or offer me a ride, but I wanted to be alone with my thoughts. It was too nice a day.

Soon my mind ricocheted across my many worries: the health of the bookstore, the release of my first novel, the draft of the next, and as always, my sadness over a past I'd lost and a potential present I wasn't living. It made me angry that I had to choose between two incomplete paths. It wasn't fair.

In the early days of our migration to the ex-burbs, when Peter was still naïvely enthusiastic about slowing things down and growing old in the country together, he'd unironically taken in all the local color of Orion. We'd go for a slice at Anderson's or get a beer with my friends at the Jukebox. While the country pace fit me perfectly, Peter liked doing active, interesting things. I had everything I'd ever want or need. But I had to admit, the best Saturdays in Orion were lame compared to hip bars and cosmopolitan entertainment. Peter had traded cocktail parties in the city for casual walks along the path by the stream. There was nothing to do in Orion unless you knew how to find it.

When we'd lived in Peter's world, with his friends, he'd been perfectly happy with me. From his point of view, it must have seemed like I was the one who'd changed. I'd probably left him wishing he could return to the life he'd started with me.

Peter tried to make it work for several months, and I tried to ignore the signs that he was growing bored with the prosaic routine, exactly as I'd lost interest in his fast-paced world. My relationship with him became more practical, in the way socking money into a 401k was more sensible than investing in a failing bookstore in a backwater town.

Maybe if I'd never come back to Orion, we'd still be together in Indianapolis. Maybe we'd be sitting across from each other in a coffee shop, in separate worlds.

Silver Fox's words, "*Not every romantic relationship is something to write home about*" stung like rubbing alcohol on an open wound. We had been something once. I clenched a fist and muttered, "It wasn't entirely my fault Peter left."

I found Mom in the backyard, white hair twisted up in a chignon, dirt up to her wrists. She handed me a pair of gloves and a trowel, and I took out my frustration by yanking out unwanted plants. I tuned her out a bit when she started relaying secondhand gossip from her bunco club the night before. All the moms on the block knew each other's business, and whoever wasn't there became the topic of any group discussion. I found it boring, but at least hearing the drama of the neighborhood reminded me I didn't have the worst problems in the world.

My ears perked up when she said, "Brenda asked after you and Peter."

So they were whispering about me even out here in the hinterlands. I didn't have a response to Brenda who wasn't there, so I slammed the trowel into the earth and tugged on a stubborn root. "Uh-huh."

Mom paused in her labors. "I just can't understand why you two haven't worked this all out. I bet if you both sat down over a nice dinner, you'd resolve everything in a conversation."

As if Peter and I were the leads in an infuriating romance. Words from Silver Fox's damn email floated to mind, and I quoted them at her, sarcastically, "I guess it wasn't a love for the ages."

Her eyebrows knit together, and I felt like an asshole. Her husband, the man who would have been my adoptive dad, died before I'd even settled into my new home when I was a baby. I still called him my dad because my mom did. I never knew my original sperm donor. I liked to say I'd had a "near dad experience." Never in front of my mom of course.

Mom meant well. She'd always liked Peter. I wouldn't be surprised if she still talked to him. I think he reminded her of my elegant dad somehow, and that pinched my heart more than anything. I sometimes forgot what she'd lost, what she'd sacrificed, and then I'd go and inadvertently say something cruel.

I'd never seen my mom in a romantic relationship, so it was easy to imagine she'd always been self-sufficient. She probably could have remarried after my dad died. I used to think she didn't date because it might confuse me or because she didn't want to neglect me more than she had to for work. But when I asked her, she said, "I did it right the first time."

I only knew my would-be dad through photographs and stories, and the way she talked about him made him seem perfect. Caring, patient, handsome, funny. I envied my friends whose dads told pitifully awful jokes and let us watch questionable TV shows while their moms were away, who took us all out for ice cream and insisted on tuning the car radio to music from last century, telling us the history of bands they thought were the height of cool. Still whenever I used to picture my dad, I'd embellish him with wealth and intelligence and sophistication, every wish fulfillment trope in all of literature. My imaginary dad was better than anyone else's real one.

In reality, the universe didn't have a father for me.

I reached over and hugged my mom. "I'm sorry. I'm mad about so many things right now, but I'm not mad at you, and that wasn't called for."

She smiled. "You were aptly named." She let it go just like

that. I always found it ironic that my birth mother gave me up because she couldn't raise me alone, while Mrs. Trudi Hanson had managed to bring me up on her own. She'd done a kick-ass job.

The benefit to getting away from my apartment and the bookstore was that experiencing the world gave me food for thought and got my imagination spinning. The farther away from a keyboard I found myself, the more the words piled up in my mind, and I needed to pour them out onto the page.

My characters talked to me the whole walk home, and I was eager to dive into my writing for the first time since I'd gotten that debilitating review. Glass of pinot grigio at hand, I set my timer to force myself to shut out social media for an hour. I needed to focus. A check-in email from my editor earlier in the day lit a fire under my ass. My deadline was barreling toward me.

I stretched my fingers out, laid them on the keyboard, and then, to my horror, my mind went blank.

The cursor blinked, taunting me, discouraging me. All the words that had been bursting to get out dried up and flew away. I typed a sentence anyway and cringed. I forced out an entire paragraph, fighting against a growing conviction there was no point to this book. Why finish it?

The spidery voice of a lone douche lord insisted I couldn't write romance. Had I bungled the chemistry of the leads once again?

I'd written half the sequel in an emotional dead zone. Was it obvious?

I reread the last paragraph I'd written.

The fields burned for hectares in every direction, darkening the sky with a billowing tower of black smoke. Rane stumbled to the cliff's edge, grasping the open wound at his side. He'd heal himself once the battle was over, if he lived that long. He needed to get to Lira before the flames reached the portal. He shuddered to think what might happen if the fire breached the door between worlds.

What might happen to Lira.

*   *   *

It had sounded pretty good in my head. Now I stared at it and wondered if it was garbage. Would reviewers single out this passage to mock? Would readers roll their eyes at the melodrama? Or would they sense the urgency? Would they believe Rane's desperate need to rescue Lira even at great cost to himself? Would they say this book was worse than the first?

The impostor syndrome that usually plagued me had been given a voice. Damn that Silver Fox.

So much for *one day at a time*. I hadn't made it one full day before the hostility built up until I couldn't stand it. If I knew where he lived, I'd bang on his door and demand he retract every word. Not just his review, but his criticism of *me*.

I hit Reply on his last email and suddenly words flowed from my fingertips if for no other reason than to vent my spleen, even if I wouldn't actually send it.

Silver Fox,

Do you even have a name? Or do you go through your real life hiding behind anonymity so you can shit on people without any fear of blowback? Seriously, I know I'm not supposed to respond to reviewers. You didn't need to remind me of that. And I know what I've signed up for, but you know what? I was drunk and I made a bad decision. But you . . . You seem to think that since nobody will call you out on your opinions, you can be as hurtful as you want. Maybe it's time someone let you know there's a human being on the other end.

As for being handed a shit sandwich and expected to sit down and eat it, you have no place telling me whether my romantic life makes me qualified to write romance. Last time I checked, Buster—

Ack. *Buster?*

I backspaced over that.

—I've never stood on a planet with two moons while attempting to solve a puzzle that no man had solved for millennia.

Maybe you think sitting in your underwear, playing Zelda until your hair turns crusty and even your mom is telling you to get a shower, makes you an expert in fantasy, but I happen to know it takes more than personal experience to bring a world to life— whether that world be complete fabrication or ripped from today's headlines. You need imagination, and you clearly do not have a shred of that or an ounce of humanity.

You can kiss my ass.

Claire

I may have gone too far. My finger hovered over the Send button, daring myself to jump off this precipice a second time. I knew I shouldn't. I knew responding to reviewers was a major no-no. I wavered. He wasn't worth wrecking my career over.

But then I remembered his *"get out of publishing"* comment, and I felt righteously angry. I was Katniss Everdeen, giving Silver Fox a three finger salute.

Fuck it. I hit send.

Layla was going to crucify me. Something compelled me to read back what I'd written, and I was horrified, but I had to laugh, too. Morbidly. My career was probably ruined, but if Silver Fox was right about my novel, I wasn't going to have a career for him to destroy anyway. My books would tank on their own.

I looked at my draft, and the cursor blinked at me like a ticking time bomb. I couldn't face it, so I did what I always did when confronted with life: I pulled out a book I'd already read many times and lost myself in the familiar words of someone else. Immersed in *Jane Eyre,* I found my soul. Suffering under surly Rochester, Jane understood my struggles.

Chapter 7

※X※

The week passed by blissfully, quiet in a good way. I didn't hear back from that reviewer, so I assumed he'd turned tail and fled back to his mama's apron strings. By Friday, I'd managed to work him out of my head and write a new chapter.

The bookstore had not been quiet, thankfully. Business had steadily improved as the days grew warmer and longer.

Orion's proximity to Indianapolis made it a convenient stop along the way for antiquers or day trippers heading out to visit the various covered bridges farther west. As much as Gentry complained about my dilapidated shop, our quaint small-town storefronts were a part of Orion's appeal. The worn exterior of my bookshop frequently popped up on Instagram. The front window had twenty-five panes of old-fashioned glass with THE MOSSY STONE spelled out in colorful paint. Sometimes with an addition from local hooligans.

The inside felt as cozy as a warm blanket on a rainy day. Most visitors came in out of curiosity, but once inside, they'd catch a whiff of the coffee and be lured farther in to the café, like the couple now glancing at my displays.

The woman picked up a souvenir mug, flipped it over to check the price, then set it back down. She did the same with the locally packaged candy. The man had discovered the shelf in the front of the store with curated titles—all handpicked to stroke the ego of readers with a literary bent. I liked to call it the Willing Wall because it was filled with books people loved to urge others to read, turning them into temporary salespeople for me. "Oh, you will love this book!" was an oft-heard phrase as people scanned the list.

Today, the man lifted his eyeglasses and squinted at the titles. "Sandra, have you ever read *Lords of Discipline?*"

Sandra joined him and scanned the wall. "Oh, look. *Anne of Green Gables.*" She picked it up like it was an old friend. I knew the feeling.

I left them alone to talk themselves into buying the books they'd already read. I'd only approach them if they asked me for assistance. Or if they ventured into the stacks. Anyone who strayed from the prepackaged enticements was usually looking for something specific. Occasionally they were browsing, but then they might want recommendations.

When twilight blanketed the night sky, I closed out my cash drawer, relieved that I was still treading water. I went to drag in the books from the sidewalk. Max must have passed by at some point because the sign now read:

Q: WHAT BUILDING HAS THE MOST STORIES?

A: THE BOOKSTORE!

Heavy sigh.

My mom had offered to feed me, so I went home and changed into some running gear to jog over. It occurred to me I'd be spending a Friday night at my mom's house, and I felt a bit castigated for all the shade I'd thrown toward Silver Fox and my fictional caricature of him as a basement dweller. But I couldn't make myself feel too bad.

I stretched and started the run. As I turned the corner onto the long country road, I realized I'd been repeating *Snape, Snape, Severus Snape* with the rhythm of my footfalls and tried to empty my mind.

A pickup approached, coming from the opposite direction.

When it slowed and stopped, I saw it was Dylan's dad's truck, but Dylan himself rolled a window down, and I became acutely aware that I looked like hell from having run half a mile. My yoga pants had a hole at the knee, and I hadn't even brushed my hair before tying it in a ponytail. Why that should matter I had no idea, but maybe it was because Dylan's gaze brushed along my body from head to toe. He didn't look any fancier than me with his baseball cap and scruffy, neglected beard. I blamed the weakness in my knees to being out of shape.

"Hey, Maddie."

"Where are you heading?" The last time I'd seen him in that truck, we'd both gotten hell for staying out all night after prom. It was worth it to sleep in his arms for once, albeit in the bed of that very truck.

"I was on my way into the city." He leaned out farther. "Do you want a ride?"

He bit his lip in that way he did. He might as well have come out and told me he wanted to have sex as soon as humanly possible. I wondered how many girls had fallen for that look in smoky clubs.

But this was Dylan. "Do you mind? I'm just heading to Mom's."

"Hell no. It's a short detour."

Is that what I was to him?

The passenger door opened with an agonized creak, and I had to climb up like I was mounting a horse, but once in the cab, I was only aware of Dylan, who'd somehow become someone I no longer recognized. I knew his features, those fingers that fretted his guitar, those shoulders I'd held onto while riding on his motorcycle, those eyes that saw right through me. But he'd draped himself in someone else's aura, and while I could see Dylan Ramirez, I couldn't unsee Dylan Black.

We rode in silence a beat, until we spoke at the same time. I said, "It's really great to see you again," just as he said, "I haven't been avoiding you."

I gaped at him. "I didn't think you had been." The words echoed around my brain. "Were you?"

He dragged his fingers through his dark hair. "Can I tell you a secret?"

"Of course."

"I've been home for a month."

"But you said—"

"I know. I needed a break from it all, and I thought I could come home, work the farm, get all the bullshit out of my system."

"You've been here the whole time?"

The right turn blinker *click-clacked,* and he turned into the subdivision, glancing at me before focusing on the road again.

"I've mostly been sitting up in the barn, reading. Just trying to escape."

"So what you said about the label?"

He shook his head. "Nah, that part's true. My head hasn't been in the game. I have to make a decision if I want to try to move into the big leagues or be a flash in the pan one-hit wonder."

"That's a monumental choice."

"Sometimes I think I just want to come home and lead a regular life. Teach guitar lessons to kids with stars in their eyes."

"What would be wrong with that?"

He slipped his hand into mine, and when he looked my way, he was literally brooding. I threw up every defense against desires I'd locked away a long time ago.

"Do you ever wonder how things might have been if we'd made different choices?"

Did I tell him that was my constant inner monologue? "Don't we all?"

"More lately." His thumb ran along mine. "I'd like to find out."

I didn't understand what he was talking about enough to say anything.

Thankfully, we arrived at my mom's. I leaned in to give him half a hug. "Come out to the book club on Friday, okay?"

"*Jane Eyre,* right?"

I was surprised he remembered. I patted his arm, then leapt from the truck.

As Dylan drove off, Mrs. Beckett hollered over from her neighboring backyard, "Is that Maddie?"

I waved. "Hi, Mrs. Beckett!"

"I was about to gather strawberries, and I was thinking about how this would be so much easier with you. Do you have the time?"

My stomach grumbled for dinner, but I couldn't turn down Mrs. Beckett's request. "Sure."

The sunlight had faded and left a bruised sky behind, but floodlights shined over the expansive terrain behind the house. The Beckett's yard once held the neighborhood's best swing set and a trampoline—until we'd outgrown one and destroyed the other. Now it had become a dedicated garden. Unlike my mom's yard, flowers didn't steal the show. Blueberry bushes ran wild in the back of the lot, and strawberries grew in their shade. Mrs. Beckett's strawberries meant summer had officially begun.

When I was younger, before she'd started her catering business, Mrs. Beckett would let me help her in the garden. I realized later she was opening her home to me so that, despite never knowing my birth parents, I'd never want for family.

Not that my mom wasn't amazing in her own right, but since my dad died, she'd had to work full time and be two parents in one. A single working mom and an only adopted daughter don't form the kind of bustling household I found at the Becketts.

Because the Becketts had adopted me as much as my own mom, I got a surrogate dad in Mr. Beckett, not to mention pretend siblings in Layla and Max. On top of that, since Max had inherited his dad's more prosaic auburn hair with only a hint of Layla's glorious red, he looked more like me than her. Whenever the three of us would encounter strangers, they'd always assume I was a Beckett, that Max and I were siblings. Layla stood apart like a rare bird of paradise.

As we worked, Mrs. Beckett asked how Layla was doing, as though it was small talk, but I knew she wanted a report Layla would never volunteer. Satisfied Layla wasn't taking drugs, she switched topics abruptly. "And has Max been bothering you with his plans?"

She'd watched us long enough to know that we often squabbled like legitimate siblings. "It's okay." I dropped a fat strawberry into the basket, tempted to bite into it. "What do you think?"

She didn't even pause to consider the question. "I'll let the two of you work that out. This has always been more of a hobby for me. It's Max who wants to take on the world."

The basket filled, and she stood. "Come on inside. I set Max to work on the shortcakes, and he may need some supervision."

We entered her kitchen, and the sight of Max measuring sugar, flour dusting his chin, transported me back in time.

He spared me a glance as he set his ingredients out on the island, just like his mom used to. Her lessons were meant to prepare Layla to bake a pie and run a proper household. Layla would roll her eyes and say she had no intention of living in any proper manner. I envied her that cavalier attitude.

While Layla rejected her mom's instruction, I soaked the attention up. And since Max did everything I did, he and I both absorbed the same process for preparing a shortcake. Under Mrs. Beckett's tutelage, Max and I might as well have both been her children.

I relaxed against the fridge, watching him mix everything together, my mouth watering at the plump berries glistening in the strainer. Compared to when we first learned to roll out a pie dough, Max's hands were now much larger, much more certain. His forearms thicker, his shoulders broader, and his eyes directly on me.

I quickly glanced away, embarrassed to be caught staring again. He was going to think I was a creeper. I looked at Mrs. Beckett, who turned away with a knowing grin.

Something was up.

I half suspected Max had sent his mom over as a pawn in his plan for world domination. Was this whole baking day an exercise in proving how well we'd all work together?

Well, I wasn't playing. I had a book to write. Nostalgia and shortcake wouldn't pay the bills. Well, shortcake might, but I thanked Mrs. Beckett and told Max, "See ya later," then headed to the safety of my mom's house.

* * *

On Saturday morning, right after I'd read to the children, Max and his mom arrived, carrying boxes and a couple of containers. I peeked in one box and discovered a couple dozen shortcakes, plain. I knew what they were up to, but I relented as they moved everything into my kitchen. I was as big a sucker for strawberry shortcake as anyone.

Max returned with a plate, overflowing with strawberries and fresh whipped cream. He hollered over to Charlie, shortcake aloft, "I don't want to spoil your lunch, but look what we have!"

He played so dirty. Charlie had a sweet tooth, so this was unfair by all standards of measurement.

Charlie dropped everything and came to inspect. "Oh, wow. Are those for sale?"

I'd be a fool to fight against guaranteed customers, so I went outside to update my sidewalk sign. As I was chalking in *Fresh strawberry shortcake today!* a UPS truck pulled in behind Max's van. I signed for a trio of boxes, and Max helped me move them to the storeroom. I failed to notice one of them came from my publisher until I opened it and discovered roughly fifty finished copies of my book. Until then, I'd only ever held the advanced copies, but this was altogether different. I covered my mouth with a fist and quietly screamed with giddy delight.

I waited until Max returned to the kitchen before picking one up to run my thumb over the gold letters embossed on the cover. The man's face was half shrouded in the darkness of his hood, signaling his mysterious identity. He had Dylan's eyes.

In the book, the Shadow is a stranger who appears to Lira and entices her to go on an adventure. The Shadow eventually reveals himself to be Rane, a powerful wizard who has been accused of crimes against his own family. Lira holds the key to vindicating Rane through the magical heritage she has no idea she holds. Adopted by humans, she comes to discover she's descended from an elf race and a sworn enemy of Rane's people. Along the way, their feelings grow complicated—and forbidden.

I intended for their love story to simmer, for readers to root for them to find a way to restore their relationship and act on their, to me, obvious attraction. I guess I needed to work on that last part.

It was a couple of weeks yet before the official release, but I was still tempted to put the book on display to gauge reaction.

I lost myself in daydreams about book signings and bestseller lists and five-star reviews. I could maintain that fantasy since I'd turned off my Google alerts once I'd realized I was never going to be happy reading every random critique that came my way.

The bell rang up front, shaking me back to reality.

Thanks to the Becketts, traffic spiked for the next couple of hours. I had to bust ass behind the counter to take orders and make coffee. Patrons lingered in the café with their laptops and a mug of coffee, sucking up my free WiFi.

I had to admit it—Max had made himself indispensable for a day.

Chapter 8

✴✴

After the crazy busy Saturday, Monday morning seemed so quiet with just Charlie typing away in the corner. Max had made his point, but I wasn't convinced he could sustain that kind of traffic. Not every day could be that magical, and I didn't want to take a business risk on a fluke.

Of course if the bookstore remained an absolute mausoleum, it wouldn't matter either way.

This would have been a perfect day to set up my laptop and write another chapter alongside Charlie, but the blank page continued to taunt me. Instead, to pass the time, I sat reading on the rickety stool, engrossed in St. John Rivers' pursuit of Jane Eyre, internally screaming at her to run far away. Why did Jane even consider him? Sure, Rochester was a mess, but poor Jane deserved more passion than coldhearted St. John. I took out a piece of paper to jot down book club questions.

What does St. John offer Jane that Rochester doesn't?

The cry of *You've got mail!* broke the silence, and I made the mistake of checking my phone. The preview showed me an incoming email from Silver Fox. I steeled my nerves for the inevitable sting and clicked the link with one eye closed, bracing for a deadly attack. Here he was a total stranger, and the prospect alone of what he might say had my heart racing worse than a Stephen King novel.

I bounced my foot on the spindle of the stool and dove head-first into what I was sure would be a flogging.

Ms. Kincaid,

I don't know why I'm responding to you, but I confess that I keep arguing with you in my head, so I've finally decided to tell you a thing or two.

First, you're wrong if you think reviewers don't hear from authors. We hear plenty, and trust me when I tell you that responses can be pretty vicious. I sometimes ignore them, but believe it or not, I do realize that authors are people, too, which is why I find myself wanting to mentor you to a better mental place. My main argument is that you shouldn't respond to reviewers because your opinion is no longer valid. Or let me rephrase it—your opinion is no more valid than mine.

Second, I find myself once again in the position of defending my own personal situation. While I do enjoy video games as much as anyone of my generation, it's not my primary occupation. In fact, writing reviews is my hobby. I may do this in my underwear, but not simultaneously at my mother's house.

Third, I do have a healthy imagination, and I can read between the lines. You may have romantic experience, but I suspect you've forgotten what it feels like to truly be in love. Unfortunately for me, love is a feeling I'm all too familiar with, and I recognize when someone is faking it. If I could offer you some free advice, I'd urge you to get out and get more experience—romance, sex, heartache. Live a little. If you haven't felt your stomach flip when your hand brushes someone else's, if your spine doesn't tingle when you think back on your first kiss, you can't bring those feelings to your readers.

Or ignore me. I'm sure there will be plenty of readers who don't care about the romance anyway. You can write for them.

SF

P.S. I'll tell you my name when you tell me yours. I'm pretty sure Claire Kincaid could only be a pen name.

* * *

Heartache? He wanted me to intentionally fly into that turbulence again? It had taken me six months to nurse myself from the depths of the abyss before I could sink my fingernails into the ledge and heave myself up and out. Silver Fox expected me to just do it again? Sure.

But what if he was right? What if the cocoon I'd wrapped myself in was preventing me from writing a genuine relationship? Worse, what if it was preventing me from moving on with my life?

I poked at my bruised heart and didn't recoil in agony. Had it dried up and died?

"*Live a little.*" Like that was so easy.

I made a fresh latte and walked over to sit with fellow romance-phobe Charlie.

"What are you working on, Charlie?"

"Reading." He closed his laptop and stretched. "Why do you think so much of literature is about waiting? Why can't it all just be the good parts? Why do I have to wade through hundreds of pages lost in the mines of Moria before getting to some real action?"

"Are we talking about Tolkien?"

"It's just a metaphor. So much wandering around. My patience grows short."

"Sounds like my life. I strayed from the path in Mirkwood forest and can't find my way back."

"Have you considered flipping pages?"

"Of my life?" I laughed, trying to imagine how that would work.

"Why not? Choose your own adventure." He pointed his index finger toward an invisible lightbulb. "Stuck in the mines? Go over the mountain."

"Madness."

"Maybe, but it's still a choice. Or just go to the next chapter. It can't be that hard."

I considered his premise. "But what if you skipped over all the boring or hard parts of life? You'd go straight to your death bed!"

"Hmm. I think you can always choose to stray from the path."
He stirred his coffee. "And with that in mind, I'm going to make
a monumental decision to start a new book." His eyes sharp-
ened with sincerity. "You could, too."

Charlie the Chronicler had struck again.

"Choose your own adventure. . . ."

Peter wasn't even in this chapter of my life. How long was I
expected to wait for the return of the king? Did I *have* to return
to the original path? Did I have to wait for Peter to come back
around?

Or could I consider other avenues?

What if, instead of sitting in my own self-pity, I took a chance
on a perilous quest fraught with messy complications, whose
successful completion seemed impossible? It wasn't like there
was safety hiding in the mines anyway. I'd already spent six
months in the dark, chased by a cave troll of emotional destruction. I might not die of heartbreak, but loneliness rose up like a
flaming Balrog from the depths of hell, and only I could choose
to fly to higher ground.

I wanted to emerge as the heroine of my own adventure. A
badass heroine controlling her own destiny.

But how?

I'd tried the option of going it alone, persevering stoically in
the solitary post-jilting landscape I'd cultivated. I'd leaned on
friends for companionship. I'd spent time reading, improving
my mind, writing, improving my career, working, and improving the bookstore. I wanted more than that.

So maybe it was time to explore other options. Maybe it was
time to get out and get more experience.

Isn't that what Silver Fox had advised? Romance, sex, and
heartache?

I knew where I could go for one of those. Dylan was a phone
call away, and he gave me those tingles that Silver Fox encouraged me to stoke. If Dylan really was considering staying,
maybe I'd consider him, but I wasn't in the market for casual
sex. I'd been there, done him, and knew how that chapter
ended. I still wanted the romance. I still feared the heartache.

"Maddie?"

I came out of dreamland and looked at Charlie. Really looked. If ever there was a brand-new chapter, it was staring me in the face.

Charlie was attractive in his nineteenth-century archaeological dig way. He was easy and comfortable. He didn't make my stomach flip, but flipping stomachs were overrated. I could get nauseated on a roller coaster if that's all I was after.

More importantly, Charlie and I had no history, no memories of heartbreak and loss. He could be a fresh new start. Why not?

"Hey, Charlie. I'm planning on taking a walk along the creek after work. You want to join me?"

We'd never spent any time together outside of the bookstore, but my proposition didn't seem to faze him. "Sounds great. To that one bridge, maybe?"

That one bridge. I laughed. Obviously, he hadn't grown up around here. "You mean *the* bridge."

There was only one bridge, and I had more memories associated with that structure than most people probably had with the totality of their own towns unless they also lived where they grew up. Bringing Peter home had forced me to picture Orion from the point of view of an outsider, and from that perspective, the streets looked smaller, the stream less magical, and that one bridge was just a bridge. Newcomers like Charlie and Peter would never see the tanned legs of two fourteen year olds swinging over the side or hear the voices of a trio of kids splashing in the water as they explored the edges of summer.

Those were ghosts only a few of us had the power to discern.

"Meet you here when you close up?"

Maybe a single butterfly flew loose at the thought of a date with Charlie.

I left him to finish preparing for his class or whatever he did and tended to other customers, glancing over at him from time to time, trying to imagine what life might be like if I gave Charlie a chance to win my heart.

A professor of literature. I already knew we could carry on lengthy conversations about books, though those did end up turning into lectures or debates. Still, we'd never run out of topics. I could work up the courage to tell him about my writing and then I'd have an instant first reader. Layla could retire.

It could work if I could get past my fear of his red pen.

So confident was I in my new life choices, I sat down and wrote a response to Silver Fox that had been percolating in the back of my mind since I'd read his email. If only my own book would come out as easily as my invectives to someone I didn't even know.

Silver Fox,

You want to mentor me? Please, allow me to soak in your expertise on romance. Clearly, if you're using the word unfortunately to talk about your own experience with love, you are perfectly situated to teach the rest of us mere mortals how to successfully relate to others. Do you honestly believe love is limited to the magic of a first kiss? Or a stomach flip? Are we back in junior high school where love has no more depth than a passing crush?

Look, maybe you honestly didn't appreciate the romance in my novel, but has it occurred to you that the failing might be your own? I'd never go so far as to advise you to get out and live life to the fullest, but maybe, if instead of thinking about girls, you actually talked to one, you might discover that we want more than to swoon over a brush of some dude's hand. And when I write romance, yes, I want there to be chemistry and tension, but also respect and real palpable love. The kind that can survive obstacles, separation, or cultural differences that render them ostensibly incompatible. That is romantic.

I'll write for the readers who want to see real, substantial relationships.

Claire

P.S. And yes, it's a pen name. That's not a crime where I come from.

Pleased with myself, I hummed "Here Comes the Sun" as I worked.

*   *   *

When the store emptied, Charlie paced the sidewalk as I locked up. He'd traded khakis for navy shorts and his white oxford for a short-sleeved Hawaiian shirt. He'd transformed into a whole different person.

Maybe Charlie would help me flip to a new chapter. Or start a whole new book.

We headed up Main Street, then down past the gazebo to the path that ran along the stream without speaking, companionably silent.

As we strolled by the gurgling water, I broke the ice. "Can I ask you something?"

Charlie's eyebrow shot up. "I suppose."

"Why did you choose to live in Orion?"

He rubbed his chin, a little playful smile crossing his lips. "You know you don't choose Orion. Orion chooses you."

I chortled. Our town did have an almost ridiculous sense of self. "I've heard that beyond the borders of Orion there is nothing. Just an endless expanse of mist."

"And anyone who dares to cross it only ends up once again in Orion."

God, that was only too true. "Yeah."

What if the world did end at the borders of town? After all, Peter had walked out never to return, and nobody other than my mom remembered him. To everyone here, he was just gone. He'd been a transplanted organ that never quite took, and the town itself had rejected him.

Or really, Orion was an isolated constellation rapidly moving away from all other celestial bodies. In some respects, Peter didn't leave Orion. Orion left him, taking me with it.

Charlie kicked a rock, and it sank into the water without a splash. "Can I ask you why you came back? Rumor has it you once set foot out there. In the lands beyond."

I didn't need to explain it to him. There was something special about the town, like we were suspended in time and space, a part of the larger world, but untouched. That would sound quaint and backward to anyone who hadn't experienced it. I'd tried to explain it to my city friends, but Peter was the only one who came for a visit. I thought he'd understood, but either he'd deceived me or I'd been deluded.

"I had to return to take my vengeance on the townspeople who cheated me out of my inheritance." Two could play at his game.

He smiled. "You ever consider writing? You know your tropes."

Rather than answer him, I dodged. "Hasn't everyone considered writing? What about you? Any aspirations?"

"What reader doesn't think they could write a novel? But it's intimidating to teach the classics and then face a blank page. It leaves you asking what right you have to add one more book to the cluttered shelves."

That sentiment hit home, and it relieved me to hear it spoken aloud. "So you haven't yet?"

He tilted his head side to side, noncommittal.

I decided not to press. "Are you teaching a class on the classics right now?"

"No. Right now, I'm teaching mythology."

"Oh, I love mythology."

"Me, too." His face lit up.

"Are you doing Greek or Roman?"

"It's a summer class, so we're staying on the surface, covering a selection of myths from different cultures: Greeks, Romans, Mayans, Native Americans, even urban legend."

"That sounds very cool. I'd love to take your class."

At the bridge, I rested my elbows against the railing and stared at the quick-flowing water a few feet below, blocking out the overpowering memories woven into that particular spot like black magic.

Just on the other side of the creek, a driveway led to the raspberry cottage I loved, and I craned my neck to catch a glimpse. I walked down the lane to get a better view.

Charlie trotted along behind. "What are you looking for?"

"Nothing." A ladder leaned against the rain gutters, a sign that someone was maintaining the place. "It's just a house I like."

I'd had my sights on that little cottage ever since the *For Sale* sign had appeared at the end of the drive. Nestled between paper birch trees, the raspberry shake siding popped like the cherry on top of a vanilla milkshake. The front door arched, putting me in mind of hobbit holes and secret gardens.

I'd loved that house my entire life. It felt somehow kin to my bookstore. It was old in the best ways, filled with character and charm. When it came on the market, I started to believe all my dreams could come true. Peter said the owners wanted too much, that it would require thousands of dollars in electrical repairs alone. Ironically, Peter would have had the money to make those changes. He'd wanted something modern, up-to-date, and move-in ready. We'd go to see a Tudor set on a hill with a manicured lawn, and my mind would try to tell my heart to love it. But I couldn't let go of the idea of my perfect house. Without Peter, I had neither the Tudor nor the cottage. I had the old apartment above the pharmacy. Not that I wanted him for his money.

The *For Sale* sign still stood there, like a promise. The Palmers had long ago moved to the new active retirement community but hadn't been able to find a buyer for the home they'd shared. Whenever Layla, Max, and I used to ride our bikes over the bridge on a hot summer day to get lost in the trails through the woods, we'd ride up the drive and ring the doorbell. Mrs. Palmer would always invite us in to give us lemonade and cookies. We'd sit at her kitchen table, ruining our dinner, not worried we might be imposing, as if the cottage were an extension of our real homes. Our youth gave us an all access passkey to behind-the-scenes Orion.

"One day," I confessed to Charlie. "I'm going to buy that house."

The sky had grown darker, and the wind picked up. I looked up, and a raindrop hit my cheek. I laughed. "Of course, it's going to rain when our only option is to walk a half mile back to town." But the cool mist felt amazing on my sweaty skin.

We started walking back. As soon as we got to the gazebo, the sky opened up, and we raced the rest of the way to the door leading to my apartment.

Charlie leaned against the doorframe, wet locks clumping on his forehead, damp shirt clinging to his skin. "Guess I won't need a shower."

Hanging with Charlie had fed my need for companionship without making me hunger for physical contact. That was a definite relief from Dylan. I hoped we could do this again. "See you tomorrow?"

With a quick wave farewell, he jogged away, and I stood in the misty rain, dreaming about hazy English moors, foggy London streets, and dark and stormy nights.

Chapter 9

Chairs squeaked as people settled in for the book club Friday night. Dylan sat directly across from me and winked. I was relieved he'd come out. He looked better rested than the last few times I'd seen him, and I hoped that meant he was figuring things out.

Max carried over a plate of gingerbread cookies and handed it to Dylan, who made a production of choosing one, although they appeared to be uniform and identical. Without asking permission, Max had dropped in about thirty minutes early with a tray of uncooked dough and insisted I let him use my ovens to serve out hot-from-the-oven cookies. I wanted to say no, but Charlie was already hanging around and started making whimpering sounds when I hesitated. What was I to do? Disappoint my best customer?

And damn if the smell of gingerbread cookies hadn't filled the entire store as they baked, making the most absorbed patrons in the café stop and look around for the source. Someone eventually asked, "What smells so good?"

Score another point for Max. At this rate, he was going to move in completely, with or without my full approval. Like he always did. Like he knew best.

He now sat, looking smug and pleased with his second coup

in as many weeks, *Jane Eyre* open, facedown, on his knee, showing signs of the inevitable broken spine.

Long ago, when Max branched out from my library discards and asked Mrs. Moore for recommendations, she'd assign him massive epic fantasies, and I'd always grab the book from him immediately so I could break in the spine properly. Otherwise, he'd crack it along a single fault, and in time, his book would snap in two. He'd never lost that terrible habit, and I could identify a book Max had borrowed off my shelves just by looking at the spines.

The rain fell gently outside, and that may have contributed to the absence of Letitia. We may have permanently lost Letitia to nonfictional romance. Shawna sat between Midge and Charlie.

I cleared my throat and began. "*Jane Eyre* is chock-full of love triangles. I was wondering if we could talk about the love interests the characters encounter, and why they ultimately make the decisions they do. Do you feel they make the right choices?"

No surprise, Charlie started us off. "Interesting question. We have the obvious love triangle with Jane, Rochester, and St. John Rivers, but Rochester also feigns interest in Blanche to make Jane jealous, and lest we forget, he's married to Bertha. Meanwhile, St. John suppresses his love for Rosamond in order to pursue the more practical Jane."

Dylan leaned forward and surprised me by jumping right in. "Obviously Rochester represents passion while St. John Rivers represents a calculated partnership. Is there any question that Jane made the right choice?"

Charlie sighed, like he was tutoring a truculent student. "You give the author too little credit. I personally felt Jane faced a real dilemma. A relationship with St. John was reasonable, and given her situation, it was better than anything she could have once hoped for. Rochester, for all his passion, could have just as easily been a losing bet. Why throw away a known entity for a mere possibility? If this were real life, what would you advise a friend in a similar situation?"

He made a fair point, but I countered. "This isn't real life, Charlie."

Shawna interjected. "Has it occurred to anyone Jane could've rejected them both?"

Dylan cackled. "As if."

Shawna sat up taller. "I'm Team Helen Burns all the way."

Charlie shrugged. "Sure, why not?"

As moderator, I felt the need to force him to elaborate. "Why not what?"

Charlie threw up his hands like it was perfectly reasonable to ask why Jane didn't just subvert the patriarchy in nineteenth-century England. "If we're talking about how she might act if this were real life and not a romantic novel, wouldn't it have made the most sense for her to simply return to teaching? Or enter into a stable partnership with St. John? Why throw her lot in with the horror show of Rochester?"

Shawna nodded. "Yes, and why not fall in love with Helen Burns?"

"Um, well, she's dead," said Dylan helpfully.

"Wow." I had no idea the discussion would take that turn. "This is great. I'm just going to register my vote for Team Rochester, but you guys keep hashing it out."

"Why?" Charlie's eyes gleamed. He enjoyed debating these questions whether or not he fully believed what he was saying. He was a die-hard devil's advocate.

"Because he's the romantic hero, Charlie." Airtight logic.

"That's not a reason. Rochester is abusive. Jane's relationship with him could be called codependent. This isn't a healthy romance. If this guy existed in real life, you'd tell your friend to run far away."

"But he's not real. And on the page, he's the hero who's right for Jane. Not to mention, he gets a redemptive character arc as well, so when Jane makes that leap of faith, she finds him a changed man."

Charlie closed his eyes and shook his head, then pierced me

with a devastating look. "Do you see all relationships through the filter of author intent?"

"Fictional relationships? Yes." How else was I supposed to read them?

"I sometimes worry books like this ruin us for realistic relationships."

Now I was fully engaged. "Why? Because the romance hero doesn't exist in reality?"

Charlie unloaded his cannons. "Maybe because romance doesn't exist in reality."

"Oh, Charlie." Everyone was simply staring at us, and I felt like a cad for ending the exchange on such a personal note. I made an effort to turn it into a discussion point. "What do you all think? Does romance exist? Do romance heroes walk among us?"

That was a question I'd love to have an answer to, but to nobody's surprise, the opinions varied greatly.

Charlie said, "Not likely."

Shawna said, "Depends on your definition, I suppose. Heroes might exist, but you're better off taking your destiny in your own hands. Don't wait for one to show up."

"Heroes are real, but rare." Dylan grinned as if to say he'd made the cut.

Max spoke up for the first time since we started. "Heroes exist." He didn't make eye contact with anyone. "At least I hope so," he said more quietly.

"What about you, Maddie?" Shawna asked.

"I hope so, too, but I have my doubts."

I'd always believed in romance, but I wasn't sure I'd ever truly experienced it. Love, yes. Sex, definitely. But had I ever encountered a true romantic hero except in my imagination?

If one existed, what made me think I'd be his love interest anyway? Peter hadn't even wanted me enough to fight for me.

Could one of the men gathered in my bookstore be a hero in disguise?

Charlie was kind, smart, funny, and cute in a professorial way. We fell into an easy rhythm, a banter that bordered on flirtatious, but not once had he asked me on a proper date or dared to encroach on my physical space. I couldn't get a read on whether his cynicism about romance extended to me. Could he be a reluctant suitor?

He glanced over and tilted his head. Embarrassed, I shot my eyes away and landed on Max.

Max. Smart, adventurous, and hella persistent, he'd make a great boyfriend for some girl someday.

Since I saw him more like my adopted brother than a serious romantic contender, I didn't make a habit of appraising his appearance. He had a boy-next-door cuteness, but of course, he'd literally been my boy next door. He had perfectly proportioned facial features, a nice nose sprinkled with freckles, and soft full lips hiding straight white teeth, thanks to two years of braces. His long eyelashes framed green eyes as familiar to me as my own. When he shaved, he had smooth skin, prone to red splotches whenever he'd get embarrassed. When he neglected the razor, he could honestly give Dylan a run for his money, but then again, I had a scruff fetish.

Objectively, Max was easy to look at. If he lived in Indianapolis, I'm sure the girls would be lining up. But for me, he was off limits. When we weren't squabbling, he was one of my best friends and Layla's brother.

That left Dylan.

If I was choosing my own adventure, I could do a whole lot worse than Dylan. At least for a night. To feel his body against mine, to let him consume me in a passionate embrace, like some oversexed pirate or roguish duke in a bodice ripper. It would be tempting to succumb to his seductions.

He caught me looking, and his eyebrow rose.

I'd discovered through writing how much an eyebrow could communicate. An eyebrow could arch with suspicion or surprise or disbelief. When Dylan arched a brow, he cocked it cockily, and his sexy confidence could conquer my will. It was easy to imagine him giving me that same look as he coaxed me out of my clothes. Up against a wall.

Charlie's earlier question resurfaced. *"If this were real life, what would you advise a friend in a similar situation?"*

This *was* my real life. Dylan represented all the passion of a Rochester, but maybe Charlie was right. Maybe Rochester was a risk that paid off for Jane only because of plot. What would I find if I returned to Thornfield Hall to stake my claim on my rakish hero?

I didn't doubt for one second that, given the chance, Dylan could make my heart palpitate in that old familiar way.

The million dollar question was: What would come after? Dylan looked out for Dylan. If I let him take me to bed, would he take my heart as well?

The book club mercifully ended on an upbeat note when Midge announced that she believed true love will always find its way. It was a nice thought anyway.

I scanned the sheet. "Looks like we're going to be tackling *Gone with the Wind* in two weeks, guys. Do you think we can do this?"

Nobody objected, and I slipped behind the counter to make a few sales.

I grabbed the massive stack of *Gone with the Wind*, unsure when I was going to find the time to read since I had yet to finish writing my second novel, a panic-inducing thought.

Dylan bent forward with that glint of seduction in his eyes. His lower lip disappeared between his teeth, and I crossed my arms as if I were donning armor against an impending physical assault. If he stepped another foot closer, I might have thrown caution and respectability to the wind. A sly grin broke out across his face, like he knew exactly what kind of trouble he could talk me into. High school wasn't so long ago, I'd forgotten how easily he'd sucked me into his orbit. He never exactly asked me out or said he wanted to be my boyfriend. He simply insinuated himself into my life, and I was powerless to stop him. He'd casually slip his arm around my waist as we walked to class, and it gave me such a thrill, I might as well have been high on amphetamines. I'd kicked that addiction, though the fluttering of my heart said otherwise.

He ran his eyes across my lips, and damn if my perfidious mouth didn't tingle. "Would you consider stopping by later?"

I felt at a complete disadvantage. We had an audience, and I didn't want to shoot him down in cold blood. I hesitated. "I—"

"The thing is, you were always honest with my music, and I've just finished this song. I need some input." He tilted his head, eyes wide, all innocence.

Torn between encouraging his seduction and trampling his creative confidence, I took a chance that he wasn't lying. "Yeah, okay. When?"

"Tonight?"

I coughed. I could picture how that might go. I'd show up to find him waiting for me out in the barn, brushing a horse or maybe just leaning against a stall, shirtless, watching me until I was close enough for him to hook an arm around my waist. He'd spin me around and press me against the ladder to the loft, threading his fingers through my hair. He'd say—

"Maddie?" His eyes, the color of overcast skies, narrowed in that seductive way he always had.

"How about I swing by Sunday afternoon after I visit my mom?"

He didn't press for more, just bought a book and left me flustered.

I rang up Charlie's book, aware that he'd witnessed that whole exchange. But he spoke past me. "Thanks for those cookies, Max."

Max said, "Hey, here's an idea." He raised his voice in a staged response, like he wasn't talking to Charlie. "Think of how much more popular this book club would be if Maddie could advertise that she'd have fresh-baked cookies every time."

And there it was. His self-promotion plug.

I would have put my fingers in my ears, but I needed them to handle money.

Charlie handed me a ten, nodding. "Great idea."

Traitor.

I mustered my exasperation to moderate my tone to civility as I handed him his change. "See you tomorrow, Charlie?"

When Shawna and Midge followed Charlie out into the rain, I wheeled on Max. "What makes you think giving away cookies is going to help me. Or you for that matter?"

He threw up his hands. "It's just an idea. Lure people in with food."

"People come to the book club to talk about books. It's not a food club."

"How about this . . . Have you considered updating your reading list? Honestly, Maddie. *Jane Eyre*?"

I made a mental note to search Amazon for a pair of earplugs. "*Jane Eyre* is a classic, Max. Even you were able to contribute to the conversation."

He snorted. "Sometimes people don't want to work so hard. You should pick books that were written this century."

I went back to closing the register. "Lots of people like to reread books. It's easy and comfortable and *familiar*."

"Maybe people would come in if you gave something new a try."

I dropped the stack of bills I'd been counting and faced him. "People do come in. You were here. You saw them."

His jaw clenched. "Charlie. And Shawna. And Midge. *Your friends*. I'm talking about people who don't feel sorry for you." He bit his tongue. "I mean . . . shit. Those people all love you, Maddie. They're going to come no matter what."

I glared. "You are the most arrogant, bossy, presumptuous—"

He stepped closer, his face inches from mine. "And you are pig-headed and opinionated."

"Me? Opinionated? That's a lark coming from you."

His nostrils flared. "I used to wonder who represented pride and who represented prejudice, but you made me realize a person could be both."

"You wouldn't be referring to a book published in 1813, would you?"

"Jesus, Maddie." He pinched the bridge of his nose. "I'm only trying to help."

"I didn't ask for your help."

"You know, the fact that you won't lean on your support system doesn't make you stronger."

I gripped the edge of the counter. "Just leave."

Defeated, he grabbed his things. "Think about it, Maddie."

Then he was gone, and I sat down on the floor and cried because at the heart of his argument, Max was right. I couldn't keep doing this alone. And I was getting so tired of trying.

Chapter 10

Saturday morning, the skies were clear, and the whole town came alive. The bell over my door jangled more than usual, music to my ears. Constant activity buoyed my spirits, and I pushed Max's incessant advice out of my head.

After reading *Stuart Little* to a dozen boys and girls, I juggled the coffee machine and the register while the lunch crowd swept in.

A couple of teens wandered in later, bored and looking for something to read. I may have scared them by listing a dozen suggestions. Finally, we landed on *Frostblood,* and I sent them on their way with an invitation to start a teen book club. They looked wary, but didn't say no.

Around two, a local author had a new release and held her launch party in the children's corner. I'd ordered her picture books in advance, and she brought in a crowd of friends and family. She read aloud and signed personalized copies. We sold enough of her books to cover the rent for the day at least.

I started to believe I might one day turn this ship around and avoid the massive iceberg of failure I was heading toward.

When the store was busy with patrons, gushing over books, or happily sunning in my café, it was almost enough to keep me satisfied. Almost.

Small pieces of my soul remained unfulfilled. I'd been abandoned by the one man who'd promised me forever, but that was only one hole in my heart. Another aspiration had grown stronger with age. After so many years studying other authors, I longed to move from behind the cash register to the shelves myself. I wanted to host my own launch party. I wanted teens to read my novel for a book club. I wanted my book to sit on the Willing Wall while couples cajoled each other into reading their favorite novel. I wanted to write someone's favorite novel.

Some days that goal seemed far out of reach. I had my publisher behind me, so that was a great touchstone against the abject fear of being critically panned and universally loathed. But a single reviewer had taken a sledgehammer to my confidence.

Maybe if my mom had let me study English in college instead of insisting I get a degree in business, maybe then I'd have learned how to write a truly memorable novel.

When my author email called out *You've got mail!* my heart skipped a beat, and I prayed for good book news. I walked toward the café and sat down hard when I saw who it was from.

Claire,
Whoa. Touché. How do I turn this thing off? Can we call a ceasefire or something? Lay down your weapons. I surrender. You win.
Damn. Did you get a Master's degree in verbal warfare?
You're right. I do have blind spots based in my own experience. Yes, it is ironic for me to give romantic advice considering my current state of affairs, but you might be surprised to learn I'm not after a superficial thrill in a relationship. I, too, want respect. Not just in romance, either.
So, well played. Your arrow flew straight to the heart. Congratulations.
Silver Fox

For some reason, I didn't feel like I'd won anything. If anything, I felt ashamed of the way I'd blasted him. His response had been undeservedly measured. I would have expected him to either stop writing me altogether or deliver another blistering retort. Instead, he'd cried uncle and let slip something vulnerable.

Maybe I owed him an apology.

When the sun had passed its zenith, and I'd swept and cleaned the bathroom and done every other chore I could think of, I grabbed my laptop and composed what I hoped was a peace offering.

> *Silver Fox,*
>
> *Thank you for your last email. I shouldn't have written you to begin with, and I need to apologize for my own personal attacks against you. It was a low point. Please consider it a lesson learned.*
>
> *To be honest, you've given me a lot to think about, and I'm planning to take steps to broaden my experiences as you suggested. I don't want to get into the intimate details, but I think you may have stumbled onto a truth when you accused me of sleepwalking through my last romantic relationship. By the time I was working on my first novel, my fiancé and I were in a comfortable lull, ya know? Maybe I'd forgotten what it feels like to fall in love. Or maybe I've never truly experienced it. Oh, I've known romance, I've known chemistry, I've been on the giving and receiving end of unrequited love. But "a love for the ages" as you so eloquently put it. How many of us experience that? I'm not entirely sure it even exists, but for the sake of art, I'm thinking of taking your advice to "live a little" and see where it leads.*
>
> *Jeez, that is a lot of personal info. But I'm finishing my first draft of book 2,* The Shadow's Journeyman, *and I want to make sure I nail the chemistry this time around. Maybe you'd be willing to read an early ARC when it's available.*
>
> *Claire*

I surprised myself with everything I'd written and hesitated on sending it. Would I really want him to read my second book?

Maybe I was seeking vindication. Maybe he'd told me more truth than any of my first readers. Or possibly, he was like Severus Snape, and if I got praise from him, I'd know I'd earned it.

I hit send, worried I'd just made an entirely different kind of fool of myself.

A couple approached the register, looking for a coffee table book about the many covered bridges in our neck of the woods. After I helped them locate what they wanted, I glanced up to watch Charlie in the corner. He had a stupid grin on his face as he read something on his laptop. Then he started typing. I imagined he could be chatting with someone on Facebook, and it made me question again where he came from originally. Did he have a bunch of friends in another hometown who might one day lure him back?

I warmed up a piece of carrot cake Max had dropped off earlier and carried it over. "On the house," I added. The price of a piece of cake was a bargain if I could keep Charlie from deciding he missed his old crowd of my imagination enough to move back to wherever he came from.

His eyes went wide. "Straight up amazing, Maddie. Thank you."

"Well, you are my favorite customer," I flirted. "And my most loyal."

That last bit was too true. He'd sat at this corner table nearly every day since . . . I tried to think when exactly he'd first showed up, but it was like he'd always been here. I'd probably come to discover he was a ghost haunting my bookstore. With his rumpled hair and timeless clothes, maybe he'd been trapped in Orion since the turn of the century. The last century.

Except he went walking with me and presumably taught classes in the outer world.

"Hey, Charlie." I started to tease him. "Say you were a ghost. Where do you think you'd spend your days?"

"You think I'm a ghost?"

I should have known he'd catch on. "You're not, right?"

"Nope. Just your average run-of-the-mill modern vampire."

I snorted. "Well, you should know I come from a long line of vampire hunters."

"Hmm." One eyebrow rose above the frame of his glasses. Intrigued. "We should work out an exchange of secrets."

"Do you have an SCIF?"

"SCIF?"

"Sensitive Compartmented Information Facility. You know like for the sharing of confidential documents."

"Dare I ask why you know that term?"

I leaned in, confidential. "I'm a spy."

Honestly, I'd learned about it while researching for a contemporary thriller I'd never written.

"And that's not your secret?" He pretended to peek at my phone, but I hugged it to my chest.

"Not anymore." I shot a glance at his messenger bag. "Your secret is that you're in the witness protection program, but you still correspond with the sweet girl you had to leave behind."

He laughed. "So busted."

"Best be careful. She'll be your Achilles' heel."

He clutched his chest. "Better my heel than my heart."

"So you do have a weakness." Maybe his anti-romance posturing was armor he wore after someone hurt him. Just like me.

"Who doesn't? What's your secret, Maddie?"

I could have said, *Pick a number.* I wasn't ready to share my true secret identity, but could I reveal that I was sizing him up for my next romantic lead?

Dare I tell him? Say, *Oh, I was hoping you might ask me out on a date.* I imagined how that might go. I'd dig through my wardrobe to find that perfect summer outfit. Maybe the flirty pink flair skirt and that soft white low-cut button-down shirt. Innocent, yet sexy. He'd know not to take me to Gentry's, so we'd go to the Jukebox, laugh over dinner, then he'd ask me to dance. It would be awkward because he'd confess he didn't really know how to dance, but I'd tell him it was fine. We'd position ourselves, his hand on my hip, mine on his shoulder, bodies pressed together, and—

"Maddie?"

I blinked and I was present. "My secret is that I'm a robot who periodically reboots."

He chuckled, and I blushed. Awkwardly, I excused myself to help customers. I should have just asked him out, but it wasn't so easy to put myself out there. Anyway, I'd given him an opening. If he didn't take it, maybe it wasn't to be.

Chapter 11

The next Saturday morning, lightning crackled across the purple sky, both beautiful and terrifying. I braved a sheet of water to cross to the store and open up early to do some paperwork. The moisture permeated the air even inside, and the musty smell of ancient mildew met me as I stepped through the door.

I fetched my laptop, poured myself a mug of coffee, and set up in the café to look over my finances. Somehow, I had a bit more in my checking account than I expected. I fought the urge to call Peter to gloat, but as I went through bills, I discovered why I had a surplus. My Internet bill had a giant red overdue message with an urgent warning to pay immediately. Had I missed a bill? After I took care of two months of wireless service plus the late fee, I looked around the empty store and fretted again. I couldn't afford to lose an entire Saturday's business to rain. Peter would expect me to send him a payment against his part of the loan in a week. The only reason I hadn't gone under already was thanks to a modest advance for my book deal, but I couldn't dip into that finite resource forever.

At least I could look forward to another check when I turned in my next book. Unable to control the weather, I dreamed of selling enough of my own words to subsidize the beleaguered bookstore with royalties. If I hit it big enough, I might be able to buy Peter out of his stake. It was still early, so I opened my disaster of a manuscript to try to make some headway.

I sat at my laptop, headphones in, trying to figure out how to salvage a critical scene I'd been struggling to nail.

Rane ran a finger across Lira's cheek, but tears continued to fall unabated. Only one of them could return through the portal, and he knew it must be her. To live without her would be unthinkable, but to die meant salvation for others.

"Go and I will follow." His voice cracked under the strain of so much emotion.

Lira dropped to her knees. "I will not leave you."

The portal wavered and snapped even smaller. Soon there would be no chance for either of them.

"You must." He knelt in front of her and lifted her chin. "I must know you're safe. Go now."

She flung her arms around his neck and buried her face into his chest, anchoring herself to his body. Somehow in that instant, he found the inner strength to gather her up and carry her toward the portal—

God, this really *was* terrible.

Had it always been so bad? Or was I hypercritical, reading through Silver Fox's eyes? I couldn't tell anymore.

As if I'd summoned it, my phone announced I had mail, and I took a break to check who it was from, intrigued upon seeing a reply from Silver Fox. He'd changed the subject heading to read: *Epiphanies.* My curiosity spiked.

Claire,

I appreciate your last email. I think we both owe each other an apology. I probably shouldn't have engaged, but wow, you came at me with both barrels. Now you've left me curious to find out what kind of epiphany I might have inspired with my admittedly boorish suggestions.

Since you've made a confession, I'll throw in one of my own.

I was in a pretty bad place emotionally while reading your book. It was a great distraction from my morose mood, but my reaction to the romantic story arc may have been colored by my state of mind. You see, there's this girl . . . and I can't seem to get her out of my head, but she's a bit of a challenge.

I can give you one more olive branch and confess that one of your scenes has stuck with me. I keep visualizing it with clarity, as if I'd seen it on the screen. It was the moment when Dane places petals on Lela while she's sleeping. I found it both tender and powerful how he sacrifices his own magic without her awareness. You do a fantastic job there of showing how potent his love is, that he'd give everything up to infuse her with that illicit power, for nothing in return, knowing she might internalize it and then turn against him, as it would be in her nature.

Wow. My purple prose is showing. . . .

SF

Had it been only two weeks since he'd made me cry? Reading his much nicer words about my characters soothed my wounded pride, even if he still got their names wrong. I felt a bit vindicated and less terrified my book would meet with indifference or ridicule. He'd reminded me I was proud of what I'd written. That confidence started my pistons firing again. For the first time since I'd read his review, I didn't dread writing.

His confession had arrived at the perfect time, and I poured out pages, ignoring the near constant criticism in the back of my mind. As I stared up in the air, trying to conjure the perfect word to describe the coy expression on Rane's face, the entire store lit up like a bomb flash. At about that exact moment, an incredible rumble of thunder exploded and shook the walls. I might have enjoyed the dramatic storm, especially as it fed me energy to keep writing, but something in the back room fizzled, and my electricity cut out entirely.

The only thing I knew how to do was check the breakers, so I grabbed a flashlight from under the front counter and went back to trip the circuit box in the back room. When I flipped the switches, the power remained out.

"Hello?" Max called from the front of the store, which meant it was time to open up, and I didn't have power. Perfect.

I abandoned my futile efforts and went to help Max carry in my order. He looked around and asked, "How long has your power been out?"

"Not long. The storm must have knocked it out."

He frowned. "When I pulled up, yours was the only store that looked dark. Are you sure you paid your electricity bill?"

Considering I'd just discovered an overdue Internet bill, it was a fair question. But I wasn't in the mood to have Max dad me through this problem.

"I'm going to call the power company," I said, following Max into the back room where he repeated my already failed attempt to flip the breakers.

He opened the back door and plunged into the rain. I worried he might try something stupid, like messing with the main shut off outside, picturing him returning looking like the kids from *Jurassic Park* after they'd been electrocuted, his hair frazzled and his face covered in char. I didn't notice my fists were clenched until he came back in.

"Anything?"

He shook his head and hit the main breaker one more time, and then miracle of miracles, the silence was broken by the rumbling of the air conditioner coming to life. The lights up front flickered back on, but I'd never turned on the lights in the back room, and we stood in relative darkness.

"Sometimes," he said, "you just have to keep trying." He raised an eyebrow, imbuing his banal observation with hidden meaning, as if to emphasize where I'd failed. As if to underscore every failure in my life.

It grated to be rescued by Max in my hour of need. I knew my stubbornness was born more from a kind of near-sibling rivalry than true animosity, due to minor irritations that had built up over time. From him trying to correct my diving form, despite the fact that he himself had hit his head on the diving board earlier that summer, to him giving me the unsolicited caution against trying to take a senior level AP English class my junior year. If I hadn't ignored him, I never would have started dating Dylan.

He might have meant well, but I'd never asked him to correct me or save me or tell me hard truths. If I were Rapunzel and Max showed up at the foot of my castle, I'd cut off my own hair to prove I could take care of myself, thank you very much.

It's why I'd never shown Max my recent writing. I could only imagine how many bad habits he'd feel compelled to break. It's also why I'd disregarded the advice he gave me last Thanksgiving.

A month before my wedding.

I'd asked Peter to spend the holiday with my mom and me, but he'd said he needed to get away from Orion for a few days. He didn't even go visit his own parents. His non-American work buddies had decided to take the time off to go skiing in Vail, and Peter went with them. He didn't invite me along, claiming he knew I'd want to do the whole turkey thing. He promised he'd make it up to me—and that we'd start our own Thanksgiving traditions the next year.

I was understandably pissed. I went for a long walk along the stream, wrapped in a warm sweater. My breath made puffs of mini clouds as I marched angrily along, muttering to myself and punching my fist in the air periodically. To my great surprise, when I got to the bridge, Max sat at the apex, dangling his feet over the edge, staring morosely at the gurgling water below. If he'd fallen in, he might have sprained his ankle.

Still, I hollered, "Don't jump!"

He half smiled at me, and I sat beside him and bumped him with my shoulder. He asked me why I'd come all the way out there. I unloaded my most secret fears.

I told him, "I don't think Peter wants to stay in Orion after we get married."

I told him, "I sometimes wonder if he loves *me,* or just the idea of me."

I told him, "I'm wondering if I should call off the wedding."

He listened until I'd said my piece, wiping the occasional angry tear off my cheek. Finally, I just leaned against him. He put his arm around me and ruined the moment.

He told me, "I'm pretty sure Peter will take you away from Orion."

He told me, "I sometimes wonder if you stay with Peter because it's easier than being alone with yourself."

He told me, "I think you should call off the wedding."

It wasn't what I'd wanted him to say. Granted, I'd asked for it, but I needed reassurances in that moment. I should have known he couldn't be more like Layla and tell me everything would work out. He'd never let go of an opportunity to solve the problem of Maddie.

I resisted the urge to push him into the freezing creek.

Knowing that Max had been so right only made it hurt that much more when Peter didn't show up for our wedding, when he asked me to choose between him and Orion.

Standing in the dark back room of my failing bookstore now, I had to wonder if I'd made the right choice.

"Everything okay, Maddie?"

Max stepped closer, and I was tempted to confess it all. That I wasn't okay. That my bookstore was foundering and I was afraid I'd end up alone thanks to my pig-headed independence. That my independence was a sham and I couldn't even pass a Bechdel test in my own mind. That I was so desperate for companionship, I'd been trying to force Charlie into a lead role.

But I knew what Max would say. He'd tell me I was better off alone than stuck with the wrong man. Shit, he'd been alone since I'd returned to town, and he seemed content to remain that way. He was even succeeding at solitude better than me.

He'd tell me to let Peter go and move on with my life. But I hadn't reached that point yet. I backed away. "I'm fine. Thanks for your help."

"It doesn't have to be like this."

I paused. I told myself not to ask, not to give him an opening to plug his business proposals, but something on his face made me ask anyway. "Like what?"

"I'm not your enemy." He licked his lips and moved toward me. "I don't know why you no longer trust me."

I could have told him about the time he'd promised to hold

me up when I learned to skate, but he'd let go because he thought I could do it on my own. I ended up with a skinned knee. But I'd also skated, upright, for a full minute before I realized he'd fallen behind. Yeah, so I'd skated, but it would have been nice if he hadn't made that choice for me.

Instead, for some reason, my mind drifted to tenth grade, when we'd stolen a six pack of beer and sat on the gazebo, feeling crazy and happy and utterly unafraid. Layla, the lightweight, fell asleep on the bench. Max and I walked along the creek, laughing and pretending we were drunker than we were. We reached the bridge and leaned over to watch the water below. Imagining liberation from inhibitions, we locked eyes.

Max had said, "Have you ever wondered what it would be like if we kissed?"

My judgment was clouded by a slight buzz, and I remembered thinking he was the cutest boy I'd ever seen. Whether or not the thought of kissing him had ever occurred to me before that, once he'd said it, it was all I wanted to do. And so I did.

For a split second, a rush of relief buoyed me, eliminating my teenage fear of being ugly and unlovable. Then his hands were in my hair, and I was biting his lip. He groaned my name.

The headlights of an oncoming car illuminated us, and we jumped apart. I blurted out, "This never happened."

We never talked about it after that, and I never told a soul. Not even Layla. I trusted him enough to believe nothing bad would come of it, and maybe if we'd had a frank and earthy discussion about our natural curiosity to kiss, our friendship wouldn't have become so strained, but we were kids. To be honest, that kind of conversation had scared me. Soon after that, Max started studying all the time, trying to outshine me academically. To compete, I had to work twice as hard. By junior year, we'd established this never-ending battle for supremacy.

I looked at Max in the here and now and said, "It's not that I don't trust you, Max. It's that I don't need you."

He swallowed hard, then stormed past me and back out to his van.

The rest of the day, try as I might, I couldn't stop replaying our conversation. I probably owed him an apology, but it made me weirdly happy to see him lose his cool. At least when he was mad at me, he was my equal.

Despite Max's imaginary advice, or maybe because of it, I picked up my smartphone and texted three words: *Are you busy?*

Fifteen minutes later, Peter responded. *Working.*

On a Saturday afternoon. Of course he was.

I just wanted to say . . . What did I want to say to him? What was left to say? *I'm sorry.*

I waited, growing nervous I'd given him too much, but then my phone buzzed.

Me, too.

A few moments later, another text appeared. *What are you reading for your next book club?*

Disappointed in the immediate change in topic, I responded. *Gone with the Wind.*

Then it hit me. Was he considering . . . ? I followed up. *Are you thinking of coming to the club?*

Did I want him to?

I pictured the scene. Charlie would be midway through a lecture about the problematic nature of *Gone with the Wind* against today's worldview. The door would swing open like when Dylan arrived, only Peter would glide in like he owned the place. Because he did. He'd walk right up to me and drop to his knees, unconcerned about dirtying his tailor-made suit. He'd say, *Maddie, I've tried living without you, but how could I live without my heart and soul? I was wrong. Will you take me back?*

Except that would never happen. He cared too much about his clothes. And he'd wait me out before he admitted he'd made a mistake.

There was no answer to my question. Typical.

Even Max's imaginary advice was spot on.

I turned back to my laptop and stared at my blinking cursor through unfallen tears until I had to admit I wouldn't write anything I'd want to salvage. I'd run out of juju. Even the hero of my creation, Rane, couldn't figure out how to properly save himself and the woman he loved. At least my heroine had more than enough power to rescue them both. If only I could reach deep inside and find a well of untapped magic to rip me from one world into another.

I no longer knew which world I'd choose.

Chapter 12

✖✦✖

We didn't open our shops on Sundays thanks to Gentry's insistence that we dedicate the Lord's day to community service. Not everyone was on board with this ordinance, but at some point before my return, the council had voted to approve it, and Gentry had never let the topic come up for review.

So on Sundays, before or after church, we might organize a 5k for charity or pitch in to gather fallen limbs after a freak storm. We'd get an email sometime before seven in the morning requesting our presence on Main Street. It would be signed from the entire council, but Gentry would be the one holding a clipboard and checking off names of able-bodied citizens who'd materialized.

When my personal email dinged before my feet had hit the floor, I knew it would be a summoning.

All of the local business people showed up to help, so it took almost no time. Up the street, Max helped Shawna. He didn't even look my way, and that was fine. I kicked a bunch of twigs into the street.

Gentry called over, "You're not getting all the sticks. Make sure you get those small ones, too." He clapped his hands like he was leading a high school production of *Grease*. "Oh, and Madeleine, I heard your power went out yesterday. You need to get an electrician over to make sure you're up to code."

"But—"

"Also, your window's been vandalized again."

I turned around and saw it. Some hooligan had painted an *E* and an *R* strategically so now it kind of read the Messy Store. Shit. Now I'd have to repaint. More money down the drain.

Gentry noticed Midge handing out cups of lemonade and made a beeline for her, finger wagging. "Midge, let the people work."

After an hour or so, Gentry declared the sidewalks, streets, and other public spaces satisfactory and released everyone in time for church services. Before we left, he reminded those of us on the city council that we needed to prepare for Fourth of July activities.

"Email me your progress, please!"

I slipped away and went to scrape as much of the errant paint off my window as I could.

Max passed behind me and said, "You should install a video camera to figure out who's doing that."

I hollered, "It's probably you."

He called back, "I would have changed it to the Musty Scone."

I muttered under my breath. "If you were in charge, it would be called the Bossy Store."

That made me giggle to myself.

As soon as I was satisfied with my handiwork, I fled to my writing cave, opened my latest file, and typed in bursts of inspiration, happy once again to hide in the world I controlled.

Lira struggled with the bonds, her wrists chaffing and bleeding. The light was fading, and soon, she'd be left in the dark. Knowing what the darkness would bring made her panic, and she tugged ever harder, but the spell had been powerful. Magic had ensnared her; only magic would free her. She closed her eyes and focused on her breathing, trying to forget the shadows creeping across the floor, ever closer, carrying Creed knew what. She reached into the depth of her essence and touched the potent stream, the source she couldn't control. Maybe if she just—

Her eyes snapped open. Light filled every corner of the room. It emanated from Lela.

Dammit.

I'd mistyped my own character's name. *Thanks, Silver Fox.* I hit the backspace key, then leaned back in my chair and stretched. How had he managed to impact me in the space of fifteen days and four emails?

I wondered where he lived, how old he was, what he looked like. On the *Book Brigade* website, they hadn't posted any images of the reviewers, but the About page, listed their bios.

Silver Fox hails from the Midwest where he grew up de-tasseling corn in the summer and burying himself in books in the winter. He prefers mainstream or literary fiction, but does not feel guilty that he has a soft spot for genre fiction, especially fantasy. The first book he remembers reading was The Little Prince, *and he's been reading whatever he could get his hands on ever since. If you think Silver Fox would be the best reviewer for your book, feel free to specify him in the submission.*

Had whoever sent my book to the *Book Brigade* asked for him by name? And why? I made a note to ask my editor what she knew.

Who was this guy? The Midwest encompassed a huge area, but de-tasseling corn was a summer ritual for a lot of Indiana high school kids. Maybe it was common elsewhere, too. Dylan had worked on his parents' farm early mornings and came back exhausted with calluses thicker than anything he'd gotten from playing guitar.

The mention of *The Little Prince* reminded me of the first time Mrs. Moore read it aloud to us kids, and I resolved to add it to the summer children's reading.

I clicked the link under Silver Fox's moniker and brought up his latest posts. Coincidentally, *Pride and Prejudice* was the last book he'd reviewed. It seemed odd he'd choose a book that old—a romance at that—but maybe he did more than upcoming releases. I scrolled to the post for my book and lost whatever enthusiasm I had for continuing this line of research.

Maybe there were clues to his personality in his choice of name. I knew the phrase "silver fox" was slang for older attractive men, but he'd said he was young, so I ruled that out. I typed "silver fox" into Wikipedia and discovered that the animal was actually a red fox. Silver Fox was also a Marvel Comics character—Wolverine's lover, a woman. Another dead end. Silver Fox was the codename of some naval exercises, an island in Newfoundland, a paint color, a bus line, and a figure in Native American creation mythology. I'd have to ask Charlie what he knew about that last one.

For all I knew, Silver Fox was his actual name.

I checked the clock. I needed to finish this draft before my editor's deadline in three weeks. By this Friday really, if I wanted to give Layla time to read it. Instead, I started typing an email, feeling a little silly for wanting to respond to some random guy when we didn't know each other at all except through a handful of emails, but he'd intrigued me with his confession. I found myself wanting to know more about this Midwestern guy who read Jane Austen alongside review copies of fantasy novels.

> *Silver,*
> *Can I call you that? :)*
> *You wanted to know about this epiphany? The truth is I've been treading water for some time, but I've decided I need to open myself to dating. I hear you whispering in my ear to give it a chance. The sacrifices we make for art, right? But you gave me a push I needed, and while I haven't yet hit on any swoopy emotions I could tap into to infuse my own characters with the drug-addled sense of overwhelming love, it's given me a lot to think about in terms of what I personally want from a relationship.*
> *Best of luck with your own romantic tribulations.*
> *Claire*

I added a postscript to encourage another response.

P.S. What on earth possessed you to review Pride and Prejudice?

I hit Send, then turned on Pandora to an instrumental station and buried myself in my novel until my butt hurt.

After lunch, I grabbed a copy of my book and headed over to see my mom, knowing at least she would express undiluted pride in my accomplishments.

I found her relaxing on the patio with a magazine and a cup of coffee. I wished she didn't live all alone, but she insisted the neighbors kept her company. The Becketts lived next door, and she had her gossiping ladies nights. Still, it hurt to imagine an entire life of loneliness. She never complained, though.

I poured myself a glass of water from the tap and dropped my book on the table. Then I fell into a chair across the table from her, admiring Mom's garden. The Virginia Bluebells were stunning.

She cradled my novel and beamed. "Oh, Maddie. I'm so proud of you. I want to send it to everyone I know. Can you get me some more copies?"

I choked on my water. "Mom, I need people to buy my book. If I give them all away, my publisher won't ask me to write any more."

"I just want to brag about you." She winked. "After all, you got your writing genes from me."

I laughed. "But I got Dad's good looks."

She snorted, then sighed. "He *was* good looking, though."

He was, if the pictures showed a true likeness. Mom's eyes would linger when she'd show them to me, a finger tracing his jawline as if he were there to appreciate it.

"When did you know you were in love with him?"

"Oh, dear." She leaned her elbows on the table and brought both her hands together to rest her chin on. "I've told you about the night he asked me to dance, right?"

"Yeah. You went to the prom with some guy named Shorty or something."

"That's what your dad called him, but his name was actually James." I loved that she referred to her husband as my dad even though I'd never known him. It gave me a sense of place. "He was nice, but he wasn't Mark." She sat straighter. "Your dad crossed the dance floor like a man on a mission. He said, 'You look so beautiful tonight, Trudi.'" She fanned herself. "Excuse me, but it was just so damn sexy. There he was in that suit with eyes that could burn up a stone. I wouldn't say I knew I was in love with him then. I mean, that would've felt foolish at the time. Looking back, though, I knew it. He only proved it with time."

My heart caught in my throat, and I wiped my eyes. "That's beautiful, Mom."

"I wish you'd gotten to know him. He was something else."

How different might my life have turned out if I'd had a proper dad, a proper male role model instead of learning about men and boys either from books or from hanging at my friends' houses and watching how their fathers and brothers behaved?

She waved away a fly. "When did you know you were in love with Peter?"

"I dunno." I closed my eyes, trying to blot out memories of Peter, focusing on the feel of the breeze tousling my hair, the sound of a lawn mower in the distance, the warmth of the sun on my legs. But Mom's recollection, seeing Dad emerge from a crowd, was so like my first encounter with Peter, the memory played like a movie on the inside of my lids.

I'd met Peter in Indianapolis at my first job out of college. Whereas Layla had been happy to return home right away, I focused on growing up and growing away from Orion. I found a perverse excitement in entering the mundane world of adulthood. University had become routine and boring, but like an enthusiastic lemming, I went to the job fairs hoping to find a corporate love connection so I could get out into the "real world" and start my life.

Next came the career clothes, the job interviews, the offer letter, the apartment hunt, the new key, the old furniture, the laminated ID badge, the impersonal cube, and the team of interchangeable coworkers. Mom helped me get settled in, then with a wistful farewell, she turned around and drove the thirty-five minutes home, leaving me alone, but not stranded, in the big city that proclaimed, "Apple is our middle name."

Enjoying my first taste of freedom, I'd barely scouted out the available pool of single men when I saw Peter for the first time at a corporate party. He oozed the kind of sexy confidence that would catch any woman's attention. The premature silver streaks in his hair coupled with his Brooks Brothers elegance lent him a decade he hadn't earned. He was so ethereally beautiful, he drew all the eyes in the room, but his eyes connected with mine, and he headed straight for me, snagging two glasses of champagne off a server's tray.

He approached, offering a flute. "I'll trade you a glass of champagne for your name."

I resisted the urge to snort at the cheesy come on. "That's hardly a fair exchange. The champagne was free."

"The courage to come talk to you wasn't."

Just like that, the admission of vulnerability endeared him to me.

"I'm Madeleine."

"Like in Proust?" He winced. "Oh, sorry. That's kind of obscure. Did you know a madeleine is—"

I arched an eyebrow at his attempted mansplaining. "It's a small shell-shaped sponge cake."

His eyes widened. "Oh, of course you'd know your namesake. I shouldn't have—"

Vanity pricked, I shook my index finger at him. "If you think Marcel Proust is obscure, I'd hate to know what you'd make of Antoine de Saint-Exupéry."

His face relaxed, like he'd found a way out of the quagmire he'd stumbled into. "I'll concede your mastery of French authors, but I've actually read *The Little Prince*."

Pretty and well-read? "What's your name?"

He held out his hand. "Peter Mercer at your service."

Never were truer words spoken. For months, Peter pursued me in a way that gave me something to call home about. We flirted over the corporate messaging system, and he sent flowers to my cube on my birthday. He surprised me on our second Christmas with tickets to *Hamilton* and a weekend excursion to Chicago. He was the boyfriend Dylan had never even tried to be.

Peter came from another world, like a character out of Fitzgerald. He had an old world confidence derived from old school money, and the taste and refinement that went along with that. He was choosy, and his approbation wasn't easy to win. The simple fact that he'd chosen me had lent me borrowed confidence to do things I might not have dared. Like writing a novel or buying a bookstore. I might have found that courage on my own, but seeing myself through his eyes had given me a sense of power.

Meanwhile the excitement of my new adult responsibilities was wearing off only to be replaced by droning meetings, grammatically odious emails, eyeball-blurring requirements documents, cringe-worthy jargon, and the soul-crushing day in and day out of contributing nothing at all creative to the world. I was no more nor less competent than those around me, so I was promoted. Peter and I celebrated those milestones as if they were achievements I'd always wanted. I'd come to believe the rewards had value, and for *years,* I filled out my annual performance reviews hoping to see *Excelled* rather than merely *Achieved* because *Excelled* came with a bigger wheel of cheese, and I could buy another pair of shoes, add more books to my shelves, and upgrade to a premium cable package. But corporate life was corroding my insides.

Since cubicle conversation revolved around sports and sitcoms, Peter's tendency to read and chat about books made him my port in a storm. Our courtship was the only thing that kept me from running home with my tail between my legs.

As my job grew more mundane, I started to daydream dragons would fly into my managers' meeting and carry away the shrieking bodies of my peers. Or I'd imagine a portal opening, coaxing me on an adventure, though I feared if I walked through it, it might deposit me into the middle of a budget meeting in another part of the building. When I moved to my own office, I had the privacy to work less than anyone believed. At first, I wasted some of that precious time keeping abreast of the news, but one day I opened a blank Word doc and dumped out a scene that had come to me. Then another. Soon, the daydreaming stopped being an incidental distraction and became a serious problem, an addiction. I started typing fiction into draft emails on my phone while I was supposed to be following along with a PowerPoint presentation about the new payroll software. I started writing at night when Peter and I were supposed to be sharing our life together.

My retreat into fantasy may have been the initial blow to our relationship.

Our communication suffered first. We'd sit across from each other in a coffee shop, Peter reading stock prices on his phone while I daydreamed about magic. Rather than appreciate him, I regretted that I wasn't sitting at home with my characters, writing the book he'd come to resent.

Then came the bookstore, the second blow to our relationship. Possibly the kill shot.

At the start, we both anticipated a new adventure, and we talked about eventually marrying and settling down near town. It was all working out perfectly. He proposed to me at Christmas at his parents' house, and we set a date for the following year, last December.

When did I know I was in love with Peter? I thought I knew, but he didn't prove anything with time. "Maybe I never did."

Mom side-eyed me. "You loved him, Maddie, but you're working through your grief. Last January, all you could talk about were the good times, what you'd lost. Lately, you've started dwelling on the problems you had, but we all have problems, even in the best of times. It's never all good or all bad. Remember that."

"Maybe I should have paid more attention to the bad times before." I sucked on a piece of ice until it melted to a sliver, thinking about her words of wisdom. I wished I'd grown up watching a real couple deal with life. The Becketts were a decent stand-in, but I'd hazard a guess they were on their best behavior whenever I was over. I didn't know what to do with imperfection. "Did you have bad times even with Dad?"

"Even with Dad. We had a solid friendship at the core of our relationship. We could always come back to that."

I was well versed in their friendship.

"But you had problems?" I didn't know what answer I wanted from her. I liked to imagine my perfect dad, but if everyone was flawed, did that let me off the hook? Did it let Peter off the hook?

She shook her head. "I know you want to believe in happy-ever-after, but you don't always get an after. You have to try to be happy now."

How could I be happy? I'd been treading water for six months, waiting for my life to revert to what it once was. "Are you saying I should give up the bookstore and go back to Peter?"

"Would that make you happy?"

"That would make me feel like I'd lost."

She frowned, another one of those facial expressions that defied description. Her lips pinched together, twisted downward, more rueful than sad. Her mouth said without words that she wished she knew what to say, but we'd been over this ground often.

She'd invested in Peter, had pictured her grandkids already. It was hard for her to let go and start over. It was hard for me, too.

I asked her about her bunco game the night before, like I was throwing a stick across the yard to distract an eager puppy. She took the bait and spent the rest of our time laughing about the mistakes of others.

When we'd run out of conversation, I borrowed her bike and rode over to Dylan's.

Chapter 13

Cicadas sang in the field as I pedaled the mile to the Ramirez's farm. I had to wave away a horsefly buzzing me, attracted to the sweat rolling down my neck from the insufferable late-June sun. I didn't want to encourage Dylan's seductive assault, so I didn't even worry that I was sweaty and gross with my hair piled in a knot at the top of my head. I needed every weapon in my lady arsenal to repel him. Even at high noon on a Sunday, I wouldn't put it past him to look sexily at me.

My fortress would need to be well defended, drawbridge raised, alligators in the moat.

I turned onto the long tree-lined dirt road that led to the farmhouse and the barn behind. I hadn't ridden out this far in years.

Dylan and I had been dating a month when we started hanging out in his parents' barn. He'd set the guitar on his lap and play me the songs he'd been writing, insisting I'd inspired him to create the sensual lyrics he'd then sing to me. After a stanza or two, I'd lift the guitar out of his hands and straddle him. We'd kiss until we were breathless.

He didn't rush, but he also never hid how much he wanted to move inside me. I filled diaries with the outpouring of youthful desire he brought out: my introduction into fiction writing.

It was an unseasonably sultry October day when he wove a

magic spell so strong it pushed me from hesitation to certainty. Even then, he took his time, not worried I'd change my mind. He stripped each item of clothing from my body as he traced my skin with his fingers. I was electric.

Our bodies weren't a total mystery. We'd explored everywhere, but we'd never lain naked together, instinctively saving that for this moment.

Eager as I was to finally lay my eyes on his heavenly body, I wasn't quite so adept at helping him shed his own T-shirt and jeans. He lay beside me and touched me in ways he'd only hinted at before. I was terrified someone would walk in on us, but also exhilarated and excited and so ready.

Dylan was ready, too. He produced a condom from some unknown cache, and I watched wide-eyed as he rolled it on. When he nudged my knees apart, I let my legs fall open and held my breath, braced for the pain.

Then it happened.

Dylan pushed himself against me. And pushed again. It was obvious even to me I should have felt something inside me. He tried again and laughed. "Um. This is awkward."

Neither of us had the least experience with this, and neither of us realized it wasn't as easy to deflower a girl as books had led us to believe. He tried valiantly once more, but we were frustrated. He slid over and sat up. "I have an idea. Stay here."

He got up, got dressed, and left me naked in the loft of the barn. His motorbike started up, and he rode away. Confused, I waited, and then after fifteen minutes, he returned with a small sack from the pharmacy from which he produced a tube with the letters K-Y on the side.

The next song he wrote was entitled, "Lube in a Tube," and I'm the only person who ever heard it.

I couldn't honestly say that first time was glorious or even orgasmic, at least not for me. But all through that year, we learned how things worked, and we became an extension of each other, fused at the lips when we weren't fused at the hips. Some of those nights were spectacular.

Although we were together exclusively, and I trusted that was the case, Dylan never made promises to me. He never talked about our future. I thought I was in love with him, and it hurt that he wouldn't commit to anything long term. I did get him to at least call me his girlfriend. That was just a word, though. It didn't keep him from following a more compelling dream. I always knew his music would come before me.

I rode to the barn and dismounted my bike, coasting the final few feet with my left foot on the pedal and my right leg swinging over the seat. Nobody waited for me there, casually sexy or otherwise. I went up the wooden steps to the front porch of the house and rang the bell. Dylan answered the door unkempt, with a pair of sweatpants hanging off his hip bones, a white T-shirt barely tucked into his waist, and indecent hair that defied gravity. Unfortunately, that only made me picture his head on a pillow in his bed, and I steeled myself before entering his stronghold.

He kicked a basket of laundry out of the way, scratching his side as he stretched. "Hey, thanks for coming."

I followed him back to his bedroom, which was neater than I expected. Maybe he'd straightened for me. His cat slept on the bed, and I took a seat by the fat, lazy boy, petting his neck until he rolled over and offered up his belly. I wasn't dumb enough to be seduced by his coy flirtation. His cat could turn vicious on a dime.

Dylan stretched over to grab his guitar and his phone. Until right then, I hadn't been sure if his invitation had been a pretext for more, but he looked like he was going to play me some music. Whatever else Dylan meant to me, it always gave me a thrill of pride to be involved in any part of his music creation. I loved when he'd performed for me alone in the barn, singing his songs like they'd been written specifically for me. I liked to think that they were. He'd written more songs since. Songs about love and loss and sex and alcohol.

I almost understood why Layla spent so much time following bands. It had been a huge temptation to climb on that bus with Dylan and live like a groupie, but my mom would have killed me. She'd sacrificed too much to make sure I got an education, and I wasn't about to disappoint her.

Then I met Peter, and Dylan met whiskey. I'd never tried to find out who else might have "inspired" him during that time. He wasn't mine anymore, he was desirable as hell, and I could guess how those years were spent. He'd left the whiskey behind for the most part, and I could only speculate about the girls.

He plopped down next to me, against the headboard, with his guitar cradled in his lap and started to strum a couple of chords, just warming up. "I'm gonna play this acoustic so you can hear the underlying tune. I used Pro Tools to put together a demo that will give you a better idea how it could sound with more instrumentation." He placed a capo on the neck. "I think this could be it, Mads."

He started to play, and the first line of the new song hit me like a sledgehammer.

> *Orion, your constellation*
> *Shines in the night*
> *A million miles away*
> *A million years too late*
> *I reach for your light*
> *My past, my future destination*

"Holy shit, Dylan." I hadn't expected him to write an ode to the town, but it was working for me. He kept his eyes closed, ignoring me. Only a slight curve of his lips indicated he'd heard me.

> *Oh, heavenly body*
> *Your orbit sucks me in*
> *Want to touch your surface*
> *Need to move in your space*
> *We lie, skin to skin*
> *We burn, we burn hot, so hot*

I swallowed hard. He'd opened his eyes midway through and looked at me with those damn blue eyes. Even with his hair standing half up on one side and sleep in his eyes, Dylan was irresistible. My fortress crumbled.

I'd made a terrible mistake coming here alone. Before he could get to the chorus, which I imagined would inflame me beyond salvation, I stood.

He stopped playing and set the guitar aside, watching me carefully. I took a step toward the door, and he was up in a flash and in my space. Not menacing. Just there. In my way. Nearly skin to skin. And I could smell his scent. It was overwhelming.

"Maddie. Don't go."

"I have to. Please let me go."

He moved toward me, his energy vibrating all the atoms in my body, and then as quickly stepped back with a royal flourish. "You know where to find me."

I raced out the door and down the steps to my mom's bike, hoping to get some distance between us before I changed my mind. I rode past the lake, straight out the country road, pedaling as fast as I could, trying to burn off the physical need, hearing the words *"we burn hot, so hot"* and I knew we would. I rode through town and along the stream.

I nearly crashed into a tree when I saw Max walking across the bridge.

He waved. I kept pedaling.

By the time I got home, I was exhausted, but completely free of unwanted sexual desire. I stood in the shower, ideas swirling, and my novel characters started talking.

Rane said, *"Lira, I burn for you."*

Lira said, *"Rane, this is impossible. You and I, we were never meant to be."*

Rane said, *"We were meant to be. We were destined to be."*

I knew the words probably sounded better in my head than they would when I got to my computer, if I even remembered them that long, but I suddenly knew Silver Fox had been right all along. What was missing from my characters wasn't just romance, it was sex. It had been so long since I'd felt that kind of undeniable physical urge, and even though that was all Dylan and his charisma, my thighs ached again.

Layla sat in the kitchen when I came out, half dressed, still towel-drying my hair. She had her laptop open to a Word doc.

"Is that a résumé?"

She nodded and ignored me. I came up behind her and read over her shoulder. She closed the window. "Nosy much, Maddie?"

"Fine."

My email ringtone caught my attention anyway. I grabbed my laptop to move over to our sitting room sofa. We had a TV on a stand, but we'd never bothered to hook up the cable and mainly only used it for the occasional Netflix binge. Layla tended to do that on her laptop, though, so the TV collected dust in the corner. I put my feet up on the coffee table and opened up Silver Fox's latest missive.

Claire,
It sounds like you're taking baby steps, and that's probably not bad. I hope you end up finding the love of your life, and not just for the sake of your art.
You asked me why I was reading Pride and Prejudice. *I happened to read it recently, and I can't explain why but it resonated with me. I think I've fallen for a Lizzie Bennet, and I don't know how to get her to meet me halfway. She vexes me, but I'm more optimistic about my prospects. We're nowhere near the happy ending, but I have moments of hope. Cross your fingers.*
I'm wondering if I should give your book another read before the next time my heart gets trampled.
By the way, how's your second book coming?
SF
P.S. I prefer to be called Foxy. :)

I laughed at his postscript and hit Reply.

Foxy,
Maybe you should follow Darcy's lead and write your Lizzie a big-ass soul-baring letter? Or if she won't budge, move on and cast your net a little wider? Sorry if I'm crossing any lines here, but I'm paying you back for the good advice you sent me.
My own romantic life isn't much better. I'm identifying very

*much with Jane Eyre right about now. The ghost of Rochester
beckons me in the form of a past love interest. While I can't
deny the lure of instant gratification, I don't need the drama.
Meanwhile, I've been pursuing a less swoon-worthy romantic
prospect.*

*It's funny. In the past, I never understood why Jane gave St.
John Rivers the time of day, but there's a safety in that kind of
transactional relationship. In real life, taking a huge leap of
faith on someone like Rochester rarely works out. What if
Rochester hasn't changed at all? It's a jump into the abyss.*

*But for the sake of research, I will keep my options open and
let you know how things proceed.*

Claire

How sad was it that I was confiding more with a total
stranger from the Internet than with any of the people I knew?
Maybe that was due to the lack of risk. Or maybe life sometimes just worked that way, mocking our efforts to find mean-
ingful connections with the people in our lives while dangling
promising relationships out of reach. What guarantee was there
we'd ever even cross paths with our perfect partner?

Maybe Layla had been on to something all along.

I went to grab a soda from the fridge. As I poured it over ice,
my phone alerted me to another incoming email.

Layla looked up from the laptop. "You've got to change that
ringtone."

She was probably right, but I was afraid if I picked something
less obnoxious, I wouldn't notice it. I still got excited over need-
ing a separate email for my authoring activities. It reminded me
that I'd succeeded against all odds to produce a finished novel.
Whether my book had sold or not, I hoped I'd always celebrate
the creation of a whole fictional world. I'd lost sight of the joy of
writing when I'd read Silver Fox's negative review, but it wasn't
his fault how I chose to respond to his critique.

Speak of the devil, the unread email in my inbox was from
my new friend.

*   *   *

St. John Rivers? Ouch.

It's funny you bring up Jane Eyre. *I was just rereading that.*
I hope this doesn't come off as too forward since I don't even
know you, and maybe I'm reading between the lines again, but
don't settle for something easy over something hard (yeah, "That's
what she said," I know). Something easy is better than nothing, I
suppose. Tell me this: Does this drama-free guy give you butter-
flies? Do you feel anything above a warm friendship? I agree with
you that those feelings can grow in time, and to be honest, I'm
counting on that possibility in my own life. But don't make that
your ultimate goal. We all deserve fireworks.

I have to think that if you're comparing him to an obviously
unlikeable character, maybe you need to reconsider if he's right
for you. On the other hand, playing devil's advocate, there are
good things to be said for a practical match. Surely there are
even positive examples in literature. It doesn't have to be St.
John Rivers.

I shot back a one-line email: *Name one.*

A few minutes later, he replied, short and to the point: *I*
dunno. Bhaer from Little Women?

Oh, no way.

I returned fire. *You can't tell me you didn't root for Laurie,*
though.

I'd always been Team Laurie, even though I could see how,
on paper, Bhaer might have been the better match for Jo. Maybe
it bugged me that we only knew Bhaer from a distance, and he
didn't materialize as a suitor until late in the book, whereas
Laurie had been there all along. And he truly loved Jo.

Silver Fox replied: *It's true. I did. But there's an argument to*
be made that Bhaer was right for Jo. Love's such a strange
thing. I wonder if Jo wanted to love Laurie but the chemistry
wasn't there for her.

Interesting. I had an alternate interpretation. *Or was she simply*
so passionate about her independence that she could push romance
aside until she'd made her own way? She resisted Bhaer's ad-

vances. But in the end, Bhaer could at least offer her mental compatibility.

He replied: *Maybe it's just a case of "may the more persistent man win" since Bhaer refused to take no for an answer.*

That made me laugh. *Says he who bases his life on the romantic notion of waiting until the girl of his dreams deigns to come to him.*

Just biding my time. The butterfly has alighted. I don't want to scare her away.

This felt like flirting. *Face it, young Laurie; you're pining. Maybe you just need to tell her how you feel.*

Oh, I'm Laurie? Well, I think you're acting like Jo, to be honest. I haven't seen any indication you're following your heart in matters of romance.

Touché. *You're right. But I haven't found my romantic hero.*

Has it occurred to you that maybe people aren't romantic heroes or tropes? Maybe you're approaching this backward.

True, but books had a certain structure and direction to them that was lacking in my life. If I had the power of the pen over my real life, I wouldn't be wandering around aimlessly, stumbling into accidental heroes. I looked at the clock. It was getting late, and I needed to finish writing a chapter.

I dashed off: *That's what everyone always tells me. Thanks for chatting. You always seem to give me lots to think about.*

His response was almost immediate. *Same. Let me know how things go.*

Another followed directly after. *Hey, follow me on Twitter. It would be a lot easier to chat there.*

I opened Twitter and hunted for Silver Fox's profile, searching out any clues about what he might look like, but his picture was a cartoon fox, and he tweeted mostly links to his reviews. My Twitter profile wasn't any more revealing. I used a picture of my book in place of a headshot and tweeted mostly never.

I clicked Follow.

Chapter 14

When I opened the bookstore on Monday, the air conditioner was off, and a funky odor permeated the air. I sniffed as I walked around trying to locate the source. I expected to discover I'd left out a rotting deer carcass overnight. Whatever was stinking hadn't originated from the bathroom or the storeroom. I ducked my head in the kitchen, but the smell grew distinctly more aromatic around the register, over near the display case.

I flipped on the light behind the counter, opened the sliding glass, and gagged. Covering my mouth and nose, I stuck my hand in and cursed because the refrigeration wasn't functioning. Among other things, a leftover roast beef sandwich, yogurt, and several pints of milk had been sitting at late June temperatures long enough to turn criminal.

As I was throwing every bit of food away, Gentry strolled in. "Oh, my goodness. What is that smell?"

Without stopping, I hollered over, "What do you need, Gentry?"

The fruit probably would have been salvageable, but I didn't want to keep anything that had sat in that stink all weekend. So I tossed one after the other into the garbage bag.

Gentry made his way over. "I was stopping in to remind you to come get flags to hang up prior to the Fourth. And please make sure the area outside your store is tidy. I noticed debris on the sidewalk as I came in."

I pushed up my sleeves so I could reach the plates at the front of the case. It made me sad to throw away the double chocolate fudge cake. I stood and ran the back of my hand across my forehead, acknowledging Gentry again. "Got it. I'll take care of it."

He turned to leave but paused. "Shame about your baked goods. I wonder what a health inspector would make of this situation." I half expected him to twist his nonexistent handlebar mustache malevolently, but instead, a crocodile smile emerged. "If you'd like to send your customers next door, we can accommodate them."

As if.

"Thanks. I'll keep that in mind."

"You know, my offer still stands."

As much as I hated to admit it, Gentry's continued offer was starting to feel less like circling vultures and more like the eagles rescuing Frodo and Sam from Mount Doom. The loss of revenue from closing the shop for another day dismayed me. I was one catastrophe away from ruin. I considered calling Peter to beg him to let me delay my payment this month.

A sense of panic was taking root, and it didn't help that the deadline for my second book was nearly upon me. I'd already written my editor begging for an extension, but she told me the production schedule was fixed and if I failed to deliver, my release date would slip, which would piss off the marketing team since they were already preparing for the various book fairs where they'd promote the sequel.

I could almost see daylight, but the ending was fighting me. I needed to buckle down and crank out the working draft by Friday so I could beg Layla to read for me before I turned the pages in to my editor in two weeks.

The bookstore had picked the worst time to explode.

Most of the smell moved to the dumpster with the trash. I sprayed everything with a water and bleach solution. I couldn't tell if the remaining residue was nauseating or not. I'd already adjusted to it.

When Max showed up, I couldn't complain about the origin of my salvation. "You are a godsend, Max."

He beamed as he set the boxes next to the register. "Well, now. That's better."

I grabbed him by the elbow and dragged him on a tour of the room. "Do you smell anything funky?"

He put his nose into his armpit. "I did shower."

Hilarious. "So you don't notice anything?"

"Maybe. It's not too bad." He leaned in. "And you smell nice."

I did a double take. Was he pretending to flirt? "The display case went out."

He scratched his chin, which had a dusting of scruff I wished I hadn't noticed. "But it was working on Saturday? It just stopped?" He went around the register, bent, and started poking at the fan. "Let me see what I can figure out. Hopefully, the motor isn't burned out."

My heart sank. I didn't think I could afford to replace the unit. It might put me out of business.

He tinkered for a few minutes before he dropped to the floor with a frown. "This is beyond me. I think we're gonna need help."

"Shit." I didn't want to have to pay someone to come out, but I couldn't run a coffee shop for long without a refrigerated case. "Okay. I'll call Jack."

Jack was a friend of my mom's who ran an HVAC repair business. He could do just about anything, though. He was like rent-a-dad growing up. I'd come home from school to find his legs sticking out from under the kitchen sink or the lingering scent of his man musk after he'd been in the laundry room.

Jack came over right away and hooked up the compressor with some fancy gadget. He plugged a blinking device into the outlet, and then inexplicably got up and went outside. I followed him to the meter. Whatever he was doing was a complete mystery to me, but he rubbed his chin, a sign I interpreted as proof this was going to cost more than I had socked away.

"I think I found the problem."

"And?"

"Has anyone been tampering with the service box?"

I remembered Max out in the rain but shook my head, unable to imagine Max doing that much damage. Unless he was finding ways to make himself indispensable, like some kind of business Munchausen by proxy. But that was ludicrous. "No. Not that I'm aware of."

"Could be a loose neutral connection."

"English, Jack."

He shrugged like he'd already explained it as simply as he could. "Could've started a fire."

"Can you fix it?"

"You're gonna need to contact the power company."

Shit. I didn't have any time for this. I made the call, and about an hour later, a stranger with a tool belt came in, worked on the meter, and repeated Jack's warning that I was lucky the place hadn't burned down. He had to take my power offline, but when the electrical repairs were made, the display unit started back up. For the time being, everything seemed to be in order.

I felt like I'd been given a reprieve.

The entire morning had been wasted, but I flipped the *Open* sign around and hoped I'd get some business today.

Charlie settled into his corner of the now empty café, and I envied him. What if I did sell the bookstore? Would I be free to write all the time? Would I want to?

My deadline was so near, I had to spend every available minute writing. I plugged my laptop in and left it at a table in the corner so I could slam out the last few chapters. I was so close I could taste it. The idea that it sucked worse than my first book nagged at me, but I no longer had the luxury to get things exactly right.

Whether the muse struck or not, I burned the midnight oil, writing nonstop. By Thursday, I was exhausted. When Max showed up, he took one look at me and said, "You're sick. Go home."

That sounded brilliant. I could go and finish writing. I was on the homestretch of vomiting all the words. "The store," I managed. I'd run out of sentences. Were there a finite amount? Did I need time to recharge?

He squeezed my shoulder. "I'll stay here. Go."

I must have been exhausted because I didn't even argue. Without premeditation, I hugged him. He froze, and then his arms wrapped around me, hands rubbing my back, and it was exactly what I needed. I pressed my cheek against his chest. I could have fallen asleep snuggled against him.

He let go first, pushing me into an upright position and toward the door, and I did something unprecedented: I handed over the keys.

He clutched them like he'd caught the snitch. "Get some sleep."

I didn't. I typed all afternoon. By evening, I was ready to collapse, but I typed *The End.*

I finished!

Layla sat in her room, her red hair twisted in a messy braid, laughing about something she was reading online. I tapped on the doorframe.

She looked up. "You're done?"

"I'm done with this draft. I'm okay with the first half, but the ending is a total funeral. I can't figure out what's wrong. I'm hoping you'll give me some insight."

"You know you should ask Max to read this. He'd probably give you amazing notes. Or any of your book club people."

"Oh, well. If you don't want to . . ."

"It's not that. I'm worried I'm gonna give you bad advice. I'm less capable of figuring out a romantic arc than anyone. What if I can't help you?"

I laughed at the idea that any of the boys in town had any clue about romance. "You did a great job before. Please?"

She bit her lip. "Okay, but I do require payment."

"Oh." She'd never asked for money before. Maybe her website wasn't panning out.

"One of my favorite bands is gonna be playing the state park in a couple of weeks. I insist you go with me. I'll pick up the tickets."

Relieved, I agreed, then went to my room and emailed her the Word doc.

With no other pressing duties, I fell into bed to sleep the sleep of the dead until my phone notifications went bananas in the wee hours of Friday morning. I rolled over and blinked as my eyes adjusted to the light. The alert indicated a new direct message, but when I clicked through, I discovered three.

I can't sleep.

I think I've become a secondary character in this girl's story. How did I become the Bingley?

Does that even make sense?

He was adorable. I wanted to find this girl and tell her to snap out of it. She had a real catch of a guy on the line. But what did I know based on a few Internet exchanges. He could be nicer online than in real life. Although he'd proven he could also be a real jerk online.

Maybe he was a beast, all beauty on the inside, and she couldn't see him through his trappings. Maybe that's why there were no photos of him available. I wanted to think I'd be wise enough to see past the physical if I discerned a poetic soul, but I'd never been put in the position to find out.

I'd fallen for Dylan's sexy charisma, but while he wasn't conventionally beautiful, he was objectively beyond attractive. His face had been used to sell a line of cologne, as if those two things were somehow related.

Peter was beautiful, and I'd fallen for him despite his lack of poetry. So maybe I was a hypocrite, and I valued outer beauty over inner. Was it wrong to want both?

It didn't matter where Silver Fox fell on the spectrum. Even if his heart wasn't taken, he was elsewhere. I wanted to ask him where, but I worried I might stalk him, so it was better I didn't know. Instead, I sent a lame reply, giggling that anyone would ask me of all people for dating advice.

I'm in a bit of a quandary myself. I wish I had the answers. It seems to work out better in books, right?

Here I was with two failed relationships under my belt, and I wasn't sure if I had a future with either of those two men because we didn't talk about it.

I'd never before now pictured my life through the prism of a romance novel. Sure, I identified with plenty of female protagonists: Anne Shirley, Lizzie Bennet, Belle, Hermione Granger, and Jo March. Especially Jo. Smart, driven women. But my main plot thread had never been a romantic arc.

I mean, I had Peter, so I figured I could focus on what would fulfill me, apart from my relationship to a man. Everything else was falling into place on its own, and I could project how our lives would play out. We'd get married and the big events would unfold in the proper order.

I'd always pictured us in the house we'd eventually settle on (the little raspberry bungalow). We'd share breakfast and exchange a quick kiss as Peter raced out with his travel mug of coffee in one hand and the generic financial pages of my imagination in the other. I'd spend my days encouraging young readers to learn to love The Chronicles of Narnia and Harry Potter. Peter would whisk me on a surprise romantic weekend to keep the love alive (because I would have hinted at something I'd read in a novel).

We'd talk about kids and argue over names and whether the public school I'd gone to was good enough.

In reality, we'd argued about the raspberry bungalow and when I was going to give up my hobby and get a real job.

Somehow, I'd ended up with almost everything I'd ever wanted, the town, the bookstore, the writing career, but I'd lost the romance hero in the process. Maybe he'd never been a hero. Maybe we'd never had a romance.

Chapter 15

✴✴

I never got around to rereading *Gone with the Wind,* but I knew it well enough to come up with a handful of discussion questions before book club Friday night. I hoped I could wing it from memory and a cursory refresher.

To keep the attention off me, I straight up lobbed a grenade. "Rhett tells Scarlett, 'I'm not in love with you, no more than you are with me.' What do we think? Did Rhett love Scarlett? Did she love him? And apart from Melanie, did anyone in this novel truly love anyone else?"

Charlie guffawed. "Sure. They all truly loved themselves." I sat back to let him pontificate professorially. After his usual dry warm up, he pulled the pin. "Honestly, I've never understood why Rhett pursued Scarlett or why Scarlett continued to humor Rhett."

Dylan scoffed. "Gonna disagree. Rhett Butler's the most interesting character in her life. He was the best man for her. If only she'd realized it in time. . . ."

Charlie leaned forward, engaged. "You have to admit Scarlett was just using Rhett because she was bored and lonely. First she used Charles Hamilton to make Ashley jealous, then Frank—"

Dylan snorted. "Are you holding a grudge on behalf of your namesake?"

Until right then, I'd forgotten Scarlett's first husband and our Charlie Hamilton shared a name. I couldn't help but snicker until Charlie shot me a wounded look, like I was supposed to choose sides.

He turned his laser focus on Dylan. "I'm not mad. I just find their romance implausible. Rhett Butler was too smart to fall into Scarlett's web. And Scarlett was too self-absorbed to ever appreciate Rhett. I'm with Shawna's 'Team Nobody,' only instead of rooting for Scarlett to choose nobody for her own good, she should spare all of mankind from her selfishness."

Shawna shook her head. "Don't put words in my mouth, Charlie. I'm with Dylan on this one." At Charlie's tense body language, Shawna lifted a hand. "Hear me out. Yes, Scarlett is utterly flawed, but do you think Rhett doesn't see that in her? She's the most interesting character he encounters, too. And yes, Scarlett's to blame for failing to examine her own feelings and discover that the man best suited to her, the man she could have truly fallen in love with, had been there all along. My God, she married him and still pined for the wrong man. How tragic is that?"

Charlie was shaking his head. "What would it have taken for her to recognize that, though? Time? She had years to figure it out. Losing Rhett? How many times did he walk away without waking her up?"

This conversation was making me uncomfortable to say the least. I stole a peek at Dylan who, thankfully, was casually studying his own foot, bouncing on his knee.

Midge spoke up, "I loved the moment when he tells her she needs kissing, but then he doesn't kiss her."

Everyone stopped and collectively tilted their heads at her.

"Go on," I prodded.

"I just found it amusing the way her head fell back and she just stood there waiting. Reminded me of when I was dating."

"You mean, in the movie?" asked Charlie.

The conversation stalled out, and I checked my notes for another prompt, but Max spoke up. "I always felt a bit sorry for Rhett."

Although he hardly ever participated, and I assumed he'd only come to pimp his business, I didn't doubt he'd read the book. He read everything.

"Elaborate."

He scratched the scruff on his jaw. His eyes moved around the group. "Rhett says he couldn't wait around to catch Scarlett between marriages. He's always taken what he wanted and directed his own destiny—" He sucked on the inside of his cheek and hesitated.

Charlie nodded. "Yes?"

"I don't know." Max ran his hand down the back of his neck. "Just, everyone sees him as this strong, roguish, cynical hero, but he's kind of a pathetic figure."

I coughed. "You called Rhett Butler pathetic?"

His head jerked toward me. "I don't mean he's a loser." Whatever embarrassment he'd been battling was forgotten, and he regained that know-it-all tone I knew so well. "I mean, pathetic, pathos. You know, tragic. The minute he meets Scarlett, he loses his heart to her, and all his bluster and sarcasm hide his vulnerability."

Charlie's finger shot in the air. "See? He would've been better off if he'd never met her."

Max cut his eyes over. "I didn't say that. Actually, I think he's lucky he did because it's very likely if he hadn't, he would've hardened his heart and lived his entire life without love."

"But he doesn't get her in the end." Charlie crossed his arms and leaned back, like a lawyer who'd made the final plea to the jury in a case he was about to win.

Max took a breath before continuing. "It doesn't matter, Charlie. Love isn't about how things end up."

We all stared at him, and I remembered what my mom had told me. "Tomorrow might be another day, but tomorrow may never come."

Max met my eyes. "Right. Rhett grew because he allowed himself to love her against all odds. And for a time, he believed he was loved in return."

Charlie finally shrugged. "Fine, but I still don't think she deserved him."

Max laughed and relaxed. "She deserved so much more than she allowed herself to have."

Shawna said what we were all thinking. "Wow. Are you for real?"

I'd never heard him talk like that before, and I had to intentionally close my gaping mouth.

Max winced, and splotches of crimson crept up his cheeks like elongated shadows.

I glanced at my notes. "I have one last question for the group. Why do you think Scarlett was so damn fixated on Ashley?"

Charlie summed it up with, "Because of plot," and we all laughed.

Dylan snorted. "It sure as hell wasn't sex appeal."

Midge said, "I once knew a young man who was so handsome, but he wasn't interested in me." She waved dismissively. "I think the rejection made him even more attractive to me if that makes sense."

Max tilted his head toward her. "Ashley was the one she couldn't have?"

"What?" asked Midge. I doubted she was talking about Ashley.

"I think—" Max started. He tapped his finger against his lip for a moment. "I think it might be a little bit that he was out of her reach, but Ashley continued to make her feel like she had a chance. He strung her along out of kindness, not realizing it was so cruel."

"I have an alternate theory." Dylan looked around the group, like a performer checking in with his audience. "Ashley represented home to her. In the end, what mattered to her more than anything or anyone? Tara, her home, her land. Ashley came from that increasingly lost world, and the more the world changed, the more she latched on to him as a connection to her past, to her youth."

Shawna laughed. "Projecting much?"

He chucked her softly on the shoulder. "Nothing wrong with wanting to return home." He cast a glance at me, and I had to avert my eyes.

Shawna took her turn. "I agree with Midge. She was collecting trophies. Scarlett didn't need any man. She wanted to win."

On that sad note, it was time to end. I picked up the list. "Next time we're reading *Little Women*."

As soon as Dylan bought his copy, he turned and announced, "Don't forget to come out to my show tomorrow night."

That was a land mine–fraught proposition I didn't know how to negotiate. After Sunday, I figured he'd understand if I didn't show. In fact, I worried that by going, he'd think I condoned or even encouraged his behavior. He hadn't called or tried to come by to see me, and I didn't know whether he felt chastened or if I didn't matter enough to him to follow up. I never knew what Dylan thought about me until he sang it to me.

Charlie was next in line and said, "Why don't we go together?"

I empathized with Scarlett, looking for her Ashley when he wasn't looking for her, surrounded by Rhett Butlers and actual Charles Hamiltons. If I were a character in a book, would readers be yelling at me to run toward or away from any of these guys? I wanted to skip ahead a few chapters and find out how everything would turn out.

Chapter 16

❋❋❋

The entire population of Orion was at the Jukebox. By the time Charlie and I arrived, after I'd closed up the bookstore, all the seats near the stage had been taken. Layla waved from a big round table in the corner where Shawna and her wife Rebecca had already ordered a few drinks.

I slid into the booth, making room for Charlie.

The lights flickered, and conversations abruptly stopped as people scurried to their tables or moved closer to the stage.

Layla's hands flew up. "I forgot to set up my camera!" She shoved me aside, pulled a collapsed tripod out of her backpack, and telescoped it out. Then she screwed her camera on and messed with the focus and lighting until she was satisfied. Once everything was in order, she hit record and sat back. "I hope nobody kicks that over."

The club owner, Kyle, climbed up on the stage to a smattering of applause. As the room quieted, Charlie laid his forearms on the table, hands wrapped around his beer. For a heartbeat, I imagined snaking my hand around his wrist to twine my fingers with his to see how he'd react. But before I could, Kyle announced, "Ladies and gentlemen, please welcome back to the Jukebox Orion's own Dylan Black!"

The crowd erupted in applause as Dylan bounced onto the

stage, guitar strap over his neck, and spoke into the mic. "Hey guys."

The spotlight lit him from above, and he looked perfectly at home.

Layla nudged me. "I haven't seen him perform in months. I've missed this."

Dylan began, "This is the club where I got my start, way back when. I'm forever grateful to all of you for supporting me for so long."

Several people said, "Aw," and more people clapped, happy to claim credit for his success.

"Since you've all been there for me, I want you all to be the first to know I've been writing new songs I'm so proud of. I couldn't think of anything more fitting than to share them with you here tonight."

I hooted: "Yeah!"

Layla shouted: "Dylan! Dylan! Dylan!" and others picked up the chant.

He ducked his head and rubbed his neck in the most adorable display of gratitude. I knew it was sincere. He'd left Orion a cocky brat on the verge of fame, but I'd watched him transition into a more serious artist, focused on the music instead of glorying in the adulation.

Onstage, he performed with the confidence he'd earned through competence and professionalism. He played a set of his new songs, then took a break promising to come back out and accept requests or play covers the rest of the night. That met with laughter.

The lights came up, and Layla fanned herself. "My God. Dylan is on fire. I still can't believe you walked away from that."

Charlie got up and headed toward the bar, leaving me scowling at Layla.

"Revisionist history. We were two trains rushing in opposite directions."

"Don't you ever wonder what it might've been like, though, out on the road, living the life of a touring musician?"

"You're free to date him if you want."

She shook her head. "As much as I love a sexy song-writing guitar player, Dylan's way too intense for me. Although I'm sure if he sticks around, the townies will try to set me up with him. At least Peter fled or I'm sure someone would've sniffed him out as a potential partner for me. They really have no concept of what's appropriate at all."

I had to laugh at that. "I'm surprised they never tried to set you up with your brother."

"Right. But there's no reason *you* can't be." She ducked to suck on her straw as if that topic of conversation had come to an end.

"That's never going to happen."

She frowned. "You know, I'm your friend first, but can you blame me if I'm still a little Team Max?"

She interpreted everything through the lens of fandom. Team Max indeed.

I scanned the crowd, waving at Letitia and her new boyfriend, Rico, who I only knew through her Instagram photos. Charlie chatted with them, and I hoped he might bring them over to our table. I turned my head and ended up staring directly at Max, who sat alone, typing furiously into his phone.

Who did he know who wasn't here?

"Hey!" Dylan smacked the table with both hands, and I jumped out of my skin.

"Holy shit, Dylan."

"How's it going? I mean, honestly. Is it okay?"

Just like old times. "You're *en fuego,* Dylan. But why are you out here. Everyone's waiting for your next set."

Ross Anderson slapped Dylan's arm on his way past. "Great set, Dylan."

Dylan said, "Thanks!" over his shoulder, then focused all his heat on me. "Saw you out here and wanted to catch you. Can you stick around after?"

Everyone at the table stared.

"I don't know."

He folded his hands together in supplication, bending slightly, like he might kneel before me. "Please, Mad?" He waved his hand out toward the rest of the club. "We'll be right here in public. I just wanna talk."

My curiosity was piqued "We'll see." I raised my eyebrows. "But you, you need to get on that stage."

He took my hand. "Are you sure you can handle it? I'm gonna play my new song."

Sweet Jesus.

"Bring it." I went to snatch my hand away, but he gripped tight and pulled it up to his mouth. When he pressed his lips to my skin, I tugged hard and laughed. "Brat."

Gentry scurried past. When he glanced over, he did a double take and his eyebrows rose. Scandalized.

Dylan winked and skipped back gracefully, turning to weave into the crowd. I followed him with my eyes and caught Max staring. I waved, and he turned to face the stage.

The lights dimmed, and Charlie appeared out of nowhere to slide into the booth beside me, handing me another beer. "Was that Dylan?"

Rather than answer, I took the proffered beer and downed half of it in one pull.

I didn't think Charlie believed we were on a date, but maybe I shouldn't have flirted with Dylan, even if he was technically flirting with me. But Charlie probably hadn't even noticed the flush undoubtedly coloring my face without the help of the stage lights.

Dylan came out and settled onto his stool, one foot on a spindle so he could prop his guitar on a knee. "Thanks again for coming out, everyone. And for sticking around for this next set. I want to play you all a song I've been working on for the past several months. It's a special song. I think you'll see why."

My cheeks flamed already. I considered getting up to leave, but it was dark enough to hide. As soon as Dylan began to play, my fears subsided. He slapped the body of the guitar in a syncopated rhythm and started singing the same song he'd sung to me, but in a Latin rhythm that made everyone bounce and move.

Then he hit the chorus.

Your body's a supernova
Come, come back my lover
Come, come, come in my bed
Scream my name over and over

I looked at Layla, who immediately made an okay sign with one hand and started poking it with her finger. Charlie shifted slightly away, and I wasn't sure he even knew he'd done it. Shawna waggled her eyebrows at me. I dropped my face into my hands.

The song was incredible, though. It had an amazing melody that worked with the acoustic guitar. I didn't have to hear his Pro Tools version to know it would be even better with a backing track added.

But the entire town would have the song stuck in their heads and would be singing "Come, come back my lover" around me.

Mortified was an understatement. And yet, my pants were on fire. Hot, so hot.

I cursed Dylan. My body had been in suspended animation for the past few months, like it was in stasis on some spaceship, but now it was waking up too soon, before I'd reached my destination.

I didn't necessarily need Dylan to take care of the need he'd kick-started, but it would be so easy to sink back into his familiar embrace. Dylan performed, eyes closed, sexy little sideburns, lips that could kiss a woman good and hard. I needed to be kissed good. I needed to be kissed hard. Could I get back with Dylan for a one-night stand?

Come, come, come in his bed?

Could I live with the emotions that would unleash?

His eyes opened, and like earlier, he pegged me, inviting me right in front of the whole room. The club became a furnace. I focused on my beer, and soon the song came to an end.

"Damn." Layla's jaw had dropped, and even Shawna was fanning herself.

As soon as Dylan finished the set, I pushed past Charlie and didn't stop walking until I hit the street, abandoning both my friends and . . . whatever Dylan was to me.

Outside, I leaned against the box office window, a supernova exploding in my pants.

My body was well and good out of hibernation, and I wasn't sure how best to deal with it. I pulled out my phone and DMed Silver Fox.

Guess who remembers what sexual frustration feels like?

I waited, hoping he'd respond so I could unload on someone who might have good advice, but my phone remained silent, and I felt increasingly foolish for sending it. What an embarrassing thing to message. That seemed to be the story of my relationship with Silver Fox.

"Hey, are you okay?" I looked up to find Shawna standing a few feet from me.

I side-eyed her. "Yeah. Maybe."

She put a hand on my arm. "Life's kind of funny, isn't it?"

I hadn't as yet found life to be particularly funny, unless she meant more funny strange. "How so?"

"It just seems like things tend to happen at the wrong time, in the wrong order. Do you ever get that feeling?"

"Yeah." I hadn't expected her to be so philosophical. "Seems sometimes like a haphazard mess that only makes sense when it's too late."

She stared up at the pale moon. "Right. That's it exactly. But sometimes things fall right into place."

Was she talking about Dylan? I rolled my eyes.

I wasn't even thirty yet, but the freight train of time bore down on me. I was lucky in a lot of respects. I had a business. I was going to be published. Those were things that gave me a sense of accomplishment, but nothing was permanent. If even a relationship of years could go belly up over the course of a single day, what faith could I have in anything lasting?

And here I was starting from the beginning. Chapter one.

The doors opened, and Midge emerged. She tapped my shoulder. "Dylan was wonderful, Maddie."

A few more people filed out, and then the trickle became a stream. I weighed my options. I could go back in and wait for Dylan, or I could go home.

Rebecca exited and slipped an arm around Shawna. "Tell Dylan he did a great job."

"Tell him yourself," I called as they moved with the crowd along the sidewalk. Dylan wasn't an extension of me, for Christ's sake.

Charlie flowed out with the crowd, and I pretended I'd been waiting for him. I owed him an apology for bailing on him, but I didn't know exactly how to explain why I'd fled without making things worse. When we got to my front door, I faced him and said, "This was—"

I searched for a proper adjective to describe a night where he'd paid for my drinks and ended up abandoned in the club with my ex-boyfriend.

After one loaded moment, he said, "Well, thanks," and bent forward. Assuming he was heading for my lips, I leaned toward him, only realizing halfway across the breach that his face was angled toward my ear rather than my mouth. Mortified that I'd mistaken a hug for a good-night kiss, I quickly adjusted my own trajectory to match his intent. Sadly, our movements ended up colliding, and he stepped away, confused, then took my hand to give it a good shake.

I wanted the shadows to swallow me.

"Uh, well. Goodnight, then." He let go and backed down the sidewalk. "I'll see you Monday?"

I wished I knew if Charlie had potential to be my romantic lead. The mountain overpass was turning out to be far more treacherous than I'd anticipated.

Once I was alone, I dropped onto my sofa, propping my feet on the coffee table beside the photo album I kept there. I flipped it open with my toe. On the first page, there was a picture of Layla and Max and me in front of their house. We sat on the steps, eating bright red Popsicles. The juice ran down our chins, making us look like very young vampires.

I leaned forward and turned the page. My mom fifteen years ago, when her hair was more yellow than white. I'd caught her asleep on the porch, a book lying open across her chest. She looked beautiful.

Pages devoted to Max and Layla gave way to pages of Dylan. Dylan on his motorbike. Dylan playing his guitar in the hayloft. Dylan boarding the bus to New York City.

I swallowed a lump as the vivid memory consumed me. I could hear the bus idling and smell the exhaust as we said our final farewells, and then he climbed the steps, and I watched his silhouette move through the aisle until he found a seat.

There he was waving from the window. If only he'd asked me to go with him, told me he loved me and needed me with him . . . I would have been tempted. I might have even boarded the bus with him, embraced the adventure, until my mom tracked me down and reminded me of my obligations. Still, if that had been our history, it would be easier to take a chance on him now. Instead, as always, he'd put his own needs before mine and left me, literally, on the curb.

As I looked at the picture now, a weird detail caught my eye: The logo on the side of the bus read SILVER FOX BUS LINES.

What the—?

My phone buzzed, and I marveled at the coincidence again before closing the photo album.

I reached over to grab my purse and fumbled until I found it. The phone buzzed twice more, and the Twitter notification number changed from one to three. I opened the app to find direct messages from Silver Fox. Was there black magic at work?

I curled up on the sofa in anticipation of a sudden improvement to my evening.

You can't leave a message like that and then not clarify.

Is this your St. John guy?

Did he turn out to be Rochester after all?

Relieved I hadn't scared him off completely, I started typing:

Different guy, old flame. More Rhett Butler than Rochester.

He's infuriatingly arrogant and sexy, and I've gotten myself into the kind of burning lust you encouraged. And I'm regretting it. So thank you.

He was fast to reply. *Care to share?*

I mulled it over. Flirting with him was a pale replacement for actual physical contact, but it was more fun than wallowing in self-pity. *Shouldn't I be saving it for my art? Fire of my loins yada yada.*

Your loins are on fire?

Actually, yes.

So why are you messaging me? Why aren't you quenching your loin fire with Rhett's tumescence?

I snorted and had to sit up farther to type easier. *Tumescence? Are you serious?*

I've read a lot of historical romance, believe it or not.

Romance, truly?

Pretty much anything I can get my hands on.

That's a far cry from The Little Prince.

Ah, yeah. You've read my bio.

So where do things stand with your tumescence, Foxy? Any progress with yon vixen?

Setback—I suspect she's interested in someone else.

Ah. So here we sit on a Saturday night engaging in literary dirty talk.

May I ask why you're alone if you've managed to light the wick, so to speak?

I laughed again. *Would you find me quaint if I told you I want more than passion?*

Is that considered quaint these days?

I want someone I can talk to, someone who wants more than passion from me. I want sex but not without friendship and love and stability.

That's exactly what I'm looking for.

Sigh. *Really? I was starting to believe a man like that only exists in novels.*

I exist. I want companionship, but would you consider me a caveman if I told you I want the passion, too?

Not at all. My problem is that I could have the passion right now. Or the companionship. But not together.

That leaves you in a state of unrest, I take it.

My bosom heaves with desire. I giggled as I waited to see if he'd volley.

Fair lady, you are clearly in distress. How may I be of service?

Bingo.

I cannot breathe for this bedeviled bodice.

A few seconds passed where I feared I may have crossed the line, but then he came through.

Shall I loosen these ties?

I couldn't contain a stupid grin. *Scandal. Good sir, you have caused me to swoon into your arms.*

What's a gentleman to do?

Gentleman or ne'er-do-well?

Ha. Ha. A little of both.

He was too cute.

Rhett Butler, then?

If only.

Who, then?

We already established I was Darcy.

Why did it always come back to *Pride and Prejudice*?

You're not seriously so vain you think that book is about you?

See? So misunderstood.

But he's a fan favorite. Everybody loves Darcy.

Everyone. Except Lizzie.

Arrow through the heart. *So you wait?*

Worth waiting.

Wow. *I hope your Lizzie figures out how lucky she is.*

And I hope your Rhett Butler finds a way to prove himself so you can satisfy your hot-blooded yearning.

You think I should take a risk on a ruffian with a heart of gold?

For your art . . .

I shook my head at his teasing. *And maybe you should put some skin in the game. Tell Lizzie you ardently admire her?*

Ha ha. I'm working up to it.

Good night and good luck, Darcy.

Strangely, flirting with Silver Fox hadn't raised my blood pressure, and in fact, I felt less flustered, and more balanced than before. I'd missed that kind of simple fun.

My phone buzzed a minute later.

But you know, if you happen to write a scene in which your characters act on their attraction, I wouldn't be opposed to taking a look.

I blinked rapidly. *You want me to write you a sex scene. . . .*

A series of messages followed in rapid succession.

Only joking.

Unless you do write that, then I'm serious. He posted an emoticon of little praying hands.

Oh, God, scratch that. I've probably offended you. Have I offended you?

I giggled. *Laughing.*

Good. Then I was only joking. (Not really.) Good night, Jane. Or Scarlett?

As I snuggled against my pillow, I wondered what Silver Fox was like in real life.

Suddenly my mind raced with a scene I'd already written for my second book that would have worked so much better if I'd taken it all the way. I snatched my phone up again and messaged Layla. *You up?*

Yep.

Have you reached the scene where Lira writes the rune on Rane's back?

Yeah—hot.

What would you think if I turned that into a full-on sex scene?

Send that to me.

I'll take that as approval.

I slid my laptop over and opened my writing software to the scene that began:

She lay in the wasted field under the wreckage of the portal. Exhausted, Lira crawled across debris, coughing up soot and blood, until she saw his twisted body. Somehow it had worked. She'd brought them both through, but at what cost?

I read to the point where she'd rolled him over and worked his shirt off far enough to begin using up the last of her stored magic to trace onto his back the rune that could restore him.

In the current version, Rane was only supposed to wake up and then declare his everlasting love for Lira. I couldn't believe I'd never thought to make that statement more overt. I started writing a more physical demonstration of their love, thinking I could just extend the scene, but the characters fought me, and I ended up failing to make them even kiss properly.

Rane drew Lira to him. For a heartbeat, she held back. What would happen if any magic remained in reserve? But when she pressed her mouth against his, his lips parted, and in response, she deepened the kiss.

Ugh.

My book was becoming a proxy of my own frustrations.

Chapter 17

Preparing for the upcoming Fourth of July festivities called for all hands on deck. I'd sent out newsletters and spent Sunday with a group of elementary school kids, helping them decorate their bikes with streamers and foil. The older kids were working on small floats they could either drag, push, or pedal through the town during our obligatory parade. There was something kitschy and old-fashioned about our celebration.

All Sunday afternoon, I climbed up and down a ladder, hanging flags along my side of the street, waving at Letitia on the other side as we exchanged the occasional passing comment.

Monday was another busy day, and there was a frenetic energy in the air as we anticipated the momentary escape from the ordinary. Orion was small, but we made a big deal out of celebrations.

I didn't close my shop on Tuesday because I didn't want to waste the commercial opportunities afforded by the holiday. The parade and excitement would attract anyone in the vicinity who didn't live a bit closer to a bigger town. I'd get more foot traffic to the coffee shop than on most days.

However, at exactly noon, I chased everyone out and flipped over the *Be Back Soon* sign so we could stand on the street and observe the first of the holiday floats rolling down the short street, followed by a half dozen girls from a Brownie troop, a procession of the high school band, their majorettes and drum line, and a demonstration from the kids from the karate school. The 4-H club handed out candy as they passed, and vets in crazy miniature cars driving loop-de-loops made everyone laugh. POWs on motorcycles formed two columns and were met with applause. In between groups, random kids rode their decorated bikes or marched in patriotic garb, waving at the sparse crowd lining the sidewalks. Parents walked out into the middle of the street to shoot photos of their kids. The local newspaper crew did the same. I waved at little kids who came to my reading corner and older kids whose bikes I'd helped decorate.

Yet another July Fourth parade in Orion finished up in a record forty-two minutes.

As the last of the parade passed, the street filled with the bystanders, now returning to their point of origin. A small hubbub at the corner turned out to be Dylan, trying to make his way down the sidewalk, surrounded by folks who must have recognized him. He'd take a step, then pause, answer a question, flash a smile for a picture, then try to move forward again. No wonder he hardly set foot outside his family's farm. That would get exhausting fast.

I knew he was more than a celebrity caught in the wild, but I found myself rooted in place, mesmerized by the star that he'd become. When he made it as far as my bookstore, I was inclined to say, "Shoo! Shoo!" like the crowd he trailed was an invasion of unwanted pests. I wanted to grab the broom just inside the door and sweep them away.

Instead, I held the door open, secretly hoping he might draw all of these potential customers inside. I couldn't help but feel special when he said, "Hey, Maddie," in front of a gaggle of gaping girls.

When had I started valuing myself by the jealousy of teenagers?

I wasn't sure if he'd come to talk to me or if he was just passing, so I made safe small talk. "Are you going to the fireworks tonight?"

He smoldered. "I bring the fireworks, Maddie."

It should have made me laugh, but I let my gaze fall on his deceptively soft lips. If I asked him to, he'd let me kiss him today. Right now. I swallowed. The words slipped out. "Will you take me there?"

"I'll take you there. Or here. Anywhere you want." He grinned, and I smirked at his innuendo. "Pick you up before sunset?"

With the parade over, Gentry barked at us to pick up the streamers and other trash left behind on the now empty street. I had no practical reason to keep the shop open, but there was no reason to close up early. The big event of the evening would be the fireworks over the little lake after sunset.

It was a long wait until sunset.

Bored, I sat on the stool behind the cash register and read *Little Women* for probably the fourth or fifth time, but after a couple of chapters, I started wondering about Silver Fox and what he was doing. I clicked on his Twitter feed and noticed he'd posted a review of *Jane Eyre,* which made me smile considering he and I had discussed it.

Max came by to deliver an obligatory apple pie and promised it would keep until the next day. He coaxed me into trying a piece along with a cinnamon coulis he squeezed from a condiment bottle. Damn, was it good.

He said, "It's my treat for the holiday."

I knew he was trying to wear me down, and the thing was, it was working.

As he was about to go, he asked, "Will you be at the fireworks?"

For some reason, I thought of the day in eleventh grade when he'd asked me to homecoming. He'd said, *"I figured we could go as friends. Like old times."* It had surprised me since he'd only talked to me about how best to prepare for the PSAT for weeks prior. I had to tell him I'd already agreed to go with poetic, brooding, artistic Dylan. He took it well, though, saying, *"No biggie."*

He'd shown up to that dance with Emma Harkness, a pretty girl nowhere near good enough for him.

"Yeah." I tilted my head. "I'll see you there."

He didn't push it and left me to my empty store where I opened my laptop and used the quiet to revise. Fortunately, or unfortunately, Layla had finished reading my novel and had given me insightful notes. I was starting to understand what Silver Fox had found lacking in my characters, but I hadn't cracked the code to infuse them with palpable desire.

Just before sunset, the rumble of a distant engine announced the arrival of my knight. Dylan's motorcycle turned the corner, and he pulled up to the curb beside me.

He took off his helmet. "Need a lift?"

"My prince has come," I said.

"Not yet." He laughed and tossed me a spare helmet.

"Brat."

I put on the helmet and straddled the seat behind him, knees pressed into his thighs, arms wrapped around his torso. His T-shirt couldn't hide his broad back. I rested my cheek between his shoulder blades. Memories crashed like waves, and that motor purring between my legs didn't exactly help keep my thoughts pure.

The sun hung low on the horizon, and when Dylan turned west on the county road, we were blinded. If anyone else were driving, I might have gripped him for dear life, but I trusted Dylan completely. On the bike anyway. I'd logged hours riding with him, and he'd never given me the slightest cause for concern. We didn't have far to go in any case.

When we reached the lake, the last of the golden light sparkled across the purple water.

We said "lake" despite the fact you couldn't take a boat out on this little body of water. By normal standards, our lake was a glorified pond. I could wave at people on the other side. I could have swum across it easily. And I had. Naked.

Dylan parked his bike and waited until I dismounted before taking off his helmet and swinging his leg over. He set his helmet on the seat and hooked his foot against the kickstand, then put both his hands on my waist. "Was it good for you?"

I tilted my face toward him. It would have been easier than anything to close my eyes, drop my head back, and let him kiss me.

I needed kissing, and I needed it badly.

Dylan loosed his grip, slipping his hand easily into mine. "Come on, M. Let's see who's here."

Frustrated that he'd let pass a chance to good and properly seduce me, I trotted along beside him, looking for people I wanted to talk to among the clusters of folks chatting or setting up blankets.

Our fireworks display would be more suggestion than spectacle. We couldn't afford to put on the kind of elaborate display they'd have in other towns, but we had our traditions, and it gave us an excuse to gather and mingle.

Dylan nodded a greeting to the people staring at him. Most everyone had known him since before he'd made a name for himself, but a couple of teen girls gawked at him, whispering behind their hands. He winked and they broke into giggles. When one raised her phone to snap a picture, Dylan let loose with a megawatt smile. I waited for him to stop vamping and walk with me.

I waved to Mr. Anderson and his oldest son Connor before I noticed they were chatting with Gentry. Gentry cast a glance at my hand in Dylan's and pointed a snooty grimace my way as if I cared about his opinion. Then it occurred to me he'd been the only person in town who'd truly welcomed Peter at our events. He'd lost the closest thing he'd had to a friend when Peter left. That cheered me up immeasurably somehow.

Dylan dropped my hand to wander over and slap backs with some of the guys who worked on his dad's farm, slipping easily into Spanish. I glanced around, smiling at anyone who looked my way. I spotted Layla and made a beeline for her.

She'd brought one of my blankets and spread it out next to a cooler. An opened beer bottle poked between the circle of her crossed legs, like a glass phallus. She waved her phone around, trying to find a signal.

I stepped behind her. "Your fly's open."

She tilted her head. "Huh?"

I pointed at her bottle. "Your hard-on's showing."

She scooted over and made room for me, still concentrating

on the phone. "I can't get reception out here, and there's a fan war brewing."

Oh, the horror. Fearing she might decide to go home and deal with imaginary drama, I said, "Don't you have other people who can handle it for you?"

"Sure. I have moderators, but I'm missing the fun."

"This will be fun, too. Look at all the people here." I scanned the huddled masses and noticed Charlie edging around the far side of the lake.

Charlie was attractive, funny, and kind, exactly the kind of guy I might have written for myself, though he lacked Dylan's sensuality. The differences between the two men couldn't have been starker. But of course Charlie hadn't shown me the least sign he might be interested in my pathetic attempts to draw him out. So there I was with Dylan. What did that say about me? Did I fall into the worst cliché of women who needed to be with a man, any man, no matter the risks? I knew hanging out with Dylan was like playing with fireworks. He'd burn bright and light up my night, but he'd likely leave me alone in the afterglow.

Layla said, "Man, people will come out for any stupid thing."

Dylan found us and sat behind me. Layla offered him a beer, and he rubbed my shoulder with his free hand.

Layla kept talking. "Do you remember when we had that Pumpkin Festival last year?"

Of course I did. As with all things Orion, that dinky festival was only a success because our town would turn out for any excuse for a gathering. Like tonight.

"I had to drag Peter to that."

The only reason he'd shown up to it was because I'd organized it. He'd griped about attending, but he put on a brave face and pretended to enjoy chatting with Midge and Shawna and Letitia. It shouldn't have surprised me when he decided to bail on Thanksgiving.

Dylan's hand clenched and pinched my neck. "Yeah, he told me."

Layla said, "That's right! I forgot you were here that weekend."

"Thanks a lot," he said.

I shifted so I could face him, but by now, his features were obscured in dusk. "What did Peter tell you?"

His hand had slid off my shoulder when I turned, and now it rested on my knee. "We were making small talk. I wasn't sure what to talk to him about. I didn't even know what kind of work he did."

"Finance," I offered. He was a CFO now, but it wasn't important. "Go on."

"He made some disparaging remark about how little there was to do here, how we had to make up these nonevent events to pretend to have any kind of culture. I wasn't sure if I should agree out of politeness or defend my home, defend your participation. I ended up saying something like, 'Well, Maddie loves it here.'"

This wasn't exactly a revelation.

"He knew that." I looked over the lake at silhouette shadows.

"He seemed to take my response as tacit agreement the town was lacking and said something like, 'Just between you and me, once we're married, we won't be living here.'"

"What?" My head jerked back to face him. "That wasn't our plan at all. You must have misunderstood."

"No, that's why I remember the conversation at all. He said he had his eye on a house on Meridian he planned to buy once you'd tied the knot."

Meridian Street ran straight through the center of Indianapolis.

"And you said . . ."

"I told him that was something he should discuss with you before the wedding, that it would be unfair to spring it on you once you were legally married."

My eyes were bugging out of my head. "Why didn't you tell me that?"

It didn't shock me that Peter wanted to leave, but the idea that he'd premeditated such a deception was outlandish. I didn't even know if I could believe what I was hearing. But I squeezed my fists and waited for an explanation.

Dylan said, "I figured you'd think I was jealous, and I didn't think you'd believe me."

I tried to look at Layla, but she was nothing more than a shape in the dark. "Can you believe this?"

Layla's head bobbed. "You had to know he wasn't happy here. It was obvious to everyone else."

That was a fair observation, but it was like the rain recognizing the ground was wet. They hadn't exactly made him feel at home.

One of the men setting up the fireworks yelled over, "We're about to start." The lake was small enough we could hear him.

The crowd let out a pitiful cheer.

"We're not done with this conversation." I turned toward the water, short-circuiting the fireworks between us just as a star burst overhead.

Was I a hypocrite for being pissed Dylan had kept his opinion to himself? I'd been annoyed with Max for six months for speaking his mind too freely.

What if it had been Dylan instead of Max who had spoken to me in the weeks leading up to the wedding?

Honestly, I wouldn't have listened.

I was dead set on following through on the wedding I'd planned. I had a dress, a cake, and my mom's approval. Apart from our emerging differences, which were exacerbated by the people I called my friends, our relationship had been everything I told Silver Fox I wanted. Peter was easy to talk to, easy to look at, easy to kiss. Sex, companionship, and stability. Wasn't that enough?

Of course, I hadn't been enough for Peter, and the fact that he'd so easily walked away left me wondering if I was inherently unlovable.

The pyrotechnicians made the display last longer than it should have by spacing out the fireworks. Kids ran around handing out sparklers, and we all wrote our names in swirling, fizzling light. Then another lackluster star would burst overhead, and we'd all say "ooh" or "aah" even at the duds that made up about 20 percent of the total.

Dylan was a perfect gentleman during the fireworks for the most part. He sat behind me and tugged my shoulders to make me lean against him, and it felt too nice to resist. He wrapped his left arm across my chest and drank his beer with his other hand.

Overall the whole thing lasted about twenty minutes, and we knew it was at the end because they managed to shoot off two fireworks at once and then called across the water, "That's it, guys!"

We mingled a bit more with everyone while drinking a few more beers and swatting mosquitoes. Dylan moved with me as I wound through different groups to try to catch up with people I rarely saw unless they came into my bookstore. Some of the kids I'd known in high school spent all their time out on family farms and almost never came into town.

Using our phones as flashlights, we worked our way around the chattering groups, but Dylan managed to steer us around Charlie, deep in conversation with Letitia's new boyfriend. I started to swing over to meet Rico and ended up locking eyes with Charlie. I took a step toward him, but as if he hadn't recognized me, he turned away without a nod or a wave.

I found myself at Layla's blanket where Max now shared a corner, both of them trying to get their phones to work.

"You ready to leave yet?" I asked Layla.

Dylan laid his forehead above my ear. "Hey," he whispered. "I thought you were with me."

His breath tickled, and I shivered. It took every ounce of my strength to resist the temptation of a passionate night burning up his bed, but I managed to break our physical connection. "Thanks for the ride over, Dylan. I need to go home."

"I can take you." He twined his fingers into mine, in his old way of claiming without making any overt declarations. He was so familiar and comfortable, it would be easy to let old patterns repeat.

But I was in control of myself and peeled my hand free. "Thanks, Dylan. Not tonight."

Besides, I couldn't go home with Dylan even if I'd wanted to.

I only had three more days to finish revising before my book was due to my publisher.

When I got home, I opened my laptop to take another stab at the sex scene that had resisted me over the weekend, but when I settled in, I found Silver Fox had just messaged me.

Evening, Claire. Scarlett? Curious to find out how things are going.

So much for writing. His timing was impeccable because I needed someone to bounce thoughts off, and normally I might have talked to Charlie, but since he was one of the people I needed to talk about, he was no longer my best confidant.

Hey there, Foxy. Or Darcy. Things are a bit weird, to be honest.

How so?

How could I explain? *My two potential suitors are polar opposites of each other.*

Right. St. John v. Rhett. So who's winning?

More like who's losing? St. John is a great guy with so much possibility. We have a solid friendship, but there's no spark. Rhett, on the other hand, is a powder keg of combustible heat, but I suspect he doesn't want anything more than a hookup. If I could combine these two guys into one. . . .

That made me think about Peter again. Peter had been right in between Charlie and Dylan in so many respects. On paper, he was an amazing catch, and we did have a physical connection. Maybe not as white-hot as with Dylan, but at least Peter wanted me for more than a night. Well, not anymore, but when we'd been together, he'd take me places and tell me he loved me.

My phone buzzed. *Sounds like they both need to up their game.*

Enough about me. *How goes it with your Lizzie?*

Not good. I think maybe I should give up.

Why haven't you? What makes her so special to you?

That could take a while.

Please. It might make me have faith in the possibility of real romantic feelings again.

You have no idea what you're opening yourself up for.

Tell me one thing.

Three little dots appeared and disappeared by his name, and I stared, impatient until the message posted.

I ought to start with her personality and kind spirit, but the thing that kills me are her eyes. I think she sees herself as a bit tough, maybe even jaded, and if you didn't know her, you might fall for it. But her eyes give her away. To describe them by mere color wouldn't do them justice. They're soft with humor and wide with curiosity. If I were an artist, I'd try to draw them for you. I want to hope only a select few are privy to the seductive gaze she casts unwittingly.

I was gutted. *That was truly gorgeous, SF. I wish you good luck and hope she finally realizes what a catch you are.*

When he didn't respond right away, I started to put my phone away, but then it buzzed one last time.

I hope you find the man who can prove himself in word and deed to be worthy of you.

God, why couldn't I find someone like him?

Does she know how you feel?

I'm sure she has an inkling.

What was wrong with her? *I'm sorry. You're such a great guy.*

Well, you don't know that. I'm the dick who publicly accused you of having no love life.

Snort.

But he'd become more. *You've also given me a great idea for fixing my sequel. (The sexy times scene. Blush.) I was supposed to be writing it tonight, but it's not working.*

Need inspiration?

I perked up. *Yes!*

When a man kisses you, do you like him to take his time, or do you like it to be sudden and overpowering?

A shiver rolled down my spine. *Why Silver Fox, I do believe the answer is yes and yes.*

So you like kissing?

Definitely. God, I miss it.

Then start with that. Get your characters to kiss and see whether it opens any other doors. Imagine yourself there.

I'd done that to no avail, but he didn't need to know that. *That's great advice. You need to do the same ... (in real life.) I need to get to sleep.*
Same. Thanks for chatting.
You, too.
I lay in bed a while longer, conjuring up fictional images of Silver Fox. What did he look like? What did his voice sound like? Was he a great kisser? I pictured him being the kind of guy who would whisper something perfect as he brushed his lips across mine. He was right about the visual. I sat up and typed the start of a new scene fueled mostly by a stranger somewhere far away who was hopelessly in love with someone who wasn't me.

Chapter 18

Layla woke me up cranking some song only she knew. I dragged my carcass into the kitchen, where she stood at the stove over a pan of scrambled eggs.

"Morning," she said. "Eggs?"

"No, thanks." I stretched. "Why in the hell are you awake?" I craned my neck to look into her bedroom just in case she was harboring a secret rendezvous. Who would she have hooked up with? So far as I could tell, Internet people didn't have a corporeal state.

She fixed her plate and sat at the table. I went over to turn down the music, poured coffee, and sat across from her. "Talk."

"I've got good news!" She grinned over her mug. "Guess what!"

I hated guessing, so I lobbed, "Um. You have a meeting with the pope?"

She guffawed. "Nope. Nope to the pope."

I tapped my fingers together. "Let's see. You've decided to become a vegan?"

She rolled her eyes. "Stop."

"You told me to guess. I'm guessing."

"Guess something realistic. I'll give you a clue. It's something you've been telling me to do for a while now."

I pondered our history. I didn't think she'd be so excited if she'd cleaned the bathroom. I had been on her about one thing, and I remembered her résumé and mysterious interest in my wardrobe.

"You found a job?"

She beamed. "I did!"

Now my grin matched hers. "What? Where?" She'd vowed she'd only get a job if she could work in New York City, but she'd never been able to get even an interview for any positions there. I was nervous she'd finally succeeded and would abandon me.

"It's a cosmetics company just outside Indy. I start today!"

She *was* going to abandon me. I rubbed my eyes, trying to wake up still. "Where will you live?"

"Relax. I can commute there from here for now. See how it goes. Guess what else?"

I groaned at her for making me work at this. "It's a night shift?"

"Shut up. No. It's in social media, so I can totally up my game. Maybe this will be a stepping stone to getting a job in Manhattan after a year or so."

"That sounds perfect." I scooted over and pulled her in for a quick hug. "I'm excited for you!"

She jumped up. "Do you mind if I pilfer from your never-ending stash of respectable clothes until I can build up my own non-pajama-based wardrobe?"

It was like we were reversing polarities, her rushing headlong toward the life I'd fled. As we picked out a week's worth of outfits that would present an image of success, I wondered if I'd moved too far in the opposite direction. Max always dressed like he was going to a real job while I treated the bookstore the same way I had as a kid, like a place to curl up in my comfiest clothes. I held up a pink pin-striped shirt I'd always loved and paired it with a dark gray skirt, considering.

My eyes drifted to the prettier dresses, and for the first time in months, I had the urge to put one on, imagining Dylan's reaction without meaning to. I toyed with the hem of a flirty purple skirt and blurted out a confession.

"I'm thinking of hooking up with Dylan." I braced for her reaction.

She merely cocked her eyebrow. "Yeah. Okay. I guess."

"What?"

"TeamMadDylan doesn't work. It sounds too much like your name. Mad Dylan. Madeleine. It's no good." She appraised a white silk Banana Republic blouse, shook her head, then let the hanger swing, dismissed.

"You know there's more to a relationship than a couple nick-name."

"Just saying. TeamMadMax. That's a keeper."

"You're relentless, but Max and I would kill each other."

She considered a light blue Ralph Lauren oxford. "You're too much alike. You push each other's buttons."

"It's not just that." I sat on the edge of the bed, thinking about the myriad ways he drove me crazy. "Did you know he tried to talk me out of marrying Peter?"

"Well . . ."

"Well, what?"

"Uh." Her face contorted in several different expressions, from wide-eyed surprise to a guilty grimace. She squinted like she was prepared to be hit by a flying object.

"Spit it out, Miss Beckett."

She relaxed and sat next to me. "That wasn't totally Max." She threaded her fingers together on her knees in front of her, like she was at an interrogation. "People in this town are so pro-tective of you. They were concerned about your happiness."

"What are you saying? Max was put up to it?"

She shrugged.

"By who?"

"Specifically? I'm not sure, but I told Max it was your deci-sion to make, that you were a smart girl and you'd never forgive him if he interfered."

"Thank you." Was that such a hard concept? Still. "Did you have the same concerns?"

"I always have concerns. But who can know what the future holds? Were there red flags? Yeah. But I didn't wanna lose your friendship over some guy."

"You wouldn't have."

"Max kind of did."

I blew a raspberry. "Not the same. I just can't believe everyone had these objections and, besides Max, only one person told me upfront."

"Dylan?"

"No. Charlie, actually. He said Peter was an alphahole and in a few years I might fake my own death and swim to freedom." She looked confused, so I clarified. "*Sleeping with the Enemy.* Julia Roberts creates an elaborate boating accident to escape an emotionally abusive relationship."

"I know that, but alphahole?"

"Alpha male asshole. Controlling, domineering." I paused to consider whether that was a fair assessment of Peter. "I figured Charlie would object to any wedding on principle. You didn't think Peter was abusive, did you?"

She shook her head. "Manipulative maybe. Mainly cold and never quite present."

"He was serious and reliable."

She wrinkled her nose. "So are most vibrators."

I snorted. "Well the busybodies were right. Now I'm alone, struggling to keep the bookstore afloat. They stripped away my plot and left me here, a forgotten footnote."

"Maddie, is that the worst ending to a story? Do you honestly think you'd be living happily-ever-after in a castle with your Prince Charming if Peter hadn't run off at the stroke of midnight when he discovered all your nicely dressed friends were just jumped-up mice?"

I giggled and flipped her orange hair. "And a pumpkin."

"But do you get my point? The big fat map of your life has a giant *You Are Here* arrow and it's pointing to right now. Nowhere else. The question is whether you're going to live here or if you're going to keep trying to overlay reality with a fantasy."

"I get it. I'm trying. I am, but that arrow doesn't point me in any direction. And the map has to be redrawn because the land-marks are all gone."

She reached out and took my hand. "Nobody gets to rely on the landmarks, Maddie. They're rarely permanent."

Inspired by Layla's newfound professionalism, I picked out a blue-and-white striped pencil skirt and a pale yellow silk blouse. Leaving it strategically unbuttoned gave it a more casual feel. I even fixed my hair in a style other than my habitual braid, rolling it into a tight chignon. I disregarded the dress shoes for more comfortable sandals and headed toward my job with a new mind-set.

Despite my upgraded attitude, the morning felt ominous. There was a pressure in the air and not a soul on the street. Not even Charlie showed, which was worrisome. I'd been throwing him mixed signals, convinced he'd missed every single one of them. But maybe I'd only managed to create fissures in our friendship. Whenever he showed up, I should sit down and clear the air.

The morning continued its foreboding aspect. I peered out-side, nervous a storm might be brewing that would keep every-one in their homes for the remainder of the day. The arrival of Max's van reassured me that the rapture hadn't taken the town and left me behind, but when he jumped onto the sidewalk and rushed inside without fetching any boxes, flipped the *Closed* sign around, and locked my door, I wondered if maybe we'd skipped straight to Armageddon.

"What are you doing, Max?"

"Didn't you get an alert?" He strode across the open space, looking around the shop. "There's a tornado warning for our area. Is there anyone else here besides you?"

The windows rattled, and a random stick or debris hit the door. I dropped the books I'd been carrying on the counter. "No. Shit."

Without warning, he grabbed my hand and pulled me after him toward the storeroom, like a scalawag throwing me on his black steed and riding straight to his lair. Or my lair to be accurate. He flung open the door to the infrequently used cellar, a room too small to be called a basement and too damp to be used for anything other than a hole in the ground. A hole in the ground was our safest location.

My heart raced.

If you live in Indiana, a few things become second nature. One of those is hunkering down in a basement during tornado season. Which is pretty much all year round. We don't take our chances. We've all seen the devastation they can leave behind. A single house among dozens might get knocked down. Or an entire town could get leveled. I'd never mess around with a tornado even if it meant being entombed with Max.

Max hit the switch to flip on the lights. Nothing happened.

The room wasn't perfectly dark, but so dim, I had to feel along the wall to avoid tripping over the small cot I'd inherited. "I have a flashlight here somewhere." Soon my hip hit an old workman's table along the back wall, and I groped in the top drawer until my hand hit solid metal. I turned on the flashlight and pointed it at the bare lightbulb hanging from the ceiling.

Max stretched his arm up, but the metal chain only hung down a few inches, and even on his toes, he couldn't grasp it. He squatted and patted his knee. "Here. Stand on my thigh and see if you can reach it."

I put my hands on his shoulders and stepped onto his leg. He held me by the waist as I caught the chain and pulled. No change. "Shit. The bulb's probably dead."

The flashlight lay on the table, bouncing our shadows against the wall.

I stepped down, and Max straightened, but rather than drop his hands, he pulled me closer to him. "This reminds me of that time we took those ballroom dance classes."

My skirt must've jogged that image loose.

"Max." I tried to sound stern, but I chortled at the memory. I assumed the awkward position, laying my left hand on his shoulder and holding my right hand up, waiting for him to take it. Instead, he pressed his lips against my forehead.

Shocked, I let my extended hand drop onto his upper arm and then froze. His bicep was solid muscle. My fingers toyed with the edges of his sleeves, wanting to explore under the fabric. What must his shoulders feel like?

I should have pushed him away, but my grip tightened, and as if invited, his lips moved to my temple.

Imperatives exploded in my mind. *Stop! This is Max!* My mouth formed the words, but when he laid a gentle kiss on my cheek, I said nothing.

Then his lips brushed mine, and my brain short-circuited completely. The only word in my head sounded like *mmm*. Every ounce of my attention focused on the delicious luxury of his mouth, parting slightly. We fit together like a puzzle. I sucked on his lower lip, and his tongue darted out against mine. Bolts of lightning shot straight through my stomach, and the rest of my body came online, bit by bit, as if powered by the electricity of his kiss.

My fingers dug into the muscles I'd only just noticed, and he groaned softly. His awakened desire should have cautioned me, but it only made me want more.

He shuffled forward a step, and like an obedient dance partner, I followed his lead, letting him waltz me slowly until my back hit the wall, and he pressed against me, hard, so very hard. My mind caught up to my body with an urgent message: The cock grinding into me belonged to Max. But I didn't want him to stop.

I hooked an ankle around his knee and forced my hips into him. My skirt rose.

What had been a quiet, low energy cranked up to full power, and the tornado found us. His fingers twined through my hair, loosening the clasp, and he grasped hold to tilt my head so he could drag his lips and teeth down my neck. My hands found the hem of his shirt and plunged under to touch his skin, to claw those tempting muscles along his back.

He broke his kiss to press his cheek against mine and whisper, "Maddie."

I stilled his lips with mine, savoring the taste of him. His hands roamed across my shirt, territory he'd never explored. Not once. Rather than douse the heat, the violation of our taboo relationship perversely turned it up, turned me on.

He slowed, waiting for a refusal I didn't give, before tentatively slipping a hand under my blouse. The calm in the storm broke, and he made up for lost time, skimming my stomach, my ribs, the lace of my bra. Before either of us could stop the momentum, I steered him toward the decrepit cot, and he fell more than sat on the rickety death trap.

As I climbed on his lap, where I solemnly swore I was up to no good, a violent crash upstairs brought us both out of our delirium.

I jerked my hands back and jumped up. "What was that?"

Max panted and drove his fingers through his hair. "Probably nothing."

It had sounded like major destruction. I straightened my shirt and moved toward the stairs.

Max sighed. "Wait." He brought out his phone and thumbed at it until he'd found what he wanted. With a resigned frown, he stood. "Okay, I think it's safe to go up."

He adjusted his pants and exhaled a nervous laugh. My hands shook with frustrated desire as we climbed upstairs.

I was worried we might find a wall or ceiling caved in from tornado damage, but the lights were all on, and outside the storm seemed to have blown past. In the café, we discovered the cause of the disruption. A tree branch lay on the floor surrounded by glass and pieces of green-painted wood that had clearly come from the front window that now had a massive hole in it.

That was going to be expensive to fix. With a sigh, I fetched the broom.

When I leaned down to pick up a large piece of glass, Max bent to grab the branch, and our eyes met. Max swallowed, then he stood and went out front to examine the window from outside.

While I swept up glass and wood, Max called through the opening, "It's weird. There's no damage out here."

"What do you mean?" My heartbeat throbbed in my fingertips, and I wanted to believe it was from the shock of the catastrophe, nothing more. I pushed an image of Max on the cot, in the dark, out of my mind and focused on the task at hand, dumping the contents of my tray into a trash bag.

"I mean, there are leaves down, but no other limbs. Not even a stick." He had to be as flustered as me, but he was matching my tone.

"What do the trees look like?"

All along the sidewalk, the city had planted trees during a beautification project when I was barely old enough to remember. They weren't enormous, but a strong storm would often leave the streets strewn with leaves and small sticks. It struck me as odd that an entire branch would come off, especially with no other debris.

He asked, "What kinds of trees are these again?"

"Linden."

He came back in and kicked the branch. "What is this, then?"

I wasn't a botanist, but even I could tell the leaves on the branch weren't the same as the little fans on the trees on the street. Not to mention the tree outside my shop was flowering. "I don't know."

Was it possible one of those little hooligans had broken my window?

As we crouched over the branch, puzzling over the long thin shape of the leaves, my phone rang out *You've got mail!* and I excused myself to check on whether I had something new from Silver Fox.

A jolt of terror froze me when I saw my editor's name. I still hadn't fixed the ending of my novel.

Maddie,
Just checking in. How are things coming along? I don't want to pressure you, but as you know, I'm expecting to see your manuscript by Friday. I wish I could extend the deadline, but

we've already set the production schedule. Do you think you'll
be able to finish on time?
  Best,
  Liz

Max carried the branch outside, and I sat in the café and
composed a quick response.

·Liz,
I'm nearly finished.

Lies.

Based on feedback I've gotten on the first book, I'm trying to
take a stab at punching up the steam when I do a second pass.
Let me know if you concur.
  Hey—do you happen to know how an ARC of The Shadow's
Apprentice *ended up at a blog called the* Book Brigade?
  Maddie

I closed the email app and noticed my text message icon had
a number above it. I clicked through to find unread messages
from Gentry and Peter.

I checked Gentry's first. *Tornado warning. Take cover.* I
deleted it.

There were three messages from Peter, over a week old.
Sorry. I got called away.
Do you want me to come to your book club?
Maddie?

I stared at the messages, confounded. What would it have
looked like for him to show up at the last book club? What did
it mean that he was even asking?

I responded, *We're reading* Little Women *now. I would love*
for you to join in, if it's what you want.

If he was willing to try, to come here and integrate, there
might be hope for him. For us. It could be a step on the path to
redemption.

Max came back in and went to the storeroom. He returned
with some duct tape and plastic wrap and proceeded to create a
fake window.

I said, "I'm going to call Jack and see if he knows of someone
who can fix the window."

Once I'd talked to Jack, my phone told me I had another mail
from Liz, so I plopped down.

Maddie,
That sounds intriguing. I can't wait to see what you do with
it. I've noticed that readers seem to want to see more romance
between your characters, which is a good thing. I'm all for
punching that up in the second book.
As for the reviews, we sent over a hundred copies to various
bloggers. I'm not sure about that specific blog you mentioned,
but congratulations. It's a good sign if your book cut through
and caught a reviewer's attention.
Just get the second book to me by Friday morning.
Best,
Liz

Yeah, no pressure at all.

When Jack finally showed, he said, "There's a hole in your
window, Maddie."

Ignoring his statement of the obvious, I walked with him over to
look at the damage, explaining, "The wind blew this branch in."

Jack looked outside. "What wind?"

"From the tornado watch earlier?" I threw a quizzical look
at Max.

Max held up his phone. "I got a text alert."

Jack shook his head. "There were some scattered showers on
my way here, but nothing serious." He peeled back the
makeshift patch and appraised the hole once more. "Call your
insurance company and start a claim, and I can send someone
over to fix this. Won't be till tomorrow, though."

We did as Jack advised, but the busted front window gave me

a pretext to avoid dealing with Max. "I'm gonna close up and go home."

The foot traffic in town appeared to be minimal, and the bookstore was empty. Running the air conditioning with a barely covered hole didn't appeal to me at all.

Max rubbed his neck where a small hickey was developing like a mortifying Polaroid picture. The memory of what we'd just done was too fresh. I'd be lying if I denied wanting to drag Max back to the cellar, but that was pure lust, and I'd recovered enough to resist physical impulses. On the other hand, if he took the lead, I might have been persuadable. But it had taken extraordinary circumstances for him to cross that line once, and I knew he respected me enough to keep his hands to himself. After all, he wasn't Dylan.

He let out a long shaky breath, like he'd been through the exact same mental gymnastics and came to his own conclusions. "Why don't we just—"

I cut him off. "I don't want to talk."

All I could think to do was reset our relationship before I said something in the heat of the moment that I couldn't take back later.

He winced. "I was going to say, Why don't we just finish cleaning up first?"

It was a temporary reprieve. I couldn't put him off forever, but for the moment, I had more pressing business. I ushered him out and headed home to stare down my blinking cursor.

I wanted to forget what had happened in the cellar, but as I climbed the stairs to my apartment, my mind bombarded me with visions I wasn't equipped to handle.

The memory of his lips on mine came rushing back and physically hurt. My stomach lurched, and my heart squeezed tight with guilt I'd buried since the last time we'd kissed and complicated what had been a simple, easy friendship. Even if the window hadn't broken, I would have needed to flee the store to avoid a messy confrontation. Of course, if the window hadn't broken . . .

What if we hadn't been interrupted? Would we have ended up with our clothes pooled at our feet? I blew out a sharp burst of air to get a handle on my runaway fantasies. What did he look like now under that shirt? My libido was an erupting volcano, and nobody was safe in the flowing lava of my out-of-control need for physical contact. Dylan had started this, but I couldn't ignore that Silver Fox had given me permission to act.

For a wonder, when at last I sat down to write, the words flowed easily, and I finished the new steamy version of the scene that had eluded me. I didn't have time to read the chapter over to fix the ordering, to excise repetitive or weak words, or to correct grammar errors if I wanted Silver Fox's feedback before my deadline. I jotted a quick email.

> *Foxy,*
> *This is outside my experience in so many ways. First, I can't believe I wrote a sex scene. Second, I can't believe I wrote it for you. (You reveal that anywhere, you will die an excruciatingly slow and agonizing death by feral spider monkeys. You've been warned.) Third, I can't believe I'm sending this to you. (Seriously, this can't be reproduced anywhere or the spider monkeys will be accompanied by actual spiders.) So here goes. Please be kind.*
> *Oh, God, I can't believe I'm sharing this. Spoilers ahead.*

I attached the file and, before I lost my courage, hit send.

May he burn with an unquenchable lust.

I suddenly realized what I'd done. I'd sent a reviewer, a guy who'd ripped apart my last novel, a first draft of a new scene. He was going to skewer me.

> *Rane's body lay limp, despite Lira's efforts to revive him. Crossing through the portal might have killed either or both of them, but it was a risk she'd needed to make. If she'd abandoned him, his death would have been guaranteed. He would never have left her behind. She was furious he'd nearly sacrificed himself trying to save her.*

They lived together or they died together.

She wrapped her hands around his solid bicep and heaved him onto one side, a trial even if she'd had all of her strength. Exhausted, she dropped on her knees and buried her face in his side, breathing him in. She had no time to process the familiar scent, to fall into the only home she'd ever known. She ran her fingers along the fabric of his shirt until she found a small tear. She slipped her thumbs in and ripped until she could free him from the tatters. His torso was chiseled marble. How often had she longed to run her hands along his skin?

Pushing regrets out of her mind, she began the ministrations that would cost her the last of her magic and possibly her life. It was a life she didn't want if it meant an eternity alone. If Rane lived, the cost would be worth it. A single day more would be worth it.

Although she needed to hurry, she took great care to trace the right shapes across his chest, curving an arc with her finger, leaving behind a burnished crescent. She reached deep down to the bottom of her well where the source had run like liquid for her once. Now it was dry. She sought for a drop here or there, pulling them to the surface and pushing them into Rane's body. So close, so close now. The rune took shape.

As she traced the last line, the symbol glowed golden for a moment, and she could do nothing more but wait. Her magic was gone, but she didn't even care. She wouldn't need it as long as she had Rane.

She laid a kiss on his brow. "Don't leave me, Rane."

Her mortality weighed on her and left her on the verge of un-consciousness. She slumped forward, but a hand caught her shoulder and held her tight. Arms wrapped around her and pressed her against a chest that rose and fell with every breath. Lira dragged her hands over the rune, down the ridges of Rane's muscles.

She lifted her head and her gaze was met by his steely eyes.

"Lira. What have you done?"

"I have become like you."

"*Like me?*" *Understanding dawned, and his hard expression softened. "Your magic?"*

"*It's gone, Rane." She was certain it was gone, and with it the taboo that had kept them forever linked but forever forbidden from joining together.*

Selfishly, she was pleased. If she were no longer Creed, she could give herself fully.

Rane looked deep into Lira's eyes. "Are you well?"

"*I am well. And you?"*

In response, he drew her to him. For a heartbeat, she held back. What would happen if any magic remained in reserve? But his lips were irresistible, and she'd longed to taste them, never believed she'd ever know the feel of his skin against hers. Her heart raced as she leaned in closer, as his fingers wound into her hair, as their lips met for the first time. They paused, savoring the press of flesh on flesh, their pulses pounding in the same rhythm. Rane groaned and coaxed her mouth open, his tongue brushing hers.

Her energy renewed as he whispered, "I've wanted you for so long."

Lira dropped her head back and let him unfasten her cloak. He loosened her tunic and slipped it off. He paused to drag his eyes down her torso, then clawed at her leggings. He tore off his own ruined pants and fell upon her. "You are well, Lira?"

This time when he asked that question, it was a request.

She'd used up a life's worth of magic to carry them through the failing portal, and Dane had leached the very last traces. She should be weak, but Rane's body lay across hers, held up on his elbows, and he wanted her. And she wanted him.

"*I am very well." I slipped my hands around his neck and forced him close enough to kiss.*

He sucked on my lips, and I wrapped my ankle around his thigh. When he entered me, my back arched, and we crashed together. He lost control and rode me until he cried out. My screaming rose to meet his, pleasure building until every last atom of my being concentrated on that one all-encompassing need.

Every last atom but one.

At the height of Rane's passion, Lira's mind was pulled deep down into her essence where the smallest particle of magic had survived and pulsed. She wanted to call out, "Stop, Rane!" but her body bucked against him, as unable to break away as he was. Her nails dug into his arms, and he let go, pouring his seed into her.

He slowed, smiling, panting, laughing, overjoyed, sated, covered in sweat. Lira lay with her eyes wide open, searching for the words to tell him she was still Creed, and they'd just broken every law.

Chapter 19

※◉※

My head throbbed like I'd gone to bed drunk, but I hadn't even had one beer. I'd written deep into the night, churning out a totally revised version of the last third of my novel. The scene between Rane and Lira had opened the floodgates.

I sat straight up. Had I really sent that to Silver Fox?

Oh, shiiiiiiit.

My phone sat on my nightstand, and the light flashed green. Green like the color of my stomach contents coming up. Green like the envy I had for the dead.

Green like the traffic light telling me to go. Urging me to write a *sex* scene. Inviting me to send it to a professional reviewer. Coaxing me to push the boundaries.

Would he know to treat me gently in return?

I couldn't ask Layla to read this email for me, so I forced myself to wake my phone screen up and look at the notifications.

But the email was just a Google alert for an eBay listing of my advance reviewer copy. I grumbled. What part of *Not for resale* did they fail to understand?

As disgusted as the auction left me, I was more horrified by Silver Fox's silence, rationalizing every scenario that might explain why he hadn't answered.

The most obvious reason was that he hadn't had the time to respond yet. Maybe he read it on a commute home from work and would write back this morning. Or maybe he'd finally hooked up with the girl he liked, and he was otherwise occupied.

For some reason, that gave me a twinge of jealousy.

I resolved not to assume he'd found the writing so terrible he was avoiding telling me his honest opinion. I didn't want to consider the possibility I'd grossed him out. What if I was even less convincing at sex than romance?

I put a time limit on my forced sanity. If I hadn't heard from him by this afternoon, I'd allow myself to casually DM him on Twitter.

I'd say, *"Hey, sent you an email."*

No, too obvious.

Maybe *"Did you have a good Fourth?"*

Worse. He'd know I was fishing. Maybe I'd just be bold. *"So . . . was it that bad?"*

I settled on this, memorized it even, then went to my laptop to try to get in another five hundred words on the final chapter, but a text from Jack cut my work short. *Repairman coming by this morning.*

With a lingering glance at my blinking cursor, I picked out another career-wise outfit, gray slacks and a light pink knit top this time. I headed over, regretting that I'd have no good excuse to keep the store closed until I finished my last-minute revisions.

Dan, the repairman, stood outside the front door. As soon as I let him in, he measured things while I flipped on lights. I'd spoken to the insurance company, and they'd assured me the repairs would be covered after a deductible I wasn't even sure I could pay given how tight things were. I considered foregoing my morning coffee to save money, but that would be insanity. After all, I had to brew the coffee for customers anyway.

Maybe I should ask Peter for help. Would he bail me out or watch me sink?

The white van pulled up, and I braced for a confrontation, a bit disappointed when Mrs. Beckett stepped out of the cab. I hadn't heard from Max since the previous morning. He hadn't even left me a message. Maybe he was embarrassed after what had happened the day before. Or maybe he was mad at me for blowing it off like it was nothing. It *was* nothing.

At least, it *should* have been nothing.

Sure, it felt great to kiss him, but it felt great to kiss Dylan. And a kiss was not the turning point of an entire relationship, no matter what the novels wanted me to believe.

But when I recalled that kiss, my face flamed, and I couldn't dispel the phantom softness of his lips or the hardness of his jeans pressed against my hip. My poor loins were scorched.

And all because of Max.

What had he been thinking?

If I could threaten my friendship with Charlie with nothing more than a handshake, how much damage had yet another kiss done to my already fraught friendship with Max? No matter how much he drove me insane, I never wanted to lose him that way. I never wanted to hurt him.

I refused to let myself imagine Max undressed. Especially not with his mom explaining why there weren't any apple crumb muffins today.

Charlie arrived while I was dealing with the delivery. When everything was squared away, I made him his usual latte and set a muffin on a plate.

Dan stood in the window, pulling out damaged panes and causing general disruptions. Charlie sat in the corner, his face illuminated with the glow from his laptop, and he held his fist over an obvious smile as he read something entertaining.

I snuck up and set the coffee down. "Something fun?"

He snapped the lid closed and blushed. "Not really."

I sighed. He'd never shut me out like that before, and it made me uncomfortable. He'd become a reliable part of my life, and I hoped I hadn't irreparably harmed whatever we had. It was a bad idea to attempt to mix friendship with romance. Only one or the other could survive.

I appraised him a moment to assess if he was mad at me. Maybe I'd caught him using my WiFi to watch porn. I wasn't even sure if Charlie would like porn. I wasn't sure if he even liked me that way. He'd never talked about any other women. "So just cat videos?"

He chuckled. "Sure. Let's go with that."

I took his response as proof things were okay between us.

Once Dan finished patching the window, customers trickled in. I'd pushed off the temptation to look at my phone for the entire morning, but I had to know if I was going to be ghosted. Or worse, would Silver Fox heap on criticism I didn't need?

The light blinked green, but that didn't mean anything. I held my breath and woke up the screen. There was no email icon awaiting me.

Disappointed, I swiped the rest of the notifications, and then noticed I had a direct message on Twitter. With a little grin, I clicked through, nervous, but excited.

There were five messages.

I didn't expect you'd actually write that scene. Is it wrong I feel like an all-powerful puppet master with an author at my disposal to do my bidding?

I'm not responding as a reviewer because I don't think you want that right now, but this is what I was talking about.

Btw—you slipped into first person for a bit there. Oh, and double-check the names. You mistyped at least once, which made me look them up. All this time, I've been calling your characters by the wrong names. No wonder you thought I hadn't read your book. So sorry.

For the record, I'm in need of a cold shower. Should I be admitting that?

Looking forward to your next book. I'd love to read an ARC.

It made me feel weird that I'd stirred a distant guy at a visceral level, unless he was joking about being turned on by my writing. I'd never written for that purpose, but if he felt powerful for compelling me to write it, I felt like a god for creating something that affected him physically.

I typed a hasty response. *I'm blushing, but relieved. Now you owe me something in return. I'd love to see your writing. Maybe you could burn off some of that heat.*

I slapped my hand over my mouth as soon as I hit Send. I didn't know where I'd gotten the courage to solicit what amounted to a literary dick pic. What was I going to do if he sent it? I giggled imagining our email exchange ending up in historical documents about my life—once I'd gotten famous, naturally. Plenty of authors had platonic long-distance correspondences with people who inspired their ideas. Where would this fall exactly?

He was some kind of muse for sure. Silver Fox was going to help me fix my second book, and he'd never know how instrumental he'd been in helping me find my footing.

He responded, *You want me to write you a love scene? You're just teasing, right? Although writing that may be the closest I ever come to ending my frustration.*

A bit embarrassed at my own suggestion, I focused on his personal problems. *You owe it to yourself to lay your feelings out once and for all.*

How do you mean?

You're obviously getting nowhere with your current efforts. Ask her out. Tell her how you feel, Foxy. Give her the benefit of the doubt. If she rejects you, so be it. At least you'll know, right?

I waited a beat, then added.

And then send me your titillating fiction.

Was this how people had inadvertent affairs?

Chapter 20

✣❂✣

Friday arrived, and I ran out of time to make any more changes to my book. I knew my editor would be sending me a massive edit letter anyway, so I explained to her my vision for a change in direction, praying she'd get excited and give me the freedom to infuse this book with more life.

After attaching the file, I had an urge to reread the entire manuscript. But I'd fixed the problems Silver Fox caught, and Layla had given me good notes. I'd gotten everything structurally in place. Liz had an eagle eye and a great feel for tension. She'd warned me that the middle book of a trilogy would be the hardest, but that twist I'd added at the end with Silver Fox's prodding was going to surprise her. We'd never talked about Lira carrying Rane's child in the third installment, and I hoped she'd let me run with that.

I hit send, and the second book was off. Just in time to freak out that my first book would release in a little over a week. My stomach roiled, and I wasn't sure I'd be able to keep my breakfast down.

Liz wrote back a few minutes later.

Maddie,
Thanks for getting your project in on time. I promise I'll get

*you an edit letter faster this time around. Congrats on finishing!
Go celebrate!*
  Liz

Now all I had to do was wait. Maybe I could find a way to induce a coma until I got her notes. I was going to need to invest in something to keep me from biting my nails.

The distraction arrived on my doorstep in the form of Dylan as I was closing up for the night. He looked like I'd caught him pacing.

"Maddie, can we talk?"

I shrugged. "Of course."

"Not here." He jerked his head toward my apartment. "Wanna go up to your place?"

It wasn't like I had no self-control around him, but considering what had recently transpired with Max, I could only conclude that lately my body had become a hormone factory with ideas of its own. "Take me to dinner."

"Aw, Maddie." His shoulders sagged. "Why's it gotta be like that?"

"Come on. Let's go to the Jukebox."

We got a table for two, and I took a peek around to check if anyone was watching us. Everyone was watching us.

"What did you want to talk about?" I kind of hoped he was going to present me with a royalty check for all the creative input I'd given him on his early music. That might save my bookstore from going under this month.

He put his elbows on the table and steepled his fingers. "You were always there when I needed you, and I guess I just assumed we could fall into our old relationship."

"Our old relationship?"

"Everything was so easy between us. Don't you think? Don't you miss that?"

"I did miss it. I got over it when you went your own way."

"I actually have something I want to ask you."

He took my hands in his and raised both eyebrows hopefully.

That wicked smile would be my undoing. "What would it have taken you to get on that bus with me when we were kids?"

Why was he asking me now? "If you'd only once talked about a future together . . ."

"A declaration? If I'd promised you forever? You would've come with me?"

"Maybe. But you never committed to anything. You never told me you wanted forever."

"What do you mean, I never told you? I've written songs dedicated to you."

I wrested my hands free and crossed my arms. "Lovely songs, but they don't count."

He raked his fingers through his hair. "Do you think those songs came easily? That's my soul, Mads."

If this was going to be an attempt to whitewash the past, it wasn't going to work. "If you'd made that promise, I would have definitely wanted to, but I couldn't anyway. My mom would have killed me if I left school."

His expression slowly turned into straight up mischief. "You could now."

"What are you even talking about?"

He pulled an envelope from his back pocket and handed it to me. "I sent over the videos Layla shot last week along with some demos, and they loved the new song."

I slipped a letter out. The letterhead read *Monday Records,* his label. I scanned the paragraphs quickly. The big executives wanted him back in the studio soon. He'd go back to traveling, studios, touring, girls, drinking. I pinched the bridge of my nose as the significance of this letter washed over me. When I looked up at Dylan, his expression was a mix of hope and more hope. His eyes moved back and forth between mine, and his lips seemed about to float away if he didn't keep them under tight control.

"This is incredible news, Dylan."

"Is that all you're gonna say?"

"What more is there? If this is what you want, then congratulations." I folded the letter and put it in the envelope. "I thought you were considering staying here. Living the peaceful life."

He laughed. "I can always do that. Eventually."

"So you're leaving." I was so glad I'd resisted the urge to hook up with him. If I'd given him that part of me again, this would hurt like ending an addiction. As it was, I already knew I'd always wonder what might have been. Again.

He leaned forward. "I want you to do this with me this time."

My stomach hurt. I imagined catching him between gigs and wondering about the girls. Too bad Layla hadn't been in that English class so many years ago. She would've eaten up that life. But I couldn't do that.

I didn't even have a glass of water to sip on to swallow whatever pill he was pushing. "Dylan."

"No, listen. You want a declaration, and I'm going to give you one." His tight-squeezed fist lay before him. "I need you."

Three little words that sounded nice to my ears. I rested my elbows on the table eager to hear more about how I was indispensable to Dylan, how he couldn't live without me. It would be a first.

"I tried to do this once before, on my own, and it ended in disaster. You were always my home and my muse. If you'd gotten on that bus with me the first time, I know you would've helped me stay grounded and make solid decisions."

For a minute, his words filled me with pride. That I could be the one person Dylan needed gave me a frisson of excitement. I sat a little taller and tried to picture what my life might be like with him.

For the first time since Peter left, money would no longer be a concern, but if I was traveling with him, what would happen to my bookstore?

That put me squarely in the same situation I'd found myself with Peter. Would I want to abandon my life for his?

He took my hand. "Maddie, would you at least consider being there for me?"

That's when an idea crystallized in my mind I couldn't shake. Dylan had only talked about what I could do for him. What would he do for me?

"Why should I?"

He gave me the cockiest smile he owned, one that should have made me want to punch him right in the kisser, but instead usually made me want to throw my panties at him. "Because I'm the most interesting person you know."

That was true. He was interesting and beautiful, talented and hot. He made me think dirty thoughts, and I'd always at least partially want to reconnect with him. But he hadn't changed, and I didn't know if he would.

Our server arrived, and we ordered as a loud band began to play.

He sucked on his teeth, then suddenly stood and held his hand out. "Dance with me."

Maybe it was foolish of me to agree to let him lay his hands on me, but I loved to dance. Thankfully the music stayed at a fast enough tempo that we mainly just twisted in our own spaces for a song or two. I kept an eye out for our food to arrive. We held each other by one hand as we pretended to dance a jitterbug.

Then the band played "At Last." As if he'd been expecting it, Dylan roped me toward him, and I found myself crushed against his body, his hand in mine, his other arm pressed against my back. I breathed him in, and he swayed with me, rocking his hips in a rhythm I could have set a clock to. Dylan felt like a second skin.

As we danced, he leaned in and sang the words, quietly, into my ear, and I melted a little bit. The room fell away, and there was just us. I could picture us so easily alone. I'd drag my lips down his neck. He'd groan my name and lay my hand on the cock that currently pressed into my hip bone.

When the song ended, I started to peel myself from him, but he slid his hand along my spine until he reached my neck and cradled the back of my head. I knew what came next. I hadn't spent a full year under Dylan's spell not to recognize his preamble to a kiss, but I couldn't push him away, magnetized as I was by the sultry magic he was conjuring. Mentally, I knew Dylan's seduction game was A+ but physically, I wanted him to conquer my will and take away my need to make rational decisions.

He gazed into my eyes as if he were enjoying the utter destruction of my resistance, and it occurred to me he wasn't Rhett Butler or Rochester. He was Casanova or the Marquis de Valmont, drunk on the power he held over me. Had Valmont loved Tourvel? Or was he a predator to the end?

Dylan's expression told me everything he expected to happen from this moment on, and still I let him make his move, kissing me soft, then predictably rougher, while I watched the scene play out from a distance. Was he kissing me? Or was he winning a game?

He broke off, unaware I'd been anything but overwhelmed by him, giving me that look that said, *We'll finish this later.* But would we?

Our food arrived, and as we settled into our seats, I asked, "So what happens to the bookstore while I'm following you around the country?"

He took a sip of his beer and licked his lips, and I was 99 percent sure he meant that as a distraction. "Can't Max run it for you? Or you could close it while you're gone." My face must have clued him into how stupid those suggestions were, so he amended, "Or you could sell it to Gentry, then you wouldn't have to worry about it at all."

"Do your ears work? Or can you not hear yourself talking?"

"What? Wouldn't you like to take a break? I know it's been a struggle to keep the thing afloat."

I reached across the table and stage-smacked his ear. "Dylan Ramirez, do you have the faintest reason why Peter and I split?"

He winced, like he no longer answered to his real name. "Sure. He didn't like that you had strong influences in your life."

My head was starting to throb. "That's not how I would describe it."

"What did you think? He had an aversion to the buildings?"

"You think he split because of the company I keep?"

"You tell me. Would you find it weird that he told me and Max to back off from you?"

"You? Maybe not." I laughed. "But Max?"

He grimaced as if he'd smelled something foul. "He threatened to forbid you to talk to us anymore, unless we made ourselves scarce."

"What?" My mouth went dry.

Dylan's fist tightened. "I should've pushed the issue and made him try. But I wasn't around here much anyway, so it was easier to ignore him."

"Why didn't you tell me?"

He laughed bitterly. "What would you have done? You haven't exactly kept in touch."

I gripped my fork with a pile of rice clinging to it, my hand shaking, precariously hanging on to anything solid. "When was this?"

"October."

"So you did nothing?"

"I gather Max did try to talk to you, but you weren't inclined to listen to him. You never would have listened to me."

My dinner threatened to come back up. "That was it?"

He ran his tongue across his lip, hesitating, before he confessed, "We decided someone should talk to Peter."

"Who talked to him? Please don't say it was—"

"Me."

"Shit."

No fucking wonder Peter up and fled. He'd probably gritted his teeth through this entire ordeal and hoped he could at least count on me to stay at his side. When I didn't pick him over my town, my bookstore, my friends, he balked.

"I wish I'd known all of this."

"Would you have done anything differently?"

It was impossible to answer that question. I would have been angry at everyone for butting in. I would have been angry at Peter for antagonizing everyone in the first place. Would I have changed course in time? Or would I have slammed into the iceberg anyway?

"I might've eloped."

He shook his head. "The Maddie I know wouldn't have gotten married if she couldn't be surrounded by her friends."

"What did you want me to do, then?"

"I wanted you to see the world as it is instead of what you expect to see, without all the filters you add to make everyone more interesting than they are. I wanted you to see that Peter, for all his shine and perfection, might not be the right guy for you."

"But you are."

"I could be." He sipped his beer. "I know I'm not a romance hero, and I'm certainly far from perfect, but dammit, we fit together so well."

"You're wrong about one thing: You are the quintessential romance hero." He really was, too. Charming, sexy, artistic, and full of passion. We had the friendship. We had the chemistry. That should have been enough. Why wasn't that enough?

His eyes twinkled, but he didn't smile. "Will you at least consider my proposal? Live a little, Maddie."

My breath caught at the phrase. But that was the exact advice that had gotten me into this mess, and it wouldn't get me out. I considered his offer, but it wasn't what I wanted. "You know I love you, right?"

He frowned like he saw where this was going. "I love you, too."

It was maybe the first time he'd said that when we weren't mid-coitus. It was nice to hear, but he should have led with that. A tear rolled over my lower lid and fell heavily onto the back of my hand. I dragged my thumb across my cheek and took a deep breath.

"I'd be lying if I told you I didn't think about what it might be like to get back together with you." Total honesty. A part of me would always regret what I was about to say to him, and I hesitated long enough that a shadow of his cocky grin reached his lips. I had to make a hard choice, now or never. "But my life is here, Dylan."

He hung his head. Then his eyes rose, and he produced a smile like it was his only armor. "Promise me that when we're forty, if we're both still single, we'll end up together."

I sob-laughed at that. "It's a deal."

Chapter 21

✠✠✠

Saturday morning, I was getting out of the shower, when my phone rang. I expected to see spam from an unknown number in Colorado and was surprised the screen said *Peter*.

I nearly dropped the phone as I answered. My stomach fluttered, and I realized I was chewing on my lower lip.

"Hey, Maddie. I'm, uh . . . I've got business out your way and was hoping to stop in and talk."

Speechless. I swallowed anger and tears I thought I'd buried.

"You there?" His voice caressed me like a worn pair of jeans. Familiar and comforting, although I hadn't heard it in months.

"Yes."

"Will you be around?"

"I'm in the bookstore all day."

"Noon okay?"

"Works for me."

"Thanks, Maddie. And . . ."

His pause hung there like an invitation for my imagination to fill in the words that would make Peter the hero I needed him to be. If he'd followed that *and* with *I made a mistake*, it would have gone a long way to heal something broken in me. He also owed me an apology for abandoning me. But if Dylan was right, if he'd chased Peter away, I owed Peter an apology, too. Maybe that's all he'd needed in the first place.

But he finished, ". . . let me know if your plans change."

As soon as I hung up, I flipped through my wardrobe, indecisive. Did I want to dress to impress him or play nonchalant? Did I want to make him rue the day he left or tempt him to want to woo me back?

I pulled out the polka-dotted A-line. The last time I'd worn it, we'd fought over a dance lesson, but it was more than that. It was about his unwillingness to share me, not just with the town, but with my own aspirations. The argument represented Peter past, and I needed him to prove I could still consider a future with him. Short of a wedding gown, it was the most passive-aggressive dress I could have worn. I slipped it on and tugged at the zipper on the side, but it stuck at my first rib. I barged into Layla's room and woke her up to help me.

Pinching the fabric together, she managed to move the zipper another inch, but a hole gaped open below the eyelet.

I sucked in my stomach as if that would shrink my rib cage. "Keep trying."

She frowned. "It doesn't fit anymore, Maddie."

I laughed out loud at the symbolism. I couldn't get literal or figurative closure from a stupid dress. I pulled the zipper down and let it fall to the floor. "You can have it."

Tempted as I was to wear worn jeans and a soft T-shirt, I didn't want to yield the advantage to Peter so easily. In the end, I dug up a white gauze skirt he'd given me to wear on our honeymoon. It still had the tags on it. Playing dirty, I paired it with a ruched off-shoulder crop top that he'd always loved.

As I was unlocking the bookstore, Mrs. Beckett pulled up in the van again. I got out my phone and texted, *Maximilian Beckett, have you quit your day job? Do you ever intend to show your face again?*

I didn't expect him to respond, so I was more than a little surprised an hour later when he sauntered through my front door. His eyes popped out of his head when he saw what I was wearing. He bowed deep, and I imagined him in a long coat like we were at some royal ball, and he was about to ask me for a dance. He straightened. "You beckoned, my lady."

"Where were you yesterday?"

He kept a poker face. "I had something to do."

"That doesn't explain this morning."

"And it's Maxwell."

"What?"

"I figured you'd know my name is Maxwell, not Maximilian. Maxwell Jude."

I knew his middle name. His parents had named both their kids after song titles. Layla often complained Max won the name jackpot while she was saddled with Layla Prudence. I'd never stopped to ask what song Max had come from.

"I guess I always thought of you like Maximilian de Winter from *Rebecca*."

"Oh. I like that." He smiled, then leaned against the counter. "Debonair beats serial killer."

It took me a minute to mentally flip through the songs Mr. Beckett often played before I landed on the obvious, and I blurted out, " 'Maxwell's Silver Hammer.' "

Max chuckled. "That would be me."

"Why would your parents name you after *that* song?"

His eyebrow rose. "You didn't know I was lethal?"

I bit my lip, trying not to crack up. "I may have had my suspicions."

"I'm a lady killer."

That made me burst out laughing, and his whole face lit up. He was really beautiful when he smiled. God, those lips. My libido cried in frustration at the thwarted sexual chemistry from the memory of those teeth dragging across my throat, and I flushed.

Surely I could resort to hiring someone if necessary.

Before I could say something I'd regret, kids started to roll in for story time, and I forced my brain out of the gutter. We'd finished *Stuart Little* the week before, and Silver Fox had given me the perfect suggestion for the next book. I settled in and announced, "Today we'll be reading *The Little Prince*."

Max waved and raced out the front door. I'd chased him away from my store often enough I didn't understand why I was disappointed to see him leaving before we'd had a chance to talk. I hid my confusion with a smile as I showed the cover art to the children. Some fidgeted, and some stared with wide eyes. I'd always loved this book, and I could still remember sitting on this same floor as Mrs. Moore read it when I was little.

I'd almost finished the first chapter when the door burst open and Max came running in like a man pursued. He grimaced when he realized he'd disrupted the reading and had all the kids watching him. He tiptoed over dramatically and put a finger over his mouth to show he'd be quiet. The kids fell apart laughing, which only exacerbated the chaos.

I arched an eyebrow at him, reproachful. He dropped to the floor, cross-legged like one of the kids, and I had an image clear as day of him in elementary school. He showed the same wide-eyed wonder as he'd ever had.

Pretending nothing had happened, I cleared my throat and continued the chapter, but it was too late. I had to read at double time to keep their attention and finish before the kids began to misbehave.

When I closed the book, Max jumped up and declared, "Show and tell!"

He reached behind him and produced a bag. "Now, you've only just started, so you don't know all the amazing characters you're going to meet, but I'm going to leave you some pretty cool amigurumi figures. Do you know what amigurumi is?" The kids shook their heads. He held up the first blob, the little prince himself, made out of yarn and stuffing. It was kind of pathetic, but also kind of adorable. "See how this is knit? My mom made these for me when I was about your age. Pretty neat, huh?"

He revealed a long lumpy brown object and asked, "Is this a hat?"

The kids yelled, "No! It's a snake!" in a raucous chorus.

"Right. A snake that swallowed what?"

"An elephant!"

"Good. And later, you'll meet these guys." He proceeded to show them a rose, and then . . . "This is my favorite." He revealed the fox. "You won't meet him until later, but you're going to like him."

The parents were starting to look at their watches, so I took over. "Everyone tell Max 'thank you.' "

A cacophony of shouted thanks ensued, and Max smiled. "I'll leave these here." He lined them up on the shelf next to the row of books standing open for display. "Don't take them, okay? But you can touch them if you want."

While most kids returned to their parents, Jason Epstein and Marta Lewis wandered over to the ugly little knit toys and poked each of them. Marta asked, "Is there really an elephant inside the snake?"

She turned her huge eyes to Max, who said, "Yes. Of course there is."

"Wow." She lifted it and squeezed it. "It's a soft elephant."

Jason picked up the little prince. "Who's he?"

"That"—Max opened the book to chapter two—"is the little prince himself. See? You'll meet him next week. You'll be here, right?"

Jason nodded seriously. His mom called, and he wandered off. "This is pretty great, Max. Thanks."

Kids and parents mobbed the single exit once story time was over, though a few parents hung back and kindly purchased something before the store emptied out.

The bell over the door rang again with an incoming patron. I glanced up, and there stood Peter, looking like he'd stepped out of some billionaire romance. Gatsby himself.

Reflexively, I ran a hand over my braid and tucked in any strays.

Despite the fact it was a Saturday, he wore a sharp suit and tie, and his salt-and-pepper hair fell in perfect, smooth waves from an expensive cut and the best products. He sported a tan he'd probably brought back from a recent business trip to Miami or maybe he'd relaxed for once on a beach in Cancun.

Peter dropped a briefcase on the table and looked at me and Max as though he'd found us playing in a sandbox. He scanned

Max from head to toe, like he was deciding if he wanted to buy the clothes Max was wearing.

Max narrowed his eyes and tensed. I couldn't tell if he was worried for my sake or his.

"There's something I'd like to discuss with you." Peter cast a glance at Max. "Alone if I could."

Max crossed his arms and planted himself on the spot as if to defy an order. "Only if Maddie asks me to leave."

Jesus Christ. I hoped they wouldn't piss on my floor. "Max, it's okay. I'll see you later."

His face dropped into a mask of exaggerated disappointment, and I felt a little guilty for making him think I was siding with Peter, but I had agreed to talk with him, and I didn't think I should have to explain my every move to Max, despite whatever had happened between us in the cellar on Wednesday.

Just like that, my stomach flipped over in a kind of sharp physical pain that somehow also felt delicious. Like when we used to go sledding down a narrow trail in the woods by the creek in the winter. Every time, I was convinced one of us would end up slamming into a tree and breaking our necks. But it was a thrill, and we'd keep going until the trail turned to mud from overuse. My mind returned to the cellar and the moment Max's lips brushed mine, and there it was again. Like I'd swallowed a baggie filled with sugar, and it just now exploded.

What the hell was that?

Meanwhile, Peter, unaware of my confusion, opened his briefcase and took out a manila folder that he laid on the table. "Come look at this."

I moved to his side and watched as he spread out several printed pages. His light citrus aroma blanketed him like a scent shield that couldn't be breached by ordinary odors. He always smelled like he'd just come from a day spa. He emanated luxury. I leaned in to look at his documents.

The top left paper showed a photo of a commercial street. The others were interior shots of an empty space.

"What is this?"

"This building is right in downtown Indy, close to where I work. And it's for rent."

"Uh-huh. So why are you showing it to me?"

He pulled out a chair and offered it to me. Once we were sitting catercorner at the table, he continued. "I never meant to make you feel like I didn't support your dream of running this bookstore. I know how much it means to you."

"Do you?"

"I think so, but you have to recognize by now it isn't practical to try to keep a business like yours afloat way out here. Imagine how much easier it would be if you had a store downtown where there's always traffic?" He started dragging over the pages with that light in his eyes he got when he was dogging a trail. He'd probably already talked to the owners and convinced them to hold off any other tenants until he'd gotten my consent.

"You told me you had business out this way."

"I do." He sighed. "This is business."

"You went to all this trouble because you're worried about my bookstore?"

"No." He dropped the pages and folded his hands together. His nails were clean and perfect. "Maddie, I made a mistake."

I blinked several times. Had I misheard him? Was he ready to compromise? "Go on."

"The truth is, I'm hoping you'll reconsider your decision to stay here. I've been waiting and watching for something to open that might lure you back to me."

"So you think you can waltz in here and spring a business proposal on me? Did it occur to you to just talk to me first?"

"And say what? You told me not to come back, so I've stayed away until I could come to you with a valid compromise. You once wanted me, but you also wanted the bookstore and this town. You can't have all three, but I'm hoping that if you could pick two of the three, you'd take the combination that includes me."

It was at least a concession. Selfishly, I still wanted to ask him why I couldn't hold out for all three, but I'd heard enough from everyone to know he'd never consider it. I didn't exactly blame him, but he was once again asking me to make a choice between him and my hometown.

As long as I had a bookstore, couldn't I be happy?

"What's changed your mind about the bookstore? You didn't think it was a wise investment."

He spread out his hands as if to show me he wasn't hiding anything. "That's a fair question. I've been keeping up with the finances, and I've noticed some trends, times when your revenue spikes. I think we could maximize that in a prime location."

"What spikes?"

"When you have events for example. Imagine how many more book signings you could get downtown."

That was true. I practically lived in the bookstore anyway, so what difference did it make where it was? Dylan was leaving. Layla was working. And Max . . . I swallowed. Max had nothing to do with this.

When I said nothing, he pierced me with his steel-gray eyes. "Come on Maddie. Think about it at least. I want you back. I miss you."

Three little words.

I'd come into this world unwanted, and my mom had raised me to know I'd been chosen, that they wanted me, and that I belonged to them. I was theirs regardless of biology. Still, a part of me always feared being unwanted, and part of my draw to Orion was that here, I'd never had to wonder where I belonged.

But something about how Peter wanted me, something about how he made me feel I belonged to him, crossed from a sense of family to a sense of ownership. He'd always let me think I was making my own decisions, but he'd been the one driving the narrative. I'd made two decisions for myself—to become a writer and to buy this bookstore—and he'd hated them both. Or at least he hated that they both took me away from him, took me away from where he wanted me.

Still, he'd come all this way to bring me this opportunity because he missed me, and I couldn't deny my temptation to seize the life I'd once dreamed of with him.

"Two questions."

"Go."

"How long do I have to decide?"

"I don't know. They just listed it last week, and they've already had interest. Maybe a week. Maybe a month."

"That's not a lot of time, Peter. This is a huge decision."

"What's the second question?"

"Could I run that bookstore and still live here?"

He looked like I'd slapped him, but he nodded. "It would be a long commute."

"You were planning to make it."

He looked away, and I knew then that he'd never intended to live in Orion. He'd always planned to string me along until after the wedding and then whisk me off to the big city.

"Well, then, I guess we'll be in touch." I held out my hand to shake and end this transaction.

He wrapped both hands around mine, so warm. "I never should've walked away. Biggest mistake of my life."

It was the best of times. I'd waited seven months to hear that admission. And it hung in the air with no resonance. It wasn't a magic incantation that could transform everything from bad to good. At most, he returned a modicum of my pride, but a bruise doesn't go away with words.

However he felt now, he'd hurt me then. It was the worst of times.

"So why did you? Why didn't you just ignore everyone and show up for your own wedding?"

"Because whenever we'd do anything in this town, it was obvious nobody wanted me here."

"Except me."

"Not even you. You were one with this crazy community. And I understand the lure, Maddie. Here you're always the star of your own fiction."

All the air left my lungs, like I'd been punched. For a second, I couldn't breathe. "What do you mean by that?"

"You aren't the same person here as the girl I met, the girl who had set a goal to start a real career and build a life with me. You came here and became the queen of the struggling artists."

I actually guffawed at that. "And you assume this is the fiction?"

"I'm just saying I was trapped in a love triangle here, and I lost you long before our wedding day."

"Love triangle? With who? Dylan?"

He snorted. "Not with Dylan. With this whole place. I couldn't compete with whatever draws you here, and everyone here made sure I knew that. I hoped I could deprogram you and get you back. I still hope I can, but the clock is ticking, Maddie."

"This is my home, Peter."

"I'd kind of hoped I was."

I had, too, once. "I'll think about it."

He tugged my hand and brought my face inches from his. "Think about this, too."

He planted a kiss on me like bestowing a gift. It caught me by surprise, much as Max's had. I thought, *This should be right. This should be okay.* I'd kissed him thousands of times.

In my parallel universe, this kiss would have been a part of my normal life, but on our wedding day, when he hadn't kissed the bride, when he hadn't even appeared at my side, he'd instead turned our relationship into blackmail. *Love me or leave me.* He might as well have said, *It's me or them.*

"Stay or go," I'd told him later. *"I'll be here either way."*

Then my future forked, leaving me stranded over in this time line. Now here he was, looking to carry me back through the portal. But that gate had already closed, and the world had rebuilt itself without Peter. And just like he'd said, I'd become the hero of my own adventure.

I broke the kiss. "Thanks for coming out, Peter. I'll let you know."

He lifted his head. "We have an audience."

Sure enough, Gentry peered in through the front door window. Satisfied we were no longer sharing a private moment, he let himself in. "Peter! It's so good to see you!"

Peter held out his hand. They clasped like a couple of sharks. "Nice to see you again, Gentry. How's business?"

Gentry looked around, and his eyes landed on the photos Peter had left on the table. Peter immediately stacked them and dropped them into his briefcase. "Convinced her to unload this sinking ship finally?"

I straightened to my full height. "This ship still belongs to me, Gentry."

He glanced at me, then at Peter. "Well, you know where to reach me."

"What did you need, Gentry?" I didn't think for a minute he'd come in for any other reason than to suck up to Peter and pressure me to abandon my post, but he at least attempted to put on a show.

"Ah, right. Don't forget we have a town meeting tomorrow. See you at nine?"

To give Gentry a hint and usher him out more quickly, I said to Peter, "Let me walk you to your car."

He'd parked his Lexus around the corner. I hadn't anticipated the level of interest Peter would attract, but the rumor must have spread as soon as Max said the first word to whoever he'd griped to. No wonder Gentry had raced over. Shawna peered out her door and made a face like we were a couple of worn-out zombies ambling down the sidewalk with our guts hanging out. Team Peter was not represented in Orion.

The whole town would know about that kiss soon enough as well. Gentry was the worst gossip.

We approached from the back of Peter's car, and I giggled at his license tag that read EQUIFOX, a nice play on words for someone in finance.

"I'd forgotten about that," I said.

"It was your idea."

"Was it?"

He ran a finger across my forehead and brushed a strand of hair behind my ear. "Have you forgotten so much?"

"Survival mechanism."

"It's been a hard year. I wish things had worked out differently."

"They could have."

"I hope they still will."

With one last glance, he gracefully slid in and started the engine. As his car pulled away, I watched him exit scene left before I dropped onto the sidewalk and pulled my knees to my chest, fighting the urge to call him back.

Chapter 22

✖✖

Everything around me suddenly bustled, as people who must have frozen to observe my conversation with Peter went about their own business. Heads that had been poking out of shops withdrew and doors closed as soon as my drama was no longer on full display.

Sometimes I questioned why I fought so hard to stay here.

Then Layla sidled up beside me and sat down. "Hey, I was just, you know, out for my afternoon stroll as I do."

I laughed. Someone must have called her to get her to emerge from her cave.

"And I thought, you know what would be great? A beer. You wanna go grab a six-pack from Wilson's and get drunk?"

That was why I stayed. Where could I get nosy friends who knew who to call to be there when I needed a shoulder. "Nah. I'm fine. I've been through a black moment, but that must mean there's daylight on the other side, right?"

Layla said what everyone else always did. "Can we keep at least one foot in reality? Come on. One beer?"

"Thanks. I need to get back to the bookstore."

Before she could react to that, Gentry intoned, "Ladies, please do not block the sidewalk."

It wasn't as if he couldn't have gone around. A couple of kids on skateboards turned the corner, caught sight of Gentry, and jumped off to run the other way.

Rather than argue, I said goodbye to Layla, leaning in for a hug. As she went back to her own dramas, a light rain began to fall, chasing me to the world of books, where I at last felt at home.

Before the rain could damage my inventory, I rushed to pull the table covered in books back inside. When I came back for the sidewalk sign, I saw the joke Max had scrawled at some point.

BOOK LOVERS DO IT BETWEEN THE COVERS!

It would have made me laugh, but it only served to remind me that my covers would remain very cold unless I could find a way to take my bookstore to bed. Was I crazy to stay in my sinking ship? Was I so stubborn I was willing to drown rather than let myself be rescued?

I was about to drag the sign inside when I saw Max on the step outside my apartment.

"Why are you sitting out in the rain?" I called over.

My hair started to stick to my forehead, and a drop of water broke free and rolled down my cheek and into my mouth. I licked my lips. When Max crossed the street, he looked like a brooding hero striding across the moors.

"Do you want to come inside?"

He shook his head. "What did Peter want?"

Just like that. As if the question wasn't fraught. "I don't want to talk about Peter."

"Are you going to take him back?"

"That's none of your business." My fists clenched, and I nearly turned and left him standing there.

"Isn't it? Do you really think that people who care about you are required to stand back and watch you make a mistake?"

"Oh, and you always have all the answers?" I brushed a raindrop from my cheek. I could have been crying for the river tracing a jagged path down my face. "I'm a big girl, Max. I can make my own decisions."

He looked down at his hands, at an envelope he held. "Look. Last year, you didn't want to hear what I had to say. I had a lot to say."

I leaned against the doorjamb, curious enough to listen.

"I've heard you say over and over that you were living in an alternate dimension. You seem to think you can bring two worlds together, that you can fix what Peter broke and find a happily-ever-after. I know this is crazy, and I shouldn't show you this." He lifted the envelope. "This is the road not taken."

I took it and started to open it, but he said, "Not here. You're probably not going to want to talk to me after you read it."

When I stepped away, he laid a hand on my wrist and said, "I'm sorry."

As soon as I got inside, I ripped open the envelope and pulled out four pages handwritten in his distinctive print-cursive combo. I sat down to read.

Maddie's Unparallel Universe
With no objections from the unconcerned onlookers, the bride and groom say I do, *sealing their union in the eyes of God and man. Henceforth, no one can put their marriage asunder. The couple is now yoked. Whither the groom goeth, so goeth the bride.*

They leave the church, man and wife, and head straight to the reception. The bride dances with her groom before the rest of the wedding party. When a friend of the bride's asks if he can cut in, the groom scowls but acquiesces. He doesn't leave the dance floor, but he also does not ask another to dance. At the next opportunity, he reclaims his bride, only jealously allowing another to take his place. Soon, the requests stop altogether, and this pleases him. She no longer belongs to anyone but him, and he doesn't like to share.

When at last the party comes to an end, the couple runs out into the night toward the rented town car that will whisk them to the honeymoon he carefully planned. While the bride has always dreamed of a big trip to England to visit all the places she's read about, her groom believes a traditional honeymoon to St. Lucia is in order. The bride agrees this is a sensible trip. They can spend the time getting reconnected at a romantic destination. After all, this trip isn't about her, she thinks.

Alas, business never sleeps. After the first night of wedded bliss, which, to be honest isn't that different from an ordinary Wednesday, she finds herself searching for breakfast and bringing him back a plate filled with local fare from the hotel restaurant. He waves her off so he can hear the conference call and drink the coffee. Each morning, she spends a little more time away, watching the other honeymooners, envying them as they feed each other pieces of fruit or sneak kisses between bites.

She reasons these people haven't been together as long as she's been with her groom, and so it makes sense she and her ball-and-chain aren't displaying the same level of intimacy they once did. Don't all relationships grow more practical over time?

Soon, they return home, except not to the home she expected. During his many business calls, the husband has finalized an offer on a house closer to the city where he works, miles away from where she expects to move. He knows where she wants to live and spent a year letting her dream of buying that raspberry bungalow in her hometown, all the while proposing houses she'd never choose, never intending to stay.

What can she do now? She's his wife.

What will happen to the bookstore she runs in her small town? Will she have to commute back and forth?

Maybe that's fair since she expected the same of her husband. They both need to make sacrifices. Surely she can still spend time with the people she's grown up with. Surely she can invite her friends to visit her at her new house.

Right?

But her husband wants her home after work. He doesn't like her friends and makes them feel uninvited, so they quit coming over in time. And she wonders: Am I an independent person, or have I been reduced to a piece of property?

If only her friends had known where this would lead and warned her. Why didn't they warn her?

The day she sells the bookstore to the neighboring proprietor, she rationalizes, "Maybe I wanted too much. Maybe I'm not so special. Maybe I don't deserve anything more."

But she's wrong.

The words ran out. I folded the pages and pushed them into the envelope. Max thought I'd be angry with him for writing that, but it only made me want to cry. Reading his concerns on paper drove home how well he understood what I wanted, how much he cared about my happiness. I couldn't say his vision of my intended life was entirely off base. I'd had those same fears. If anything, he confirmed the doubts that had prevented me from leaving with Peter in the first place and the reason I needed him to meet me more than halfway.

Maybe Max thought I'd be annoyed at him for calling me out on my tendency to rationalize Peter's behavior and shift the blame to my own unrealistic expectations. But he was right. Peter appeared to be the kind of romance hero that fueled wish-fulfillment novels. He had it all, and I'd once allowed myself to think that was enough. But no matter how hard I tried to have it all, it was always going to come down to a choice with Peter.

Peter's proposal was another fork in the road. He was right that I could be more successful in the city. It would give me the illusion of having what I wanted: Peter and the bookstore. In exchange, I'd merely lose my identity.

No. As long as I could eke out a living, there was nothing appealing about swapping one bookstore for another, or my town for his. Not even if it meant swapping loneliness for companionship. The spell had broken. The Wardrobe had closed. My choice was made. I was ready to make this new world my reality.

I took out my phone and sent a text. *I've made a decision.*

No response. He was probably driving. I didn't need him to ask me to elaborate. I was done playing games.

Thanks for coming all the way out here, but I'm going to stay here.

Even though I knew I was making the right decision, it still twisted my gut. All that waiting had been in vain. We'd had so much potential, it was killing me to concede defeat, but as long as neither of us would bend, we had different paths to follow.

I owed Max an apology and a debt of gratitude for daring to express his unwanted advice. I was lucky to have him as a friend.

When I closed up for the night, the rain had stopped, leaving a clear sky. The rain had fit my mood better, but with the cooler temperature, I decided to walk out to the creek and think. I stopped at the bridge, sat down, and dangled my feet. As I stared at the water below, I tried to figure out where I was going, what I was going to do. Peter would most likely want me to buy him out of his share of the bookstore, something I wasn't able to do.

My worst fears were coming true.

From the other side of the bridge, a voice said, "Don't jump."

I looked around and saw Max coming down the end of the driveway from my raspberry cottage. "What are you doing?"

He shrugged. "Picking up a little extra work. The Palmers needed a pair of hands, and I had the time."

I scooted over so he could sit next to me. "You need extra work?"

"I know, right? You'd think the catering business in a small town would be booming." He frowned. "Truth is, I've tried everything I can to get my mom's business off the ground. When Gentry took on his own pastry chef, we lost a chunk of business, and now I'm working odd jobs to balance the ledger and pay rent."

"Adulting sucks." I sighed, watching the water weave around smooth round stones. "Do you remember when we decided to follow the creek to see where it went?"

"Yeah." His voice rose half an octave. "We got in so much trouble."

"Layla kept telling us we should turn back, but it didn't seem that late."

"Then all of a sudden it got dark."

"It took us twice as long to find our way back, and everyone was out looking for us."

We both laughed. He leaned against me. "Some of my best memories were in those woods."

As kids, Layla, Max, and I used to roam all over the trails, and we knew all the weird places to explore. "Do you remember that old abandoned concrete monstrosity? I wonder if it's still there."

He stood. "Let's go see."

The rain had left the air sticky. A mosquito buzzed near my ear, and I knew the woods would be teeming with insects waiting to eat me alive. I swatted my neck. "You sure you want to hike in this humidity?"

He arched an eyebrow, challenging. "It never used to bother you."

That was true. When we were kids, I never noticed heat or cold, rain or snow. Whatever we did, we'd get so lost in our world, the weather couldn't distract us. In the winter, after we'd go sledding, my toes would turn so numb I could kick a wall and feel nothing. In the summer, air conditioning was an intermittent luxury confined to libraries, convenience stores, and home. Exploring the woods on a humid July afternoon would have been ordinary. We never called it hiking then.

I fanned my face. "I'm getting old."

"Hardly." He held out his hand. "Come on, Tigger. Let's go for an explore."

Only Max would reference *Winnie-the-Pooh*.

The narrow trail wound down. The forest hummed with life—life that was taking an active interest in me. Max bushwhacked ahead, while I waved off gnats. And then, there it was, the massive cylinder in the middle of the woods. It was a complete mystery to us as kids, but later, we were told it had been intended to become a part of a large well or aquifer. Now it rested at such a steep angle we could step over its ledge on one side and lean against the high wall on the other.

It wouldn't have surprised me to see a younger Max pop up

from behind the far wall and shoot me with a water pistol. The structure made an excellent fort, hiding place, rendezvous point, or make-out spot. Not that Dylan would have set foot in the woods for anything. Peter had never known about its existence.

Max pressed his palms against the slanted curve. A line of sweat ran down the back of his shirt.

I climbed in and sat on the ledge at the point where my feet could dangle. He sat beside me, which was also a little beneath me, so that I naturally leaned into him. I scooted up to no avail. Gravity only intensified with the curve of the wall.

We sat quietly. I'm sure he wanted to ask what I thought about the pages he'd given me to read. I stared at a moth squirming against a spider web where it had gotten itself tangled.

I finally confessed. "You were right. Everything you said. Spot on."

He picked at his thumbnail. "So, Peter?"

"He wanted to show me a rental space in the city. It was tempting." I figured I might as well admit why. "I'm worried about the future of the bookstore."

"Yeah. About that." His lower lip disappeared between his teeth.

I kicked his foot. "You're not seriously going to pitch me your proposal right now?"

"Not that. I owe you an apology." He closed his eyes for a moment and inhaled deep like he was meditating. "I know this is a kamikaze mission, but I've been thinking about what happened in the cellar for the past three days."

"Yeah." I didn't know what to say about that. My libido had finally gone full supernova, and Max had borne the brunt. Not that he'd seemed to mind. Maybe I owed him an apology, too.

"I shouldn't have kissed you like that. I'm sorry. That wasn't fair to you."

Maybe if we'd had an adult conversation about that kiss when we were kids, our friendship wouldn't have taken such a hit. I laid a hand on his knee. He slid his hand underneath and threaded his fingers with mine. In all the years I'd known him, despite kissing him twice, despite spending hours and days in his company, he'd never held my hand like this. It was nice. Familiar. Comfortable.

He traced my thumb with his, and it sent a jolt up my arm. My crazed sex drive was going to destroy our equilibrium. I closed my eyes until he started talking again.

"Maybe I was wrong to kiss you, but it felt right." He sat perfectly still. "Tell me you didn't feel it, too."

I said nothing. If I spoke, I'd have to lie. His kiss felt . . . like an oasis in a desert. But I'd been parched, and he'd been the nearest source of cool, delicious water. I glanced at his lips now, and my heart pulsed in my fingertips, in my thighs.

I couldn't keep denying that my body responded to him like a furnace, and it would be nice to finish what we'd started the week before. But what I'd told Silver Fox held true. I wanted more than passion.

He sighed. "Say something?"

I thought back to that morning, to how we'd gone into that cellar together, chased by a storm. How I hadn't been thinking of Max like that, how that kiss had forced me to think of Max like that. Yes, I'd liked it, but I hadn't seen it coming. Like that night on the bridge, we weren't kissing, and then suddenly we were. No preface. No foreshadowing.

Or had I missed the signs?

"Why did you? Why'd you kiss me?"

"I thought that was obvious." When he looked at me again, he had a hard resolve I didn't recognize. "I love you."

I caught my breath. Three little words that flipped my world upside down, flipped my stomach like a Tilt-a-Whirl.

"You had to know it, Maddie." He hadn't broken eye contact, and I couldn't look away. "I've loved you for as long as I can remember."

Impossible. I took my hand back. "No way."

Max as a romantic hero? I shook my head to clear it. Max was my friend. Apart from Layla, he was my best friend. Why was he putting that at risk?

That kiss had been one thing. A loss of control between two

people who shared an attraction we'd never truly acted on. But love? Romance?

I rubbed my eyes. Silver Fox's phrase came to mind: romance, sex, heartache. If we tried and failed, then I'd lose more than a boyfriend. I'd lose Max. What could be more heartbreaking?

Max chuckled. "When we were kids, I had an unrealistic fantasy about how one day you might look over and notice me. I blew it by making a joke of kissing you. I was terrified to show you what I really thought, so scared you'd reject me if you knew. I just buried myself in school and tried to survive the humiliation."

I sat for a full minute processing all he'd said. Max stared at his hands, waiting. All that competition in high school, had I misread it? Had he been trying to beat me—or win me?

That was the thing. Max probably only thought he loved me because romance was the one area where he'd never come in first. Surely, this was just one more contest.

"You're not in love with me, Max." I don't know why I was whispering. "You're in love with an idea." I had to swallow the urge to hedge. Maybe, maybe I was wrong. The world was changing faster than I could keep up. My throat constricted.

He exhaled. "No, Maddie. *You* are the one in love with an idea. You're so enamored with this narrative you've constructed you can't even see the story unfolding before you."

I steeled my resolve. One of us had to preserve the status quo. "You know I care for you with all of my heart."

He guffawed. "Are you quoting *Little Women*?"

Busted. "Paraphrasing."

"Maddie, I'm not Laurie, and you're not Jo." He took a breath and let it out. "But I can channel Laurie and tell you I'm tired of standing by while you try to fall in love with someone else."

"While I try to?" My irritation rose to the surface. "What the hell?"

"Oh, come on. Everyone has a role in your fiction. Once Peter was knighted as your romantic savior, you stopped paying attention to how wrong he was for you."

"And you're so right?"

I was working up to give him a good piece of my mind, blast him for his presumptuous letter, and put my finger in his face to ask him to stop telling me how to live my life, but then a tear spilled over his eyelash and hung before dropping. My heart rose in my throat.

"I thought—" He twisted his mouth in a frown. "You made me believe your feelings had changed." He looked me in the eye, ignoring the tear rolling down his cheek. "Because yes, I think I'm so right. I don't think there's ever been anyone more right for you."

My hands clenched. He always thought he knew better. But he'd put his heart on the line, so I said, "You'll be right for someone."

God forgive me, my body warred with my mind, urging me to scream *Yes!*, demanding I lean over and kiss him forever. But I was the only one of us fighting to salvage our friendship.

His battle raged on. "I'm not proposing to you. I'm just asking you to date me. It's a simple yes or no. Won't you at least give it a chance, give *me* a chance."

Date. I pictured us at the movies, laughing at the bad dialog, but this time, his arm around me, his lips brushing my cheek. I imagined him walking me home, waiting as I unlocked my door, then kissing me good night. The kiss would heat up, and I'd invite him up. A whole fantasy could have played out, but then I looked at him and saw the expectation in his eyes.

And I recognized it. It was the same look he'd given me whenever he caught me watching him.

This feeling wasn't new to him. Nothing had changed for him, while everything had changed for me. I needed time to sort it out.

"Can't things just go back to the way they were?"

I reached up to touch his cheek, but he turned his face away.

"I'm tired of being whatever it is I am to you."

"You're tired of being my friend?"

"If that's what this is." He sat up straight, moving slightly out of reach.

"Oh, Max. I—"

He held up a finger, and I gestured that I was zipping my lips. "Look. I knew you'd probably reject me. I didn't want to say I never tried, but this was my last shot."

"What are you saying?"

"I'm moving on."

"Moving on? And go where?"

"Indianapolis."

I froze. "*Indianapolis?* Doing what?" Oh, God. I sucked in a shaky breath. He was hitting the eject button anyway. I was going to lose him no matter what I did.

He tugged at his shirt and looked away from me. "Layla's company has an opening in marketing. That's where I went yesterday, to interview. I'm lucky they're considering me. It's been a long time since I worked a legit job, and nobody's overly impressed with my Frankensteined list of half talents."

"I'm impressed."

He smiled, weak. A ghost of an emotion. "Yeah, well. Anyway." He fidgeted. "I told you I can't stay here, but I found out I don't have enough experience to leave. It's time I started planning for my future." He picked up a leaf and began peeling it in half.

"Is that what you want to do?" I blinked back tears. He was leaving me.

He became still and quiet. "No, Maddie, that is not what I want to do."

"What do you want?" *Say you want to stay.*

"I want you." He pinched his lips, then relaxed. "I want to stay, but the catering business isn't working out either. I would have loved to partner with you in the bookstore, and I still think that would have benefited us both, but you won't even consider it. And honestly, I don't think I'd consider that anymore. You can't possibly understand how vexing it is to be me, always with you, but never with you."

"Max." He'd never know how close I was to telling him to fight harder, make me change my mind.

"It's like . . . I keep opening a book to the same page, and the spine is about to crack. I need to try something different."

Turn the page, flip to the next chapter. He was bailing from our story line. "I get it."

I did get it at an intellectual level. After all, I'd been attempting to change the plot of my own book for the past month. But I couldn't wrap my head around the implications. He loved the town as much as I did, and it gutted me to think of him leaving because of me.

Maybe it was time to throw in the towel, give up, sell to Gentry, and follow up on the place in the city. I hated to let Gentry win. I hated to crawl to Peter to ask if the offer still stood. But if I let Max take over the bookstore, he could stay, run his business his way. If this town wasn't big enough for the two of us, I should cede it to Max. It meant more to him.

He jumped off the ledge and faced me. "Anyway. I'm sorry. I wish I could feel differently, but I can't."

There was only one path to follow back out of the woods, and I saw the metaphor. There was only one way forward because all paths led to the same destination: I was going to lose Max.

Chapter 23

I saw it as a good sign Max showed up on Monday morning to deliver my order instead of his mom. I'd slept poorly worrying that there was no way to salvage his friendship. He'd laid it out so black and white: He had to become more. Or less.

Choose him or lose him.

And it struck me that he was no better than Peter threatening to leave me because I couldn't be who he needed. It might not be an explicit ultimatum, but it might as well have been. I was damned if I'd be emotionally blackmailed into a romantic relationship.

Not even if I wanted to be.

But as he moved across the store, I couldn't help but follow him with my eyes, watching him for any evidence of what he'd confessed, trying to reset my worldview. He looked the same as always. Just Max, carrying a stack of boxes. But when he set them on the counter beside me, he cast a glance my way, radiating so much heat and longing, I nearly swooned. Had he always stood so close to me when I signed for the delivery?

I fumbled with the pen, and he caught it before it dropped. His fingers touched mine briefly as he handed it back. Had he always crackled with electricity?

When I said thanks, my voice broke, and I blushed at my sophomoric awkwardness. This was just Max.

I'd fought back the advances of expert seducer Dylan with ease. Peter had nearly crawled back, yet I declined his proposal with barely an afterthought. I'd been right to reject Max. Why wasn't I more sure of my decision in the aftermath?

It didn't help that he acted like he'd failed to get the memo. He carried a cake to the kitchen. The space behind the register was tight, and I heard his breath hitch as his jeans brushed against me. He placed a hand on my waist for the briefest moment, and the potential energy charging around him shot up my spine.

I turned to face him, and it was like we still stood in the cellar, the tempest raging on, my body trapped in a whirlwind of lust. I was Francesca da Rimini, suspended in the second circle of Dante's *Inferno,* helplessly tossed by unquenchable desire.

What would he do if I pushed him against the refrigerator, if I planted a kiss on those kissable lips? I must have been blushing like a sunrise. Maybe my eyes lingered too long on his mouth, because he licked his lips, and I had to force myself to step out from behind the counter. It was like fighting a riptide that wanted to pull me out to sea. I wanted him to pursue me, catch me, take me, but that had never been his way. I moved out of range of his magnetic field, and soon gravity held no power over me. I floated off into the open space of the bookstore, drowning on *what-ifs.*

What was I supposed to do?

I liked him so, so much, maybe even loved him, but that didn't mean we'd make a good romantic couple. I wished he could understand his friendship was more important than that. Maybe it was better for him to go before I lost control and acted on this crazy desire. Could he feel it pulsating off me like a power source?

At last he left, and my body thrummed as I worked in a dreamy haze.

My phone buzzed. I hesitated when I saw the incoming text was from Peter.

Give it some thought, Maddie. We can work this out.

But Max had been right about Peter. He could never be my

Prince Charming. I didn't need to compromise to make him fit my narrative. I needed to burn my last bridge with him.

Please don't call or text me. We need to move on.

And with that, I could no longer pretend my solitude was only temporary. I was on my own.

I messaged Silver Fox.

This has been a hell of a strange weekend.

I wondered if he'd had better luck than me. I could imagine the scene. Maybe he sat in a coffee shop like Charlie, daydreaming about a girl like me. At the idea, I cut a piece of spice cake and carried it over. Charlie pushed the chair out and reached into his bag. As I sat down, he pulled out a red leather-bound book.

"Check this out."

He bit his lip with a coy smile threatening to break out when I gingerly took the book.

The cover was embossed with a gold title that read Northanger Abbey and Persuasion. I ran my fingers across the cover before tentatively opening to reveal the brittle pages, browned and slightly stained, with a typeset no publisher had used in a century. At the bottom of the title page, the year of publication read 1818. My eyes darted back to Charlie. "This is a first edition?"

He nodded, eyes twinkling. Clearly enjoying my confusion and excitement.

"But how? Why?"

He shrugged. "As you know, I'm a ghost, and while I was out haunting, I happened upon—"

I flung a napkin at him. "Seriously."

"Seriously." He took a deep breath and released it. "My family has a rather extensive collection of this and that." He pointed toward the book in my hands. "I came across this in my father's library recently, and I knew he would only see its worth as a function of money. I purloined it to show you. Did you know that, though this book is quite rare, it fetches well below what other Jane Austen books can command."

I shook my head, dumbstruck by all he had revealed. Was

Charlie hiding an eccentric millionaire father? Was he secretly the heir to a fortune?

Shit. I was doing it again. Maybe Max was right. Maybe I was trying to fall in love. I set the book down and took a deep breath. "Charlie, I've been meaning to talk to you."

"Oh?"

How did I begin?

"Back when you told me to choose my own adventure, I considered you might be flirting, and my imagination went a little crazy. I'm a bit worried I've been sending you mixed signals, and I wanted to clear the air."

"Maddie—" He shifted in his seat and I braced for whatever he'd have to say. "I like you."

As far as three little words went, those were probably the best he could have offered.

"I like you, too, Charlie. But I think I've been trying to create a romance hero out of thin air when what I should have been doing is finding out how to be my own hero."

His fingers traced the edges of the book. "Look. I'm not romantic. At all. I'm just a guy who comes to a bookstore to sit in the corner to think and work. Despite how much you struggle to keep your business going, you've shared your food and your company, and that's not nothing. You could have stayed aloof and treated me like a paying customer, but what you do here, you do it because you love the books and the people, and that's why you'll ultimately succeed, Maddie." He dipped his head to come into my field of vision since I'd begun to stare at my own hands to fight back the tears. "As far as I'm concerned, you already are the hero in this story."

Those were the exact words I needed to hear. Relieved I hadn't screwed up at least one relationship, I left him to go shelve some inventory.

There was a simple pleasure in handling books. As I unboxed them, I loved to read the blurb on the back and imagine the world inside the covers. I'd never be truly alone as long as I had a book to read.

It hit me right then and there that I liked my life. That parallel universe I'd wanted so desperately to return to had collapsed in on itself, and I was okay. Things weren't perfect by any means, and part of that was my fault. I could make peace with the here-and-now, although I'd mucked it up a bit.

My phone buzzed, and I reached into my back pocket to read the message from Silver Fox. *How so?*

How so what?

I glanced back at my earlier message where I'd told him about my weird weekend. Oh, right. My thumbs tapped. *I'm back to zero heroes, but I think I'm okay with being alone.*

As I closed up for the day, I discovered the sign out front had been vandalized to read:

Q: WHAT HAPPENED WHEN THE VERB
ASKED THE NOUN TO CONJUGATE?

A: THE NOUN DECLINED.

I frowned at Max's subtle jab and erased the chalkboard. He'd get over it, and we'd stay friends. That's what mattered.

Silver Fox's next message came as I was climbing the stairs to my apartment. *I'm out as well. I did as you said and laid it out. She knows how I feel. She shut me down.*

Was it horrible of me that I was a little bit glad? It was strange to feel a twinge of jealousy over someone I didn't even know, like somehow he owned a piece of my heart and he could hurt me without ever laying eyes on me.

I plopped on the sofa, hoping he was still online.

I confessed, *I've come to the conclusion that there may be romance heroes, but maybe the modern-day princess wants something else. I want too much.*

He didn't take long to respond. *Don't say that. You want what you're worth. Nothing more.*

Aw. *Your Lizzie is a damn fool. You're a sweetheart.*

I sometimes wish I could write to her, just like this. If I could

*just talk to her without her automatically filtering what I want
to say to her through her idea of me, I might break through.*

I paraphrased a relevant line from the fox in *The Little Prince.*
It's only with the heart we can see what is invisible to the eye.

Ha. Yes, exactly.

Why don't you write her, then?

*I think that time has passed. . . . She noped pretty decisively.
So what are your plans with your experiment?*

*I think I'm done. I dated around, but all these guys want me
on their terms. I want a partner, someone who considers my
needs. Why is that so hard to find?*

I want the same thing, actually.

His next message came on the heels of that one.

It's too bad we don't live near each other. . . .

I'd had the same thought, though Layla had given me many,
many lectures on online safety, so I was reluctant to share my location or even my photo in case he was a psycho stalker. What
if he showed up in town and I couldn't shake him?

Surely there was a way we could meet without risking our
lives.

I threw out a query. *Yeah. Where in the Midwest are you, exactly?*

Indianapolis area.

So close. Dare I tell him we were neighbors? What could it
hurt?

*You're not terribly far away. I go into Indy once in a blue
moon.* I bit my lip and added, *In fact, I'm supposed to go to a
concert there Saturday night.*

Yeah? Where at?

I hesitated. The park was big and crowded, and I'd be safe
enough. *It's at the state park.*

*I know it well. No pressure, but if you decide you'd like to
meet, let me know. I can get there easily.*

I took a deep breath. I did want to. No pressure. I had time to
figure it out still.

Feeling courageous, I asked, *Whatever happened to that steamy scene you were supposed to write me?*

I was met by humiliating silence. Why did I keep doing stupid shit like this?

Mortified, I shot off a less salacious message to Silver Fox. *Oh and I was wondering—any chance you put your copy of my book on eBay?*

To my relief, my phone buzzed. *Oh, ha. Yeah. I wrote that thing. It was . . . Uh . . . inspired by what you'd written me.*

Fifteen minutes later, I received an email, and it had an attachment. Even though I'd never laid eyes on Silver Fox, I was as excited to read his fictional scene as I once might have been to hear Dylan's new music. But one of these things was real, and the other was not. How was it possible I felt something for Silver Fox without really knowing him? I didn't even know his name. Was that infatuation? Or was he stroking my ego, releasing dopamine into my drug-starved brain, and making me feel like I was falling in love?

I'll take dopamine for two thousand, Alex.

Double jeopardy!

As soon as I could, I closed the bookstore and carried my laptop upstairs to my little study. I could clean up and deal with inventory and money later. I was dying of curiosity.

Claire,

To answer your first question—no. I wouldn't auction your book. It comes out next week, right? Exciting!

On to your second question . . .

I wasn't going to send you this because it felt wrong while I was seriously pursuing my Lizzie, but that seems to be done. I hope this isn't creepy. Remember, you did ask for it.

While you had fictional characters to play with, this is a scene without context. As such, it reads like a letter to Penthouse. *Still, I think I needed to write this. Imagine if you will that this is what might have happened after I shared my feelings with her.*

I don't know if it's what you're expecting, but it is what it is. I can never run for political office now, lest you uncover my identity and share this with the world. Seriously, though, I hope you know this is for your eyes only.

True confession, I'm nervous. Is this how you feel every time you send your works off to be read? If so, I suddenly empathize and would like to formally apologize for not couching my original review in more praise. If I tell you now that you're a gifted storyteller and wordsmith, will you refrain from any harsh criticism? I can dish it out, but I can't take it.

Without further ado—assuming you're still reading this email instead of jumping straight to the climax . . . Enjoy.

SF

I opened the attached file into Word, praying it wouldn't be a total train wreck of poor writing.

A half-empty bottle of wine stood sentinel from the bedside table, watching silently as I lay upon the black-and-white checkered comforter, waiting for her to emerge. Would she return fully dressed, putting her shoes on as if we hadn't turned a new corner? Would she make an excuse and leave me again with unfulfilled desire?

I wasn't greedy. As long as she stayed, I wouldn't ask for more.

The door cracked open, and she stood, lit from behind. Her hair had escaped her braid when we'd first kissed, and a halo of brown and gold surrounded her obscured features. The silhouette of her shape teased my raw desire with promises.

"Turn off the light," I said, emboldened by her sultry gaze.

With a click, the room plunged into darkness temporarily, until my eyes adjusted again. I felt more than saw her settle next to me. The mattress dipped. The cover shifted. Her hand laced through mine. I sat half up and roped her toward me.

If she had second thoughts about where things were heading, she hid them well. Before I overcame gravity, her mouth was on mine, satisfying one need, birthing another exponentially more demanding. We fell together, tangled, a blur of hands. Fingers unbuttoned, hands gathered fabric, shirts dropped to the floor, and pants, slowly, excruciatingly, slid down legs.

The urgency abated as reality caught up, and I saw her at last as she appeared in my dreams. I savored the moment, drinking her in, a sea of beauty washing over the desert of my impoverished imagination. She hesitated, too, as her eyes dragged down every inch of my body, lingering on some inches longer than others. Her devilish smile was all the approval I'd ever need.

When she moved, it was a languid dance. Her arm rose and fell on my shoulder. Her finger left a trail of gooseflesh in its wake as she mapped the path to my ever-growing passion. I stayed her hand before she could transform the potential into the transactional. She pouted, but I kissed her until she purred, and then I touched her at last.

Her skin, like cream, silky smooth and soft, rippled wherever I sailed. Her mouth made a perfect O when my thumb caressed her nipple. Helplessly, I wrapped my hands around the small of her back and pulled her closer, and when I pressed my lips to her breast, she groaned. Her hips rocked toward me, inviting me, and I sighed. I'd dreamed of her for so long, and now she was here. In the flesh.

My fingers slid across her flesh until I touched between her legs. With an effort, I drew my mouth away and watched her as my middle finger glided across her slick heat. She writhed, twisting like a willow in a storm.

A soft moan became a rasp. "I need you."

I needed to be inside her, but I would die happy watching her face contort with the pleasure I gave her. She reached for me. I caught her hand and pressed my lips against her palm.

She said, "Let me touch you."

Instead, I moved down, away from her grasp. When I slipped a finger inside her, she said my name. And when I bent to run my tongue against her, she screamed it.

Time stood back, swirling, biding its despised return. I lost myself in delicious delirium, wanted, wanting, and she gave herself to me in soft sighs and shouted interjections. She wrecked my sheets with her fists. She guided me with her yeses and encouraged me with her hips. The bed shook, and she snapped her thighs together.

Time clawed its way to dominance, and I crawled to her side. The peace of her post-ecstasy would be enough to satisfy any man. Her eyes opened slowly, and she said, "I want you."

When I started reading Silver Fox's scene, I half expected him to spend entire paragraphs extolling the virtues of the breasts, but by the time I reached the end, I was—how did he say it?—in need of a cold shower. This exchange was not conducive to my health. I almost hoped Dylan would show up on his motorcycle and invite me to his place.

Or Max. If I was being honest, while I read Silver Fox's fantasy, I wasn't picturing Dylan at all.

The door slammed, and Layla came in talking to someone. I cleared my throat, and she spun to face me, saying, "Gotta go. I'm home now," into her phone before hanging up.

"Who was that?"

She almost never talked on the phone. Typed, yes. Spoke, not so much.

"One of my moderators. Something happened while I was driving home, so she called."

"What happened?" I imagined the band breaking up or a stage collapsing.

"Some trolls were flooding the comments section of the blog with all these nastigrams. Ashley's freaking out." She laughed. She got off on all the craziness of her online world. "We're troll proof, though. My posters live for flame wars."

She headed toward her bedroom, but I suddenly wanted to pick her brain. "Hey, Layla?"

Her hand rested on the door handle. "Yeah?"

"Have you ever fallen in love with anyone online?"

Her mouth twisted as she thought. "No. Fallen in hate, yes. Gotten into plenty of feuds. I've flirted with some people. I assume they were men. It's hard to know for sure." She side-eyed me. "Why, are you using a dating app?"

"I was just curious. You never date anyone here, and you're always online. I just assumed . . ."

She came and sat on the sofa by me, one foot under her knee. "Yeah, well. Unlike you, I have no intention of remaining here. So I'm not gonna get tied down."

"Nobody online either?"

"First of all, people who flirt with me on my site are usually after something. They think I have connections, backstage passes, something. I don't. But I never trust that anyone is pursuing me for me."

"So what if I met someone online?"

Her one eyebrow rose just as her jaw dropped. "Talk."

"Nothing much to tell. Remember that reviewer?"

"The three-star guy? You're still talking to him?"

"Crazy, huh? Turns out he's pretty great."

"Just be careful. I've seen real relationships form online, but at the best of times, people are presenting a fiction of themselves."

I considered that. "Maybe, but what's odd is that I've been more honest and open with him than with people I know in real life."

"It makes sense. When you don't have to deal with small talk or the realities of the physical world, you can get to the essence of a conversation. I see that a lot, and many friendships form between the most unlikely of people over some common point of view. I'm always amazed at how quickly total strangers will jump straight into sharing intimate details online. Things you wouldn't imagine telling the neighbor you've known for twenty years."

That sounded familiar. It had been easy to tell Silver Fox things about my love life that even Layla didn't know. "So what's wrong with that, then?"

"It's easy to project onto them what you want them to be."

"Like the people who think you're all-powerful."

"Yeah. Maybe you're letting this reviewer guy stand in for working things out in the real world?"

"I think I'm done with the real world. It's a bit disappointing."

She patted my knee. "Preaching to the choir."

At that, she stood and started toward her own online kingdom where she reigned supreme, but I had one more question. "Do you happen to have the review copy I gave you?" I didn't want to outright ask if she'd sold it on eBay. Surely, she wouldn't do that.

She scrunched up her nose, and I braced for disappointment. "Sorry. I lent it to Letitia."

My stomach lurched. "What? Why?"

"Relax. I didn't tell her it was you, but she came up to ask me to help her get some malware off her laptop, and when I finished cleaning it up, she was curled on the sofa, already into chapter three, and she wanted to keep reading."

That appeased me, and I let Layla slip back to her game of trolls and grabbed my phone to hop on Twitter.

So I read the scene you sent. How did I love it? Shall I count the ways?

Dots appeared, and I waited for his reply. *Really? Can I beg for you to count the ways? I've been trying to write an actual piece of fiction for a while. I don't know how people do it. I feel like everything I write is inferior.*

I knew that feeling well. *We all do. But you pulled me into the scene, and while it had me fanning myself, I was also taken in by the emotion. Is that seriously how you'd proceed with a woman? Because, damn.*

My thighs ached, honestly. Would it be weird to take care of my own needs while thinking about words Silver Fox had written about another woman?

Moments later, he responded. *Why do you say that? Is that not your usual experience?*

I laughed. *Not hardly. I mean, you didn't write one word about your own physical pleasure.*

Had I actually written that? I blushed.

Yes. I did.

The back of my hand hit my forehead, and I nearly swooned. *Break out the smelling salts, I'm heading to the fainting couch.* Layla's admonition to maintain a high alert for pretense brought me down to earth.

You can't be for real.

Ha. I'll admit, I haven't always been as attentive in the past, but I chalk that up to youth and inexperience.

So what changed?

I came to see sex as more than a one-time fulfillment of desire. It's a slow dance. Don't go thinking I'm talking about a marathon tantric lovefest. It's just that I can no longer imagine being involved with a woman if I can't take the time to appreciate her, savor her, make her happy.

Holy shit.

What are you doing Saturday night?

Are you serious?

Was I? Or was I just horny? No, it was more than that. We'd developed a real connection. Or at least a virtual one. I could no longer find the difference.

Would it be wrong to want to meet? Layla was going to kill me.

Where?

I took a breath. *I'll be at the White River State Park for that concert I mentioned.*

I can get there. Where do you want to meet?

What if this was a bad idea? What if he turned out to be nothing like I imagined? Then again, what if he turned out to be exactly what I wanted him to be?

Do you know where the big totem pole is?

Beside the NCAA Hall of Fame?

That's the one. Could you get there by seven?

Wild horses wouldn't keep me away.

I set the phone down and processed my mix of emotion. I went straight past nervous to curious and landed on excited. I probably wouldn't sleep well for the rest of the week.

Chapter 24

✺✺✺

I wasn't sure if Dylan or Max would show up for the book club on Friday. I'd let them both down in the past week, yet for some reason, they came.

Since my life had become a chess game of love triangles lately, I decided to clear that area of discussion off the board and delve into other aspects of *Little Women*.

"Raise your hand if you think Jo should have chosen Laurie." I waited for everyone to agree so I could say, *Great. Let's move on.* But only Midge and I raised our hands.

I sighed. I guess we were doing this. "Right. So Shawna and Charlie, you both think Jo should have remained alone. Max, you're being contrary." I raised an eyebrow. "And Dylan doesn't care either way. So why don't we talk about—"

"Wrong." Charlie held up a finger to draw further attention his way. "I felt that way about Scarlett O'Hara and Jane Eyre, but Scarlett was a brat and Rochester was a brute. Jo's smart, and Bhaer is sensitive and well-suited to her. Jo's world is not Laurie's. She never could've been happy with him."

I narrowed my eyes at him. "If Bhaer's so well-suited, then why does Jo set aside her literary career to run a school with him? Why would she give up her identity for her husband?"

Dylan piped in. "Don't you find Laurie to be a simpering wimp? Bhaer had an artistic temperament, like Jo. And he was out in the world, where Jo wanted to be. He could meet her intellectually and keep her life exciting. All Laurie has to offer is a childhood devotion. Why would that ever be enough for Jo?"

Dammit. They were making good arguments.

Midge said, "Ah, but does she love Bhaer?"

Exactly my point. "Right!"

Max dropped the anvil. "Your question is moot. She doesn't love Laurie."

"But . . ." I had no answer.

"You love Laurie, but Jo does not. She could've tried, but she did the right thing by not leading him to believe there could ever be more." His frown matched mine.

Were they all using this book club to take revenge on me?

At last Shawna raised her voice. "You were right about me, Maddie. Bhaer surprises her and convinces her against her own resistance to take him. There's definitely a basis for a good friendship, but to me there's always something sad about Jo's choices. Her imagination is so powerful, I don't think any man could ever satisfy her completely. I wonder if she could truly be happy with either of the two men, or if she'd be better off living in a fictional world of her own creation."

I heard her, and I took her meaning. It was clear to me everyone present knew I'd turned down every flesh and blood man who'd shown any interest. Rather than acknowledge their subtext, I gave them all a pointed look. "Could we get back to talking about the book!"

Everyone's eyes sought out someone else's, and they all pulled faces like I was the one in the wrong.

"Fine. Talk amongst yourselves, then. I'm done." I stood and dropped my book on my chair. As soon as I got outside, I knew I'd overreacted, but they couldn't pretend they weren't all talking about me.

The door opened, and Shawna slipped out. "You want to tell me what that was about?"

"You're all giving me advice disguised as literary analysis."

"Oh, Maddie. You really identify far too much with central characters."

"See? Isn't that what you just said?"

"Close. But I also said Jo is probably better off without any of the men in her world. You know I don't think that about you."

My voice cracked. "You think I should go with Dylan."

She laid a hand on my shoulder. "Look. You were happy when you were with Dylan. I don't know if you'd be happy with him now. I'd just like to see you take a chance on someone. You're going to over-judge every single guy against unrealistic expectations, and nobody will measure up."

"Well, you'll be happy to know I *am* taking a chance."

She tilted an eyebrow. "Max?"

I laughed. "No." Then I frowned. "No, not Max. Wouldn't that be easy, though?" It would solve ninety-nine problems. He'd be happy. He'd stay.

I imagined walking along the stream together, hand in hand with Max, kissing on the bridge at sunset. My heart cramped at how nice that could be, but then I pictured myself sitting on the bridge, alone, after things ran their course, and we'd lost it all. We were attracted to each other, but would we be compatible as more than friends? I couldn't risk him to find out.

"So who?" Shawna brought me back to reality.

"Would you believe I met this guy online?"

"Letitia's dating service?"

I winced. "No, we just started talking, and we're gonna meet. Tomorrow night."

She grimaced. "Is that safe?"

"Don't worry. I promised Layla I'd go to see a concert to-morrow over at the state park. We've agreed to meet in public before the show. You know that totem pole?" She nodded. "It's gonna be like *Sleepless in Seattle*."

She didn't look convinced. "What do you know about him? Have you exchanged pictures?"

I laughed at the valid questions. "I don't know much, and I've never laid eyes on him. I don't even know his real name. Crazy."

"So you're just going to go and hang around, waiting? What if he never shows? Or what if he's, I dunno, a teenager?"

I chortled. "I don't think he is, but I've thought it through. I can scope out anyone hanging around and bounce if he seems too sketchy." I tried to conjure an image of that meeting. "I don't think he'll be sketchy. I hope not. I hadn't considered he might not even show up. What if he comes and scopes *me* out, then leaves?"

"That would never happen. Look at you. This guy doesn't stand a chance."

A clank from the alley revealed that we had company. I peered around the corner to discover Gentry behind the trash bins, closing a lid.

"Evening, Gentry. Nice night for eavesdropping."

He harrumphed and continued past us into his restaurant.

Shawna said, "Good luck tomorrow. You know I just want what's best for you. I hope you figure things out."

So did I.

Chapter 25

✖✕✖

As tempted as I was to message Silver Fox Saturday morning, I knew I'd be seeing him later, and I didn't want to seem overeager. I wished I'd pressed him for his name or his picture, but then I would have had to give him mine. I got to the shop early to take care of some inventory so we could head out to the concert. I heard the toilet flush and carefully set down the books I'd been unpacking so I could make sure I didn't miss a customer.

I caught Gentry's backside as he headed toward the front door and called out to stop him.

He spun back. "Ah, here you are. I seem to have a bit of your mail."

I reached out and took the proffered envelope. It would be just my luck for the electricity bill to go errant. A quick glance showed it was nothing more than a credit card offer.

"Thanks, Gentry."

He lingered. "I was wondering if I could get you to do me a small favor this evening. I hate to ask, but my pastry chef has me in a bind."

"Oh?" I didn't like where this was going.

"He needs extra refrigerator space. Just for this evening. I thought maybe—"

I cut him off. "I'm not going to be around tonight. In fact,

I'm closing the store a little bit early." I fake winced. "Sorry. Can it wait until tomorrow?"

"I'm afraid not." His face brightened. "Perhaps when you get back. How late will you be gone?"

"I don't know, Gentry. Late."

He blinked. "If you left me a key—"

That was not going to happen. "Nope."

He pouted. "What if you left it with Max?"

"Sorry. He'll be with me."

Because of course Max had invited himself to tag along to the concert. Secretly, I was glad because I had a friendship to repair, and it would be easier in the comfortable trio of yore. We could pretend like it was old times, and maybe it would be. Maybe he'd change his mind about leaving.

As Gentry was heading out, Dylan showed up, and my heart skipped a beat.

"Hey," he said. "Just stopped in to check on you."

I pulled out a chair and beckoned him to sit. I took a seat across from him. "Are we good, Dylan?"

"Always."

Those stormy eyes made me almost wish he'd pushed a little harder. *That's what she said,* I thought. "I wish . . ." I trailed off, wanting to share with him every possibility I would've loved to have written into existence, but I worried such admissions would reopen a door I'd already closed.

"Me, too." He shrugged, like I didn't need to put it into words. "But you were right. I shouldn't have asked you to tie yourself to my goals."

"Dylan . . ."

He slid his hand into mine. "You know, when I left the first time, I was full of myself with confidence, but it wasn't long before I lost my way. I thought I needed you with me this time because you always give me courage." He sat a little straighter and tightened his grip. "But I can do this on my own."

"I know you can."

"Will you promise to come see me whenever you can?"

"Of course." My heart broke a little, and I suddenly wished I could clone myself so one of me could run away with Dylan and lead a life of adventure. "When do you leave?"

"Tuesday." He checked his watch. Dylan was the kind of guy to still wear one. It wasn't expensive, just a plain black leather strap with a functional clockface.

I squeezed his hand. "We'll talk later?"

"I have to be somewhere this evening, but I'll try to catch you before I head out."

I didn't know if he meant for the day or forever, and the reality hit. He was leaving again. What if he never came back this time? But I'd made my choice, so I couldn't cry about losing him now.

Layla spread out the blankets and shot pictures. I checked my phone. It was almost seven, and I didn't know how long it would take to get to the totem. I stretched casually and was about to make an excuse to leave when Max jumped up.

"I think I'm gonna go walk around a bit. I wanna see how small the children's maze looks now."

Perfect. I could walk that far with him, then ditch him. I stood. "I'll come with you."

Layla called after us. "Don't be too long. You don't wanna miss the show."

We moved against the crowd until we exited the concert area and found ourselves along a path that led toward the totem.

Max snapped pictures. "Why do they even call this a maze?"

Good question. It was nothing more than a bunch of long bench-height stones arranged in concentric circles. While he went through his photo roll, I walked ahead, hoping he'd linger, but he caught up and stayed at my side. I worried he might have created this moment to get me alone, but he didn't look up from his phone, and I had to steer him around a couple pushing a stroller.

A bit farther, we passed a tall modern sculpture. Max stopped again to take a picture, then messed around, typing in his phone. I tried to take the opportunity to leave him behind again, but he said, "Hold on."

He was going to make me miss Silver Fox. "Can you do Facebook later?"

"I wasn't doing Facebook. I was sending a picture to Layla."

"I'm sure she can wait for the photo gallery, but she'll kill us if we miss the opening act."

"You can go back."

Not an option. I could see the totem from where we stood. A series of narrow canals ran along the path to our left and ended just beyond the meeting place. We walked along the path until we reached the Hall of Fame directly across from the totem, and I climbed the steps as if that had been my destination. I peered through the glass doors, then glanced at the statue.

Would I know Silver Fox on sight?

A woman posed for a picture, and a couple strolled past arm in arm. My fears of a throng of possible Foxies was mitigated. Instead, I might have been stood up. I checked the time on my phone. It was a little past seven. Maybe he'd come and left. Maybe he was late. Or maybe he had the same idea and stood watching for me from a distance. Max at my side would have thrown him off. He wouldn't be looking for a couple.

Max left me to walk beside the canal, taking pictures and stopping to upload them.

He acted like nothing had happened between us the week before, like he always did, and I realized that what he'd said must be true. He'd been living with this reality for years and acting like he wasn't suffering with an unrequited emotion.

I pulled up my Twitter app and DMed. *Where are you?*

A moment later, I had a response. *I'm here.*

I rubbed my forehead and messaged. *I don't see you.*

Was I waiting for Godot?

Max started to walk around the end of the canal, but I didn't follow. I was too intrigued now to figure out where Foxy was. My phone vibrated.

Now do you see me?

There was still only Max there. I started to type, *No.*

"Maddie?" The voice came from my left.

I turned and there stood Peter, taking the last few steps toward me. Max started back, but when he saw Peter, he froze.

Peter casually relaxed, with a hand in his pocket. He didn't seem surprised to see me.

I descended the steps. "What are you doing here?"

"A little bird said you might be here." He winked, like I should understand.

Who knew I was coming here besides—"Layla?"

"Nope."

I scanned the people passing through the area again but didn't see anyone who appeared to be looking for me. Except Peter. The only person who knew I planned to come here besides Layla and Shawna was . . . Silver Fox.

I clapped my hand to my mouth. *No.*

"Silver Fox?"

He laughed and ran his hand through his hair. "Why, thank you."

"How?"

"How what?"

"How is it possible? You're . . . Are you—?"

"You wanted to meet. I'm Peter." He held out his hand like we were being introduced for the first time, and I shook it in a total stupor. "What a funny coincidence."

I blinked, trying to clear my head of assumptions and preconceptions. Had I been talking to Peter this whole time?

Nothing made sense, and I couldn't understand my disappointment. What had I been hoping? I'd wanted Silver Fox to be someone new, someone who could surprise me. But if Peter had been capable of saying everything he'd written, maybe I'd underestimated him.

I stood there, mouth hanging open, gobsmacked, reeling with another mind-shattering world flip, trying to formulate a coherent question, but he just raised an eyebrow. Mischievous.

"I don't understand." Before I could fully interrogate him, the screech of guitars alerted me that the show was beginning. I'd promised Layla I'd sit through the whole thing. "Do you have a ticket to the concert?"

"I can get one."

I called to Max, and he looked around once more, like he'd lost his keys or something. He waved us away. Clearly, he didn't want to be a third wheel.

Before we moved out of view, I looked back. Max paced back and forth, probably killing time to avoid seeing me with Peter. I felt a twinge of guilt for the loss he must be feeling.

If I was being honest, I was feeling it, too.

Layla gave me a dirty look when Peter and I sat on her blanket. I couldn't figure out if it was because I'd missed most of the opening act or because I'd brought Peter with me. After Peter had bought a ticket, I'd stopped to get four cups of beer, assuming Max would eventually get over his disappointment and make his way back. When I handed one of the beers to Layla, she begrudgingly took it with a sneer.

I wanted to quiz Peter on every aspect of the correspondence we'd been having. There was so much that didn't make sense. When did he start reviewing books? Why had he given me such an unfavorable review? How'd he even get a copy? Had he known it was mine all along? He knew I wrote, but I'd never told him my pen name.

And those chats . . . He'd never been so flirtatious with me over text messages before. Silver Fox did say he'd changed. Had Peter changed?

Did I owe him a chance to find out?

I'd chided Silver Fox's girl for failing to see past her preconceived notions of him. Had I misjudged Peter? Everything about Lizzie Bennet . . . had that been about me?

As soon as the opening act left the stage, Layla launched into a monologue to bring me up to speed on the main band we'd come to see. "So, the lead singer is the brother of the girlfriend of the lead singer of the band I run the fan forum for. Got it?"

I shared a glance with Peter. "Uh. Sure." My questions would have to wait until later.

"Micah is stunningly beautiful, but so is his lead guitarist, Noah. Noah is pretty like a girl, like a Duran Duran. Like a Hanson. He's pretty."

"Like Scarlett Johanson?" I asked.

Peter chuckled. "Did we come to hear a boy band?"

Layla's eyes went wide, and her cheeks filled with color. "Never! This is a rock show."

When she'd stopped enthusing, I turned to talk to Peter, but two things happened at once. First, Max appeared and kicked over the beer he didn't know was there. Second, the featured band ran out onto the stage and started to play.

We missed half the first song from checking everything that might have gotten wet, then moving the blanket over several feet while Layla cursed us out for talking over the music.

At last we settled in and watched the show. I didn't know the songs, and I was focused internally, walking back every conversation with Silver Fox. Had Peter written me a sex scene? Had I sent him a sex scene? My cheeks flamed.

It came as a surprise when the sound system went silent, and the crowd chanted for an encore. I started to get up to leave. Encores were the time for beating the crowd out of the parking lot, but Layla grabbed my wrist. "Oh, no you don't."

By the time we left, we had to shuffle out of the exits like zombies, one lumbered step at a time. Peter had brought his own car, but Layla would never forgive me if I bailed before the obligatory concert postmortem on the drive back. Peter asked if he could follow us to town. I agreed.

We had a lot to talk about.

Chapter 26

✖✖

It was late when Max pulled up along the curb to let me and Layla out. He hung his head as Peter's headlights swung around the corner. I told Max I'd see him later and slammed the door.

As I waited on the sidewalk for Peter, something caught my eye in my bookstore. A light was on, and someone was moving inside. I jogged over and noticed the glass on the front door was shattered, and the door stood ajar.

Max got out of the car. "What's going on?"

I walked inside and flipped on the overhead light. I stopped dead. I was standing in a stream winding across the floor.

"Maddie?" It didn't even surprise me to find Gentry poking his head in. "I noticed water out on the sidewalk and called Jack. We had to break your window to get in. If you'd left me a key . . ."

If I'd left him a key, how would that have kept my bookstore from turning into a flood zone?

Jack emerged from the bathroom, wearing rubber shit-stomping boots and carrying an augur. "The valve wasn't closing properly in the tank. Looks like the water could've been running over for hours."

"Holy shit!" said Max, pushing past the others and treading carefully around the puddles. The wooden floors would be forever ruined. God only knew if this reached into the storeroom to the boxes all over the floor. I'd have to close down to deal with this.

I'd be lucky to sell this place at all now.

Then again, Gentry wanted to demolish it anyway.

"This is too much," I said to nobody in particular. "I can't do this anymore."

I backed out of the store into Peter waiting on the sidewalk. He put an arm around me. "We'll call the insurance company in the morning and—"

"I'm going to sell it. You were right the whole time."

"What?"

"That bookstore has been treating me like a rejected transplant ever since you left. It clearly doesn't want me here. There's nothing for me here."

"Maddie, you're in shock." He rubbed my back. "Come on. Let me take you home, and we can make plans in the morning."

I started toward my apartment, but he tightened his arm around my back and urged me toward his car. "Peter, this isn't the way home."

He stopped and spun to face me, grasping both my shoulders. "Come home with me, Maddie. You can't fix anything tonight, and we need to catch up." That was true. I had so much to ask him. He stepped in close. His forehead slowly met mine, more by inertia than by its own propulsion, like an astronaut touching down on the moon through weak gravity. Something about that gentleness cracked me, and I started to sob.

His thumbs brushed my cheeks, then tucked loose hair behind my ear. His fingers tangled into what had started out as a braid, and he tilted my head up so I was forced to face him.

His lips pressed against mine, but they might as well have been made of wax. He'd won. After all my efforts, he'd get everything he wanted.

And why not? All the people I cared about would soon leave me. I could open a new bookstore and start over. Maybe Peter and I could take up where we left off.

Everything he'd said to me as Silver Fox had proven he could be more than I'd given him credit for. I'd never suspected him of the level of adoration he'd written in that one steamy scene. I'd fallen back in love with him through his words in the end after all.

I broke away from him, and sighed. "It's weird to think that all this time, I've been your Lizzie."

He scowled. "My what?"

"Lizzie? From the book? You know—" Did he? "—*Pride and Prejudice?*"

He shot double finger pistols at me. "Oh, right! Because Elizabeth Bennet's such a stubborn character."

How could he forget something so critical to our conversations?

I took a step back. "Do you remember talking about this?"

He frowned. "Uh—"

I narrowed my eyes. Gears turned. Maybe this all felt wrong because it was.

"By any chance, have you ever de-tasseled corn?"

"Done what?"

"And what's your opinion on *The Little Prince?*" I pictured the ugly little knit figures sitting even now on the shelf of the bookstore.

"I haven't read that book in years. Why are you asking me all this? Is it about the bookstore? You know I'll support you when—"

"Have you read my book?"

"Well, yeah, of course." He scratched his neck. "I mean the parts you showed me before. It's really great. I was surprised at how good."

"Oh, God." I dropped my face into my palms, and my shoulders slumped. It was a miracle my bones held me upright at all. I looked up at him. "Would you excuse me? I need to think."

I walked down the sidewalk past the bookstore. Max had found a Shop-Vac and was sucking up toilet water. I continued until the sidewalk ran out. How had Peter known to meet me if I hadn't been talking to him?

Under a streetlight, I got out my phone and opened Twitter to find a series of messages from Silver Fox.

The last I'd read before I met Peter said, *Now do you see me?*

They continued for about ten minutes, all variations on, *I'm at the totem. It's the one by the Hall of Fame. Is there another one? And the last one. I don't know why you've stopped responding. I'm gonna assume you came but changed your mind for whatever reason. I'm sorry. I thought we'd made a pretty solid connection. It's okay, though. Take care.*

Fuck. I'd totally blown my chance to meet him. Where had he been? What was Peter playing at?

I hit reply. *So sorry for earlier. I never did see you even though you were clearly right there in front of me.*

When I strolled back up the sidewalk, I caught a snatch of conversation and paused.

"I promise she'll sell." Peter's voice. He no longer stood where I'd left him. "You just have to offer her enough to pay off her mortgage. Hell, you could just assume her mortgage. That would be even faster."

I inched toward the voices, stopping when I came close enough to their origin—a narrow alley beside my shop, where the trash bins lived. Fitting.

"Well, hallelujah. It took long enough. So she'll go with you tonight? And you'll keep our deal? I've done everything you asked." Gentry.

"We'll talk tomorrow. I need to make sure she doesn't change her mind."

"I'd like to start the paperwork as soon as possible."

I rounded the corner. "Hello, boys."

Gentry turned around with a dramatic dawning of surprise that almost made me laugh. I suppressed the urge to wave my index finger aloft and demand to know, *What sort of villainy is this?* But I'd gathered enough from what I'd overheard.

I spun on my heels. I needed to get far away from Peter before I completely lost my shit, but he chased after me and laid a hand on my shoulder. I shrugged him away and attempted to storm down the sidewalk.

He called, "Maddie, you don't understand."

That stopped me dead. I faced him. "Don't I?"

"It's not what you're thinking."

"If you know what I'm thinking, I must be on the right track."

"Maddie, I just missed you."

"But do you care about me? Do you worry about what I might need? About my dreams? About the future I want? Or do you just look for ways to manipulate my life to get your happily-ever-after, never mind mine?"

He shook his head. "I'm just urging along the inevitable. I've kept an eye on your finances, Maddie. You're on a collision course with bankruptcy. It's better to get out now while you can. Gentry's willing—"

"Don't you talk to me about my finances or about Gentry. Did he somehow rewire my electricity? Did he throw a branch through my front window? Which of you is going to reimburse me for the flood now destroying what's left of my store?"

He held up his hand. "I don't know what you're talking about."

"Don't you? Tell me this, then. Who was the little bird who told you to meet me at the park?"

He glanced away. "You did. Online."

"Bullshit. You don't even know what we supposedly talked about. Who was it?"

"Can we drop this? You're overreacting. You always imagine more drama than exists in reality."

"Do I? Let me guess. Gentry overheard me telling Shawna I was meeting someone. And you both thought maybe if you showed up, you could deceive me into believing I was looking for you."

He swallowed. I'd hit my mark. He stepped closer. "Maddie, listen. You wouldn't even talk to me."

I looked up at the dark sky, searching for a star to wish on, but they were drowned out by the town's lights. Appropriate. "It almost worked, but I don't know how long you thought you could sustain that. You weren't the person I was looking for."

This broke through enough to bring a wrinkle to his perfect brow. "Maddie, exactly who were you meeting?"

"A friend. Someone who understands me. Someone who's listened to me and spoken to my heart." I let my mind drift to the park, where I would have met Silver Fox if Peter hadn't come. If I'd waited. He'd said he was right there. But the only person there had been . . . My hand flew to my mouth. I whispered, "Someone who cares about me."

I backed away, and Peter reached out as if he were trying to catch a fleeting ghost. But I wasn't even in the same plane of existence anymore. "Maddie, come back. Let's talk."

I wanted to run, but I knew there would be no freedom as long as I owed him money. Panic fluttered in my gut as I envisioned how much harder my life would become if I leveraged more debt to buy him out. I'd have to find a way. "An accountant or lawyer or someone will be in touch about your stake in the bookstore. You don't want it. Please don't make it difficult."

He laughed. "You can't be serious. You don't have equity. You don't have collateral. You can't raise the money."

I'd find a way. "Goodbye, Peter."

I wished I felt as confident as I pretended to be. I'd only managed to keep from crying due to righteous anger. As I walked away, for good this time, I was hit by a wave of despair and bitterness for my insecure future and my lost past. I questioned my judgment for letting myself be manipulated again and again into thinking I was making my own decisions when even the ones I thought were mine were mired in duplicity. How could I trust anything or anyone?

Yet, there was one person who'd warned me not to trust Wickham. I'd faulted him for trying to take away my agency at the time, for selfishly manipulating the arc of my life, but Max had risked our friendship to save me from myself.

I raced back and stopped in the doorway, taking a good look at him. Seeing him true for the first time. Silver Fox. He had to be.

He glanced up. "Still here?"

I stepped in and grabbed the mop. "Well, it is my bookstore."

We rolled up our sleeves and started cleaning together. Thankfully, the storeroom door had been tightly closed when all this happened. Max had already done the literal shit job of carrying the water out and disposing of it, God knows where. We mopped and bleached the floors, and I watched him out of the corner of my eye, trying to reconcile two different people into one.

How would he feel if his identity was blown? If I confessed to him that I knew his secret alter ego, I'd have to reveal mine. He'd know he'd given me that terrible review. Worse, that he'd sent me word porn.

He put the mop into the wringer and twisted, those biceps tightening and reminding me of how I'd discovered them through his clothes when he'd kissed me. My breathing sped up, and I put more effort into dragging my own mop against the wood, back and forth, as I recalled how he'd lost control of whatever constraints he normally kept in check when he had me in his arms in the cellar.

I gasped as I realized that he'd inspired me to write a sex scene. I'd emailed him a sex scene. I definitely couldn't tell him that. Could I? If I was being honest with myself, the only reason I'd even broken through my own barriers to write it was because of that kiss.

Waves of revelations continued to hit me. How had I been so stupid?

I pushed my sponge into the wringer as the truth reverberated again. Max was Silver Fox. My Max, the boy who'd kissed me on the bridge when we were kids, the man who'd put his heart on the line last week, that Max was the author of my palpitating heart.

I needed time to process my new world. Had this happened in any books I'd read? Surely, I could find one example from literature to glean some answers from. Was this how Simon felt in *Simon vs. the Homo Sapiens Agenda*?

We left late and exhausted. I avoided Layla. If I told her everything, she'd force the issue. I hadn't even begun to sort out how Max might react. I fell into bed and drifted off replaying every exchange I'd ever had with Silver Fox, trying to picture my Max as the flirty, confident, beautiful soul I'd fallen in love with. Because I had. I'd fallen in love with Max.

* * *

Max showed up Sunday and Monday to help empty the front of the shop. The whole place needed to be evacuated, so to speak. I took inventory from the shelves, furtively casting glances at Max while he packed the books away in boxes. He was the same boy I'd always known, so why did he make my stomach flip so hard?

He'd grown more distant since we'd talked, since I'd told him no, like he was preparing to give up on me, biding his time until he could start the next chapter.

What if I told him the truth, that we'd been connecting anonymously for weeks? I couldn't get him to make eye contact with me, let alone listen. What if it didn't matter?

The sad truth I now realized was that it shouldn't have mattered. The only thing Silver Fox had done was peel the blindfold from my eyes, the cloak from my heart. Silver Fox allowed me to recognize what I should have known already. I'd loved Max for a very long time.

My insurance adjuster, Ross, came in Monday and cataloged the damage. Fortunately, my policy covered overflow. I couldn't prove Gentry had tampered with the toilet machinery, but I wasn't buying his explanation for breaking my front door.

Once Ross had examined everything, he invited me and Max to take a look at the paperwork.

"I have great news." He pulled out a yellow notepad. "We'll get solid numbers on this in a couple of days, but I'm recommending all this flooring—" he waved at the boards from the entry past the register "—needs to be replaced. It's old and absorbed a lot of water. But we'll do the whole floor since you'll want it to be consistent. You'll need to document the cost of any damaged inventory. The best news is that you can also make use of business interruption insurance, which will cover loss of income while these repairs are made."

Holy shit. "That's great."

We spent another hour talking details and getting a list of approved contractors to start the work. Then it was just me and Max, alone in an empty bookstore.

I stared at the paperwork Ross had left. "I don't know what

I'm going to do. Even if this weren't going to end up costing me a dime, I'm barely keeping my head above water. And now I need to buy Peter out. Why am I bothering with all this?"

Suddenly, it all seemed hopeless. I was never going to pull myself out of this hole.

"What if—" I couldn't believe I was thinking this. "What if I sold this to Gentry and then found another space, maybe for lease?" I'd never get another mortgage on my own. Peter's signature had covered my own lack of credit. "Maybe the empty video store over on Wabash."

Max slouched. "Yeah. I suppose you could do that. But it would be a shame. No other place would have the history of this bookstore."

We both looked around from the coffee shop where we sat, which hadn't existed when Mrs. Moore was alive, to the rows of now half-empty bookshelves. Max smiled. "Do you remember when we used to sit in beanbags over there on rainy days?"

"Yeah. When it was sunny, we'd ride our bikes to town. I can't believe our parents let us do that."

"I think we told them we were going to the pool."

I laughed. "Yeah." We did go to the pool sometimes, too. Or sometimes we just rode into the woods or down back roads. We knew every square inch for a square mile. No place on earth would ever feel like home like this town did.

He shifted in his seat and said, "You could try talking to my mom. She might be willing to buy in to help you out, though to be honest, she's looking to downgrade the business once I'm gone."

My eyes widened. "What?"

"Don't worry. She's going to keep helping you out, but she's thinking of going back to specializing in wedding cakes. The whole bakery expansion was mainly my idea."

I should have listened to him before. "Tell me your idea."

He side-eyed me. "Now?"

"Please?"

He gestured back toward the register. "Well, first off, you

have this amazing kitchen. I know it all works because I tested it when I made those gingerbread cookies."

"Is that what you were up to?"

"I wanted to make sure my plan was viable. Right now, you're selling the bare minimum to offer something to your existing customers. I was thinking that my mom or I could come here early mornings and fill your case up with the most amazing baked goods. We could continue to take orders, but we'd function more like a real bakery and let people come pick up their own stuff. And I had other ideas. . . ." He trailed off.

"Like what?"

"You have so much unused space." He glanced toward the ceiling. "Your upstairs—"

"Is an office."

"An unused office. I've been up there. You keep boxes and a desk up there. You could be using that."

"For what?"

"I dunno. What if you moved the children's area upstairs?" A lightbulb visibly went off over his head. "Or a space to accommodate teens? They need a place to hang out."

"So you did plan to take over." I knocked his foot with mine so he'd know I was teasing, but the truth was he made total sense. I'd fixated on the smaller children because moms were always looking for a Saturday morning enrichment opportunity, but it was the town teenagers who wandered around trying to kill the boring hours after school. It was the teens who'd left dick pics on my window.

Or had that been Gentry, too?

It might work.

"What if we did it? What if we partnered up and put your plan in motion?"

The smile melted off his face like I'd thrown acid on him. "I already told you why I can't." He scooted his chair back. "I'd better finish emptying the shelves."

I stayed seated, watching Max work. He wasn't very efficient. He'd pull down four or five books, then flip through one of them, either smiling as if at a fond memory or raising an eyebrow like he was making note of a book he'd need to remember later. At one point he asked, "Hey, maybe I can take some of these home?"

He'd earned a few books as payment for all the extra work. "Sure, why not?"

I grabbed a box, too, and started loading up everything I could from the children's corner. I came across the ugly knit *Little Prince* toys Max had brought, wondering how I'd managed to miss so many signs. I lost myself in fond memories, dating back years.

Mrs. Moore told us to gather 'round as she read the story of the taming of the fox. I sat and listened with wonder as the prince talked to the wise fox, who insisted the boy was nobody, nothing to him. The fox didn't need the boy because the boy hadn't yet tamed the fox. The fox said, if the little prince could tame him, the fox would regard the boy as unique in all the world. Once tamed, the fox would depend on the boy, and in return, the boy would be responsible for the fox. The fox told the boy that being tamed would be like the sun shining on his life.

The boy's very footsteps would be like music.

I didn't understand why Mrs. Moore cried as she read this. I didn't understand why I cried now. Had I been tamed? Or had I tamed the fox?

All this time, I'd been looking for a romance hero. I'd never realized he was waiting for me.

Chapter 27

In the early evening, I was in the storage room, taping and labeling boxes when the bell tinkled up front. Hearing voices, I went to see what was going on and found Dylan and Max chatting amiably.

Dylan smiled at me. "Hey, Layla told me what happened. I'm at your service."

"Thanks for coming, Dylan."

"That's what she said, am I right?" He held up his hand for a high five, but Max just rolled his eyes and headed toward the large shelves that needed to be cleared out.

"Do you think we can lift these?"

The bell rang and in stepped Charlie. "I heard you needed a burly man."

I tried not to laugh at that joke, even though Charlie himself had made it. He might not be strong compared to Dylan or Max, but he was more helpful than me. "I can't believe you're here."

"Why wouldn't I be? A damsel in distress such as yourself must need heroes to rescue her." He winked. "Even though I know you could handle this by yourself."

"You are all my heroes." My voice caught.

"And your friends."

I reached over and pulled him into a hug.

He didn't seem to know what to do with his arms at first, but then he wrapped them around me. "Is this what you call friends with benefits?"

I pushed him away, laughing. "Now get to work."

It took them a couple of tries to get the hang of it, but once they found the best way to move the shelves, they got into a rhythm and had them all stacked in the storeroom in less than an hour. When they'd started on the last units, I called in an order for pizza and a couple of six-packs of beer from Anderson's.

By the time the food arrived, the guys were done, but they'd moved all the tables and chairs to the back, too. We had nowhere to eat.

I yelled, "Hey, you guys hungry? Let's go somewhere else."

Max grabbed one of the boxes he'd loaded up with the booty he'd decided to hoard. "If you guys will help me carry these, we can eat at my place."

So it was settled.

I told him he'd never get around to reading all those, but then I remembered I'd never once seen him without a book except when he was reading his phone. His phone was probably loaded with more books. Or did he write his reviews with his thumbs?

Or was he writing messages to me?

I still couldn't believe I'd been corresponding with him all this time, and the ramifications struck me hard. He'd been warning me through his alter ego that my image of him had been layered over from years and years of knowing him as my best friend's brother. As my best friend. As my brother. But there was more to our relationship. So much more. I'd been lying to myself for longer than I could remember about how much I loved him. I'd packed a closet full of pent-up desire, and the door had blown off the hinges.

I ran my eyes down him from head to toe, still trying to reconcile Silver Fox with the boy I'd written off as a mere friend. The man I'd dismissed as a brother had slowly seduced me without knowing he was doing it.

I drew even with Max as we crossed the street and followed

him up the narrow stairs to the landing. He hadn't even bothered to lock his door, but it appeared the only petty crime around these parts was perpetrated by neighboring business people. And Gentry had nothing to gain from looting Max's man pad.

Once inside, I set the pizzas on his kitchen table. I hadn't been to his place in almost a year, not since before everything went bananas. It looked pretty much exactly as I remembered.

There was a corner desk where he kept his laptop and now apparently a copy of my book on top of a stack of others. Was it weird to feel a stab of jealousy toward the woman he'd been writing to, even if that woman happened to be me?

I excused myself to use the bathroom. When I crossed the threshold into his bedroom, I stopped dead. On his bed lay a black-and-white checkered bedspread I'd never seen before. I immediately flashed back to the story Silver Fox had sent me, connecting the dots. The full impact of what Max had unwittingly revealed to me hadn't hit me until that second.

He'd written fan fiction. About me.

I'd never known one could have a spontaneous orgasm standing completely alone, but the thoughts of what he'd imagined doing to me made my knees buckle. It took supreme willpower to rein in my immediate impulse to tell Dylan and Charlie to beat it.

When I came back to the table, the boys were eating messily, laughing, and telling stories.

Max said, "Hey, Maddie, we just had the best idea. Instead of our regular book club, we should get a liquor license and have an adults only night with food and beer. We could still talk books."

He was saying *we* as if he was subconsciously moving forward with the plan he'd abandoned. I pulled out a chair and fixed a plate.

"And movies?" asked Dylan.

I tuned out of the conversation and simply watched Max, the way his eyes lit up when he talked, the way his neck muscles moved, the way his long fingers held on to the bottle of beer I wished was my hand. I pictured those fingers on my skin the way they'd been in the cellar. I imagined them running across my stomach, between my thighs, on a black-and-white check-ered bedspread. I saw myself in his bed.

Charlie said, "On nights you have musicians, you'd be more competitive with the Jukebox if you also served beer."

Max held up his bottle. "Plus Gentry would hate it."

One mention of Gentry dampened my building lust and left me angry. "What am I going to do about him? You know he's responsible for that mess. What if he doesn't stop?"

"Two words," said Max. "Security cameras."

I sighed. "Can't I sue him?"

"If you catch him."

Dylan leaned in and pointed the end of his crust at me. "What you need to do is run against him for the town council. You could beat him easily. Everyone loves you, and you've been here longer than him."

Max nodded. "You could promise to overturn his stupid Sun-day rule. You could cater to the antiquing crowd. And the kids are always bored."

Charlie added, "I'd love it if you were open on Sundays. I get so much more writing done when I'm in the shop."

We all looked at him. "You write?"

He said, "Well, yeah. What do you think I'm doing all that time? Grading?"

This seemed like a good time to confess my own secret. I took a breath and opened my mouth.

"I write, too," said Max. "Or at least I'm trying to."

"So do I," said Dylan. "Poetry, mostly. And lyrics, obvi-ously."

I laughed. "And me. Novels."

"Well, damn." Charlie shook his head. "We could've been an author club all this time."

Max leaned on his elbows. "That's another thing you could do to attract people to the shop, Maddie. Start a writing group. If all four of us are writing, I'd imagine there are others."

Those eyes. I'd seen them my entire life, but had they always been so green? Had he always been so beautiful? The scruff on his smooth, freckle-dusted cheeks made me yearn to graze my face against his.

I'd learned more about him in the past few weeks than I'd known our whole lives. What else was he hiding? What else did I have to learn about him? He laughed at something Dylan said, and I tried to catch up on the conversation, but everything became white noise as I watched him. His eyes cut over and shot back to Dylan, but returned again to find me lingering on him, drinking him in, sucking him to me like an unquenchable void at the center of the universe.

He looked back a third time, and his gaze stuck.

Could he read my mind? Could he sense the seismic shift in our relationship through mental telepathy and the heat of my wanton desire now radiating off me like the shimmering distortions on a scorched summer highway? His black-and-white comforter lay only a few feet away. Want piled on want.

What would he do if I crawled across the table and bunched his shirt in my fists?

Chairs scraped.

Dylan said, "Uh. I guess we should be going."

Charlie said, "See you later."

A door clicked shut, and I couldn't drag my eyes away from Max.

Max.

I inhaled like I'd just come up for air.

He set his beer bottle on the table, and that was enough of an invitation. I stood, but the table was too damn crowded with pizza trash for me to make my triumphant crossing, so I just leaned forward and grabbed him by the collar. I hadn't planned this out very far, and as it turned out, I couldn't reach my mouth to his. He didn't seem to know what I was doing and had the panicked look of a murder victim. Frustrated, I swept my arm across the barrier, knocking bottles and cardboard to the floor. Only then did it occur to me to simply walk around the table.

I stalked over to where he sat, and he leaned away from me, like he expected me to strike him. "What are you—"

"I'm attempting to kiss you."

"Why didn't you just say that?"

He grabbed my wrist and pulled me onto his lap, our faces inches apart. For a moment, I just wanted to stare at him. His features were so familiar, but somehow altogether new.

I traced the scar high on his cheekbone from when he'd attempted to do a back flip off the diving board and clipped the board on the way down. I found it so sexy; he could have gotten it from racing motorcycles. I laid my lips there. His eyes closed, and he sighed.

I shifted so I could swing my leg over him and face him straight on, straddling him in a way that left no question about my intention.

Then I did what I'd set out to do. I wrapped my fingers in his locks and drew him near. When I kissed him, his hand slid up my back to my neck and twisted in my hair. I rocked forward and ground against him, thrilled at the moan that escaped him.

His chair tilted against the refrigerator, and I nearly let out a giggle as I recalled words he'd written in his review: "*I've felt more chemistry between my kitchen appliances.*"

Me, too. I was feeling serious chemistry between his appliances.

I reached for the top button of his shirt.

He groaned. "Maddie, stop."

"Stop?"

"Or slow down. Let me catch up. What is happening here?"

"Isn't it obvious? Didn't your parents teach you about what happens when two people like each other very much?"

"No, the school did." He smiled, and I pressed my thumb against that lower lip, dragging it across, savoring his breaking resistance. He wrapped his hand around mine. "What are you doing, Maddie?"

"Seducing you."

"Why?"

"Because I want to." Why was he fighting me? "I thought you wanted me, too."

He grasped my forearms tight. "I want you so bad it hurts."

I could feel that through my jeans. His pain was my torture. "Then what's the problem?"

"Just not like this."

"Like what? I don't understand."

His hands relaxed and wrapped around my back, ignoring what his mouth was saying. He tilted his head. "Do you remember the first time you kissed me?"

"Of course." In retrospect, that kiss had felt like home.

"You said it never happened. Do you remember that, too?"

My face flushed at the memory. "Yes."

"Well, it did happen, and I told myself to forget it, but my body wouldn't forget. I lied to myself to force myself to tolerate seeing you with Dylan, then with Peter."

"I was wrong about Peter. I know that now."

"Maddie, you've known that for a while. If you'd really loved him, do you think a dilapidated bookstore in an isolated town would've been enough to keep you from him? Why did you stay?"

Had I stayed for the bookstore?

I answered the unasked question. "I don't want you to leave Orion. I don't want you to leave me."

He ran a hand through his hair. "How did we get here?"

"I was wrong, Max." How could I make him understand it when I'd only figured it out for myself. I opened my mouth to tell him I'd fallen in love with him, but he spoke first.

"I'm trying to make sense of your capricious interest in me. As much as I want you, I need to understand. You can kiss me and walk away without a scratch. But you have the power to devastate me. If we take this any further, I would be sealed to you for life."

I scoffed. He'd started everything with that kiss. "You didn't seem to have those concerns a week ago."

He lifted his hands, fingers splayed. "Do you understand that every second of every day, it takes an effort to not be kissing you? I let my guard down last week, and you can't deny you reciprocated. I thought maybe, just maybe, things might change.

Then I laid everything out, put it all out there, and you shot me down. That was a week ago, Maddie. Can you understand why I'm hesitant?"

I knew I could make him break. I knew I could kiss him, drag my teeth across his neck, grind against him, and he'd cave. He'd as much as admitted that he was holding out by a force of supreme willpower.

Maybe if I told him I loved him, he'd relent, but I respected everything he'd said, and as disappointed as that left me, I was ready to show him I was serious. We could build from here. If he was still here.

"So you'll stay, right?"

His shoulders sagged. "Is that what this is all about? Is this some kind of con?"

"Seriously?" I climbed off him, entitled words spilling out. "I thought you loved me. I thought you'd be happy I wanted you, too. I thought—" On the fridge, I saw a magnet quoting *The Little Prince* and lost it. "I thought you'd want to stay here *with me.*"

He came up behind me and rubbed my shoulder. "You were right. I do love you. Of course, I want you to want me. But Maddie, I'm at a crossroads, and I need to be thinking of my future. What I told you the other day about wanting a career wasn't a sudden decision. Yes, I want to stay here with you, but if that's the only reason I stay . . . I don't mean this to sound as awful as I know it will, but it's too much of a risk."

I turned to face him. He meant I was too much of a risk. Could I blame him? I'd been an absolute idiot. His eyes were soft, sad, but without blame. Maybe he needed me to fight harder, make him reconsider.

"There's more here than just me. You've got friends, family. Home. You could have the bookstore. I would *give* you the bookstore. You could work there with me. Together."

"I'm not saying no, Maddie. How could I say no to you?" He wiped a tear off my cheek. "I was so sure of everything this morning. You're making it hard to keep my resolve. I can't believe after all this time, I'm having to ask you to wait for me. But I need to invest in myself. Can you understand?"

"Gah, Max. You've thrown a plot twist at me." I laid a hand on his cheek, gently, no dirty tricks up my sleeve. I just wanted to comfort him despite how terrible I felt. "I used to think you were my Laurie, but you've always been my Gilbert Blythe, haven't you? Gilbert was always going to end up with Anne Shirley."

"Maddie, I've never been Gilbert Blythe. I've always been Max Beckett." His nostrils flared, but his voice remained calm. "I'm not a hero in a book. I'm just me. I've been waiting for you to get your head out of the clouds long enough to see me, right here, just me. I just wanted you."

I traced his cheekbone with my thumb, a little bit sneaky perhaps. "All you have to do is ask, Max."

"It would be the easiest thing in the world."

"So stay." It came out more question than statement. My voice wavered on the brink of a wail.

"As much as I want to, I can't. I have to think about what happens tomorrow."

Dammit. I'd missed my chance to gain his trust. I'd have to go the long way now. Fine. I'd prove my love with time and stoic determination. After all, Max had waited this long.

"Then go. I'll still be here tomorrow." My hand slid around to the back of his neck, and I let my fingers tighten, relishing the pink dots advertising how much it was costing him to resist. "I'm not playing around. I'll be ready when you are." I straightened and laid a kiss on him I hoped would curl his toes. Cheating, maybe, but as they say, "All's fair in love and war."

I released him and backed away. "Please don't accept that job right away. Please see how you feel at the end of the week."

He shrugged. "I can do that. They haven't offered me the position yet."

"So you're saying there's a chance they won't?" I waggled my eyebrows, shamelessly rooting for a deus ex machina to come to my rescue.

"If they don't, I'll still have to look for another job."

"You have a job." If he stayed.

"I don't have a career, Maddie."

I had no answer to that. I'd had a career once. Maybe I had one still. I loved what I did so much, it didn't feel like work. "Just take the week." I opened my arms to give him a hug, and he stepped into it. "Will I see you tomorrow?"

"Sure. I'll come help you pick out flooring."

It was a relief. I regretted all those times I'd rejected his proposals for the past year. All that time, we could have been working toward a common goal. For that matter, I could go back years and think of how much time I'd lost for my own blindness. I had to stop myself. That way lay madness. I needed to focus on fixing what was broken now before we lost even more time.

When I got out to the street, I stood blinking back tears. No surprise he'd been the reviewer who passed judgment on my novel. In some way, he'd always been a reader of my life, reviewing my decisions and weighing in with his honest critiques. Now that he'd found himself a character in the story at long last, he went and flipped the script. Ironic since he'd been the one to call me out on a lack in my romantic arc.

That made me laugh hard enough to dry away my tears. After all, tomorrow was another day.

Maybe he'd believe my intentions were real if I told him we'd been corresponding for weeks. I thought about going right back to his apartment and confessing everything, but maybe I'd waited too long. Would he feel betrayed I hadn't told him right away? Or would he find it as funny as I did? I wished I'd walked into the bookstore that night and explained it all like an adult.

What would a clever heroine do?

I took my phone out and typed in a quick direct message to Silver Fox. To Max.

Would you be willing to try to meet again? Name the time and place and I'll be there.

When he agreed to meet, I'd act surprised by the revelation. If he thought I was finding out at the same time as him, he couldn't

get mad. And then he'd understand that my feelings were genuine. He'd know I wasn't using him to save my store. He'd have
to believe he meant so much more.

The next morning, I was awoken with a familiar greeting:
You've got mail!

I stretched and reached for my phone, hoping for the response from Max as Silver Fox. Silver Fox had gone dark since
Saturday night. Maybe because he was helping me clean out my
bookstore.

Instead, I had an email from my editor congratulating me on
the release of my first novel. Somehow I'd forgotten my book
went public today. Why didn't it feel like a much bigger deal than
this? Actual readers would be buying my book, leaving reviews,
judging my work. And yet, I felt oddly Zen about it. Somehow
working through my worst fears with Silver Fox—with Max—
had prepared me to deal with whatever came my way.

I moved into the kitchen as Layla came out of her room. "Hey."
Rubbing her eyes, she shuffled to the coffeepot and started going
through the motions of waking up to head to work. "Oh, I ran
into Dylan last night. He said to tell you he's leaving for New
York this afternoon."

"Last night? He could've told me himself."

"Mm-hmm." Layla shot me a sly glance. "He might've mentioned something about that, too."

"What did he say?" I blushed, thinking of how obvious I'd
been and exactly how much damage Dylan and Charlie might
have sustained had they remained in my heat-seeking lust path.

She reached into the pantry and retrieved a bag of bagels.
After she sliced one and dropped it into the toaster, she fell into
a chair. "So . . . what's going on with my brother?"

Why had I insisted on living in this town? Could nothing stay
private?

"Nothing. We were just talking. We need time to figure
things out."

She squealed. "So, not nothing."

I wanted to be the voice of reason and tell her there was no

Max and me, but I loved the idea of it, and I loved that her exuberance matched my own spinning internal giddiness ever since I'd allowed myself to entertain the possibility I could truly be in love with Max Beckett.

Squeamish nerves threatened to engulf my lovesick butterflies. What if I lost the boy right after he won me?

"After work, I'm going to buy a bottle of champagne! I wanna hear how this happened." She grimaced. "But no details, please. After all, he is my baby brother."

I held up my finger. "Now you understand."

Her forehead wrinkled. "What?"

"Why it's taken me so long to work this out."

"Not really. I was always the other half of your brain, but Max is the other half of your heart."

She'd been right all along. I should have listened. "But he's leaving."

"And? Surely you can convince him to stay. He belongs here with you."

Her words had the opposite effect than she intended. Make sure Max stayed? How would I be any better than Peter if I couldn't let Max go?

"Or you could work around it. He could commute with me. It's not like he'll disappear forever if he steps out of the town."

I burst out laughing. So practical. All of Layla's relationships were by definition long distance. Even if Max picked up and moved, he wouldn't be that far away. We'd still see each other. It sounded wise and practical. But now that I knew how I felt, I didn't want to wait. I wanted everything, and I wanted it now.

Chapter 28

✖✖

Before heading to the shop, I opened Twitter and sent out a handful of promotional tweets and thank-yous in response to lovely congratulations from my editor. When my phone announced *You've got mail!* I experienced a thrill to find Silver Fox in my unread emails at last.

> *Claire—*
> *I saw all the tweets about your book release today. How exciting! My one contribution to your big day is a revised review. I reread your book, and maybe I'm a bit biased now that I know you, but I think it definitely deserves more than three stars. After all, you ended up teaching me more about love and romance than I'd learned in my whole life. It's thanks to you I took a risk.*

So I'd flirted my way to four stars at least. I doubted that was the most efficient way to up my rating, but it left me beaming. When Max found out the truth, I'd expect no less than five stars.

> *That's why it's so hard to tell you I have to decline your invitation. I did want to meet you, but I think it's better if we didn't. I hope you can understand.*

* * *

I didn't. How else was I going to safely reveal this secret?

I've treated you like an extension of this girl, like an alternate, and that's not fair to you or to her. I don't know what you were anticipating, but I can't do anything that might feel like a betrayal to her.

I imagined walking to his apartment to knock on his door and tell him I wasn't an alternate, but I kept reading.

You pushed me to share my feelings, and doing so, I at least know better where I stand. Would you believe she says she loves me? That's all I ever wanted to hear, and yet I'm more confused than ever. I've been burned twice now. Do I want to touch the sun again?

See, I'd made this huge decision to move on, but now she wants me to stay—with her. I'm torn between my mind and my heart. Am I letting fear stand in the way of what I truly want? Or am I being pragmatic? To be honest, I'm a heartbeat away from changing my mind, but I'm terrified of making a mistake.

What if I give up this opportunity and find myself right back where I was before?

I can hear you asking me why I don't do both, chase the opportunity and the girl? That's what I'm weighing. Honestly if I knew I could trust this new thing with her, nothing would drag me away. I love my life here. I just need a sign this is for real. There's a fork in the road, and one path leads downhill toward promising vistas of paradise. I desperately want to believe it isn't all a fleeting illusion.

Best wishes,
SF

I felt like a horrible, dirty, no-good rotten spy for having read all of that. Before, when I didn't know Silver Fox was Max and that I was his Lizzie, there was nothing at all unethical about the things I got him to tell me. I hadn't anticipated such an outpouring of his heart. I hated myself for driving him to the point where he had to choose between the happiness within reach and this grasping for a lifeline to stay afloat lest I should chuck him out to sea yet again. I couldn't blame him for wanting to run screaming away from me.

How was I going to fix this? I had to tell him, even though he was going to be hella pissed at me for conning him into expressing his feelings, knowing it was him.

But would it convince him to stay?

Would it convince him I truly loved him?

I came up with a new scheme to reveal the truth in a way that would still exculpate me. With my book releasing, I'd trick him into giving away his identity and location to Claire, and then I'd spring a trap.

My plot was to mock up a flier announcing a book release event with one Claire Kincaid. Max would wonder how I'd managed to swing it, but since my book was in the shop already, I could tell him I'd discovered a local author. I'd pretend my phone had died and beg him to please write to inform her the event was canceled. He'd send the email, and it would come to my author email account, and I could say, *Oh my goodness! You're Silver Fox?*

We'd laugh, and everything would fall back in place.

What could go wrong?

I knocked on wood quickly and swallowed back nerves, hoping I hadn't just jinxed my plan.

I had to work fast. I printed up a fake flier announcing a book signing of *The Shadow's Apprentice*. When I got to the bookstore, I taped it to the front of the cash register, next to Dylan's and the other local-interest advertisements.

The contractors were scheduled to arrive at ten, and Max strolled in a few minutes early, looking like he'd slept poorly. I fought my urge to rush over and fling my arms around his neck. I couldn't tell if he'd be receptive or if he was still in "resist Maddie" mode.

I didn't have a moment to do damage control because the contractors arrived to survey the store. I looked at floor samples, pretending to understand the different grains and stains. I asked Max his opinion, and he pointed at one randomly. It worked for me. Once they had everything they needed from me, they swarmed around taking measurements, and I just wanted to get out of the way, so I huddled in the corner on the stool.

I picked up my phone to kill time and discovered an email from Peter. Or actually, it turned out to be a forwarded scanned letter from his attorney. Peter said, *This will be arriving in your mail this week. I'm giving you a month to comply.*

I opened the attachment, and my stomach dropped to my feet. He was demanding out of his partnership and suing me for his share of the money. In other words, he'd taken my threat and turned it against me. I'd have to assume the entire mortgage. I wasn't sure he was legally allowed to walk away from a loan he'd cosigned, and I started laughing at the absurdity of it. Workmen were gearing up to start repairs on a place I wouldn't be able to keep if Peter got his way. I couldn't even fight him in court over it. I had nothing to fall back on.

Max emerged from the back room. "What's so funny?"

At least Max had a plan to get out. I was about to lose him, the bookstore, and everything. Peter would win, but it would be a Pyrrhic victory. He'd finally force me to give up on everything I wanted, but he wouldn't win me back.

What could I do?

The bookstore became a whirlwind of activity, taking measurements, signing long forms, setting a schedule. When the contractors left, it was time to put my plan into action.

"Hey," I said. "I have a slight problem."

"Yeah?"

"I forgot I had an author coming in later today. Do you think you could email her and tell her we need to cancel? My phone is dead. Otherwise I would." I pointed at the flier, fighting a giggle. "I don't want her to drive all this way for nothing."

He walked over and looked at the flier. His eyes widened. "This author is coming here, today?"

"Right. Obviously we won't be open."

"How on earth did you—"

"I hope she isn't already on her way. That would be pretty awkward." I folded my hands together in prayer. "Please? Her email address is right there on the flier."

He huffed but put his phone a foot from his face and started typing. As soon as he hit send, my phone screamed *You've got mail!,* giving truth to my lie that the phone was dead.

I went for the *Princess Bride* humor. "It was mostly dead?"

He twisted his mouth and dropped his phone in his pocket. "You need to get over your aversion to technology. How did you even connect with that particular author anyway?"

"Uh." I landed on an answer that had the benefit of being true. "Letitia knows her."

"Oh, that makes sense."

Phew. "Yeah?" I moved around the counter to surreptitiously peek at my phone while he talked. "Why's that?"

I dragged down the notifications. My heart sank as I encountered the first fly in my plan. Max had emailed from his personal, non-Silver-Fox account. Why had I stupidly assumed he would use his Silver Fox email account?

"Yeah. Would you believe I've read her book?"

I opened his email, not expecting much, so I wasn't disappointed. It only explained that we'd need to postpone. Nothing further. Nothing revealing any connection to Silver Fox.

Absently, I asked, "What did you think?" My mind was spinning.

Maybe I could write back to claim that Claire didn't get the email until she was already in town. I couldn't figure out how that could be used to lure him into meeting her—me. But that would only compound the lies.

Max had stopped talking, and I blinked a few times to clear my imagination and see what was right in front of me.

He leaned against the counter. "Why did you ask me that if you weren't even going to listen?"

"I was listening." I went to my memories of comments from his review. "You liked the world-building aspects, but you thought the author didn't handle the romance well."

"That's true." He narrowed an eye. "But that's not what I just said."

Without looking away, he slid his phone from his pocket. He had to break his eye contact to type something, and I only realized what he was doing too late. We both heard *You've got mail!* at the same time.

That ringtone had seemed cheeky when I installed it. Now it was foiling my plot. I coughed, hoping to cover the traitorous tone, but Max ran his tongue over his teeth and typed again. "Wonder what will happen when I hit send this time."

He whistled like a bomb as he dramatically let his finger fall toward his phone. "Boom!"

You've got mail!

His eyes went wide. "All that time? Claire Kincaid?" He staggered back a step, a cloud of confusion crossing his features as he processed the same revelations I already had. I held my breath, waiting for him to laugh or cry. "That was you?"

The room fell dead silent as it became apparent Max was waiting for me to say something. He crossed his arms, patient. And my imagination shut down. I couldn't wrap this all up into a neat dramatic package to present to him as a happy ending after some funny shenanigans. He'd caught me out. This was happening in real time, and I couldn't think of a scene from any book or movie to guide me.

I tried something new. Reality.

"So. Did I mention I wrote a book?" I tap-danced a ball and chain and ended with a jazz hands. Ta-da!

That earned me a smile, but it was followed by a hostile response as he quickly got under control again. "How long have you known?"

"Since I started writing it."

That joke didn't provoke even a groan. "How long have you been playing games with me?"

"Since we were kids."

That time he did groan. "God, just answer the question I'm asking."

"That's not a question. It's an imperative." I bit my lip, trying not to laugh.

He sucked in a huge breath and took two steps until he was right up in my space. "This isn't funny."

I knew he was trying to look intimidating, but this was Max. I snorted. "It's kind of funny."

It wasn't until he turned and headed toward the door that the magnitude of the fire I was playing with hit home. I followed and grabbed his wrist. "Max."

He spun around, mouth rounded, words at the ready. I winced, expecting a torrent of all his pent-up frustration with my levity, anger at my deception, and renewed vows to leave and never come back. But he only said three words. "Just tell me."

"I didn't know, Max. I only figured it out Saturday."

"That's why—"

"That's why I knew I'd fallen in love with you. You've been a friend. You've been family. But it took getting to know you on-line, just your words, your soul, your essence to figure it out."

He blinked rapidly. "In love with me?" He covered his mouth as the new reality hit him. "Oh, my God, what did I write to you?"

I stepped closer. "Lots of things."

"And that scene I wrote. You know I would never have sent it but—"

I stepped closer again. "But you didn't think I cared for you like that. I know."

He pressed the heel of his palm to his forehead. "And everything I wrote you last night. Maddie—"

"Yeah, I'm sorry. I wasn't trying to get that confession out of you. I just wanted to trick you into meeting. I wanted to have this amazing revelation."

He threw his hands up in the air. "You're fucking kidding me, right? You wanted to trick me? Did it once occur to you to just say, 'Hey, Max, guess what? We've been talking to each other online for weeks. Funny, huh?'"

"Yeah, that did occur to me. I liked my way better."

"And how did your scene end?"

"Maybe with a kiss."

"And then?"

"Happily-ever-after."

He shook his head. "That's the sticking point for me. Because that scene has been set up for us again and again."

"I get why you don't trust me. I do. I can't believe how blind I've been, how it took words from an apparent stranger to break my heart open enough to find in you what you always could have been. I won't try to make you choose between me and another path, Max. Go ahead and pursue this other opportunity, and I swear, I will be here, waiting for you for a change."

I must have finally hit the right combination to unlock something because he leaned forward and put his forehead on mine. "Secret author, huh?"

It was such a small gesture, but I'd been swimming against a strong current and had finally reached solid land. I didn't realize how starved I was for contact from him until he was so close I could have kissed him. What would it take to get him to move another inch toward me?

I sighed, my whole body melting. "Secret reviewer."

His lips nearly brushed mine, but then he jerked back. "Do you think everything will be like a fairy tale? What happens when we fight? What happens when the business struggles and we have economic hardships? Are you prepared for that?"

"Max, you just described the past six months. I still want this. I don't want to force you to do something, but I wish you'd take a chance on me."

A smile curled the corner of his lip. He wrapped his hands around the back of my neck and granted my wish. It wasn't a seductive kiss. He just pressed his lips to mine, then broke away again. "Hold that thought."

Then he walked out of the store, leaving me alone to worry he wasn't coming back.

Meet me on the bridge.

That was all his text said. I raced out the door and ran the entire distance without stopping to catch my breath once. I arrived before him, panting and leaning over the rail, hoping to catch a faint breeze to cool off my now perspiring skin.

The sun was just starting to set, and the sky over the trees was a bruise of blues and reds and purples. Crickets and frogs sang out in a chorus from the woods and stream. It was the kind of twilight that felt like magic when we were children. The last burst of daylight, the last grasp of freedom before darkness would drive us home. I could almost hear the laughter as Max, Layla, and I tore across this bridge on our bikes, racing to get home before we'd get in any more trouble. I could see us on another day, when we were old enough to stay out later, swinging our feet from the bridge, making plans for the future, dreaming about what our life might turn out to be.

The light slipped from pink tinged to purple hued, and I discerned a dark shape strolling along the side of the stream, hands jammed in his pockets, like he had all the time in the world. His confident gait gave him an air of nobility, like a duke disguising himself as a commoner, unrecognized for who he truly was. I stopped myself. Max wasn't a secret duke or a renegade knight or a billionaire down on his luck. He wasn't a romance hero at all. He was my best friend, my soul mate, and the man I loved. He didn't need to be anything more.

When he reached the bridge, he said, "Have you considered my proposition?"

I laughed. "Has this all been a long con?"

"Indeed it has been." He took my hand. "But we took a different route to get here."

"Where did you go?

"I went to talk to my mom."

"And?"

"She'd be thrilled if you wanted to partner with us. We can refinance the mortgage to remove Peter from the loan."

"What if the bookstore fails? You'll lose your business, too. You could lose everything."

He kissed the back of my hand. "Not if I don't lose you. And besides, we're not going to fail. We're going to turn both businesses into so much more than either was before."

My mind raced. If I wasn't always tapping into my savings to pay Peter . . . "And we can use my advance."

He blinked, confused.

"From my book. I'm expecting another check. It's not a lot, but we could make some renovations."

His face brightened, and he laid a hand on my cheek. "Have I told you how proud I am of you?"

I blushed. "Max."

"Maddie." He smiled. "TeamMadMax."

I didn't laugh, too fixated on his lips inches from my own. As he leaned closer, my heart pounded in my chest. I looked around for anything to spoil the magic—a car, a jogger, a noisy goose. But we were alone at the center of the bridge. The sky turned deepest, darkest black as I lost myself in a kiss so magical it made me forget about everything and anyone but Max.

Chapter 29

I closed and locked the door after the last book club patron left.
Max looked up from the cash register. "Can you believe how
many people showed up tonight?"

He'd been right that choosing recent releases would interest a
more diverse readership. Dylan had been right that serving liquor
would interest everyone else. Even my mom and her neighborhood bunco buddies showed up tonight since we were reading a
hot new Kelly Siskind novel. I'd had to borrow chairs from Letitia.
I needed to invest in my own since we'd brought in crowds for the
writing group that met on Tuesdays and the teen reading group
on Sundays. Yeah, as my first order of business as town council
president, I put the Sunday ban up to a vote. The consensus was
that each business could make that decision autonomously.

We'd kicked off our new book club format with my own
book (plus complimentary wine). I'd been terrified to hear criticism to my face, but most everyone lauded me with praise,
though that might have been obligatory. Two weeks earlier,
most of the town had turned out for my book signing as if it
were a Dylan concert. I cried at how supportive everyone was
and pretended it didn't bug me when friends asked me for free
copies or told me they'd borrow it from the library, or worse,
that they'd wait for the movie to come out. They meant well,
and I ended up selling out of my stock. It was fun to personalize

and sign each novel as if I were a real author. I still didn't feel
like a real author. Was that something that came in time or had
Jane Austen suffered from impostor syndrome, too?

While Max dealt with the money—a task I'd been more than
happy to let him take over—I went to fetch the broom. Max's
dad had stayed to help fold up the chairs, and I found him in the
storeroom, putting on his jacket. Ever since Max and I had become partners in all things, his family became mine in ways I'd
never dreamed possible. I was never on my own. Not only had I
gained three extra sets of hands to help around the bookstore,
I'd gained an extra pair of parents.

Max's dad paused and turned. "Maddie, you are a remark-
able young lady. Look at everything you've accomplished."

I blushed. "I had the help of your son."

He shook his head. "Max may have helped, but you took the
leap of faith. You made all of this happen. I'm so proud of you."

My throat constricted, and I didn't know what to say. I gave
him a hug. "Thanks, Dad."

He laughed. We were still trying that out, but I liked it. A lot.
I think he did, too. He squeezed extra hard and said good night.

I'd started sweeping up front, but Max snuck up behind me
and grabbed the broom, leaning it against a wall.

"This can wait. Take a walk with me?"

I'd spent the entire day dreaming of the moment I'd finally be
able to act out the fantasies he inspired. I was particularly interested in running my lips across the day-old scruff he'd allowed
to grow. He'd learned fast how that affected me.

"I don't want to walk with you." I grabbed his hand. "Take
me home."

He reeled me in for a quick kiss but drew back before I could
get going. He knew from experience I wouldn't hesitate to have
my way with him in the bookstore. Nobody would ever know the
things we'd done in the teen rec room upstairs. And I couldn't
pass the cellar door without blushing.

"I want to get some fresh air." He stepped toward the front
door. "Come on. Just up to the bridge."

Pouting, I put on a coat and braced for the cold. Despite the crackle in the air, the promised snow hadn't started to fall. I slipped an arm under Max's jacket to absorb his warmth and touch him. After six months, I still hadn't convinced myself that this was real, that Max was mine, totally mine.

As we walked, I said, "Did you see that Dylan's song moved into the Top 40?"

"Oh, hey. Good for him." He was humoring me. He wasn't invested in Dylan's career, but Layla had been using her blog to promote the new single, and she kept me up to date.

"Layla says he'll be opening for some band at Market Square Arena in a few months."

We passed the gazebo in silence. Then Max said, "You know Layla's moving out, right?"

"Yeah." She'd grown tired of the commute. "It was inevitable."

I'd been wondering when Max would suggest I give up the apartment and move in with him. It would make sense now that my roommate was leaving. It would make sense because we made sense.

At the bridge, I hopped up on the rail so I could pull Max closer. He wanted to talk. I wanted to wrap my legs around his waist. Once upon a time, I might have checked for witnesses, but whenever we were alone for a moment, I couldn't resist stealing kisses. He could be working in the kitchen, elbows deep in sudsy water, and I'd slink my arms around him and lay my head on his back. No motorcycle ride had ever felt so sexy.

Tonight, our only witness was the moon. I unbuttoned the top of his shirt and lay a kiss on his chest. He laughed. "You're gonna do that right here?"

Like he didn't know me at all. "Uh-huh."

"I have an idea." He reached into his pocket and produced a key ring. "Let's go somewhere warm."

He took off at a jog, and I raced after him up the driveway to the raspberry cottage, laughing as he unlocked the door. "We cannot break and enter."

"Is it breaking and entering if I have the key?"

I wasn't aware Max was still maintaining the house for the Palmers. I couldn't imagine they'd approve of our current plans for the place.

As soon as we were through the door, he pressed me against the wall and planted the kiss I'd been trying to coax out of him since the book club ended. As much as I wanted him, I couldn't get past how wrong it would be to defile this house, and I pulled away, groaning. "Max, we cannot have sex in the Palmers' foyer."

"You're right."

Instead of opening the door to leave, he angled my body so he could walk me backward farther into the house. In the kitchen, he removed my coat and dropped it on the hardwood floor. His followed. He had a determined look in his eyes, and I said, "Max, we cannot have sex in the Palmers' kitchen."

He pulled off his boots and dropped them one at a time. "We are not going to have sex in the Palmers' kitchen."

Without warning, he put his hands on my waist and picked me up. I let out a startled cry and wrapped around him as he stumbled down the hall. I realized where he was carrying me. "Oh, God, Max. We are definitely not going to have sex in the Palmers' bed."

Despite my protest, I'd already unbuttoned his shirt and had it halfway down his arms when he kicked open the door and dropped me on the side of the bed. As he pulled my shoes off, he said, "No, we aren't going to have sex in the Palmers' bed."

He slid his hands under my shirt and pulled it over my head. I told myself the Palmers didn't live here anymore, then popped the button and tugged at the zipper on his pants. Off they came. As he stood to grab my jeans by the ankles, I raised my hips to help him out and noticed a bottle of wine on the bedside table.

He knelt and kissed the inside of my thigh. My eyes closed, and I thrilled at how his every touch brought me to the edge of ecstasy. He'd spend an entire night seducing me if I let him, but I needed him next to me, in me.

I dug my fingers in his hair and compelled him to crawl up onto the bed. I knocked him over so I could straddle him. He was so hard, all I had to do was lean forward and push back, and he was deep in me. I rocked forward to kiss him and accuse him of lying to me. We were definitely having sex in the Palmers' bed. As I looked down at him, I realized he lay on a black-and-white checkered bedspread.

I gasped. "This is not the Palmers' bed."

"No, it is not." He flipped me over onto my back.

My mind wrestled with the need to solve a mystery when he slid in me again.

"What is going on? Did you buy this place?"

"Rented for now." He pressed his lips to my throat. "Buy later."

My brain shut off entirely as he kissed me. Not a short teasing peck. He sucked on my lower lip, then coaxed my mouth open and ran his tongue across mine. My body responded to him like we were created from the same cosmic energy, and stars burst, constellations formed, planets aligned when we were together. My fingers dug into the muscles in his arms, dragged across his shoulders, scratched his back, and followed his spine to the curve above his ass. Sweat dripped from his hair onto my temple as he increased his pace, grunting, muttering prayers to God in heaven or whispering my name.

The universe collapsed into the smallest pinprick and then exploded like all the fireworks going off at once. My body went stiff just as Max cried out, and a second orgasm hit me with his. We fell beside each other and gazed into each other's eyes.

"I love you," he said. He was so cute with his hair a mess and sexy sweat beading on his forehead.

I touched his nose. "I love you, too." Then I sat up on my elbow. "So what, you're going to live here now?"

He took my face in his hands. "I hoped *we* could. Would you want to live here? With me?" His eyebrows drew together, and his lower lip disappeared between his teeth. God, he was cute.

"Do you even know me?" I played it cool, but I wanted him to be happy, too. "Is this really what you want?"

He dragged a finger through my hair. "This is what I want. I don't care where." He pressed his lips against mine. "But I can't think of a more appropriate place to live with you."

Butterflies flew loose. Silver Fox would be pleased. I should tell him . . .

"You know you make my stomach flip, right?"

He grinned. "I am your romantic hero, after all."

"You're my happy-ever-after."

I'd ended up with everything I ever wanted, although it wasn't exactly how I'd imagined it. The things I'd fought against turned out to be the things I needed most. And all because I'd been lucky enough to meet my best friend as a total stranger and discover how perfect he was for me.

"So, Lizzie . . ."

"Darcy?"

"Looks like we're going to be coauthors from here on out."

I groaned at how corny he could be. "You ready for the sequel?"

"Sequel so soon?" He arched an eyebrow. Ever competitive. "I'm just getting started."

Acknowledgments

The creation of a book takes a whole cast of characters and comes with its own plot twists, black moments, and ultimately a satisfying conclusion.

The inciting event for this novel was a conversation with my editor, Wendy McCurdy, in which a seed of an idea was proposed. Like a god with the power to create, Wendy said, "Let there be book," and a world was born. If it weren't for her help in shaping the concept and her continued support for my writing, this novel literally could not have existed. I am so grateful to have had the opportunity to bring it to life.

Along the way, a ragtag group of misfits offered their many strengths to propel me through myriad obstacles so I could slay the dragon of drafting and revising. Huge thanks to my mage, Kelli Newby for soothsaying and plot wizardry, and to my constant companion Kristin Wright for always knowing where the hidden treasure is buried and for providing the map. Summer Spence, you are the wise caretaker at the crossroads, showing me the paths I need to take (even if they look forbidding). Elly Blake, you are the deceptively cute woodland creature that turns into a dread beast at the stroke of midnight and devours my words. And Ron Walters, you bring the much needed comic relief. To the CD, you are all the magic system that powers my universe.

A huge special thanks to my deus ex machina, Riki Cleveland, for reading as a reviewer and providing insight as a real-life book blogger. I chewed my fingernails awaiting your verdict. I am ultimately responsible for any missteps, but your input helped me level up.

There are many unsung heroes involved in this process, from copy editors to cover designers. I'm so appreciative of how hard they work to take a manuscript from concept to finished product. Thanks to Jane Nutter, Norma Perez-Hernandez, and Paula Reedy for the countless things you do to shepherd my books out in the world. Thanks also to my agent Mike Hoogland for his guidance and support.

To my kiddos, Eve and Zoe, thanks for rolling with your mom's author alter ego.

Finally, as this book is about books, I can't neglect to thank you, the reader, for taking the time to peruse these pages, and you, the reviewer, for sharing your opinions on Amazon or Goodreads or on your blog. Reviewers are so important to authors because you help the right readers find the right books. Thank you.

DATING BY THE BOOK

Mary Ann Marlowe

About This Guide

The suggested questions are included
to enhance your group's reading of
Mary Ann Marlowe's *Dating by the Book*.

DISCUSSION QUESTIONS

1. What do you think would have happened if Maddie had never responded to Silver Fox's review? Who do you think she would have ended up with?

2. Which of Maddie's suitors did you root for? Did your opinion evolve over the course of the book? What qualities made you think that one would be the best choice for Maddie? (Or for you?)

3. What does Maddie see in each of the men in her life? What does each offer her that she thinks she needs?

4. Maddie's initial exchange with Silver Fox is antagonistic, but it eventually turns into a constructive conversation. Have you ever gotten into a fight with strangers on the Internet? What types of comments or topics compel you to express yourself in a confrontational manner? Can you think of any disagreements you've had that stayed civil? How does this differ from debates people might have if they were face-to-face?

5. Why do you think that Silver Fox and Maddie were able to open up to each other in writing in a way that they didn't with their friends in real life?

6. Did Maddie make the right choice? Have you read books where you thought the heroine ended up with the wrong guy? Are there any love triangles in fiction where you're firmly on a "team"? Care to confess which ones?

7. Do you understand why Peter left Maddie at the altar the way he did? Would you ever be able to forgive something like this?

8. Are you familiar with the 1998 movie *You've Got Mail,* starring Tom Hanks and Meg Ryan? How about the 1940 movie *The Shop Around the Corner,* with Jimmy Stewart and Margaret Sullavan? If so, how are they similar to and/or different from *Dating by the Book?*

9. Maddie has had a long love affair with books. Do you recall which book made you fall in love with reading? Do you have a favorite book?

10. Do you fall in love with fictional romance heroes? Who are your book boyfriends or girlfriends?

11. Is there a kind of hero who appeals to you more than others: enemy-to-lover, best friend, second-chance love, etc? Which types of hero does Maddie encounter in her world?

12. Do you believe that romance heroes exist in the real world? Why or why not?

13. Have you ever wanted to own a bookstore? If you could have your own bookstore, what kind of place would it be?

14. Why do you think Maddie is so connected with her hometown? Is there a place where you feel so at home or where you long to return?

Do not miss Eden and Adam's story in

SOME KIND OF MAGIC

by Mary Ann Marlowe
Now available in bookstores and online!

What if you could seduce anyone in the world. . . .

In this sparkling novel, Mary Ann Marlowe introduces a hapless scientist who's swept off her feet by a rock star—but is it love or just a chemical reaction . . . ?

Biochemist Eden Sinclair has no idea that the scent she spritzed on herself before leaving the lab is designed to enhance pheromones. Or that the cute, grungy-looking guy she meets at a gig that evening is Adam Copeland. As in *the* Adam Copeland—international rock god and object of lust for a million women. Make that a million and one. By the time she learns the truth, she's already spent the (amazing, incredible) night in his bed . . .

Suddenly Eden, who's more accustomed to being set up on disastrous dates by her mom, is going out with a gorgeous celebrity who loves how down-to-earth and honest she is. But for once, Eden isn't being honest. She can't bear to reveal that this overpowering attraction could be nothing more than seduction by science. And the only way to know how Adam truly feels is to ditch the perfume—and risk being ditched in turn . . .

Smart, witty, and sexy, *Some Kind of Magic* is an irresistibly engaging look at modern relationships—why we fall, how we connect, and the courage it takes to trust in something as mysterious and unpredictable as love.

Read on for a preview. . . .

Chapter 1

My pen tapped out the drumbeat to the earworm on the radio. I glanced around to make sure I was alone, then grabbed an Erlenmeyer flask and belted out the chorus into my makeshift microphone.

"*I'm beeeegging you . . .*"

With the countertop centrifuge spinning out a white noise, I could imagine a stadium crowd cheering. My eyes closed, and the blinding lab fell away. I stood onstage in the spotlight.

"Eden?" came a voice from the outer hall.

I swiveled my stool toward the door, anticipating the arrival of my first fan. When Stacy came in, I bowed my head. "Thank you. Thank you very much."

She shrugged out of her jacket and hung it on a wooden peg. Unimpressed by my performance, she turned down the radio. "You're early. How long have you been here?"

"Since seven." The centrifuge slowed, and I pulled out tubes filled with rodent sperm. "I want to leave a bit early to head into the city and catch Micah's show."

She dragged a stool over. "Kelly and I are hitting the clubs tonight. You should come with."

"Yeah, right. Why don't you come with me? Kelly's such a—"

"Such a what?" The devil herself stood in the doorway, phone in hand.

Succubus from hell played on my lips. But it was too early to start a fight. "Such a guy magnet. Nobody can compete with you."

Kelly didn't argue and turned her attention back to the phone.

Stacy leaned her elbow on the counter, conspiratorially talking over my head. "Eden's going to abandon us again to go hang out with Micah."

"At that filthy club?" Kelly's lip curled, as if Stacy had just offered her a *non*-soy latte. "But there are never even any guys there. It's always just a bunch of moms."

I gritted my teeth. "Micah's fans are not all moms." When Micah made it big, I was going to enjoy refusing her backstage passes to his eventual sold-out shows.

Kelly snorted. "Oh, right. I suppose their husbands might be there, too."

"That's not fair," Stacy said. "I've seen young guys at his shows."

"Teenage boys don't count." Kelly dropped an invisible microphone and turned toward her desk.

I'd never admit that she was right about the crowd that came out to hear Micah's solo shows. But unlike Kelly, I wasn't interested in picking up random guys at bars. I spun a test tube like a top, then clamped my hand down on it before it could careen off the counter. "Whatever. Sometimes Micah lets me sing."

Apparently Kelly smelled blood; her tone turned snide. "Ooh, maybe Eden's dating her brother."

"Don't be ridiculous, Kelly." Stacy rolled her eyes and gave me her best *don't listen to her* look.

"Oh, right." Kelly threw her head back for one last barb. "Eden would never consider dating a struggling musician."

The clock on the wall reminded me I had seven hours of prison left. I hated the feeling that I was wishing my life away one workday at a time.

Thanh peeked his head around the door and saved me. "Eden, I need you to come monitor one of the test subjects."

Inhaling deep to get my residual irritation under control, I followed Thanh down the hall to the holding cells. Behind the window, a cute blond sat with a wire snaking out of his charcoal-gray Dockers. Thanh instructed him to watch a screen flashing more or less pornographic images while I kept one eye on his vital signs.

I bit my pen and put the test subject through my usual Terminator-robot full-body analysis to gauge his romantic eligibility. He wore a crisp dress shirt with a white cotton undershirt peeking out below the unbuttoned collar. I wagered he held a job I'd find acceptable, possibly in programming, accounting, or maybe even architecture. His fading tan, manicured nails, and fit build lent the impression that he had enough money and time to vacation, pamper himself, and work out. No ring on his finger. And blue eyes at that. On paper, he fit my mental checklist to a *T*.

Even if he was strapped up to his balls in wires.

Hmm. Scratch that. If he were financially secure, he wouldn't need the compensation provided to participants in clinical trials for boner research. *Never mind.*

Thanh came back in and sat next to me.

I stifled a yawn and stretched my arms. "Don't get me wrong. This is all very exciting, but could you please slip some arsenic in my coffee?"

He punched buttons on the complex machine monitoring the erectile event in the other room. "Why are you still working here, Eden? Weren't you supposed to start grad school this year?"

"I was." I sketched a small circle in the margin of the paper on the table.

"You need to start applying soon for next year. Are you waiting till you've saved enough money?"

"No, I've saved enough." I drew a flower around the circle and shaded it in. I'd already had this conversation with my parents.

"If you want to do much more than what you're doing now, you need to get your PhD."

I sighed and turned in my chair to face him. "Thanh, you've got your PhD, and you're doing the same thing as me."

When he smiled, the corners of his eyes crinkled. "Yes, but it has always been my lifelong dream to help men maintain a medically induced long-lasting erection."

I looked at my hands, thinking. "Thanh, I'm not sure this is what I want to do with my life. I've lost that loving feeling."

"Well, then, you're in the right place."

I snickered at the erectile dysfunction humor. The guy in the testing room shifted, and I thought for the first time to ask. "What are you even testing today?"

"Top secret."

"You can't tell me?"

"No, I mean you'd already know if you read your emails."

"I do read the emails." That was partly true. I skimmed and deleted them unless they pertained to my own work. I didn't care about corporate policy changes, congratulations to the sales division, farewells to employees leaving after six wonderful years, tickets to be pawned, baby pictures, or the company chili cook-off.

He reached into a drawer and brought out a small vial containing a clear yellow liquid. When he removed the stopper, a sweet aroma filled the room, like jasmine.

"What's that?"

He handed it to me. "Put some on, right here." He touched my wrist.

I tipped it onto my finger and dabbed both my wrists. Then I waited. "What's it supposed to do?"

He raised an eyebrow. "Do you feel any different?"

I ran an internal assessment. "Uh, nope. Should I?"

"Do me a favor. Walk into that room."

"With the test subject?" It was bad enough that poor guy's schwanz was hooked up to monitors, but he didn't need to know exactly who was observing changes in his penile turgidity. Thanh shooed me on through the door, so I went in.

The erotica continued to run, but the guy's eyes were now on me. I thought, *Is that a sensor monitoring you, or are you just happy to see me?*

"Uh, hi." I glanced back at the one-way mirror, as if I could telepathically understand when Thanh released me from this embarrassing ordeal.

The guy sat patiently, expecting me to do something. So I reached over and adjusted one of the wires, up by the machines. He went back to watching the screen, as if I were just another technician. Nobody interesting.

I backed out of the room. As soon as the door clicked shut, I asked Thanh, "What the hell was that?"

He frowned. "I don't know. I expected something more. Some kind of reaction." He started to place the vial back in the drawer. Then he had a second thought. "Do you like how this smells?"

I nodded. "Yeah, it's good."

"Take it." He tossed it over, and I threw it into my purse.

The rest of the day passed slowly as I listened to Kelly and Stacy argue over the radio station or fight over some impossibly gorgeous actor or front man they'd never meet. Finally at four, I swung into the ladies' room and changed out of my work clothes, which consisted of a rayon suit skirt and a button-up pin-striped shirt. Knowing I'd be hanging with Micah in the club later, I'd brought a pair of comfortable jeans and one of his band's T-shirts. I shook my ponytail out and let my hair fall to my shoulders.

When I went back to the lab to grab my purse and laptop, I wasn't a bit surprised that Kelly disapproved of my entire look.

"I have a low-cut shirt in my car if you want something more attractive." She offered it as though she actually would've lent it to me. Knowing I'd decline, she got in a free dig at my wardrobe choices. We were a study in opposites—she with her overpermed blond hair and salon tan, me with my short-clipped fingernails and functioning brain cells.

"No, thanks. Maybe next time."

"At least let me fix your makeup. Are you even wearing any?"

I pretended she wasn't bothering me. "No time. I have a train to catch."

She sniffed. "Well, you smell nice anyway. New perfume?"

"Uh, yeah. It was a gift." Her normally pouting lips rounded in anticipation of her next question. I zipped my computer bag and said, "Gotta go. See ya tomorrow, Stacy?"

Stacy waved without turning her head away from whatever gossip site she'd logged on to, and I slipped out the door.

As I stood on the train platform waiting for the 5:35 Northeast Corridor train to Penn Station, I heard someone calling "Hello?" from inside my purse. I fetched my phone and found it connected somehow to my mom, whose voice messages I'd been ignoring.

Foiled by technology and the gremlins living in my bag, I placed the phone to my ear. "Mom?"

"Oh, there you are, Eden. I'm making corned beef and gravy tonight. Why don't you come by before you go out?"

I didn't know how to cook, so my mom's invitation was meant as charity. But since she was the reason I couldn't cook, her promise of shit on a shingle wasn't enough to lure me from my original plans.

"No, thanks, Mom. I'm on my way into the city to hear Micah play tonight."

"Oh. Well, we'll see you Sunday I hope. Would you come to church with us? We have a wonderful new minister and—"

"No, Mom. But I'll come by the house later."

"All right. Oh, don't forget you've got a date with Dr. Whedon tomorrow night."

I groaned. She was relentless. "Is it too late to cancel?"

"What's the problem now, Eden?"

I pictured Dr. Rick Whedon, DDS, tonguing my bicuspid as we French kissed. But she wouldn't understand why I'd refuse to date a dentist, so instead, I presented an iron-clad excuse. "Mom, if we got married, I'd be Eden Whedon."

Her sigh came across loud and clear. "Eden, don't be so unreasonable."

"I keep telling you you're wasting your time, Mom."

"And you're letting it slip by, waiting on a nonexistent man. You're going to be twenty-nine soon."

The train approached the station, so I put my finger in my ear and yelled into the phone. "In six months, Mom."

"What was wrong with Jack Talbot?"

I thought for a second and then placed the last guy she'd tried to set me up with. "He had a mustache, Mom. And a tattoo. Also, he lives with his parents."

"That's only temporary," she snapped.

"The mustache or the tattoo?" I thought back to the guy from the lab. "And you never know. Maybe I'll meet Mr. Perfect soon."

"Well, if you do, bring him over on Sunday."

I chortled. The idea of bringing a guy over to my crazy house before I had a ring on my finger was ludicrous. "Sure, Mom. I'll see you Sunday."

"Tell Micah to come, too?"

My turn to sigh. Their pride in him was unflappable, and yet, I'd been the one to do everything they'd ever encouraged me to do, while he'd run off to pursue a pipe dream in music. So maybe they hadn't encouraged me to work in the sex-drug industry, but at least I had a college degree and a stable income.

"Okay, Mom. I'll mention it. The train's here. I have to go."

I climbed on the train and relaxed, so tired of everyone harassing me. At least I could count on Micah not to meddle in my love life.

Chapter 2

At seven thirty, I arrived at the back door of the club, trailing a cloud of profanity. "Fuck. My fucking phone died."

Micah exchanged a glance with the club owner, Tobin. "See? Eden doesn't count."

"What the fuck are you talking about?" After two hours fighting mass transit, I'd lost my patience. My attitude would need to be recalibrated to match Micah's easygoing demeanor.

Micah ground out his cigarette with a twist of his shoe. "Tobin was laying a wager that only women would show up tonight, but I said you'd be here."

I narrowed my eyes.

Micah's small but avid female fan base faithfully came out whenever he put on an acoustic show. His hard-rock band, Theater of the Absurd, catered to a larger male following and performed to ever-increasing audiences. But he loved playing these smaller rooms, bantering with the crowd, hearing people sing along with familiar choruses.

Before Tobin could get in on the act, I blurted, "Can I charge my phone in the green room?"

I made a wide berth around Tobin's plumage of cigarette smoke and followed Micah down the shabby narrow back hall. Dimly lit eight-by-eleven glossy posters plastered the walls, advertising upcoming bands and many other acts that had already passed through. Nobody curated the leftover fliers although hundreds of staples held torn triangles of paper from some distant past. A brand-new poster showing Micah's anticipated club dates hung near the door to the ladies' room. That would disappear during the night as some fan co-opted it for him to autograph, and Tobin would have to replace it. Again.

The green room was actually dark red and held furniture that looked like someone had found it on the curb near the trash. And it smelled like they'd brought the trash, too. God knew what had transpired in here over the years. I tried to touch nothing. Micah flopped down on the sofa and picked up a box of half-eaten Chinese food. His red Converse tennis shoes and dark green pants clashed with the brown-gold hues that stained the formerly whitish sofa.

I plugged in my phone, praying I'd remember to fetch it before I left. I fished out some ibuprofen and grabbed Micah's beer to wash it down. I waved off his interest in the drugs I was popping. "Birth control," I lied.

Without looking up from his noodles, he said, "Oh, good. I was starting to worry you'd joined a convent."

When Micah finished eating, he led me to the front of the club and put me to work setting up his merch table. His band's CDs wouldn't sell, but his self-produced EP of solo work would disappear. Mostly for girls to have something for him to autograph. They'd already own his music digitally. A suitcase filled with rolled-up T-shirts lay under the table. I bent down and selected one of each design to display as samples.

Micah moved around onstage, helping the club employees drag cables and whatnot. Not for the first time, I envied him for inheriting some of Mom's Scandinavian coloring and height, while I got Dad's pale Irish skin and raven hair. Micah repeated "one-two-three check" into the mic a few times and then disappeared around back to grab one last smoke before he had to transform from my sweet older brother into that charismatic guy who held a crowd in the palm of his hand.

Right before the doors opened to the public, one of the guys I'd seen setting up the stage stopped by the table and flipped through the T-shirts and CDs. He picked up Micah's EP and then raised dark brown eyes. "Micah Sinclair. You like his music?"

He wore faded jeans and a threadbare T-shirt from a long-forgotten AC/DC concert under a maroon hoodie. His black hair fell somewhere between tousled and bed head. I saw no traces of product, so I assumed he came by that look through honest negligence rather than studied indifference.

My quick scan revealed: too grungy, probably unwashed, poor. I resisted the urge to pull the merch away from his wandering fingers. But I wouldn't risk the sale, so I leaned in on my elbows, all smiles.

"He's amazing. Will you get a chance to hear him perform?"

"Oh, yeah. Definitely." He set the EP down and held out his hand. "I'm Adam, by the way."

I wrapped my hand around his out of sheer politeness and proper upbringing, but I couldn't help laughing and saying, "Just so you know, my worst nightmare would be dating a guy named Adam."

He quirked his eyebrow. "That's kind of discriminatory."

"My name's Eden." I waited a beat for the significance to register, but I guess any guy named Adam would've already dealt with such issues of nomenclature. His eyes lit up immediately.

"Oh. Seriously?" He chuckled, and his smile transformed his features. I sucked in my breath. Underneath the dark hair, dark eyes, and hobo wardrobe, he was awfully cute. "I'll rethink that marriage proposal. But could I get you anything? You want a beer?"

This was a new twist. Usually, the ladies were offering drinks to my brother. I loved getting the attention for a change. "Sure. Whatever lager or pilsner they have on tap."

He walked off, and I snickered. *Maybe some guys like pale brunettes, Kelly.* As he leaned against the bar, I assessed him from the rear. Tall enough, but too skinny. Questionable employment. Either an employee of the club, a musician, a wannabe musician, or a fan. Shame.

Micah strolled up. "Is everything ready?"

I forced my gaze away from Adam's backside. "Are you?"

He scratched his five-o'clock chin scruff. "That's the thing. I may need some help tonight. Do you think you could maybe sing backup on one song? I was hoping to harmonize on 'Gravity.' "

"Sure." What were sisters for? I had his whole catalog memorized, even the music from his band, although that music ran a little too hard rock for my tastes.

Micah left me alone at the merch table, and Adam returned with a glass. "Did I just miss Micah?"

He'd pulled his hoodie up so his face fell into shadow, giving him a sinister appearance. With the nonexistent lighting in the club, I could barely make out his features. This odd behavior, coupled with his interest in my brother, made me worry maybe he was in fact one of the crazy fans who found ways to get closer than normal, and not, as I'd first thought, an employee of the club. How had he gotten inside before the doors opened?

Before I could ask him, a woman's sharp voice interrupted. "Will Micah be coming out after the show?"

I looked toward the club's entrance, where people had begun to stream in. I took a deep breath and prepared to deal with the intensity of music fandom.

"I assume so. He usually does."

She didn't move. "It's just that I brought something for him." She held up a canister of something I guessed was homemade. I'd advised Micah not to eat whatever they gave him, but he never listened. And so far he'd never landed in the hospital. I knew his fans meant well, but who knew if those cookies had been baked alongside seven long-haired cats?

"I could take it back to him if you like." I made the offer, knowing full well it wouldn't do at all.

"No. Thank you. I'll just wait and give them to him later. If he comes out." She wandered off toward the stage.

I spotted one of Micah's regular fans, Susan something-or-other, making a beeline for the merch table. She looked put out that I was there before her. "Eden, if you like, I'm more than happy to man the merch."

I never understood what she got out of working merch for

Micah. He didn't pay except possibly in a waived cover charge. And she was farther from the stage and possibly distracted from the performances. Perhaps it gave her status. Whatever it was, it made her happy, and I was glad to relinquish the duty to her.

"Thank you, Susan."

She beamed. "Oh, it's no problem." She began to chatter with the other women crowding up to the merch table. I overheard her saying, "Micah told me he'll be performing a new song tonight."

Adam caught my eye, and we exchanged a knowing smile. So okay, he wasn't a fan. He stepped beside me as I walked to the bar to get a seat on a stool. "So you're not the number one fan, then?" he asked.

I smiled. "Of course I am."

Before we could discuss our reasons for being there, the room plunged into near-total darkness, and Tobin stepped onto the stage to introduce the opening act, a tall blonde whose explosion of wild hair had to weigh more than the rest of her.

She pulled up a stool and started into her first song without further ado. Out of respect, I kept quiet and listened, although her performance was a bit shaky, and the between-song banter didn't help. It pleased me that Adam didn't turn to me to say anything snarky about the poor girl or talk at all. I had to glare over at the women hanging around the merch table a few times, though. They'd shut up when Micah came on, but they didn't seem to care that other musicians preferred to play to a rapt audience, too.

In the time between acts, Adam ordered me another beer. At some point he'd dropped his hood back, but with the terrible lighting in the club, I had to squint to see his face. Normally, I wasn't a big fan of facial hair of any kind, but Adam's slight scruff caused my wires to cross. On the one hand, I worried he couldn't afford a razor out there in the cardboard box he lived in. On the other hand, I had a visceral urge to reach up and touch his cheek. And run my finger down the side of his neck.

He caught me staring when he leaned closer to ask me how long Micah had been performing.

I wasn't sure what he was asking, so I gave him the full answer. "He's been singing since he was old enough to talk. He started playing acoustic when he was eleven, but picked up electric when he was fifteen. He formed a metal band in high school, and the first time they performed live anywhere beyond the garage was a battle of the bands."

Adam's expression changed subtly as I recounted Micah's life history, and I could tell he was reassessing my level of crazy fantardness. I laughed and said, "I told you I was his number one fan."

His smile slipped, but he managed to reply politely. "He must be very talented."

Something about the timbre in his voice resonated with me, almost familiar, and I regretted my flippant sarcasm.

Before I could repair my social missteps, the lights faded again, and the girls near the stage screamed in anticipation. A spotlight hit the mic, and Micah unceremoniously took the stage. He strummed a few notes and broke directly into a song everyone knew. The girls up front sang along, swaying and trying to out-do each other in their excitement.

Adam twisted around and watched me, eyebrow raised. Maybe he expected me to sing along, too. I raised an eyebrow back and mouthed the words along with Micah. Wouldn't want to disappoint him. Finally, Adam straightened up to watch the performance, ignoring me for several songs.

Micah performed another well-known song, then a new one, introducing each with some casual-seeming banter. I knew he planned every word he said onstage, but the stories he told were no less sincere for that. He controlled his stage presence like a pro.

Before the fourth song, he announced, "This next song requires some assistance. If you would all encourage my sister, Eden, to come join me, I'm sure she'd hop up here and lend me a hand."

The audience applauded on cue. As my feet hit the floor, Adam's eyes narrowed and then opened wide as he did the math. I curtsied and left him behind to climb up onstage to perform— Micah's support vocals once again. Micah strummed a chord, and I hummed the pitch. Then he began to play the song, a beautiful ballad about a man with an unflagging devotion to a woman. The ladies in the front row ate it up. Micah knew I got a kick out of performing, and I suspected he asked me up so I could live his musician life vicariously.

When the song ended, I headed back to the anonymity of my stool. The hard-core fans all knew who I was, but if they weren't pumping me for information about Micah, they didn't pay much attention to me. There was a fresh beer waiting, and I nodded to Adam, appreciative. He winked and faced forward to listen to Micah. That was the extent of our conversation until Micah performed his last encore and the lights came back up.

Then he turned back. "You were right. He's very talented." He tilted his head. "But you held out on me. Your opinion was a little bit biased."

"I was telling you the truth," I deadpanned. "I am his number one fan."

"You two look nothing alike. I'd never have guessed."

"We have a crazy mix of genetics."

As we chatted, the area behind us, near the merch table, filled up with people waiting for a chance to talk to Micah, get an autograph, or take a picture with him. The lady with the cat-hair cookies had nabbed the first place in the amorphous line. I scanned the rest of the crowd and discovered that Tobin had lost his bet. A pair of teenage boys holding guitars stood on their toes, trying to get a glimpse of Micah over the heads of the other fans, but he hadn't come out yet. They were most likely fans of his edgier rock band, taking advantage of the smaller venue to meet him, pick his brain about music, and have him sign their guitars. They'd still be competing with at least thirty people for Micah's time.

If I wanted to go home with my brother, I'd be hanging out a while. I could still catch a train back to New Jersey, but Micah's place in Brooklyn was closer. I decided to stay. It had nothing to do with the cute guy paying attention to me. I just didn't want to navigate Manhattan alone and drunk.

Adam leaned in and asked, "So what do you do? Are you a musician, too?"

"Actually, no. I'm a biochemist."

"Finding cures for Ebola?"

That caught me off guard, and I snorted. "No, nothing like that." I didn't know what to tell him about what I actually researched, so I half lied. "My company's developing a perfume."

"What's it like?"

I scooted over. "I'm wearing it. Can you smell it?"

He met me halfway, eyes dilating black. I knew I shouldn't be flirting. He didn't appear to meet a single one of my criteria and, in fact, actively ticked boxes from the "deal-breaker" list. I didn't want to lead him on only to have to give him the heave-ho in the next thirty minutes.

He took my hand and kept his dark eyes on mine as he lifted my wrist up to smell the fragrance Thanh had given me. "Mmm. That's nice."

Without dropping his gaze, he brushed his lips across my skin, and an electric current shot up every nerve in my arm. I drew my hand back, shrugging off the shiver that hit me like an aftershock. "And you? What do you do?"

He laughed and scratched the back of his neck. "Well, I'm a musician."

I blinked back my disappointment. From Adam's appearance, I hadn't had high hopes, but he might've been dressed down for a night out. Way down.

On my list of suitable professions for my prospective mate, *musician* wasn't at the absolute bottom. There were plenty more embarrassing or unstable career choices. I wouldn't date plumbers or proctologists for obvious reasons. Salesmen either because, well, I didn't like salesmen, but also because their financial situation might be uncertain. Plus they tended to travel. My ideal guy, I'd decided, would be an architect. But there weren't many of those swimming around my apartment complex in Edison, New Jersey.

I had nothing against musicians. On the contrary, I loved them. I'd supported my brother in his career, but the lifestyle was too precarious for my peace of mind. Even the most talented had a hard time making ends meet. Traveling and selling merchandise became a necessity.

Which is why I never dated musicians.

Unfortunately, all the doctors, lawyers, and architects I encountered were usually not interested in jean-clad, concert T-shirt wearing me. This train of thought brought me around to the realization that I'd judged Adam for dressing exactly the same way.

Micah saved me from sticking my foot in my mouth when he appeared at our side. "Adam! I'm glad to see you here. I see you've met my sister." He turned to me. "Eden, do you mind if I steal him for a few?"

Adam threw me a glance. "Will you be here when I get back?"

The jolt of butterflies this simple question gave me came wholly unexpectedly. "I'll be here. I'm leaving when Micah does."

He flashed a crooked smile at me, and I traced his lips with my eyes. He was going to be trouble.

They headed toward the green room, leaving me as confused as Adam must've been when I went onstage. I didn't know who he was, or why my brother wanted to see him.

I weighed the possible options.

Option one: The most logical explanation was that Micah was hiring Adam to temporarily replace his bassist, Rick, who was taking time off to be with his wife after the birth of their first child. I congratulated myself for solving the mystery on my first try.

Option two: Maybe Adam was a drug dealer. No, other than smoking and drinking, I'd never known Micah to try a recreational drug. And surely, this wouldn't be an ideal location for such a transaction. Besides, Adam already said he was a musician. Option one was looking better and better.

Option three: Or maybe Adam was a homeless man Micah was going to take in out of charity. A homeless man who'd just bought me three beers. I rolled my eyes at myself, but then felt awash with guilt. He probably wasn't homeless, but it did seem like he might be struggling to get by, and I'd accepted three drinks I could've easily afforded. *Good job, Eden. Way to drive a man to starvation.*

Every new option I came up with to explain Adam's presence

here defied logic and stretched the imagination. I gave up and watched the crowd thin. When Micah and Adam came back out, the bar was empty, save me and the staff.

Micah poked me. "We're going over to Adam's. You can come or just go straight back to my place." He bounced on his feet. I looked from him to Adam, standing relaxed up against the bar. From the looks of things, Micah had a boy crush. I might be interrupting a bromance if I tagged along.

Adam stepped toward me. "I have a fully stocked bar, and I don't like to drink alone." His smile was disarming. The whole situation seemed so contrived, and I had to wonder whose idea it was.

Micah stifled a yawn. "Come on, Eden. Just for a drink. Let's go see how the other half lives."

Did he know what that expression meant? "Okay, but let's get going. Some of us have been awake since this morning."

Connect with U s

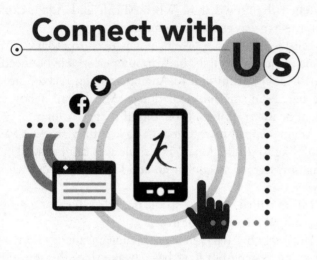

Visit us online at
KensingtonBooks.com
to read more from your favorite authors, see books
by series, view reading group guides, and more.

Join us on social media

for sneak peeks, chances to win books and prize packs,
and to share your thoughts with other readers.

facebook.com/kensingtonpublishing
twitter.com/kensingtonbooks

Tell us what you think!

To share your thoughts, submit a review,
or sign up for our eNewsletters, please visit:
KensingtonBooks.com/TellUs.